THE LOGICAL RESPONSE

"I was with John for all the wrong reasons," Celeste admitted. "I wanted to belong to someone, to love someone and be loved back so badly. . . . " She blew out a sigh. "I guess I just deluded myself into thinking something was there that really wasn't."

"That's why decisions need to be based on logic," Rand said.

"*All* decisions?" she asked.

"Sure."

"Oh, come on. Some things just aren't logical."

Rand slanted a grin at her. "Like you?"

She rolled her eyes, then smiled back. "Yeah, like me."

"Okay, well, I admit that some things"—he shot her another teasing grin—"and some people aren't logical. But there's a logical response to everything."

"Oh, yeah?" Her eyes held a playful challenge.

"Yeah."

"So what's the logical response to this?" With a mischievous grin, she put her hands on his chest and pushed him backward.

"This." Grabbing her arms, he pulled her down on top of him. She laughed as she landed on his chest.

And then he heard her breath hitch. Or maybe it was his—because as he gazed into her face, a surge of desire kicked in, hard and fast and urgent. Her eyes were all smoky need, her lips a plump, parted invitation. His arms wound around her, and the next thing he knew, he'd pulled her down and covered her mouth with his.

Other *Love Spell* books by Robin Wells:

OOH, LA LA!
BABY, OH BABY!
PRINCE CHARMING

ROBIN WELLS

Wild About You

LOVE SPELL NEW YORK CITY

LOVE SPELL®

July 2003

Published by

Dorchester Publishing Co., Inc.
276 Fifth Avenue
New York, NY 10001

ISBN 0-505-52535-6

The name "Love Spell" and its logo are trademarks of Dorchester Publishing Co., Inc.

Printed in the United States of America.

Visit us on the web at www.dorchesterpub.com.

Wild About You

Chapter One

"Handlin' a horse is a lot like handlin' a woman," Emile Armand declared, his Cajun accent as thick as gumbo roux. "An' b'lieve you me, I'm an expert on handlin' the ladies." The overweight oilman placed a dun-colored ostrich-skin boot on the bottom rail of the pasture fence and tugged at the alligator belt that served as a retaining wall for his enormous belly. Every time he inhaled, the pearl buttons on his tight blue western-cut shirt threatened to pop off, and his pants slid a little lower. "Yessirree—with both horses and women, you gotta let 'em know who's boss an' keep 'em on a tight rein."

You're the one who needs a tight rein, Rand Adams thought darkly—*a rein as tight as your shirt, wound around your over-active piehole.* To hear Emile tell it, he'd bedded more women than Warren Beatty and knew more about horses than Mr. Ed. The old windbag had blathered nonstop for the past two hours as Rand showed him around his ranch, and Rand was sick of listening to his obnoxious boasting.

1

But Rand could put up with just about anything in the short term if it would help him in the long run, and it was in his best interests to humor this braggadocio moron. Landing the account to train Emile's horses would bring Rand one step closer to achieving his goal of building his Circle A Ranch into the largest quarter horse breeding and training facility in Louisiana. The old blowhard had deep pockets and a young wife with a penchant for showing quarter horses. Rumor had it she also had a penchant for young stable hands and rodeo riders, but that was beside the point.

Rand pushed back his black Stetson and wiped a bead of sweat off his brow. It was only ten-thirty in the morning, but the mid-July sun was set on broil and humidity hung heavy in the south Louisiana air.

"What's your trainin' philos'phy, son?" Emile asked.

Son. The word made Rand feel like he'd just bitten into a green grapefruit. His father used to call him that, back before he'd abandoned Rand and his mother. Every time he heard the word, Rand wanted to take a swing at whoever said it.

Rand wanted to take a swing at Emile anyway—probably because he reminded him so much of his old man. Both men shared an uncanny knack for self-delusion. Rand's father used to believe that a lucky roll of the dice would solve all his problems, while Emile thought he was a babe magnet, but it was all the same. Neither one of them had the guts to face the truth.

If there was one thing Rand couldn't stand it was self-deception. He'd spent his entire childhood waiting for his father's ship to come in, only to learn there'd never been a ship in the first place. He'd learned the hard way that the only ships you could count on were the ones you built, launched and captained yourself.

It was a lesson Rand had taken to heart. He didn't believe in wishful thinking; he believed in objectivity, logic and cold hard facts.

And the facts in this situation were that as much as Rand disliked this old windbag, he needed to get his business. He hooked his thumb through the belt loop of his faded Levi's and turned his mind to Emile's question. "I've always found that the best way to make a horse do what you want is to make him want to do it, too."

The heavyset Cajun gave a derisive snort. "You're kiddin'."

"I'm dead serious."

"How the hell do ya do that?"

"Get to know the horse. Evaluate its temperament and figure out what it responds to best, then use that to motivate him."

Emile ran a beefy hand over his sweating scalp. "Hmmph. Sounds like a load of *merde* t' me, but you're shore doin' somethin' right. Your horses, they've taken home the money in the last four shows my wife entered." He put a booted foot on the bottom slat of the pasture fence and tugged at his belt again. "My wife, she got her heart set on one of those nat'nal trophies, she. So I came over from Lafayette t'see what kinda voodoo you're conjurin' up over here."

From what Rand had heard, Emile's wife had her heart set on a young bronco rider, but he didn't intend to share that particular piece of information. "No voodoo. Just a lot of hard work. I've been lucky enough to get some good horses, and I have the best trainer in the business."

"George Wright? Oh, yeah, he's good, no doubt 'bout it." A trickle of sweat dripped off one of Emile's overgrown eyebrows. "In fac', I tried to hire him 'way from you."

"So I heard."

Emile raised his hands in a gesture of surrender, his

round face creased in a placating smile. "No offense meant."

"None taken." *Because you didn't succeed, you sorry SOB.* "Lucky for me, George has no intention of leaving Cypress Grove. He was born and raised here, and he's the town's volunteer fire chief."

"That's what he said. I tol' him I'd have more fires than he could put out, but nothin' doin.'" Emile grinned. "Can' blame a man for tryin', though." He reached in the pocket of his pants, pulled out a crumpled tissue and mopped the folds of fat on his neck. "I hear tell you're fixin' to expand your ranch."

"That's right." *And if things go my way, you're going to help finance it.*

"You gonna build more stables right 'ere?"

"I'm trying to acquire the two hundred acres next door." It was the one sticking point in his plan. Rand had negotiated for months with Lizzie Boudreaux, the elderly woman who lived in the old Acadian-style house on the adjacent property. Just as he'd finally talked her into selling the place, she'd up and died on him, leaving the property to her older sister.

Which presented a problem: Rand had no idea where the sister was. He had been out of town at a horse show when Lizzie died, and by the time he got back, the sister and her husband had come to town, buried Lizzie and left. The administrator of the trust that handled Lizzie's estate had told Rand that the sister's married name was Jones, and that she and her husband worked for a circus. But when Rand contacted the circus, he'd been told that the couple had just retired and no one knew where they'd gone. With a last name like Jones, looking for them was like looking for a horsehair in a bale of hay.

"What-all ya gonna build?"

"A new arena, new stables and a lodge."

"A lodge!"

Rand nodded. "We're going to offer seminars and clinics for horses and their riders. I'm going to renovate and enlarge the house next door so folks'll have a place to stay." When he got through, he'd have the first quarter horse facility in Louisiana to offer full-service accommodations. It was all part of his ten-year plan.

Emile let out a low whistle and shook his head. "Trainin' horses is one thing, but trainin' people—whoo-ee, that's a can of worms I wouldn' touch with a ten-foot pole. Unless, of course, the person needin' trainin' is a pretty young thing." Emile winked again. "In that case, I wouldn' mind touchin' her with my own pole, if you get what I mean."

Oh, I bet the ladies are just lining up for that. Rand gazed through the fence at the foal and its mother he'd been showing Emile, keeping his expression deliberately blank.

"Speakin' of pretty young things—I saw you with that Oklahoma rodeo queen at the Shreveport horse show last March."

Rand had no intention of discussing his love life with this randy old goat.

"Molly somethin'," Emile continued. "Lawson or Dawson or some such."

The name was Larson, but Rand wasn't about to enlighten him.

"Oo-ee, she's a real looker. She your girl?"

"We occasionally run into each other at horse shows," he said noncommittally.

Emile winked. "You do more than run into each other, from what I hear. I heard tell you two were gettin' serious."

Molly was getting serious—which was the reason Rand had broken things off five months ago. Why did women always have to ruin a good time by trying to turn it into something permanent? He'd been perfectly happy with their long-distance relationship: no strings, no pressure, no messy emotional involvement.

Things had been just fine, but Molly wasn't happy to leave well enough alone. No woman ever was. Sooner or later, the *L-* word or *C-* word or even the *M-*word would surface, and Rand would have to call things off.

"You heard wrong. The only things I'm serious about are horses and the Circle A." Rand fixed his gaze on Emile's black Cadillac, parked in front of the stables about fifty yards away. Rand was more than ready to close this deal, pack this old geezer in his fancy car and send him on his way. "So what do you think?"

"Looks like your place is first rate." Emile tugged his belt again. "I'm mighty partic'lar about my animals. I've never out-placed 'em b'fore, but looks like you take as good care of yours as I do of mine, so . . ." He picked at his teeth with his pinkie fingernail. "How many colts you think you can handle?"

A sense of victory pulsed through Rand. He frowned, determined not to show it. "How many you got?"

"Six, right now."

He rubbed his chin thoughtfully. "I imagine we could manage that."

"Good. Real good. B'cause . . ." Emile's beady eyes strayed to the pasture, then widened with alarm. His brow creased like a folded horse blanket. He jabbed a thick finger toward the mare and foal. *"Mon Dieu*—is that a bobcat?"

"Nah. Can't be. Bobcats don't live around—" Rand's gaze snagged on something that made his heart jerk to a stop.

A large, gray-brown wildcat skulked along the wooden fence about twenty yards away, creeping toward Rand's best spring foal. At first glance, it looked like an enormous housecat; when Rand looked harder, there was no mistaking it. Its large ears were tufted with white, its tail a tell-tale short stub.

"Mus' be rabid." Emile took a step back. "You'd never see a healthy bobcat out in broad daylight. Don't see 'em stalkin' horses, either, 'less they're starvin'."

No way a bobcat could be starving—not in southern Louisiana. The thick woods that surrounded Rand's property were teeming with so many rabbits and rodents that the cat probably tripped over a few just getting into the pasture.

"See there—that beast's got foam comin' out its mouth." Sure enough—the animal turned toward Rand, revealing a patch of white froth on its chin.

"Those bobcats, they're nothin' to mess with," Emile said. "They go straight for the jug'lar. I have a huntin' buddy in Colorado who lost a foal and a calf to a bobcat las' winter."

The large cat crept closer to the foal, who was now nursing at its mother's side. Rand's fingers curled in his palms, and his lips pressed into a hard line. "Well, that's not gonna happen here. I've got a twenty-two in my truck."

Rand had no sooner started toward his pickup than a loud whinny made him whip back around.

Oh, dear God—the mare had spotted the cat. She backed up, nearly knocking down her colt, and let out a shrill neigh.

The air left Rand's lungs. Walleyed in panic, the mare reared up on her hind legs, pulling black lips back over blunt white teeth. Her front hooves flashed silver in the morning sun, directly over her colt's head.

"*Mon Dieu!*" Emile gasped.

Rand's blood iced in his veins. Time slowed to a horrifying freeze-frame pace as the mare's front feet came down like a blacksmith's hammer, missing the colt's skull by a scant inch.

It was a long moment before Rand could breathe. He watched the mare and the colt race away, the colt awkward on long, spindly legs. Rand's heart galloped with them.

"Blessed Mother, that was close," Emile breathed.

Too close. And the damn cat was still there, sitting by the fence like it owned the place, unmoving except for the twitch of its stubby tail.

Well, he wouldn't be sitting there for long. Rand covered the remaining five yards to his Silverado in about as many strides, yanking his keys out of his jeans pocket as he went. He didn't bother with the tailgate, but hoisted himself onto the bumper and over it, climbing into the truck bed like a swimmer out of a ladderless pool.

Squatting in front of the black built-in metal toolbox, he rapidly unlocked it, yanked out his .22, then slammed the lid shut. He knelt on top of it, cocked the rifle and leaned over the top of his truck, bracing his elbows on the roof of the truck cab. He'd just aligned the crosshairs with the wildcat's head when a woman's voice overrode the roar of blood in his ears.

"Bite me!"

Rand froze. He would have thought he'd imagined it, but the bobcat froze, too.

"Come on, baby. Bite me!" The woman's voice wafted out of the thick woods beyond the pasture, directly behind the bobcat.

"Who the devil is that?" Emile asked from his position beside the truck bed.

"Damned if I know."

"Bite me!" the woman called. Her singsong voice sounded nearer. "Come here, you naughty boy."

Aw, hell. The property next door had become a popular necking spot ever since Miss Lizzie had died. A couple must have gotten tired of doing it in the car.

"Come on, sweetheart." The sound of snapping twigs

accompanied the still-closer voice. "Come to Mama and I'll give you a special treat."

"What's goin' on here?" Emile asked.

Damn it all to everlasting hell. First a rabid bobcat, and now this. The woman sounded as if she were in the dense foliage directly behind the cat, right in Rand's line of fire. Rand was a good shot, but he couldn't risk accidentally hitting her or her playmate. He muttered an oath and lowered the rifle.

The branches of a red oak swayed and parted behind the bobcat. Rand caught a flash of blond hair and a long stretch of pale skin before the branches snapped back together.

Emile's jaw fell open. "Holy Moses—is that girl *nekked?*"

Great, just great. Lady Godiva was about to walk right into a rabid wildcat. Even if no one got hurt, Emile was going to think he was running a side show instead of a ranch.

The branches swayed again, and a blonde charged out of the woods like a bronco out of a rodeo gate. She wasn't naked—not entirely. She wore a leopard-print bikini, black rubber boots and an assortment of leaves stuck in unruly golden hair pulled up in a ponytail on top of her head. She stood on the other side of the fence about five yards from the bobcat, directly in Rand's line of fire, and smiled.

"There you are! Come here, sweetheart, and I'll rub your special spot."

Who the heck was she talking to? A playmate still hidden in the woods? Emile?

Rand?

Under any other circumstances, it would have been a tempting offer. The blonde was all lush, full curves and smooth, pale skin. She bent and climbed through the slats of the fence, stepping into the pasture.

The bobcat turned to face her, its head low, its muscles

tensed, as if it were about to spring. White foam gleamed on its chin. There was no time to sort things out.

"Get back, lady!" Rand shouted.

The blonde whipped up her head, her expression surprised. "W-what?"

Apparently she hadn't been addressing him. If he weren't so worried about the rabid bobcat, Rand might have been disappointed. "Step back, nice and easy, and I'll take care of that thing."

Her eyes grew as large as Frisbees as she stood still and stared at him. "Is that a *gun?*"

"Yeah. Now take a couple of steps back."

"Why? So you can *shoot?*"

"That's the general idea."

"You'll do no such thing!"

Great, just great. She wasn't just kinky but a bleeding-heart wildlife-hugger as well. "Lady, that cat is rabid."

"Bite me."

That was a hell of a way to talk to someone who was trying to save your life, Rand thought darkly.

"Who is this?" Emile demanded. "What's goin' on?"

"Good question." Rand's gaze was locked on the bobcat. The creature was now sitting down and licking a front paw, calm as a kitten in a Little Friskies commercial—a sure sign it was sick. Rand needed to take it out, but the woman too close for comfort—and her boyfriend was still out in the woods somewhere.

"Okay, lady—where's your partner?" he called.

"My what?"

"Your partner—or friend or date or whatever you call him. Whoever you're frolicking with in the woods."

"Frolicking?" She stared at him, her eyes wide and wary, as if he were the one with rabies. "I don't know what you're talking about."

"Look, lady. I don't know what you call it or what kind

of sex game you're playing, but that cat is—"

"Sex game?" Her eyebrows flew up in surprise, then pulled hard together. She put her hands on her hips and stared at him. "Are you crazy?"

Boy, was that the pot calling the kettle black. "Look— I need to deal with this rabid bobcat, and I don't want anybody to get hurt."

"He's *not* a bobcat."

This dame was clearly lacking the fruit in her loops. "You just worry about where your pal is and I'll handle the wildlife ID. Now, I'm a pretty good shot, but if your playmate is in my line of fire . . ."

She placed her hands on her hips and glared at him. "I don't have a playmate, I'm not frolicking and I'm certainly not playing sex games!"

"So who the hell were you talking to?"

"I told you. Bite me." She knelt down, held out her hand to the bobcat and made little smooching sounds. "Come here, sweetheart."

"Is there a mental hospital somewheres 'round here?" Emile asked in a low voice. "Mebbe she escaped."

The nearest institution was forty miles away, but this woman would have had no trouble hitching a ride, not with a body like that. Rand was in no mood to be admiring feminine assets, but hers were pretty hard to miss— especially when she leaned forward like that, causing her cup-runneth-over breasts to nearly spill out of her bikini top.

"Come on, baby. Come here. Bite me," she murmured.

Judging from the way the bobcat was creeping toward her, the woman was about to get her wish.

Well, she needed to find a place besides his property to indulge her masochistic fantasies. Rand uncocked the rifle and jumped out of the back of his pickup. Tucking the weapon under his arm, he ducked between the slats of the fence and strode through the pasture toward her. "For the last time, lady—get away from that bobcat before he attacks."

"He's not a bobcat. He's a little sweetheart."

Oh, jeez—she was certifiable. He considered yelling to scare the beast away, but he was afraid that might cause it to attack. No telling what the woman might do, either. His best bet was to get close enough to get a clean shot if the cat lunged for her.

Rand stopped a few yards away from the woman. The cat continued slinking through the grass, creeping ever closer to her outstretched hand. Rand raised the rifle, his heart in his throat. If he was going to shoot, he needed to do it now. The cat was only about a yard away from the woman. Rand peered through the scope, his finger tensing on the trigger.

And then the woman's hand appeared in the crosshairs. With a muttered oath, Rand jerked down the rifle, only to stare in shock at the scene before him.

The bobcat was on its back, its paws in the air, letting the woman rub its stomach.

"See?" The woman shot a triumphant I-told-you-so glance at Rand. The cat's purr reverberated through the air, loud as a motorboat. "I told you he was a sweetheart."

Rand cautiously eased closer. "He's tame?"

The woman nodded. "As tame as I am."

Which might not be saying a whole lot. Rand regarded them both warily. "You've got a bobcat for a pet?"

She blew out a how-many-times-do-I-have-to-tell-you sigh. "He's not a bobcat. He's a Highland Lynx, which is three generations removed from a wildcat. He's completely domesticated, and he can't have rabies because he's had all his shots."

Rand continued to eye her with suspicion. "Well, then, why does he have foam on his jaw?"

"That's just shampoo lather." She reached down and

brushed it away with her finger. "I was giving him a bath when he ran away." Her fingers stroked the animal's fur and the cat closed his eyes, apparently in the throes of feline ecstasy. She gave the beast a chiding smile. "Bite me—you're a naughty, naughty boy, aren't you, fella?"

There she went, weirding out again. "Why the hell do you want him to bite you?"

"I don't."

"But you keep saying—"

"That's his *name*." Her voice held an exasperated, explaining-the-obvious-to-an-idiot tone.

"*Huh?*"

"His name is Bite Me. He got it from his first owner. Apparently he liked to nip at fingers when he was a kitten, and he heard the phrase 'don't bite me' so often that he began to think it was his name. The *don't* part got dropped somewhere along the way."

The damned bobcat was named Bite Me—only it wasn't a bobcat but some kind of half-assed hybrid. Rand wasn't sure if she'd played him for a fool or he'd simply acted like one. Either way, he felt stupid, and it irritated the hell out of him. "Why didn't you just tell me all that?"

"I tried to, but you wouldn't listen."

Rand felt his temper rise. "You didn't try too damned hard."

She lifted the cat and stood up, her eyes indignant. "If I wasn't clear, it's probably because I'm not used to having a rifle trained on me."

He scowled. "I was aiming at the cat, not at you. I thought I was saving your life."

"And *I* thought you were threatening my pet."

The adrenaline in his bloodstream was running as high and fast as the Mississippi at flood stage. "Dammit, lady, do you have any idea what kind of havoc you've wreaked here today? While you were playing Jane of the Jungle in the woods on *my* property, your cat there spooked my mare, causing her to damn near trample her own colt. I nearly shot both you and your precious pet, and to top things off, I've got a potential client over there who . . ."

Rand turned and motioned toward his truck, only to see Emile waddling toward his Cadillac.

"Hey—wait up!" Rand called.

The heavyset man flapped one arm in a dismissive gesture. "I'm outta 'ere," he yelled. "No way I'm bringin' my foals to a place with crazy women and wildcats."

The morning was going from bad to worse. Muttering a low oath, Rand jogged across the pasture, the rifle in his hand. He ducked under the fence and fell into step beside the large man, who didn't even slow his pace.

"This whole thing was just a big misunderstanding," Rand said. He forced a chuckle, trying to give the incident a lighter spin. "Turns out that isn't a bobcat after all. It's some kind of domesticated hybrid."

"My horses are jus' like your mare—they won' know one wildcat from another. An' that woman—she's *fou*." Emile made a circle in the air by his head. "You're not runnin' a ranch here, Adams; you're runnin' a three-ring circus."

"If you'll just wait a moment, I'm sure . . ."

But Emile was already stuffing his huge belly behind the steering wheel of his car. Frustration filled Rand's chest as he watched him slam the door and crank up the engine. The tires crunched on the shell drive as he sped away, taking a prime piece of business with him.

Damn.

Rand blew out a long breath. Blast that woman and her half-breed pet! Who the devil was she, and what was she doing on his property, anyway?

He turned around, ready to head back toward her, only to discover she'd followed him. He strode over to the fence where she stood with her infernal cat.

"You said that was a potential client?" she asked.

"Yeah."

"Oh, gee." The smooth skin between her light eyebrows furrowed. "I guess Bite Me and I cost you some business."

"Only about thirty-thousand dollars' worth," Rand said tightly.

Her eyes were the color of moss, the green-gold kind that grew on the north side of the live oaks in his front pasture. They narrowed in a wince. "That's a lot of money."

"You can say that again."

"I'm *so* sorry."

Dammit, he was angry and indignant. He didn't want to forgive her—and he sure as hell didn't want to feel attracted to her. But it was impossible not to, not with those big eyes turned on him, all full of remorse and chagrin. Not to mention those lush breasts spilling out of that leopard-print bikini.

She caught him staring at her chest and shifted the cat higher in her arms. "What kind of business are you in?"

"I raise and train quarter horses."

"You must be awfully good at it, to make that kind of money." She gazed at the horses in the distance. "You've got some beautiful animals here."

"Yeah, well, I try to take good care of them. So when I saw your cat creeping up on them with foam around his mouth, well, I was more than a little upset."

"I would have been, too." Her eyes were still focused on his horses. Her brow wrinkled in a frown. "Hey—did you know that black mare has a toothache?"

Rand looked at her in surprise. "What makes you say that?"

"Well, she's holding her mouth funny as she chews. We had a dog at the shelter I used to work at that did the same thing, and he had an infected molar."

She had a good eye, he had to give her that. Beyond

good; amazing was more like it. He regarded her with new respect. "You're right. She cracked a back tooth and the vet removed it a couple of days ago."

"She's on the mend, then. Good." A look of relief crossed her face. "I hate to see animals in pain."

"That makes two of us."

"It tears me up to see that look in their eyes," she continued. "But you know what really gets me? It's the way they just *deal* with it, the way they just go on the best they can, without whining or complaining. I think animals are braver than people that way."

Rand nodded in agreement. She was different than he'd first thought. Apparently she had a real respect for animals. Most of the people he worked with saw horses as commodities, but he'd always seen them as creatures a lot like himself—creatures with will and pride, who felt pain and pleasure. His challenge in training them wasn't to break their will, but to coax them to align their desires with his own.

"Well, I'm really sorry I messed things up for you."

Rand shifted his rifle to his other hand. "Well, what's done is done."

She gave him a tentative smile. "You know, it may not seem like it now, but in the long run, you'll probably be glad this happened. You might even thank me someday."

"Oh yeah?" The annoyance Rand had just tamped down flared to life. She had some nerve, acting as if she'd done him a favor when she'd just put his horses in danger. "And just how do you figure that?"

"Because everything happens for a reason. If you were meant to work with this guy, your meeting would have gone smoothly. But Bite Me ran away and I followed him and we stumbled into this situation, which seems like an unfortunate coincidence, only there's no such thing as coincidences, so that means this was meant to happen."

He fixed her with an appraising stare. Maybe she'd fallen in the woods and injured her head or something.

She gave him another one of those little half-smiles. "A lot of people don't realize it, but nothing happens by accident. Everything is part of a larger plan. And when something out of the ordinary like this happens, it's a sign."

"A sign of what?" *Besides the fact that you're seriously disturbed.*

"A directional sign. Like an arrow, pointing you toward your destiny."

Oh, brother. She was one of *those.* To Rand's way of thinking, people who believed that the cosmos was cheerfully conspiring to grant all their wishes were less in touch with reality than compulsive gamblers. Rand's lip curled. "Well, I must have one hell of a destiny in store, if the powers of the universe saw the need to drop you and your mutant cat in the middle of my horse pasture."

Instead of being offended at his sarcasm, the woman nodded, causing the curls on top of her head to bob. "I'm sure you do. Because there was another coincidence I thought was quite striking."

"Is that a fact."

The high ponytail bobbed again. "I heard your client say your place is like a circus. Which is very odd, because that's what the Joneses did for a living."

"What?"

"They worked for a circus."

Rand stared at her. "The Joneses—you mean the ones who own the place next door?"

She nodded.

"You know them?"

"Well, I didn't know Mrs. Jones—she died last January. But I knew Mr. Jones. He passed away just a few weeks ago." She shifted the enormous cat in her arms. "That's why I'm here. He left me the property."

Rand's stomach took a sudden dip, as if he'd gone over a large bump in a speeding vehicle. "Left you . . . you mean, *you* own it now?"

She nodded. Shifting her cat, she stuck out her right hand and flashed a wide smile. "I'm Celeste Landry—your new neighbor."

Huh.

Rand prided himself on his ability to stay in control of his emotions, yet he found himself at a complete loss for words.

"I didn't catch your name," she prompted.

"Rand. Rand Adams." It took a moment for him to register that her hand was still extended. He took it, then immediately wished he hadn't. The feel of her soft, warm fingers made him feel hot all over. Against his will, his gaze wandered to her cleavage. He gave her hand a quick shake, then pulled away.

She fixed him with those earnest green eyes. "Look— I'm sorry we got off on the wrong foot. But don't you worry. From now on, Bite Me won't get out unless he's on a leash." She hoisted the squirming cat higher in her arms. "Well, I guess we'd better get out of your hair."

Rand was still trying to process the information as she turned to leave. It was such a shock that it took him a moment to connect the dots.

She was a fruitcake. She was his neighbor. *She was the ticket to all of his plans for property expansion.*

"Wait!"

She paused and turned around.

He pulled off his hat and ran a hand through his hair. "You, um, don't want to carry that huge beast all the way back through the woods. Let me give you a ride."

"Thanks, but I've already caused enough trouble for one day."

A day? More like a week. Make that a month. Hell, she'd

caused enough trouble to last a whole damn year.

But she held the key to the future of his ranch. "It's no trouble. What are neighbors for?"

"I really don't want to impose on . . ." The cat squirmed in Celeste's arms.

"The way he's wiggling, he's likely to escape all over again," Rand warned. Bite Me writhed like a full-fledged wildcat, helping his argument.

"Well . . . okay. Thanks." His neighbor shifted her grip on the animal and gave a sheepish grin. "He *is* quite a handful."

Takes one to know one, Rand thought. From every indication, this woman was a handful and a half.

Chapter Two

Clutching her wriggling cat, Celeste edged past Rand as he opened his pickup's passenger door, painfully aware that she was wearing only a bikini. Her discomfort wasn't helped by the fact that her new neighbor's gaze kept straying to her chest then flicking away, as if he was trying not to get caught looking.

She was having the same problem with him. He drew her eye like a T-bone drew a bulldog. He was tall and muscular, with thick dark hair, tanned skin and strong-features. His face was all planes and angles, with high cheekbones, a deep-clefted chin and a pair of eyes that grabbed hold and wouldn't let go. He was rugged and tough and uncompromisingly masculine—like the Marlboro Man without the cigarettes.

He was sexy as sin.

"I really appreciate this," she said, sliding onto the seat. Its black leather was hot against her bare legs. She tried to arrange Bite Me to cover her upper body, but the beast refused to cooperate.

"No problem." Rand closed the door, then leaned through the open window. "Let me lock up the rifle and we'll be on our way."

He was putting away that gun—thank goodness. Not that he'd be much less intimidating without it.

He climbed into the truck bed, causing the pickup to rock, making Celeste's stomach rock as well. This was a big man, over six feet tall and powerfully built. His navy knit shirt stretched over wide shoulders and well-developed biceps, and his worn jeans clung to muscular thighs. Yet it wasn't his size that made him seem so formidable—it was his eyes. Deep-set under heavy black eyebrows, they were dark and razor sharp. She suspected they didn't miss a thing.

Which made being nearly naked around him especially unnerving. Celeste tensed as the truck door opened on the driver's side and Rand climbed in, bringing the scent of leather and sweat with him. It immediately made her think of sex.

She shifted nervously and rearranged Bite Me on her lap. She'd never considered herself a highly sexed individual, and she certainly wasn't in the habit of entertaining bedroom thoughts about men she'd just met, but something about her neighbor had her doing just that. He was good-looking—there was no question about that—but she wasn't usually so attracted on the basis of mere physical appearance. There was something else about him, something invisible and compelling.

Maybe it was an aura or pheromones or the pull of personal magnetic fields. Maybe it was because she was wearing next to nothing. Or maybe it was the fact that sex had been introduced into the equation before they'd ever met. He'd thought she'd been playing a sex game, for heaven's sake.

The thought made her face flood with heat. A sex game, indeed! Celeste didn't even know any.

She bet he did, though. That would explain why he'd jumped to such a rapid conclusion. She wondered if he played them often, and with whom.

What kind of games would they be, anyway? Certainly not board games or card games. And not anything involving a court or a course, like tennis or golf. More than likely they'd involve tying someone to a bedpost, or wearing a blindfold, or . . .

"Aren't you worried about getting all scratched up?"

His words jolted her out of her musings. She saw him looking at the still-wriggling cat. "Oh, Bite Me's been declawed," she told him. "His first owner did it—not Mr. Jones, but the owner before him. I personally don't approve of declawing cats; it puts them at a terrible disadvantage against other predators. Of course, Bite Me doesn't have that problem because he's an indoor cat. I only took him outside to give him a bath."

"I wasn't aware that cats needed baths."

"This one does. You see, he develops a skin condition and starts losing his hair when he's upset, and he's been very upset by this move. I didn't want to upset him further by bathing him in the bathtub—he hates bathtubs because he likes to be able to see over the rim, and bathtubs are too deep. But there's a big sink in the barn, so I thought . . ."

She was babbling. She always babbled when she was nervous, and Rand made her as nervous as a rabbit around Glenn Close.

His mouth curved into an amused smile as he turned the key in the ignition. He no doubt thought she was the classic dumb blonde.

People always thought that. She clamped her lips together and bit down on them, forcing them to stop moving, then coaxed her cat onto his back and rubbed his tummy. The animal immediately relaxed and began a throaty purr. At least her thighs were covered, Celeste thought. She felt Rand's eyes on her and wished she had another cat to drape across her chest.

She was relieved when he turned his attention to putting the truck into gear, backing up and maneuvering it onto the oyster-shell driveway. He guided the truck down the curving drive, past a large white farmhouse with a wraparound porch.

She started to ask him if that was where he lived, but when she turned toward him, she found him sneaking a glance at her. Their eyes locked, and she felt a blast of heat. Attraction crackled in the air like dry wood in a campfire.

"So . . . does your wife help with your horses?" she found herself asking. Oh, jeez—what a lame way to fish for information. Could she possibly be more obvious?

He shot her a smile. "I'm not married."

"Oh. Well, the only reason I asked was that your house—I'm assuming that was your house we just passed—well, it looked like a house for a family, so . . ."

"No wife, no family. You?"

"Um . . . No. Me, neither. I mean, I don't have a husband. Or a family." Why, oh why, did everything she say make her sound like an idiot?

"So you moved here by yourself?"

"Well, I'll live by myself. But I had some help moving."

"When did you get in?" he asked.

"I arrived around eight last night, but the truck with my stuff didn't show up until nearly midnight. It was close to two before the driver and I got it unloaded."

He shot her a questioning look. "I didn't know moving vans unloaded at that hour."

"Oh, I didn't use a moving van. Mr. Jones's will said that the house was furnished, so I didn't bring any furniture—not that I really had any, anyway. A friend's brother drives a cattle truck, and he dropped me and my animals off on his way to Florida."

Rand drove past a stand of trees that shielded his house from the road, then braked at the end of his drive where it intersected with a two-lane blacktop road. He glanced over at her. "So how long did you know Mr. Jones?"

"Only about four months."

One eyebrow shot up. "That's all? And he left you his property?"

Celeste stroked the large cat. "Well, we hit it off right away."

"You must have." His gaze flicked down to her chest, then back up to her face. "How did you meet?"

"He was going into the hospital for heart surgery."

"What were you? His nurse?"

"No. Just a friend."

The eyebrow edged higher. "You must have been an awfully good friend for him to have left you his land."

Indignation made her spine stiffen against the leather seat. "I wasn't his Anna Nicole Smith, if that's what you're implying."

"I didn't say that." He made a left turn onto the two-lane road.

"No, but that's what you were thinking. I could tell by the way you were looking at me."

His lips tilted up slightly. "How was that?"

"Like . . . like you think I'm some kind of floozy gold digger who prances around half-naked preying on sick old men."

His eyes flashed with amusement. "I said all that with just a look?"

"Yes, you did. And I'm not. Not a floozy, I mean. And not a gold digger." She was babbling again, but she couldn't seem to help it. "And I don't usually go around dressed like this, either, but Bite Me always splashes water everywhere when I bathe him, and I didn't expect to be seeing anyone, so I thought I'd put on a swimsuit instead of getting my clothes all wet, and . . ." She paused for a breath. *Stop talking,* she ordered herself. "Anyway, I would have worn more clothes if I'd known I'd be meeting you, and you can rest assured that Mr. Jones never saw me in anything remotely this revealing."

"Too bad." His gaze swept over her, heating her skin.

She didn't know which rattled her more—the frank male appreciation in his eyes or the fact that he still questioned her relationship with Mr. Jones. She shot him her iciest look. "What is that supposed to mean?"

"Just that the old guy didn't know what he was missing."

There was a compliment hidden in there somewhere, but she was fairly certain it didn't warrant a thank-you. "For your information, Mr. Jones wouldn't have cared if I'd been stark raving naked."

"I believe the expression is stark raving mad."

Which is what you're making me! Celeste bristled. "I'm not stupid."

His dark eyebrows rose again, and his mouth curved into a maddening smile. "I didn't think you were."

You did, too. People *always* did. People looked at her hair and her bustline and immediately assumed she didn't have a thought in her ditzy blond head. But she did. She had lots of thoughts. They just sometimes got all jumbled up when she tried to put them into words; then they poured out in a confusing torrent—especially when she was nervous, like she was right now. She drew a deep, calming breath. Slow and easy, she told herself. Compose yourself. Compose your thoughts.

"When I met Mr. Jones, he was not only very ill but grieving for his wife. He'd absolutely adored her, and she'd died only three months earlier."

Rand braked for a turn in the road. "How did you meet him?"

"I managed an animal shelter, and he came in, wanting to know if we could keep his pets while he went into the hospital for an operation. The shelter couldn't handle them, so I offered to go out to his place twice a day and care for them."

"That was awfully nice of you." His eyes took her measure. "Where did he live?"

He still suspected she'd had an ulterior motive for being nice to the elderly man. Irritation flashed through her. "In a huge mansion with gold gates and a diamond-studded front door," she said dryly. "The minute I saw it, I thought to myself, 'Oh, boy—here's an easy mark. I'll take this old guy for all he's worth.'"

She was gratified to see a sheepish look cross Rand's face. He shifted uneasily on the seat.

"That's what you thought, isn't it?" she prompted.

"No, of course not."

"Liar."

He shot her a sidelong grin. "Okay," he conceded, "but that part about the diamond-studded door was a real surprise."

She'd heard the term *disarming smile*, but this guy actually had one. Against her will, she felt her irritation dissolving.

"Actually, I was wondering what prompted you to take on such a big commitment to a complete stranger," he said.

"Well, it sure wasn't money. Mr. Jones had less than me, which means he was practically broke." She looked out the window at the towering pines, her mind picturing the way Mr. Jones had looked when he'd shuffled into the shelter: pale and frail and out of breath, the bones of his shoulders visible through his threadbare gray sweater, his eyes shadowed with grief and worry.

"He reminded me of my grandfather right before he died," she admitted. "He was weak and ill and facing surgery, and he was all alone in the world, except for his pets. He loved those animals like children. In fact, he said they were the children he and his wife never had. I happen to love animals, too, and he didn't have enough money to board them, so . . ." She turned up her hands and lifted her shoulders.

"Why was he so broke? He and his wife must have inherited at least a little cash from Lizzie. Plus they inherited the ranch."

"After Mrs. Jones's sister died, they planned to retire and move here. Evidently Mrs. Jones had always yearned to come home, but her family had disowned her when she'd run away and gotten married. But then she took ill and was diagnosed with cancer. Houston has good medical facilities, so they stayed there. They spent just about every cent they had on medical treatment."

"Where did they live?"

"In a beat-up old trailer on a little piece of rented land just outside Houston."

Rand gazed out the windshield, a thoughtful expression on his face. "No wonder I couldn't find them."

Celeste looked at him, her eyes wide with surprise. "You were looking for them?"

Rand hadn't intended to broach the subject quite yet, but what the heck? Might as well get right to it. "Yeah. I wanted to buy their property. Lizzie and I had reached an agreement on it, but she died before we could sign the papers."

Celeste's eyes grew incredulous. "She was going to *sell* it?"

Rand nodded. "It was practically a done deal. In fact, my attorney had gone to her house to get her to sign the contract when he discovered that she'd died in her sleep. When she didn't come to the door, he went inside, and . . ."

Celeste covered her mouth with her hand. "Oh, dear!"

Oh, dear, indeed. "I was at a horse show in Oklahoma at the time. By the time I got back to town, the funeral was over and the Joneses had come and gone. I tried to find them, but no one knew where they'd gone after they left the circus."

"I can't believe she was going to sell the place," Celeste murmured. "It was built by their great-great-grandparents, and it was supposed to stay in the family as long as there were any living family members. There was supposed to be some kind of trust that made sure of that."

"There was. But Lizzie said her sister was dead as far as the family was concerned, and my attorney was able to find a loophole. There was evidently bad blood between Lizzie and her sister."

Celeste nodded. "The way Mr. Jones explained it, they came from a weird family—their parents were very domineering and possessive and didn't allow either daughter to date. Apparently they wanted both girls to stay single, live at home and take care of them in their old age. But Mrs. Jones defied them."

Rand had heard bits and pieces of the story. "She actually ran away and joined the circus, didn't she?"

Celeste nodded. "She met Mr. Jones when a small show came to town, and I guess it was love at first sight. He was an animal trainer and a clown. They corresponded for a few months after the circus left. When her parents found out, they hit the roof. They forbade her to have anything to do with him and threatened to disown her if she did."

"But she married him anyway."

Celeste nodded. "He came back for her, and they eloped."

"And her parents never forgave her."

"No. Her sister never forgave her, either. It was Mr. Jones's one regret, that he'd come between his wife and her family."

"Sounds to me like he did her a big favor." Rand turned the truck into the drive of Lizzie's property. He might as well get right to the point. "I'd still like to buy the place."

Celeste shook her head. "Sorry, but I'm not interested in selling it."

"You haven't even heard my offer."

"I don't need to. I can't sell it."

"Why not?"

"Well, Mr. Jones promised his wife on her deathbed that he'd bring their pets here just as they'd planned, and that he'd make sure they were loved and cared for for the rest of their lives. I intend to help him keep that promise."

She wasn't just half-baked; she wasn't baked at all. Dogs and cats didn't care where they were. How was he supposed to reason with someone so unreasonable?

Very carefully, he decided. "You can care for pets anywhere. You could buy a nice place near Houston for what I'd pay you for this."

"It wouldn't be the same." Her voice held an alarming note of conviction. "Mrs. Jones always wanted to come home, and when she realized she wouldn't be able to, she wanted her family to come here. It was her last wish."

"But you're not a family member," Rand pointed out.

"No, but the animals are."

Surely she wasn't serious. "Oh, come on. Animals aren't people."

"That doesn't mean they're not family. The Joneses saw their pets as children."

"But they're not. And the pets won't know if they're here or in Timbuktu."

"But I'd know. Mr. Jones promised his wife, and a promise is a sacred thing." Her lips firmed in a determined line. "Besides, the ranch is a perfect place for me to start a new business. I was supposed to come here. It was meant to be."

Oh, jeez—here she went with that destiny junk again.

"There've been too many coincidences for this to be an accident," she continued. "For instance, it's awfully odd that Mrs. Jones's sister died right before she sold you the property, don't you think?"

Oh, no. No way. He wasn't about to encourage her. "That wasn't a coincidence. It was just something that happened."

"Well, the timing was sure significant. It was a sign. And I'm convinced that the way I met Mr. Jones was a sign, too."

A sign of what? That you're nuttier than a pecan praline?

"It's all just too perfect to be an accident," she said.

Perfect? The only perfect thing about this whole mess was the fact that she was perfectly nuts and he was perfectly screwed.

Well, he refused to be dissuaded so easily. He parked in front of the weathered old house, hitting the brake a little harder than he intended.

Celeste gathered her drowsy cat in one arm and put her hand on the door handle, then hesitated. "The place is a mess, but I've unpacked the coffeepot. Would you like to come in for a cup?"

"Sure," he said. He had a million and one things to do today, but none of them were more important than acquiring this property from Little Miss Headcase. He intended to do just that.

Chapter Three

Rand studied the rundown Acadian-style house as he followed Celeste up its brick steps to the wide wooden porch. The white paint on the two-story building was peeling like a bad sunburn, a couple of the dark green shutters hung at precarious angles by a single hinge and the roof was missing a few shingles, but from the real-estate appraisal he'd already had done on the property, he knew the structure was basically sound.

No need to tell Celeste that, though. Better to point out all the repairs that needed to be made. She'd said something about not having much money. With any luck, she'd realize she'd gotten in over her head and sell out to cut her losses.

"This place sure needs a lot of work," he remarked. "The exterior paint job alone was estimated at seven thousand dollars."

"It won't cost anywhere near that if I paint it myself."

"Do you have any idea of the amount of work involved?

You'd have to scrape off all the old paint, then prime it, then apply at least two coats."

"I've painted before. I enjoy it."

How could anyone enjoy scraping paint off a house in the middle of a Louisiana summer? That was crazy. He watched her unlock the large cypress door, determined to find the key to convincing her to sell.

He followed her inside, then froze as two tiny gray balls of fluff assaulted her feet. When they quit moving at the speed of light, he realized they were toy poodles. "Hello, babies," Celeste crooned to the little dogs. "I brought your buddy back." She set Bite Me on the floor, and the two dogs eagerly licked the enormous cat's face. To Rand's amazement, the cat purred and rubbed up against one of them as if it were a human leg before calmly stalking off.

Celeste scooped up the dogs, one in each arm, and turned to Rand. "Meet Bruiser and Killer."

"Do all your animals have such cuddly names?"

She laughed. "Pretty much all of the Joneses' do. They enjoyed the irony." The tiny dogs looked like a pair of wriggling pom-poms. Rand gingerly reached out to pet one of them, only to have the other try to nudge under his hand.

"The dogs were part of the Joneses' circus act," Celeste said.

"Oh, yeah? What did they do?"

"Lots of things. They walk on their back legs, do handstands and balance on large balls. They also ride on the backs of other animals and jump through hoops. Mr. Jones said they wouldn't perform for anyone but him and his wife—but they'll do their tricks for me, too."

Rand's gaze drifted from the dogs to Celeste's bikini. For a moment, he could understand their eagerness to please.

He followed her down the hall, which was painted a sickly shade of institutional green on one side and covered with faded floral wallpaper on the other. "You'll have to excuse the appearance of the place," she said. "I haven't had a chance to freshen it up."

Rand was well aware of how the place looked. He'd already had an architect draft plans for enlarging and renovating it. "This place needs more than freshening," he remarked, pointedly looking at the cracked plaster, peeling wallpaper and dangling cobwebs. "It needs a major overhaul."

She lifted her shoulders. "A few patches and a little paint, the place will look terrific."

"That'll cost thousands of dollars," he pointed out.

"Not if I do it myself."

She was either a regular Bob Villa or completely clueless. Either way, it would do no good to argue the point. He needed to try a different tack.

Rand followed her through the living room, which was dominated by a large curio cabinet filled with Miss Lizzie's doll collection, and into the large kitchen. Boxes sat on the scarred oak table and in piles on the worn plank floor. An open box sat on the white-and-black-tile countertop, alongside a Mr. Coffee machine. Celeste washed her hands at the sink and filled the coffeemaker with water, then pulled a filter and a bag of coffee from one of the open boxes.

Rand leaned against the counter on the opposite wall and watched as she measured out the grounds. He needed to be figuring a way out to convince her to sell this place, but the sight of her bikini-clad bottom distracted him. It was round and well-shaped, and her swimsuit didn't quite contain it; a tiny bit of cheek escaped from each side of the fabric. Rand's gaze locked on the shadowed spot below the swell of her bottom, the spot where her leg ended and her backside began. It was one of his favorite spots on a woman—curved and sexy and seductive. Man, how he'd like to cup those sweet buns, squeeze their fullness, pull her flush up against his—

"All set." She turned around and caught him staring. Rand jerked up his gaze, but when their eyes met, a jolt of sexual awareness ricocheted between them.

She felt it, too; the attraction was too strong, the eye contact too prolonged for it not to be mutual. They stood there and stared at each other for a long, sexually charged moment, and then she jerked her gaze away. She took a step back. Color flooded her cheeks and she folded her arms protectively across her chest. The gesture only accentuated her cleavage.

"It'll take a few minutes for the coffee to brew," she said. "Why don't you go relax in the living room, and I'll go throw on some clothes."

Rand stifled a pang of disappointment as she hurried from the room, the pair of poodles trailing after her like fuzzy gray shadows. He should be grateful she was going to cover herself up, he thought as he ambled into the living room; it was impossible to keep his mind on business with those curves on blatant display.

Besides, he deliberately avoided dating women who lived less than thirty miles away. Distance was the key to keeping a relationship manageable. From what he'd seen of Celeste, nothing much about her seemed manageable at all.

Rand settled into a ratty brown armchair, set his Stetson on the floor beside him, and eyed the doll collection displayed in the enormous curio cabinet against the wall. It had always struck him as sad that Miss Lizzie collected dolls. In addition to delicate porcelain ones, the elderly woman apparently had a penchant for life-like baby dolls and plastic trolls.

Celeste soon joined him, wearing a pair of denim shorts and a navy t-shirt. She'd combed the leaves out of her hair and pulled it into a ponytail, and put on a soft pink lipstick. Was the lipstick on his account? Heck, he was having enough trouble keeping his eyes off that cupid's-bow mouth as it was.

Rand couldn't help but wonder if she still was wearing the swimsuit underneath or if she'd changed into normal undergarments. If so, what would her idea of "normal" be? A woman who bathed her cat in a leopard-skin bikini was not likely to have conservative tastes when it came to Skivvies.

"So . . . tell me about yourself," she said, perching on the edge of a dust cloth–covered sofa. "Are you from around here?"

Okay. Get your mind off her underwear and onto convincing her to sell you the property, Adams. Rand shifted in his chair. "I moved here six years ago."

"Where were you before that?"

"Here and there. Mainly Baton Rouge."

He was here to talk about her, not himself. He needed to gather information that would help him discourage her from staying. "What about you? Are you originally from Texas?"

She nodded.

"It must be tough, moving away from your friends and family."

"Actually, I don't have any family. My parents were killed in a car accident five years ago. And all my friends have gotten married or moved away."

So much for the homesickness ploy. He'd try a career angle. She'd said she intended to start a business here, and that she'd moved in a cattle truck, so apparently she was planning on cattle ranching. "Did you grow up on a ranch?"

"No—in a Houston suburb. But I've always dreamed of living in the country."

Finally here was some information he could use. He'd

try to dissuade her by pointing out how difficult it was to make a living raising cattle. "Do you have any experience with ranching?"

"No."

"It's a lot harder than you think."

Her eyes held an oddly baffled look. "I never thought it was easy."

"You have to have in-depth knowledge about a lot of things: the cattle market, diseases, breeding, bloodlines, vaccinations, what to plant on your grazing land, when to buy and sell. . . . It's all very complicated. It's hard work, too, with not much of a return on your investment. Miss Lizzie was around cattle all her life and she got out of the business about ten years ago."

"Really?"

Rand nodded emphatically. "Ranchers all over the country are having a hard time keeping their heads above water right now. If you're starting from scratch, it'll be years before you make a profit. Especially if you still have to acquire most of your livestock."

She gave him an odd, Mona Lisa-esque half-smile. "I've got all the livestock I need."

Rand doubted it. One cattle truck couldn't carry very many cows and bulls. "How many head of cattle are you starting out with?"

"Actually, I'm not going to run a cattle ranch."

Rand frowned. "You said you came in a cattle truck, so I just assumed . . ."

"Oh, no. That's just the type of truck my friend's brother happened to have. It works for other animals as well."

Rand would never dream of transporting his horses that way, but not everyone was as particular as he was. "You're going to raise horses, then? How many do you have?"

Her smile widened. "Two."

"Just two?" Boy, was she ever a neophyte. "You'll need a

whole lot more than that to turn any kind of a profit."

From the corner of his eye, Rand thought he saw some movement on the floor. He looked down, but only saw his cowboy hat sitting there.

He turned his attention back to her. "I don't know if you're planning to breed them or show them or what, but . . ."

Once again, his peripheral vision detected some kind motion. He glanced down. His hat quivered then stilled. But it was now about a foot farther away from where it had just been.

He sat bolt upright and stared at the floor. "What . . . ?"

Celeste's eyebrows rose. "What, what?"

"My hat. It just moved."

Even as he said it, Rand realized how ridiculous he sounded. The black Stetson sat perfectly still, about a foot from his chair.

"Maybe you accidentally kicked it."

He was sure he hadn't. The hat was at his side, and his feet were in front of him. . . . Of course, he'd been so intent on talking her out of staying that he hadn't been paying much attention to his body movements. Maybe he'd inadvertently knocked it when he'd crossed his leg or something. That must be what had happened.

He turned back to Celeste, keeping one eye on the hat. "Well, as I was saying . . ."

The Stetson quivered again—then rose a couple of inches off the floor and crept forward. To his alarm, Rand glimpsed a pair of small, hairy legs underneath it. They weren't the legs of a dog or a cat, and the creature had something that looked more like tiny feet than tiny paws.

Rand jumped to his feet, his mind searching for a logical explanation, mentally sorting through various species that might possess those legs: a rodent, a gargantuan cockroach, an enormous tarantula, a space alien—each possibility was more ludicrous than the next. His mind rejected them all as his hat again settled to the floor.

"Oh, dear!" Celeste was on her feet, moving toward the hat.

Rand put out his arm, like a driver protecting a child during a sudden stop. "You'd better stay back."

"But . . ."

He cautiously moved forward, his pulse pounding, and bent down with extreme care, slowly reaching out to grip the crown of the hat. Abruptly, he snatched it up.

A tiny, diaper-clad creature with a furry humanoid face stared up at him. Rand stared back. With a parrotlike screech, the animal dashed toward Celeste and jumped into her arms.

"What in blazes is that?" Rand gasped.

Celeste laughed. "A squirrel monkey." She patted the beast on the back, then turned it to face him. "Meet Mr. Peepers."

Rand gaped at the animal. It was tiny, only eight inches or so high, and thin as a reed. It had a long tail, long arms and an expressive white face. Rand drew closer for a better look.

The monkey let out a shrill shriek and abruptly spit. A warm, wet blob landed on Rand's cheek.

"Hey!"

"Mr. Peepers—shame on you!" Celeste scolded. She turned to Rand, her eyes apologetic. "I'm so sorry. He's usually very well-behaved, but men frighten him. Let me get you something to clean up with."

Cradling the monkey in one arm as if it were an infant, Celeste hurried into the kitchen. She returned with a damp paper towel and handed it to Rand, over the monkey's squeaking protests.

Rand eyed the tiny ape as he wiped his cheek. "In addition to your lynx, you've got a pet *monkey?*"

Celeste nodded, patting the monkey's back as if she were burping a baby. "As well as three llamas, two goats, a donkey, four sheep, six rabbits, two Shetland ponies, a pot-bellied pig, a pair of ducks, a rooster, two hens and some just-hatched chicks. You've already met Killer and Bruiser. And I have a regular house cat, Duchess, that I owned before I took over the Joneses' pets."

"Holy moley." She was operating a regular zoo, right next door to his ranch. If he hadn't seen part of it for himself, he'd think this were some kind of joke. "How . . . ? Why . . . ?"

She gestured back to the chair, indicating that he should sit down again. Rand felt more than ready. Clutching his Stetson, he sank into the armchair. Celeste settled again on the couch, holding her monkey in her lap like a child.

"The Joneses were both professional clowns. They trained animals and used them in their acts. But in addition to the animals they performed with, they took in elderly, injured or unwanted animals, and they used them in a children's petting zoo concession before and after the circus performances."

"Those are the pets you inherited?"

Celeste nodded.

Rand's mind swam. He'd been thinking in terms of dogs and cats, with maybe a guinea pig or hamster or parakeet thrown in for good measure. The animals she'd just named weren't pets; they were livestock! "And . . . you brought them all here?"

Celeste nodded again.

Alarm bells clanged in his mind. Surely this was just a temporary situation. "What do you plan to do with them?"

"The same thing the Joneses did, only on a full-time basis."

Rand stared at her blankly. "You're joining a circus?"

Celeste laughed as if he'd said something clever. "No. I'm setting up a permanent petting zoo."

Rand didn't look pleased, Celeste noted. In fact, he looked downright upset. Mr. Peepers must have thought so, too, because he made a throaty grunt in Rand's direction, then lunged from her arms to the knick-knack case against the wall.

"Mr. Peepers! Come down from there right now!" Celeste ordered.

Instead of obeying her, the monkey grabbed a small porcelain doll and lobbed it at Rand.

"Hey!" Rand ducked, and the doll crashed to the floor.

The monkey bounced up and down, shrieking with glee.

"Mr. Peepers, you stop that this instant!" Celeste started toward the curio cabinet, but the monkey grabbed another china doll.

"Watch out!" Rand yelled. He grabbed her arm and yanked her aside as the doll flew past, narrowly missing her head. As Celeste watched in horror, Mr. Peepers began hurling dolls with both hands.

"Get behind me and cover your head," Rand said.

Celeste did as he directed. For the next few moments, dolls crashed around the living room like mortar shells. The sound shifted from breaking glass to hard thuds.

"What's happening?" she asked.

"He's run through the porcelain dolls, and now he's throwing trolls. Stay put until he runs out of ammunition."

As suddenly as it began, the bombardment stopped.

"He's emptied the shelves," Rand said. "The coast is clear."

Celeste peered out from behind Rand's back. Mr. Peepers stood in the middle of the cabinet, looking around for more dolls.

"What the hell was that all about?" Rand demanded.

"I-I think you upset him."

"Yeah, well, the feeling's mutual." Rand rubbed his upper arm.

"Are you okay?" Celeste asked.

"Yeah. I only took one hit—from a wayward troll."

He'd used his body as a shield to protect her. The thought made Celeste's chest feel strangely warm. "Thanks," she said. The word was completely inadequate.

He shrugged it off, as if body blocking dolls were an everyday occurrence. "No problem."

"I would have been hit in the face if you hadn't pulled me out of the way," she said. "You saved me from a nasty cut or a concussion or worse."

"No big deal. He's got a pretty good arm, but no aim." Rand shifted his stance, as if he were uncomfortable in the role of hero. "What the hell's the matter with that thing?"

"He used to belong to a man who beat him, so he's afraid of men."

"Do you have someplace to lock him up so he won't start throwing something else?"

"He has a kennel, but he's pretty nervous right now. I might have trouble catching him."

"Any way I can help?"

"She shook her heard. "Why don't you get out of his sight, and I'll try to coax him down."

Rand strode into the kitchen. Celeste made her way toward the empty cabinet, carefully stepping around shards of broken china. "Come on, Mr. Peepers. It's all right. Come on down."

With a squawk, the monkey leapt into her arms and hugged her neck. "That's a good boy." She carried the creature into the guest room where she'd set up his large wire kennel. She crooned soothingly to him for a few minutes, then opened the wire door. Mr. Peepers jumped into his kennel immediately, apparently relieved to be in familiar surroundings.

When Celeste returned to the living room, she was surprised to see Rand sweeping the broken china off the floor. The sight of the gruff cowboy wielding a broom struck her as both touching and sexy. The warmth she'd felt when he'd shielded her from the flying dolls filled her chest again. "You don't need to do that."

"I didn't want your cat or your dogs to get their paws cut."

The warm spot grew warmer. "That was nice of you."

He scowled, as if the thought of being nice displeased him. "Bring over that dustpan, would you? I put it on the table."

She picked it up, crossed the room, and stooped in front of him, holding it while he swept up the last of the broken pieces.

"There. I think that does it," he said.

"Thanks."

He followed her as she carried the pan into the kitchen. "Does your monkey do that often?"

Celeste shook her head. "I've never seen him like that. I think he was trying to protect me."

"From what?"

"From you." Celeste gave a dry smile as she opened the cabinet and pulled out two coffee mugs. "My guess is he thought you were threatening me."

"Why would he think that?"

She poured coffee into the large cups. "You were frowning. Mr. Jones said the monkey responds to people's facial expressions."

"What was I frowning about?"

"I'd just told you I planned to open a petting zoo."

*　　*　　*

Rand was glad she'd turned around to open the refrigerator, because the beginnings of another frown flicked across his face again. He rapidly assumed a neutral expression as she turned around, holding a carton of milk. "Do you want some milk in your coffee?"

"No, thanks. I take mine black." He leaned against the counter and watched her pour a generous dollop of milk in her cup. "A petting zoo, huh?"

She nodded. "I've always wanted to work with both animals and children. When Mr. Jones mentioned that they'd run a petting zoo, I thought, 'What a wonderful idea! I'd love to do that.' And then he left me the land and his pets, making it possible." She gave a contented sigh. "It's a dream come true."

More like a nightmare, Rand thought darkly. "What happens at a petting zoo, exactly?"

"Well, children come to play with the animals. They pet them and feed them and brush them, and they can ride the Shetland ponies. Most petting zoos are popular sites for birthday parties and picnics."

"Sounds like you'll need a lot of visitors," Rand pointed out. "You're an hour and a half away from the nearest city, and this is a pretty sparsely populated area. There aren't all that many children around here."

"I realize that. That's why I plan to advertise."

"Advertising's expensive."

"I've got a little set aside."

"It's going to take more than a little. Do you have a marketing plan?"

"I intend to take out some billboards along the interstate. When children see the signs, they'll be begging their parents to stop."

"The interstate is a good twenty-five minutes from here," Rand said. "Do you really think hordes of people will go so far out of their way for a spontaneous side trip?"

Celeste lifted her chin, a defensive light in her eyes. "People will come if they know it's here." She set down her coffee cup. "Do you want to see the other animals?" she asked after a moment.

"Umm. . . . Sure."

She turned back to the refrigerator and pulled out a bag of carrots and dried corn. "I fed them this morning, but they always like a little treat."

Rand clamped his Stetson on his head and followed her out the back door through an overgrown garden surrounded by a metal fence, then out the gate into a heavily weeded pasture. He walked beside her down a long path that led toward a weathered wooden barn set between two enormous live oaks.

"Do you have any experience starting a new business?"

"Well, no. But I managed an animal shelter for the past six years."

"It usually costs a lot more money to open a new business than most owners estimate. And more small businesses fail than make it in the first year."

She shot him a sardonic look. "Why do I get the feeling you're trying to discourage me?"

Because I am. "I was just wondering if you'd really thought this through. Have you done a feasibility study or analyzed the market or . . ."

She shook her head. "I don't need to do any of that."

He raised his brows.

"Look—I've got enough money to fix the place up and do some advertising and, if I'm careful, to support myself and the animals for about three months. I can either spend the time and money doing studies, or I can just give it a go."

"Three months is not a lot of time to get a business rolling."

"Well, it's all I've got. The property taxes are due then,

and if I can't make enough of a profit to pay them, well . . ."

Property taxes. They were due the first of November, and they amounted to several thousand dollars. The tight feeling in Rand's chest began to ease. Heck—he had nothing to worry about. There was no way she was going to turn a profit of several thousand dollars in that amount of time.

"What are you going to do if you can't pay them?"

"I'm not going to waste my time worrying about it. It'll all work out."

She might have moved to the state of Louisiana but she lived in the state of denial. The name Celeste fit this woman for a reason other than her heavenly body, Rand thought—her head was in the stars.

They stopped at a wooden fence. She carefully unlatched the gate and motioned him inside.

"Brace yourself," she said.

"For what?"

"An onslaught." She made smooching sounds with her mouth. "Come and get it, guys!" she called.

Two scrawny goats rounded the barn at a dead run. Close on their heels came three llamas and four sheep, a swaybacked donkey and two of the ugliest Shetland ponies Rand had ever seen. Bleating and baaing, the goats and sheep stood on their back hooves and tried to take the carrots out of Celeste's hands. A short, fat pig, its belly so large it nearly dragged the ground, lumbered forward and stuck its snout against Rand's ankle, trying to root up his jeans. Chickens and ducks soon entered the fray, clucking and quacking as they dodged the others' hooves with amazing agility. Laughing, Celeste tossed the carrots and corn in different directions, dispersing the mob.

The animals ate until the food was gone, then the donkey pushed at Celeste's arm with his muzzle, as if he didn't quite believe the carrot bag was empty.

"Sorry, Slowpoke. All gone."

A goat reached up and tried to grab the empty bag. Celeste pulled a sugar cube out of her pocket and held it out in the palm of her hand.

"There you go, Dr. Freud." The goat gobbled the sugar cube and snorted for more.

Rand's eyebrows rose. "The goat is named Dr. Freud?"

Celeste nodded. "Mrs. Jones named him. I'm sure it's because of the beard."

More than likely, it was because of her deep need for psychiatric help. A need that Celeste apparently shared if she thought anyone would want to pay to see this mangy menagerie.

The goat eventually ambled off, followed by most of the other animals. "Well, that's quite a collection," Rand said as the noise receded.

Celeste beamed like a proud mother. "Aren't they great?"

Not exactly the word that came to mind. He searched for something positive to say. "They're, um, sure friendly," he managed. Too friendly, if you asked him. "And they all seem to get along really well."

Celeste petted the donkey's nose. "They've been together for years, traveling in tight quarters. If one of them is removed for any reason, the others all get upset."

"That's certainly . . . unusual."

"Like Mr. Jones said—they're a family. That's why his wife wanted to keep them together. She never got over being disowned by her folks. She didn't want the animals to ever feel cut off or abandoned like she did." Celeste petted the donkey's neck. "That really touched my heart."

Touched your head, too, Rand thought. This chick was clearly an overly sentimental flake.

"You don't have much time to fix this place up and get going if you intend to make a profit in three-months' time."

"I'll have to hustle like crazy, but I'm sure it'll all work out." She smiled as the donkey nudged her pockets, apparently looking for more treats. "When things are meant to be, they always do."

"Has that been your experience in the past?"

"Well, not exactly, but that's because I've gone about things all wrong. My grandmother used to say that Divine Providence has a plan for all of us, and if we'll just ask for guidance and listen to the small, quiet voice inside, we'll always know which path to take." The blonde turned those earnest green eyes on him. "I never did that. But when Mr. Jones died, he left me a letter, and it made me realize that my grandmother's advice was right."

"What was in the letter?"

"All the same things my grandmother used to say. Mr. Jones wrote that he was sure we'd met for a reason, and that he thought Divine Providence had brought us together, and that he believed his little family of animals would be a blessing to me just like they'd been to him and his wife. And that if I listened to the small, quiet voice within, I'd know just what to do. And he said something else, something that gave me goose bumps when I read it."

She ran her fingers through the donkey's short mane. "He said that if I got the same message two separate times from two separate trustworthy sources, it was a sign from Heaven, and I needed to pay attention to it. Well, we'd never talked about my grandmother, so he couldn't have known the stuff she'd told me—but his letter was the second time I'd gotten that same message. So I figured, who am I to argue with fate? So . . ." She grinned and held up her hands. "Here I am."

"I see." *I see that you're seriously disturbed.* Rand shoved his hands in his pockets. "So tell me this: How do you know that you weren't meant to sell this property and buy some land closer to a large population base?"

"Because Mrs. Jones wanted the animals here at her old

home, and I want to help Mr. Jones keep his promise to her."

"What if the promise is impossible to keep?"

"It won't be."

He sighed. "For the sake of argument, let's just say that after three months, you run out of money and the petting-zoo concept hasn't taken off. What will you do?"

"That won't happen."

"But if it does?"

"It won't."

He blew out another exasperated breath. "Are you always this unrealistic?"

Her green eyes held a challenge. "Are you always this negative?"

"I'm not being negative. I'm looking at the facts. When a business needs a large volume of customers, locating it out in the boonies is a bad risk."

"Since I'm the one taking that risk, I guess that makes it my problem, doesn't it?"

"Yeah. It sure does." What the hell—let her have her little fantasy. If she wanted to pour all her money into a losing proposition, it was her business. All he had to do was wait three months for her funds to run out; then she'd be begging him to buy the place. Maybe it wouldn't even take that long.

There was nothing to be gained by arguing with her. "Well, I wish you the best of luck." *'Cause you're gonna need it.*

He turned around to leave, only to find a llama blocking his path. Rand moved to the left, only to have the creature move to the left as well. He moved to the right, stepping over the exposed root of the live oak, and the llama did the same thing.

"What's with your llama?"

"She's very protective of the other animals. She must think you pose a threat."

"Well, call her off."

"It's all right, Dolly," Celeste said soothingly. Rand dodged to the left again, only to have the llama pull back her fleshy lips and sling a wad of grass-colored spit. It landed on the brim of Rand's hat.

"Hey!" Rand exclaimed, yanking off his Stetson.

"Oh, dear!" Pulling a tissue out of her pocket, Celeste hurried forward. "Here—let me get that for . . . oh!"

She stumbled on the tree root. Rand reflexively dropped his hat and reached out to catch her. The next thing he knew, she was in his arms.

Oh, man—who would have guessed that she'd smell like that? Her scent was clean and soft and flowery, with an intoxicating undertone that wasn't shampoo or perfume, that was too elemental to be manufactured. It was just her, the heady essence of woman.

It hit him like a sock in the gut—taking away his breath, turning his brain to chicken feed, making him feel as wobbly legged as a just-born colt. And it wasn't just her scent. All of a sudden she was invading all his senses. The feel of her soft, warm breasts against his chest, the sound of her breath hitching in her throat, the sight of her parted lips as she gazed up at him, her green eyes all large and dazed: Impression after impression curled through him like smoke, blocking out everything else.

Her skin was as soft as the down on a duckling's belly, her hair as silky and seductive as a belly dancer's veil. A strand caught on the stubble of his shaved jaw.

"Sorry," she breathed, stepping back.

The strand of hair went with her, freeing itself from his face. The sensation was disconcertingly intimate—the kind of sensation usually experienced behind a locked bedroom door.

It had been a while since Rand had locked any bedroom doors. Too long, if his reaction to Little Miss Divine Destiny here was anything to go by.

Well, it was going to be a while longer, he told himself sternly. He shoved his hands into his pockets to prevent them from reaching for her again. He had no intention of getting involved with this spacey Pollyanna. He'd learned early on that people with their heads in the clouds like Celeste were nothing but trouble. They ended up suckering you into their unrealistic schemes, raised your hopes, then broke your heart.

"So . . . what's with all your expectorating animals?" His voice came out as a growl. "Do they have some kind of excessive saliva problem, or do I just look like a spitoon?"

She grinned. "Sometimes monkeys and llamas spit when they encounter hostility. Neither of these two used to do it very much, but I'm afraid they've taught each other some bad habits."

Rand could think of a few bad habits he'd like to teach Celeste. He watched her press her lips together and wished he was pressing his on hers instead.

The thought sent a wave of irritation surging through him. Did he have a latent masochistic streak, or what? This woman was trouble with a capital *T*. In the span of just one hour she'd cost him an important new client, nearly killed a colt, thwarted his expansion plans and informed him that she was opening a zoo of mangy, maladjusted, misfit animals next door to his ranch—all because she thought it was some grand plan of destiny.

She was nuts. And she was making him the same way. Maybe lunacy was contagious.

Rand bent and picked up his hat, being careful to avoid the llama loogie. "If you change your mind and decide to sell the place, you know where to find me."

"Don't hold your breath."

I won't, he thought as he stalked away. *I'll simply keep an eye on the calendar and wait until November.*

Celeste watched Rand's broad shoulders disappear around the corner of the house; then she heard the faint roar of an engine. He gunned his truck's motor, as if he were in a hurry to get away.

"Well, good," she murmured to Slowpoke as the sound disappeared into the distance. The farther away he took his know-it-all, domineering presence, the better. She didn't need someone throwing cold water on all her plans and undermining her confidence.

Which was shakier than she'd let on.

The donkey responded by pushing his shoulder under her hand. "Is your rheumatism bothering you, Slowpoke?"

The animal lifted doleful brown eyes. Celeste ran her hand gently across the coarse hair of his stubby mane. "Come on, fella. Let's put some ointment on that."

Walking into the barn, Celeste opened one of the boxes she'd brought out earlier that morning. When she'd come out at dawn, the day had shimmered with possibilities. She'd been excited to be in her new home, happy to be outdoors, full of enthusiasm and plans.

Now she'd run into Mr. Negativity, who'd fired a round of buckshot into her bluebird of happiness.

Pulling out a jar of liniment, she returned to the doorway where Slowpoke stood in a ray of sun. "Sunshine makes you feel better, huh, boy?" she murmured. "It makes me feel better, too." She unscrewed the lid, wincing at the strong medicinal odor. "I'd much rather be around someone with a sunny disposition than someone trying to rain on my parade."

Celeste dipped her fingers into the thick cream and slathered it on the donkey's shoulder. "There you go, boy."

She rubbed it into his warm hide, wishing there was a potion to rub out a memory.

Rand's opinion made no difference, she told herself. After all, he had a personal motive for discouraging her.

Because there was more than a grain of truth in what he'd said. It *was* going to be difficult to attract enough visitors to make this place self-supporting, much less profitable. She'd known the ranch was off the beaten path before she moved here—the first thing she'd done when she'd learned she'd inherited the place was to look it up on a map—but she hadn't known it was quite *so far* off the beaten path.

And she hadn't known that the place was in such rundown condition, either. Rand was right; it was going to take a lot of time and effort to make the place presentable. Even if she did the bulk of the work herself, it was still going to take money—money she'd planned to use on advertising.

Anxiety started a sickening crawl through her belly. She struggled to fight, to fend off the old insecurities. *You can't do it,* her mind taunted her. *You've failed before, and you're going to fail again.*

"That's not so," she muttered as she rubbed Slowpoke's shoulder.

Everyone made mistakes, and she'd made her share. Okay, maybe more than her share. But that was because she hadn't had enough self-confidence to trust her own judgment. She'd given too much weight to the advice of other people—people like that financial counselor who'd advised her to invest all the life insurance money from her parents' death in a software company that went belly up.

And the used-car salesman who'd sworn that the Camry she'd bought two years ago was in top-notch shape and as good as new, when actually it had been through a flood and needed a whole new engine.

And the apartment manager who'd sold her on the lakefront view but forgot to mention that every morning at four-thirty the fishing boats out her window roared to life with a din so loud it shook the floor.

And then there was her track record with men. The thought of that made her blow out a sigh. *That* particular area of her life made her other decisions look stellar.

It wasn't that she was dumb. She'd been told once in school that her IQ was actually quite high. The problem was, she always trusted other people's opinions more than she trusted her own.

There had been little signs about that investment, that car, that apartment, that man—little incidents, little obstacles, little red flags that things just weren't right. She'd known it in her gut, but she'd ignored her intuition.

Well, no more. From here on out, she was going to follow her heart—and she was deep-down certain that she was meant to be here.

So what if there were a few more obstacles than she'd anticipated? She'd work hard, keep an optimistic outlook and overcome them. She would *not* be swayed by the opinion of a man who had a personal stake in discouraging her. She would push Rand's comments completely out of her mind.

And while she was at it, she'd push away the memory of how his arms had felt around her and how her knees had turned to melted butter when he'd held her. She'd made a vow that she'd never again get involved with a man who didn't fully support her plans and dreams, and Rand was about as nonsupportive as you could get. The next time she fell for a man, it would be one who cared about her as much as she cared about him.

Rand Adams could just take his know-it-all, have-all-the-answers self right back to his fancy-schmancy horse farm and leave her alone. She refused to let his negative attitude affect her in any way.

Slowpoke turned toward her and brayed.

"My opinion exactly," she told the donkey, giving him a final pat. "You took the words right out of my mouth."

Chapter Four

"Sara Overton—is that you? Why, I haven't seen you in a coon's age."

Sara looked up from the antiquated cash register to see a frail, elderly man shuffling into Overton Feed and Seed, leaning heavily on a cane. Smiling broadly, she circled around the counter and headed down the center aisle to kiss his wrinkled cheek.

"It's so good to see you, Mr. Bouchon. How have you been? You look wonderful!"

"Better not let Myrtle hear you say that. You know how mean she gets when she's jealous."

Sara grinned. His tiny, soft-spoken wife was one of the gentlest souls on the planet. "How is Myrtle? Is she still making quilts?"

"Oh, yeah. I think she's prob'ly made one for just about everybody in the parish by now. She's doin' just dandy."

"And how about you?"

"Oh, I've managed to stay out of too much trouble. Myrtle cracks the whip and keeps me on the straight and narrow."

Sara smiled again. It was hard to imagine Myrtle wielding a flyswatter, much less a whip. "Well, good. Somebody needs to keep you in line."

Mr. Bouchon laughed, showing the gaps of missing teeth. What age was he? Sara wondered. He'd been coming to her father's store once a month ever since she could remember, and she'd turned forty-six last December. She'd thought he was ancient back when she was a child.

"I heard you'd come back to Cypress Grove to help out your dad," Mr. Bouchon said. "How's he doin'?"

"Better. He's started physical therapy, but it's slow going."

The elderly man's head bobbed sympathetically. "Those strokes are nasty things. Is he out of the hospital?"

Sara nodded. "He's at Forest Manor Nursing Home. The doctors say it'll be a while before he's able to live by himself again."

"They think he'll get well enough for that?"

The question loomed large in Sara's mind. Her future, as well as her father's, hinged on the answer. "We're hoping he will. The doctors say only time will tell."

"Well, I'm sure it puts his mind at ease, havin' you here, handlin' his store." He leaned on the counter, propping himself up with his cane. "So who's running that fancy interior design shop of yours in Chicago?"

"My business partner." Thank heavens for Christine, who was a good friend as well as the most competent businesswoman Sara had ever known. As soon as Sara received word two and a half weeks ago that her father had collapsed at work, Christine had shooed her off to Louisiana. "Stay as long as he needs you and don't worry about a thing," Christine had said. "I can handle things here."

"Your father's always braggin' about what a big success you are up there," Mr. Bouchon continued. "He said you even designed drapes for Oprah Winfrey. An' he talks about how you drive a fancy sports car an' live in a ritzy condo on the lake, an' how you're always jettin' off to Paris an' Italy an' the like." Mr. Bouchon grinned. "Yessiree— your dad's awful proud of you."

The remark took her by surprise, and Sara felt her throat tighten with emotion. Her father had never told her he was proud of her.

Funny, how you sometimes learn the most important things about a relationship from a third party. She'd thought her father had never gotten over his disappointment that she hadn't stayed and helped with the store.

"I don' know how you handle those cold winters, though," the old man continued.

"It's not bad once you get used to it," Sara replied. "A heavy coat, some warm boots and you're all set."

"Someone to cuddle with would probably be handy, too," Mr. Bouchon said, a gleam in his eyes. "Any gentlemen up there to help keep you warm?"

"Not at the moment."

"Hmm. Well, George Wright is available again, you know."

Sara's stomach squeezed into a hard ball. It wasn't the first time George's name had been brought up since she'd been back. People never forgot anything in a small town, especially anything gossip worthy or embarrassing. As for public scenes and scandals . . . well, those had the half-life of plutonium. No matter how far away you moved or how many years went by, you could never live down the past. Sara carefully kept her expression neutral. "I was sorry to hear about his wife."

"We all were. Heather was a real fine woman." Mr. Bouchon leaned forward and gave her a meaningful look. "And George is a real fine man."

"I-I'm sure he is."

"You oughta look him up while you're here."

Oh, I'm sure he'd love that. A wave of heat suffused Sara's face. She was searching for a way to change the subject when the cowbell jangled over the front door, sparing her the need to answer. She looked up to see an attractive blonde in khaki shorts and a red knit shirt entering the store.

"I'll be with you in a moment," Sara called.

"No hurry," the woman replied with a friendly smile. "I'll just look around."

Sara turned back to Mr. Bouchon. "What can I get for you today?"

"Same as always. A fifty-pound bag of oats, and a hundred of corn."

Sara circled around the counter and rang up the sale as Mr. Bouchon pulled a wad of bills wrapped with a rubber band out of his overalls pocket. The cash drawer stuck, the same way it had been sticking forever. She gave it an expert thump, wondering why in the world her father hadn't traded the thing in years ago. So many things in Cypress Grove seemed trapped in a time warp.

She seemed trapped in a time warp, come to think of it. From the moment she'd arrived in town two weeks ago, she hadn't felt like herself. Not like the self she was in Chicago, anyway. There she felt capable and confident, independent and in control. Here she felt fifteen years old all over again, unsure and awkward. Even her jeans were all wrong. She'd only packed two pairs, both of which she'd picked up in Milan on a buying trip for her store. She loved their snug fit, loved the way they made her legs look lean and long when she wore them with her Manolo Blahniks. But heels weren't practical in a feed-and-seed store, and a fit that looked just right in the city looked overly suggestive in small-town America.

She handed Mr. Bouchon his change. "You can drive

around to the back and Martin'll load them for you."

"Thank you kindly." He stuffed his loose change in the chest pocket of his overalls, then carefully placed the bills in his roll of money, refastened the rubber band and stuck the wad in his back pocket. "It was mighty good seein' ya."

"The pleasure was all mine."

"I'll stop by and see your dad on the way out of town."

"I'm sure he'd like that," Sara said. "Give my regards to Myrtle."

"Will do." His cane clicked on the hardwood floor as he ambled toward the exit. He paused and turned. "How long before you hightail it back to Chicago?"

"It all depends on how Dad's recovery goes."

"Well, you better come out to the farm and see Myrtle before you leave. You know how tough she is, and she'll give me the thrashing of my life if I let you leave town without seein' her."

"Oh, my—I can't let that happen," Sara agreed with a smile. "Tell her I'll be out this weekend."

"Okey-doke. But don't forget. I don't know if these old bones can stand another of her whuppin's."

The young woman in the back of the store followed the elderly man with a worried gaze until he pushed through the door; then she walked toward Sara, her eyebrows pulled into a frown. "He wasn't serious about getting thrashed, was he?"

"Oh, no." Sara·laughed. "Mr. Bouchon's been pulling that gag for as long as anyone can remember. He dotes on his wife, and she spoils him rotten. She's a tiny thing, not even five feet tall, and one of the sweetest people who ever lived." Giving the blonde a warm smile, Sara added, "You'd have to know Myrtle to know how funny it is."

"Good." The young woman's frown melted into a relieved smile. "I didn't think he looked like a domestic-abuse victim, but you never know. People can do some terrible things. I used to work with abused animals, and it would break your heart to see how cruel some folks can be."

"It was sweet of you to be concerned. I'm Sara Overton." She held out her hand.

The young woman shook it. "Nice to meet you. I'm Celeste Landry."

"Landry." Sara thoughtfully cocked her head. "I used to know everyone in Cypress Grove, but I've been away for twenty-something years. Are you new?"

The woman nodded. "Very new. I moved into Lizzie Boudreaux's old house yesterday."

"That's a big place. Do you have a large family?"

The young woman's mouth tilted in a wry smile. "Yes, but not a human one. It's just me and twenty-two assorted animals."

"Assorted?"

"Sheep, llamas, goats, ponies, a donkey, chickens, ducks, rabbits, a pig . . ."

"Oh, my! That *is* an assortment. So what brings you to Cypress Grove?"

"I inherited the place, along with the animals. I plan to open a children's petting zoo."

Sara was delighted. "A petting zoo—how fun! How did you come up with such a great idea?"

The reaction was sure a lot warmer than Rand's, Celeste thought. Before she knew it, Celeste found herself telling the petite brunette the whole story of how she'd met Mr. Jones and come to Cypress Grove. In return, Sara explained that she was temporarily back in town running her father's store while he recovered from a stroke.

"I'd forgotten how different this town is from Chicago," she said.

"It's a big change from Houston, too, but I like what I've seen so far."

"Everything here happens at a slower pace, and everyone knows everyone else. I'd forgotten what it's like to be on first name terms with just about everyone you pass on the street."

"I'm looking forward to it. So far I've only met you and my neighbor."

"Your neighbor? You mean Rand Adams?"

Celeste nodded.

Sara smiled. "He's quite a hunk, isn't he?"

Celeste didn't want to think about the attraction she'd felt for him. She lifted her shoulders. "If you like the bossy, controlling type."

"From what I heard when I got my nails done at the beauty parlor, plenty of ladies around here like it just fine. He's quite a hot commodity."

A hot commodity—in what way? Not that Celeste cared. It was absolutely none of her business. "You mean he's a ladies' man?" she found herself asking anyway.

"I mean he's successful, he's smart and in case you happened to miss it, he's gorgeous. From what my manicurist said, every single woman in the parish is after him."

"So he's not involved with . . ." Celeste stopped herself. She didn't want to give the impression that she was interested. She wasn't. Not in the least.

"Involved with anyone?" Sara shook her head. "I understand he used to see a woman in New Orleans, and for a while there was someone in Hammond. Rumor has it there's a girl on the horse-show circuit, but it doesn't seem to be serious. Apparently he's a commitment-phobe." Sara straightened a display of work gloves. "And a work-a-holic. He's president of the local Chamber of Commerce, a member of the volunteer fire department, and he works around the clock on his ranch."

Celeste seized on the opportunity to change the subject. "I'm going to have to work around the clock, as well. I need to get my place up and running as fast as possible."

"When do you plan to open for business?" Sara asked.

"As soon as possible. The place is pretty run down, so I'll have to do some painting and landscaping. I'll also need to create an area for parking, and install some picnic tables and swing sets. Plus I want to create some dioramas and hands-on exhibits about each of the different animals."

"Educational exhibits?"

Celeste nodded. "I want to explain things like how wool gets off the sheep and into sweaters, and how we need to preserve the habitat of South American monkeys, and—"

Sara held up a manicured hand. "Wait a minute. You have a *monkey?*"

Celeste nodded. "As a matter of fact, I have him with me. Want to see?"

"Absolutely."

Celeste opened her large shoulder bag, and Mr. Peepers's furry head popped up. The monkey pulled back his lips in an imitation of a grin and made a parrotlike squawk.

Sara's hand flew up to her chest. "Oh, he's precious!"

A feeling of something that was probably close to maternal pride filled Celeste's chest. "He's a sweetheart, but he has a mischievous side. I thought I'd left him in his kennel, but on the drive into town I discovered he'd stowed away in my purse."

The monkey looked at Sara, lifted his arms and gave two grunts.

"That means he wants you to pick him up," Celeste said.

"Oh—may I?" Sara's face looked so eager that Celeste smiled.

"Sure."

The older woman held out her arms, and the monkey climbed into them. "It's like holding a baby!"

"A very mischievous one."

The monkey hugged Sara's neck. "He's adorable. And so affectionate!"

Celeste nodded. "He always is with women and children, but he's wary of men. Apparently he was abused by a man before the Joneses got him."

"Poor sweetie." Sara patted the little monkey's back. "It's hard to believe that anyone could hurt an adorable little fellow like this."

"A lot of the animals that the Joneses adopted had sad backgrounds—neglect or illness or injuries."

Mr. Peepers pressed his lips to Sara's cheek. Her eyes grew wide with awe. "He kissed me!"

Celeste nodded. "The Joneses taught him that as part of their clown act. They'd turn their back on him and he'd get into all kinds of mischief. When they turned back around and saw the mess he'd created, he'd act all sweet and innocent." Her mouth curved in a wry smile. "It's an act he's got down pat."

"Well, he's absolutely adorable." The brunette grinned as the animal ran bony fingers through her short, stylish hair. "Children are going to love your place. There aren't many spots for youngsters around here."

"Unfortunately, as Rand pointed out, there aren't that many children around here, either," Celeste said glumly. "According to him, I'm doomed to failure before I start."

Sara's eyebrows pulled together. "That doesn't sound like Rand. I sat in for my father at the chamber of commerce board meeting last week, and one of the items on the agenda was how to generate new business development. Why, this month's program is on how new businesses help the whole community."

"Well, he doesn't see my business that way." Celeste explained the circumstances of how they'd met and how he'd tried to discourage her. "He wants me to throw in the towel and sell him the property."

"Once he realizes you're serious, he'll set his sights on the property on the other side of his ranch, or behind him." Sara gave a teasing grin. "I can't imagine he'd object to having such a pretty neighbor."

"Oh, he seems to object plenty," Celeste replied.

"Well, if there's anything I can do to help, just ask." Sara's gray eyes were warm and sincere. "I know how hard it can be to get a new business off the ground, and I'd be glad to help in any way I can."

"That's very kind of you." Celeste picked up a bag of mixed grains. "There is one thing—could you tell me who handles your advertising? I'm interested in getting a billboard on the interstate, and I don't know where to start."

"My father doesn't advertise. He doesn't have to. This is the only feed store within sixty miles, and his customers are all locals." Her eyes suddenly lit up. "Wait, though . . . I do have the name and phone number of the advertising agency in New Orleans that Lamont Grocery down on Elm Street uses. The account executive called on me last week when he was in town. I can give you his card, if you like."

It was just the kind of information Celeste needed. "That would be great. Thanks!"

She followed the older woman to the counter. Sara rummaged through an old Rolodex by the cash register, pulled out a card and handed it over. "Rand might have some suggestions, too. I understand he advertises in quarter horse magazines, so he must use an ad agency."

Just the mention of Rand's name made Celeste's stomach tighten. "I don't think he'd be very inclined to help me."

"Oh, I'm sure . . ." Sara stopped in midsentence, her eyes on the front door. "Speak of the devil—look who's coming this way."

For reasons Celeste couldn't explain, her pulse fluttered

like a flag in the wind. She turned toward the front of the store as the cowbell jangled. Sure enough, Rand was pushing through the door.

He froze for a second when he spotted her. Their eyes locked, and a jolt of electricity shot through her like a zap from a microwave oven. He felt it, too; Celeste saw the awareness in his eyes. Then he turned to Sara and smiled so smoothly that Celeste thought she must have imagined it.

"Hello, Rand," Sara greeted him.

"Morning, Sara." He turned to Celeste and gave a curt nod. "Celeste."

"I see you've met your new neighbor," Sara said brightly.

"Yes." He looked at the monkey in Sara's arms. "Both of them."

Sara turned the monkey around to face him. "Isn't he just the cutest thing?"

Rand held up his hand and took a step back. "Don't get him too close to me. He thinks my face is a spittoon."

Celeste jumped to her pet's defense. "Rand scared him. And when Mr. Peepers gets upset, he spits."

"He also likes to throw dolls and clear off knick-knack shelves."

"Sounds like there's a story there," Sara said. The phone rang at the counter. "Excuse me. I need to get that."

Sara hurried to the front of the store, still holding the monkey. Silence stretched awkwardly between Rand and Celeste as they found themselves alone.

Remembering their last encounter, Celeste braced herself. She refused to let him discourage her.

"So how are things going?" he asked.

"You'll be disappointed to hear that they're going very well," she said stiffly. "I've already painted the front fence and scraped the paint off the front porch."

He shifted his stance and had the grace to look uneasy.

"Well, good. Look—I'm sorry if I offended you the other day. I just happen to have quite a bit of insight into the type of businesses that can make a go of it in this community, and . . ." His voice trailed off. "I just thought you might want to consider all the facts before you sank a lot of time and money into the place."

"Well, thanks for your heartwarming concern."

Rand frowned. "You don't have to be so prickly. There's no shame in evaluating a situation and changing your mind."

"I'm not going to change it."

His mouth tightened. "Suit yourself."

"That's exactly what I intend to do."

Celeste was relieved to see Sara return. The petite brunette handed her Mr. Peepers, then turned to Rand. "Celeste told me about her plans for the petting zoo, and I think it sounds wonderful. I was explaining to her that the Chamber of Commerce is a strong supporter of new businesses."

A muscle twitched in Rand's cheek.

"The Chamber is holding a fais do-do a week from Saturday," Sara told Celeste.

"A what?"

"A fais do-do—a Cajun dance. They're lots of fun—very casual and high-spirited. You should come. It's a fund-raiser for a new fire truck, and it'll be a good way for you to get to know people in the community." She cast a winsome smile at the tall rancher. "Right, Rand?"

"Right." He sounded less than enthusiastic.

"One of the keys to making a business successful is getting the word out." Sara placed her hand on Rand's arm. "Say, I've got a great idea! Since you're the Chamber president and you live right next door, why don't you bring Celeste and introduce her around?"

Rand ran a hand through his thick hair. "Oh, I, um—I don't think . . ."

"I'm sure he's already got plans," Celeste broke in. She knew Sara meant well, but the last thing she wanted was to be saddled with Mr. Negativity for an entire evening.

But Sara didn't take the hint. "From what I hear, he always goes stag to these things."

"I'll, um, be tied up with Chamber business all evening."

"I'm sure Celeste won't mind. You can introduce her around in between." Sara shot him a winsome smile. "And I'm sure you'll find time to sneak in a few dances."

Celeste felt her face flame. "Actually, I'm not in to dancing. And I plan to spend the weekend doing repairs around the house."

Sara's face fell. "Oh. Well, that's too bad. Still, we need to convince you to join the Chamber—don't you think, Rand?"

"Um . . . sure." The complete lack of conviction in his voice sent a rush of irritation through Celeste.

"Rand is always saying how every business in Cypress Grove should be represented," Sara continued. "The Chamber undertakes a lot of projects that help the community."

"There's no need to rush Ms. Landry into anything," Rand said. "The dues are pretty steep, and Celeste has only been here a couple of days. She hasn't had a chance to even evaluate whether or not she intends to stay."

"Oh, I intend to stay, all right." The implication that she might not was infuriating.

Sara broke in, interrupting Celeste's thoughts. "The next Chamber meeting is day after tomorrow, isn't it?" she asked Rand.

"Well . . . yes."

"And anyone can come as a guest for three meetings before they decide to join, right?"

Rand's mouth flattened into a tight line. "That's right."

His obvious reluctance to see her become a part of the community made Celeste's blood boil. She lifted her chin and turned to Sara. "I'd love to come. When is it?"

"Thursday morning at eight. It's a breakfast meeting in the private room at the Cajun Café."

"I'll be there."

She took a perverse pleasure from the way Rand's eyes darkened—and even more from the way they watched her purchase a month's worth of assorted feed and leave the store.

Chapter Five

The Cajun Café sat across the street from the Feed and Seed in an old, two-story red brick building. Celeste paused outside the smoked glass door on Thursday morning and smoothed her sleeveless blue print dress, reading the list of daily luncheon specials taped to the window. Today's special was crawfish etouffe. Judging from the scent of garlic that hit her nostrils as she opened the door, the chef had already begun to prepare it, even though it was only a little before eight o'clock.

Bright fluorescent lights gave everything, including the complexions of the customers, a surreal greenish-yellow cast. The tables were set with blue plastic tablecloths, metal napkin dispensers and two types of bottled hot sauce.

The rumble of chatter dulled as the diners turned and stared at her. Apparently, strangers were enough of a rarity in Cypress Grove to be a cause for gawking.

A sign by the staircase opposite the front door indicated that the meeting room was upstairs. Celeste cast a nervous smile at the restaurant's customers and headed up the staircase. As she climbed, she noted that the walls were plastered with photographs of various civic groups that apparently met there—Lions, Elks, Rotarians, the Ladies Auxiliary and the Chamber of Commerce.

She hesitated at the top of the stairs.

"Come in, dearie, come in." Celeste turned to see a woman in her late fifties seated at a long registration table. The woman's hair was dyed a flat, light-absorbing shade of black, and she wore glasses as thick as the bottoms of Coke bottles. She gave Celeste a warm smile and a name tag. "You must be the gal who's opening a pet store."

Apparently, the town had an active, if not accurate, grapevine. "Actually, it's a petting zoo," Celeste said, scribbling her name on the tag.

"A zoo for pets?" The woman's eyes appeared crossed behind her thick lenses.

"No. A petting zoo. Where children can pet and feed animals."

Judging from the woman's puzzled expression, she still failed to grasp the concept, but she smiled widely all the same. "Well, welcome to Cypress Grove. Go right on in and make yourself at home."

Celeste thanked her, pressed the white name tag high on her right shoulder and strode into the noisy room. She immediately spotted Rand against the far wall. His back was turned toward her, but she recognized his tall build, wide shoulders and dark wavy hair. To her annoyance, her pulse picked up speed at the sight of him. He seemed to sense her eyes on him, because he turned around.

There should have been broken glass, the way their gazes collided. What was it about the man that made Celeste feel as if she'd been mowed down by a semitrailer every time he glanced her way—antipathy or attraction or a weird combination of both?

71

"Celeste—I'm so glad you made it!"

Celeste felt a wave of relief to see Sara hurrying toward her. The petite brunette wore a simple sleeveless black dress with a piece of bold gold-and-silver jewelry around her neck. Elegant, sophisticated and self-assured, she looked like she'd just stepped out of a fashion ad.

The woman gave her a smile and a quick hug, then placed her hand on Celeste's arm. "Come on—I want you to meet a few people."

For the next fifteen minutes, Sara took her around the room. "I'll never remember everyone's name," Celeste murmured after Sara had successfully introduced her to the local grocer, the gas station manager, a pharmacist, an insurance agent and half a dozen other people.

"That's all right," Sara assured her. "They'll remember yours—and more importantly, they'll remember your business."

Celeste glanced over at Rand and caught him watching her. He abruptly looked away, but not before she saw a displeased expression on his face. He probably resented the fact that she was being welcomed so warmly by the other Chamber members.

Sara steered her toward a balding, rotund man carrying a heaping plate of scrambled eggs. "Celeste, I'd like you to meet Dawson Adler, the president of Cypress Grove Savings and Loan." She shot Celeste a meaningful glance, indicating that the man was a important contact. "At one time or another, Mr. Adler has been of help to just about everyone in the room." She smiled at the banker. "Dawson, Celeste just moved into Miss Lizzie's old place."

The man shifted his plate in order to shake Celeste's hand. "Oh, really?"

"She inherited it from Lizzie's sister," Sara explained.

"Well, well, well!" He regarded her with interest over his towering mound of eggs. "If you're looking to sell the place, I happen to know Rand Adams is interested in buying it."

"So I heard. But it's not for sale," Celeste said.

"Celeste is going into business there," Sara contributed.

Mr. Adler's brows rose toward his nonexistent hairline. "Is that so?" He looked at Celeste with interest. "Well, good. My bank specializes in backing local enterprises. What kind are you opening?"

"A petting zoo."

The eggs wobbled on his plate. "Come again?"

"A petting zoo. A place where children can interact with animals. It'll be a site for birthday parties and picnics, as well as family outings."

"I see." From the dubious tone of his voice, it was clear he didn't see at all. "Well, that's certainly an interesting undertaking." He turned to Sara. "How's your father, my dear?"

After a brief conversation with Sara, the banker turned back to Celeste and gave her a polite nod. "Well, I wish you the best of luck. It was nice meeting you."

Mr. Adler strode away with an air of hurried importance, his eggs about to avalanche.

"Every business owner needs a banker," Sara confided, guiding Celeste between two round banquet tables covered with blue-checked tablecloths. "Never know when you might need a little financial aid. Especially when you're just opening shop."

"From the way Mr. Adler hurried away when he found out what kind of business I'm opening, it's a good thing I don't plan to need any."

Sara looked at her curiously. "Most new places have a cash-flow problem the first few months."

Celeste gave her a dry smile. "I barely have enough money to float, much less flow. But if I manage my budget carefully, I should have enough to last three months."

Sara's forehead creased in a frown. "Three months? That's not long to get off the ground."

The remark echoed Rand's words almost exactly. A quiver of uncertainty rolled through Celeste's stomach. "Well, I guess I'll just have to work extra fast."

"That's a lot of pressure to put on yourself at a time when . . ." Sara stopped short.

Startled, Celeste looked over to see her friend staring straight ahead, her face pale. She leaned toward her. "Are you all right? You look like you saw a ghost."

"I-I feel like I did."

Celeste followed Sara's gaze. A handsome man in his mid-forties wearing blue jeans and cowboy boots stood at the registration desk, pressing an adhesive name badge on his plaid western-cut shirt. He had dark hair shot through with silver, a matching mustache and a lean, muscular physique. He sauntered into the room with easy confidence, pausing to shake hands with a man at a banquet table. He smiled and laughed at something the man said, then straightened and strode farther into the room.

Until he caught sight of Sara. Their gazes locked, and he stopped dead in his tracks. As Celeste watched, he abruptly turned and headed for the exit.

"Come with me," Sara whispered in an urgent tone.

Celeste hurried after her friend, wondering what in the world was going on.

The man nearly made it out the door, but he was waylaid by an incoming Chamber member. He'd just extricated himself from that conversation when Sara caught up with him.

"H-hello, George." There was a distinct quaver in Sara's voice, completely at odds with her usual aura of confidence.

"Hi." The man nodded curtly, then turned to Celeste,

studiously avoiding Sara's eyes. "Hello. I'm George Wright." He held out his hand.

She shook it. "I'm Celeste Landry."

"You must be the gal who's moved next to Rand's ranch."

Celeste nodded. The man was deliberately avoiding speaking to Sara, she realized.

"I help out with his horses. Nice meeting you." His eyes flashed toward Sara, then rapidly looked away. "Well, if you'll excuse me . . ." He turned back toward the door.

"George—wait."

The man paused, then reluctantly turned around. Celeste noted that his eyes never quite met Sara's. Two bright pink spots colored Sara's cheeks.

"I-I was sorry to hear about Heather," she murmured.

George fixed his eyes on the floor. "Yeah. Sorry about your father, too. Hope he recovers real fast." He turned away.

"George . . ." Sara's voice held a pleading note.

"I gotta go." His voice was gruff, his tone curt. He turned and disappeared down the stairs.

Sara stood still, her eyes dark and pained.

Celeste touched her arm. "Are you all right?"

Sara drew in a shaky breath. "Yes."

"Do you want to sit down?"

Sara shook her head. Her eyes were suspiciously moist, and her face was flushed. She drew in a long breath.

"Why don't I get you a glass of water?" Celeste suggested.

"I-I'm fine. I—"

"Sara Overton!" A large elderly woman in a flowing pink dress with bright pink lipstick and heavily rouged pink cheeks barged up, enveloping Sara in an enthusiastic hug. "I saw your father two days ago when I was visiting my sister out at Forest Manor. She's moved into that nice new assisted living wing."

Celeste watched Sara compose her features and paste on a polite smile. "Is that right?"

"Yes. She loves it there." The vertical lines above the woman's pink mouth creased like a Chinese fan. "I was shocked to see how bad off your father is, though."

"He's making progress. He's actually quite a bit better than he was." Sara gamely gestured toward Celeste. "Mrs. Heath, I'd like you to meet Cypress Grove's newest resident. This is Celeste Landry, and she's opening a petting zoo."

"You don't say!" The pink lady jerked Celeste's hand up and down as if priming a water pump.

"It'll be a wonderful place to take your grandchildren," Sara told her.

"Speaking of my grandchildren, little Abby did the cutest thing the other day. . . ." The woman launched into a lengthy story. Celeste noted that Sara listened politely and smiled at all the right spots, but Celeste could tell that her thoughts were elsewhere.

No doubt on the handsome man who'd left so abruptly. What was the story between them? Celeste hoped to find out, but when the pink lady finally lumbered off, Sara looked at her watch.

"I've got to get going. My father's doctor comes by the nursing home around nine on Tuesday mornings and I need to talk to him. I wanted to stop by here first, though, and make sure you felt welcomed."

"That was very sweet of you. I really appreciate your taking me under your wing like this," Celeste said.

Sara patted her arm. "I had a mentor when I first started my business in Chicago, and helping you makes me feel like I'm paying her back. Plus, it's an outlet for all my unused maternal instincts."

"Well, I really appreciate it. Will you let me take you to lunch tomorrow as payback?"

"I'd love it."

"I'm not familiar with the restaurants around here. Where should we meet?"

"How about the Past Times Café out on the highway?"

Celeste had no idea where that was, but she figured it couldn't be too hard to find. "Sounds terrific. At noon?"

"Sounds great." Sara lifted her hand in a graceful wave and headed for the door. "See you then."

Celeste turned around to find Rand still watching her from across the room. He probably wished she'd left with Sara. Well, tough cookies, she thought, squaring her shoulders. She was here to stay, and he'd better get used to it.

She headed toward the buffet table and reached for a plate, only to have one placed in her hand.

"Here you go, Celeste," said a male voice.

Startled, Celeste turned around to find a man in his mid-thirties standing behind her. He had sandy hair, a ruddy complexion and an overbright smile. She was sure she hadn't been introduced to him.

"Thank you," she said. "How did you know my name?"

"I always make a point of learning the name of the most beautiful woman in the room."

Oh, brother. Celeste suppressed the urge to roll her eyes. She was about to make a polite escape when she glanced across the room and saw Rand staring at her, apparently trying to catch her eye. He tilted his head in the direction of the man beside her and gave his head an almost imperceptible shake, as if he were warning her not to talk to him.

Irritation flashed through her. Who did he think he was? Rand had no right to tell her what to do.

"I'm Larry Birkman," the man said.

Hoping that Rand was still watching, Celeste gave the man a warm smile, shifted the plate to her left hand and held out her right one. "Nice to meet you."

Instead of shaking her hand, Larry simply held it.

She felt the heat of someone's eyes on her and glanced to her right. Sure enough, Rand had crossed the room and was standing behind Larry, staring directly at her. His mouth was pulled in a tight, disapproving line.

Something reckless made her flash Larry her most brilliant smile as she pulled back her hand. "What business are you in, Larry?"

"Carpentry. Birkman and Sons. My grandfather did the original cabinetry work at your ranch."

Celeste gazed at him in feigned fascination. From the corner of her eye, she saw Rand scowl, then walk out of her line of vision. "You don't say. Does your grandfather still work with you?"

"No, he died a few years ago."

Celeste could no longer see Rand, but she suspected he was still watching. She moved down the buffet line, making small talk with Larry and filling her plate, although she had no appetite at all.

"The Chamber's sponsoring a fais do-do next week," Larry remarked as they neared the end of the line.

"So I heard."

Larry leaned in close. "It should be lots of fun. I hope to see you there."

Celeste had decided after her reactions to Rand that she needed to start dating again, but Larry was not her type. "I'm not planning on going."

"Why not?" Larry pressed. "Don't you like Cajun music?"

"Oh, I like it just fine—what little I know about it. But . . ."

"But what?"

Celeste gave a sheepish grin. "I'm a terrible dancer. I don't even know how to two-step."

Larry's smile widened. "That's no problem. I'm a great teacher."

"Thanks, but I don't think—"

"Come on. Just say yes." Larry's hand snaked out and landed on the small of her back. "I promise you'll have the time of your life."

Before Celeste could frame a response, Rand's voice sounded behind her. "Sorry to butt in, but Celeste has already agreed to come to the dance with me."

Startled, Celeste turned around. Her heart began to beat an unreasonable tattoo as Rand fixed a cold gaze on Larry.

The other man's hand dropped immediately. He flashed Rand a nervous smile. "Hey, buddy—I didn't see you standing there."

"I've been here for quite a while." His gaze seemed to bore holes in Birkman. "How's Linda?"

Larry's gaze flickered away. "Fine. Just fine."

"Glad to hear it."

Larry swallowed visibly. He gave Celeste a jerky nod, all of his flirtatiousness gone. "It was nice meeting you." Then he beat a quick retreat across the room.

Rand reached out and authoritatively took Celeste's plate from her.

She glared at him. "What do you think you're doing?"

He took off across the room, carrying her food. "Finding you a table. The meeting is about to begin."

She strode after him. "I can find my own place, thank you. And anyway, that's not what I was talking about. I never agreed to go to the dance with you."

"I know. I didn't ask."

The gall of the man was unbelievable! "Oh, and if you'd asked, you're sure I would have agreed?" Celeste had to hurry to keep up with him. "You think all you have to do is *ask*, and there's no doubt about my answer?"

"If you don't want to go with me, fine. Stay home."

She circled around a table and cut in front of him, blocking his path. "If I want to go, I'll do so on my own."

"Okay." he said agreeably. "We'll go in separate cars and meet up at the dance." Neatly sidestepping her, he continued to carry her plate through the maze of tables.

"I've met some arrogant men before, but you raise conceit to whole a new level." She struggled to keep up with him, regretting the fact that she was wearing high heels. "What is your problem?"

"You are, at the moment." His voice was soft, but Celeste heard an undertone of steel. "Believe it or not, I just did you a favor."

Celeste pulled on his arm, nearly making him spill the plate of food. He abruptly stopped and turned to face her, his mouth grim, his eyes foreboding.

Celeste's insides quivered, but she stood her ground. "Maybe everyone else lets you get away with this kind of high-handed behavior, but I won't stand for it."

"Well, I might be high-handed, but at least I keep those hands to myself," Rand replied.

"What are you talking about?"

"Larry Birkman is the Casanova of the parish."

Rand was trying to protect her from a smooth operator? Celeste rolled her eyes. "This may come as a shock, but I can take care of myself."

A muscle flexed in Rand's jaw. "If you're seen with Larry, the whole town will think you're 'taking care' of him."

"What?"

"He's married. His wife's job requires a lot of travel, and he cheats on her every time she leaves town. Everyone in Cypress Grove knows it. Everyone except his wife, that is. She probably knows it, too, but finds it easier to ignore than to act."

The information left Celeste at a loss for words.

"Linda is a decent person, and I respect her too much to let her be embarrassed by Larry hound-dogging you at the dance. And if you show up solo, that's just what he's going to do."

Rand strode to the nearest table and plopped her plate down at an empty place setting beside an elderly man and woman.

"Dwight, Marcia, this is Celeste Landry," he said. "Celeste, these are the Channings; they run the dry cleaning shop on the corner of First and Maple."

Celeste found herself responding to their polite hellos, irritated that Rand had found such an effective way of terminating their conversation. Mr. Channing politely stood as Rand yanked out a chair, leaving Celeste no choice but to sit down. Rand shoved her chair up to the table with a little more force than she thought necessary.

"I'll pick you up at seven on Saturday." He shot her a glance that managed to be simultaneously full of warning and maddeningly polite before he turned away and walked off.

Celeste watched him go, anger simmering in her veins. His explanation had dampened her fury but by no means extinguished it. No motive could justify such overbearing behavior. And yet, underneath her hot blanket of outrage lurked a tiny, cold coal of hurt.

Rand wasn't insisting on taking her to the dance because he was attracted to her; he was doing it out of respect for Larry's wife.

It was ridiculous that fact should make her feel as flat as the pancakes on her plate, yet it did.

"What a charming young man," Mrs. Channing remarked, her gaze following Rand. "Isn't he something?"

Celeste forced a polite smile through gritted teeth. Adding insult to injury, he'd seated her with people who apparently thought he'd hung the moon. "Oh, he's something, all right," she muttered. "He's definitely something."

But exactly what, she couldn't say.

Chapter Six

"The shrimp salad is good here," Sara said the next day as she and Celeste studied their lunch menus.

"Shrimp salad it is, then." Celeste closed the menu and leaned across the table. "So tell me all about your interior design business."

Sara folded her menu and placed it on the table. "Well, we specialize in eclectic designs based on traditional European decors. I like to use lots of antiques and rich fabrics, mixed with custom-made modern elements."

"So I guess you're not likely to stock up on any of the things for sale here," Celeste teased.

The Past Times Café was set in the back of the Past Times Antique and Curio Shop a couple of miles out of town. The store was filled with old farm implements and kitschy items from the '50s and '60s—old gas station signs, a jukebox, Elvis memorabilia, tin lunchboxes and an assortment of ugly vinyl chairs that once must have been the height of modern chic.

Sara grinned as she gazed at an old Texaco sign on the wall. "This isn't exactly my clientele's cup of tea. It makes for an adorable lunch spot, though."

Celeste nodded. "It's like dining in an aunt's attic." The place was tiny, just six tables altogether, and since it had no stove, it only served sandwiches and salads.

She turned her attention back to Sara. "Where do you find the stuff you use?"

"I travel a lot," the older woman said. "I go on buying trips abroad for new fabrics and furniture several times a year, and I attend auctions for antiques."

"That sounds so exciting!"

Sara took a sip of water. "It was at first, but after you've done it as many times as I have, it starts to lose its charm. To tell you the truth, lately I've started to dread the trips. My partner has school-age children, though, and she doesn't want to leave them for a week or more at a time, so it all falls on me." She unfolded her napkin in her lap. "We've been discussing bringing in another partner to help out with some of it."

A young waitress with heavy black eyeliner stopped to take their order.

"So how was the rest of the Chamber meeting?" Sara asked when the waitress left.

Celeste fixed her gaze on an old wagon wheel on the wall and sighed. "Things went downhill after you left."

Sara's eyebrows rose. "Oh?"

Celeste nodded. "Rand turned into a Neanderthal. He overheard Larry Birkman asking me to the dance, and before I could even answer he butted in and told Larry I was going with him."

"Really?" Amusement twinkled in Sara's blue-gray eyes. "Well, believe it or not, that was more white knight-ish than Neanderthal. From what I've heard at the beauty shop, Larry's bad news."

"Rand could have just *told* me that. I'm perfectly capable of taking care of myself."

"Larry doesn't like to take no for an answer. Rand probably figured that was the easiest way to get him to leave you alone."

"Well, it was rude and condescending. And then he had the nerve to tell me—not ask me, mind you, but *tell* me—that I'm not going to the dance unless I go with him!"

Sara laughed, her eyes sparkling. "And that's a problem?"

"You bet it's a problem! Not that I planned to go anyway. But where does he get off, thinking he can order me around?"

Sara's brows knitted thoughtfully together. "I've got to say, it doesn't sound like Rand. Everyone always talks about how he's a perfect gentleman."

"Well, you couldn't prove it by me. He's been in my face since the first time we met."

"Know what I think?" A grin crossed Sara's face. "I think he's got a thing for you."

Celeste snorted. "He sure has a funny way of showing it."

"He was watching you every moment yesterday morning."

Despite herself, Celeste felt a little thrill crawl up her spine. "He was?"

Sara nodded. "Like a hawk."

"That's just because he wants to get his hands on my property."

"I don't think that's all he wants to get his hands on." Sara's eyes held a mischievous smile. "He wouldn't have such a strong reaction to you if his feelings were purely mercenary."

In spite of her desire to remain detached about the tall cowboy, Celeste felt her face heat.

"There's definitely some chemistry between you two," Sara continued.

"Yeah—like gunpowder and matches." Celeste seized the opportunity to turn the topic around. "Speaking of chemistry, what's the deal with you and George Wright?"

Sara fiddled with her glass of water, keeping her eyes lowered. "Let's just say he and I have some history."

"The romantic type?"

Sara nodded. "We nearly got married."

"Wow. That's history, all right. So what happened?"

"I stood him up at the altar."

Even after all this time, a sense of shame washed over Sara—shame and guilt and sorrow. Twenty-eight years had gone by, but the feelings were still there, sharp as broken glass. She gave a rueful smile as Celeste's eyes widened, and she said, "I know, I know. It was a horrible thing to do."

"You must have had your reasons." Celeste's voice was gentle, her expression nonjudgmental.

"I did. But that doesn't mean anyone else can understand them."

"I'd like to try."

Sara took another sip of water, then set down the glass. She knew people had been talking about it ever since she'd returned to Cypress Grove. She'd seen the covert looks, heard the conversations abruptly halt whenever she approached. "I might as well tell you. You're sure to hear the whole sordid story sooner or later."

Sara fixed her eyes on an old John Wayne movie poster and let the memories out of their locked cage. They flapped around her like the dark wings of a tethered falcon. "George and I were high-school sweethearts. Everyone said we were the perfect couple." *And we were,* Sara thought sadly. *We had so much in common. We were able to finish each other's sentences, anticipate each other's actions.*

"Our relationship actually started before high school. Our mothers were best friends, and they'd always hoped we'd end up together." Sara smiled. "I think they started planning our wedding while we were still in diapers."

An image swirled in her mind—the way her mother looked in the photograph that her father kept in his wallet. Aside from pictures, Sara couldn't really remember her mother's face. She remembered the woman's lap and her perfume, the sound of her voice reading bedtime stories, the cool feel of her palm on her forehead when she had a fever. But that was all she recalled. "My mother died when I was eight, and George's mother kind of took me under her wing. She took me shopping and to the beauty parlor and helped me with all the girl stuff that Dad was clueless about."

Sara wiped a bead of condensation off her water glass. "Our families were close. George used to work at Dad's store in the summer, and Dad thought the world of him. And I did, too." Her mouth curved in a smile. "I'd had a crush on George for as long as I could remember."

And her feelings had been reciprocated. She and George had been the perfect pair—a small-town cliché. George had been a rodeo champion and the student-council president, and Sara had been the Four-H Sweetheart.

"Everyone expected us to marry. It was just kind of a given. It was like our lives were already all planned out: George would take over his grandfather's horse farm and I'd help my dad in the store—at least until we started a family. But during our senior year . . ." Sara hesitated, not sure how to explain what happened, not sure she even understood it herself. "I started to realize that I wanted to do other stuff first. I wanted to go away to college and spend some time on my own—to spread my wings and discover who I was."

"Sounds pretty normal to me."

"Unfortunately, I couldn't get my father or George to see it that way."

"Why not?"

Sara lifted her shoulders. "After my mother died . . . well, I became scared to death of losing my father, too. He was so silent and sad that it was like he wasn't really there, either. So I thought—in that illogical way that children think—that if I was good and quiet and never made any trouble, I could make him happy again and keep him safe. I grew into a real people pleaser who never made any waves. Dad didn't want me to leave Cypress Grove, and I didn't want to upset him."

"He didn't want you to go to college?"

"He did, but he wanted me to go to SLU in Hammond, with George. It's only about thirty-five miles away, and we could commute. I wanted to go to a bigger university and study interior design." She took a sip of water. "I've always had a thing about settings and how they make you feel, how they affect your mood and your overall quality of life. And I've always loved fabrics—how they feel and drape and hang."

Celeste smiled. "Your face lights up when you talk about it."

Sara grinned ruefully. "Unfortunately, my dad didn't share my enthusiasm. He said interior design wasn't practical, that Cypress Grove was too small to support a business like that. He wanted me to major in business or accounting and help him with the store. And being the people-pleasing, meek, dutiful daughter that I was, I agreed."

"I sense a big *but* coming."

"You're right." Sara smiled slightly. "I agreed, but I secretly applied for a scholarship to a design institute in Chicago."

"And you won it?"

Sara nodded. "But by the time I found out, I was already engaged."

"Oh, no! When did you get engaged?"

"The night we graduated from high school. George had already talked to my father before he asked me—and he'd talked to his parents, too. My father was so pleased, and George was so pleased, and George's mother and father were so pleased. . . . Well, I just couldn't bring myself to let down all those people I loved. And there was something else. . . ." Sara paused.

"What?" Celeste urged.

"Sex." Sara gave a shy grin. "We were healthy, normal kids and our hormones were raging, but we'd agreed to wait until we were out of high school. So we waited, but then George insisted we needed to be engaged to sleep together."

"*George* did?"

Sara nodded. "Isn't that sweet? I didn't even realize it at the time." There were a lot of things about George that she hadn't fully appreciated at the time, she thought ruefully. He'd had a lot of traits that she'd later learned were special and rare.

"Anyway, as the wedding plans got underway, I started feeling trapped. I tried to tell George I wanted to wait, that I wasn't ready to get married, that I wanted to go away to college and have a career, but he wouldn't listen to me. He said I was just scared, that everything would be all right, and then he would kiss me, and. . . ." Sara gave a sheepish smile. "When he kissed me—well, let's just say I couldn't think straight."

Celeste smiled. "He must have had good diversionary tactics."

"Extremely good tactics." She could still remember how good. "I tried to talk to my father, too, but he just brushed my worries aside—as if I didn't know what was best for me, or as if I wasn't mature enough to know my own mind."

A wave of old frustration swept through her. "Everyone was so used to me just being this quiet, timid, obedient, don't-make-any-waves sort of person. Worst of all, *I* was used to being that way. I didn't want to make a scene. I didn't even know how." Sara shook her head. "Isn't that pathetic?"

"It's completely understandable," Celeste said softly.

"As the wedding date got closer, I started feeling more and more like I was just being swallowed whole, as if I were losing my identity. I'd been with George so long that I wasn't sure what was me and what was him. I mean, did I like chicken-fried steak or did I just eat it because he liked it? Did I dislike Chinese food or did we not eat it because George didn't care for it? He was so sure of himself, so strong in who he was, and I . . . well, I just felt like I tagged along, like a shadow." Sara turned her hands palms up on the table. "How could I pledge my life to him when I didn't even know who I was?"

"You couldn't."

"Well, I couldn't get my father or George to see it that way. And everyone else kept telling me how lucky I was, how wonderful George was, how beautiful the wedding would be, how they'd never seen another couple so meant for each other."

An old sense of claustrophobia clutched at her throat. She'd felt so smothered by her own cowardice, so trapped by her own need to please the people she loved.

"What happened?" Celeste asked.

"Well, I tried to talk to George one last time, the night before the wedding." The memory was indelibly etched in her memory. He'd driven her home in his old Chevy pickup after the rehearsal dinner. As he turned into her driveway, the song "All I Need Is the Air That I Breathe" was on the radio. George had shifted into park, keeping the truck's engine running so they could hear the song. He'd stretched his arm around her. "Tomorrow's our big day."

Her heart had pounded so fast and hard she'd thought she was going to pass out. "George, I . . . I don't think I'm ready."

"Honey, you're more than ready. I sure know I am." He'd reached for her breast, a familiar light in his eye.

Sara had shifted away. "I mean it, George. I—I think we should wait."

"We can't, sweetheart. Everything's all lined out." He'd run his hand up and down her arm. "You've just got pre-wedding jitters. You'll be fine."

"I don't think I can go through with it," she'd whispered.

George had tipped up her chin with his finger and forced her gaze to meet his. His eyes had searched hers, bearing down like a pair of approaching headlights, straight and dead-on and almost unbearably intense. "Do you love me?"

"You know I do." And she did. It was an honest answer.

"Well, then, honey, all you have to do is follow your heart." He'd walked her to her door and pressed his lips to her forehead, a gentle, tender kiss. Then he'd pulled back and given her that rakish grin that always made her heart turn over. "See you in church." He'd turned and taken a couple of steps, then swiveled back around. "Be sure and wear something special."

The waitress set two large shrimp salads in front of Sara and Celeste.

"And then?" Celeste prompted when she was gone.

Sara took a sip of water. "The day of the wedding I just felt paralyzed. It was as if wet cement had been poured down my throat. My stomach just got heavier and heavier, and my throat kept getting tighter and tighter. On the drive to the church, I realized I couldn't do it. I just couldn't. So when I got to the church, I told George's mother I needed to talk to him."

Her throat grew thick at the memory. "She refused to let me—she said it was bad luck for the groom to see the bride before the wedding. She said I'd be fine once I got down the aisle, that my dad was outside the door and she'd send him in, that it was time for her to go get seated."

Celeste regarded Sara somberly, her eyes large and empathetic.

"I know I should have been more forceful. I know I should have insisted that she go get George. But I didn't have the self-confidence or gumption or whatever you want to call it to stand up to her. All I knew was, I couldn't go through with it. And since I couldn't fight, the only option was flight."

"What did you do?"

Sara gave an embarrassed grin. "I climbed out the bathroom window."

Celeste's eyebrows flew up in astonishment. "In your wedding gown?"

Sara nodded. "It wasn't easy, believe you me. The dress was a big ol' thing—a huge confection of a gown, layers and layers of lace and tulle petticoats and a gargantuan *Gone With The Wind*-sized skirt. I ripped it getting through the window, and when I landed in the bushes, the whole skirt flipped over my head. Some late guests were still arriving at the church." Sara grinned. "I'm sure it was a sight they'll never forget."

"I imagine not!" Celeste grinned, but her eyes were concerned. "Where did you go? What did you do?"

"Well, I grabbed my suitcase and purse out of George's car—we were supposed to go to Nashville for our honeymoon—and I ran to the bus station."

"In your wedding gown?"

Sara nodded. "It was at a gas station back then, just a

couple of blocks from the church. The man who owned it was at the wedding."

Celeste put her hand over her mouth, her eyes wide.

"I got a ticket for the next bus, and it pulled up. And just as it opened its doors, here comes George and his parents and my father, followed by the whole wedding party and most of the guests."

"Oh, no! Oh, how awful!"

It had been. Sara felt the shame, the terror, the trapped-like-a-rat-in-a-corner feeling clawing at her chest all over again, just thinking about it. "I climbed on the bus and took a seat way in the back. George tried to talk to me through the window, demanding to know what I was doing. I told him I was sorry, that I loved him but I just wasn't ready to get married. He climbed onto the bus, but he didn't have a ticket and the driver made him get off.

"Then my father ordered *me* off the bus. I told him he couldn't tell me what to do anymore, that I wasn't a child, that it was my life and I had a right to live it as I wanted. And then the bus pulled out, and I cried all the way to New Orleans."

"Oh, Sara!"

"So that's the story." She turned up her hands. "I can't tell you how much I hated hurting George and his parents and my dad like that. I know I didn't handle it well, but it was the best I could do at the time. It seemed like a matter of life or death. And in a way, I guess it was. I knew that if I walked down that aisle and made those vows, I'd just get smaller and smaller until I disappeared."

"Oh, that must have been so hard," Celeste murmured.

"Not as hard as I'm sure it was on George. After all, I left. He was the one who stayed here and had to face everyone."

"Did you talk to him after that?"

"I tried. Oh, I tried. He wouldn't take my calls, and he

returned all my letters unopened. He wouldn't let my father even mention my name to him. He said he never wanted to hear it again." Sara picked up her fork. "He got married a year later—to one of my bridesmaids."

Even after all this time, the memory felt like a stake through the heart. "She mailed me back the last letter I wrote him—unopened, of course—in a big manila envelope with the wedding announcement from the local paper and a note telling me to leave them alone. So I did."

"Oh, Sara," Celeste whispered.

"They had a couple of sons. My father used to keep me posted on how they were doing, about the events in their lives."

And it had hurt like hell, but she'd always asked for news.

"His wife died about four years ago after a long struggle with cancer." Sara's throat grew tight. It was ridiculous that she should feel envious of a dead woman, and yet she did. "George was really good to her during her illness. He took care of her around the clock. He even sold his horse ranch and took her to South America for some experimental treatments. The people in town think George hung the moon." Her mouth pulled in a sad smile. She gazed at an old movie poster of *The Wizard of Oz* mounted on the wall. "And I'm sure they think I'm the Wicked Witch of the West."

"Oh, no—absolutely not." Celeste's voice was firm and sure. "From what I've seen, you're well-liked and respected. Besides, that all happened a long time ago. I'm sure everyone's forgotten about it."

"Evidently you don't know much about small towns," Sara said dryly. "People in a place the size of Cypress Grove never forget a juicy piece of gossip. That incident will follow me the rest of my life."

Celeste's brow furrowed with concern. "It must be tough on you, then, being back here."

Sara sighed. "People keep bringing up George's name to me. Some of them are just nosy and want to see how I'll react, and others seem to think that since George is single again, we ought to pick up where we left off."

"Sounds awkward."

Sara nodded slowly. "I've avoided coming back as much as possible over the years. My dad used to come to Chicago for the holidays, and we'd always spend a week together in the summer, fishing in Colorado. But when he had his stroke, well—I had no choice. Dad needs me here. And I've grown a pretty thick skin." She took a sip of water. "But I still feel awful about the way I handled things. And being here does bring some uncomfortable moments."

"Like yesterday."

Sara bobbed her head in agreement. "I've seen George since I've been back, but it's always been at a distance, and he's always avoided me. Truth be told, I've avoided him, too." Sara sighed. "I knew we were bound to run into each sooner or later, and I knew it would be weird. But I never suspected it would be *that* weird. It's been almost thirty years, for heaven's sake. You'd think he'd at least be able to act civil."

"I'm sure it was a shock, seeing you face-to-face."

"It was a shock to me, too."

"He's a good-looking man."

"Yeah. He aged well." *To put it mildly.* He'd been attractive as a boy, but now he was downright devastating. "When he walked into the meeting, I decided it was time to face things head-on. I hated skulking around town trying to avoid him, so I thought I'd just get it over with." She gave a rueful smile. "You saw how well that worked."

"Maybe you need to try again. In a less public place."

Sara shook her head. "He'd never agree to see me."

"Well, then, maybe you need to force his hand. Get him in a situation where he has no choice but to listen to you."

"Such as?"

Celeste shrugged. "I don't know. Get stuck in an elevator with him, maybe."

Sara grinned. "The only elevator in town is in the parish jail, and it only goes up one floor. Besides, the sheriff's a friend of his."

"I guess that rules out Plan B, too, then," Celeste said with a mischievous smile.

"What's Plan B?"

"Get the sheriff to arrest him, then go visit him with a hacksaw in a pie."

Sara laughed. "You watch too many bad movies."

"Probably so." Celeste smiled back; then her face grew somber. "Seriously, Sara—it sounds to me as if you need to clear the air for your own peace of mind."

Sara nodded. "You'd think the years would make the feelings go away, but they haven't. I still feel so horribly, terribly guilty."

"You did the best you could at the time," Celeste said gently.

"Maybe so, but I still hurt and humiliated someone I loved. And he's never given me the chance to even explain why."

"You'll get your chance."

"You sound awfully sure."

"My grandmother used to say that everything happens for a reason, whether we can see it or not. She said the ultimate reason for everything is love, and that love always finds a way." Celeste's green eyes gazed into Sara's, earnest and direct and wiser than her years. "She also said that love never dies, it just changes shape—like water changing into ice or steam. And when that happens, sometimes people can't recognize it."

There is no love left between me and George, Sara thought sadly. Only hurt and pain and regret. "That's a nice thought, but I don't think it applies in this case. George won't even let me explain."

"You need to find a way to make him."

Celeste was right, Sara decided as she picked up her fork. But that was easier said than done.

Chapter Seven

It was not even ten in the morning, but the day was already so steamy that Rand's sunglasses fogged up as he climbed out of his pickup in front of Celeste's house.

He yanked them off his face and strode toward the porch, where Celeste stood on a ladder, her back toward him, painting the ceiling. She was wearing a Sony Walkman over a blue bandanna kerchief and she must have had the volume turned up, because she was oblivious to the fact that she had company—just as she was oblivious to just about every other reality, Rand thought darkly.

"Hey, there!" he yelled.

Her only response was to rhythmically wiggle her backside.

It was a shapely backside, damn it—perched atop long, tan legs and clad in tight denim shorts. It was unfair that she looked so good. He was here to give her a piece of his mind, and he didn't want his anger diluted by the annoying sense of attraction he always felt around her.

He walked around to the front of the ladder and planted himself directly in front of her. She looked down, started and promptly dropped her paintbrush on top of his cowboy boot.

"Oh!"

Oh, indeed. A muscle twitched in Rand's jaw as he gazed down at the blob of white paint oozing off the black leather toe of his favorite Noconas. Couldn't this woman do *anything* without causing him problems?

"You startled me." She pulled off her headset and rapidly climbed down the ladder, regarding him with a frown. "You really shouldn't sneak up on people like that."

He started to tell her that he wasn't sneaking, but a smudge of paint near the corner of her mouth distracted him, and his attention drifted to her lips. Oh, man, she had a beautiful mouth—a mouth just meant for kissing. Her upper lip had two provocative swells with a deep dip in between, echoing the shape of her other lush curves—curves of which he was keenly aware and at which he was trying hard not to stare. Man, how he'd love to feel those curves pressing against his body as he slid his tongue between her pink lips and . . .

"I'd better get that paint off your shoe before it dries." Before he could gather his thoughts, Celeste grabbed a terry-cloth rag hanging on a rung of the ladder and knelt in front of him. The neck of her navy tank top gaped open, giving him a clear view of her black lace bra.

A hard jolt of attraction rocked through him. "I-I can do that."

But Celeste was on her knees, rubbing his boot like a shoeshine girl, displaying a disconcerting amount of cleavage in the process. Rand gritted his teeth. He hadn't come over here to get physically aroused by Little Miss Disaster-Looking-For-a-Place-to-Happen. But it was hard not to, not when he could see her breasts quivering against their lace constraints.

She looked up at him, her face horizontal to his fly. "If I get this wet and rub it, I think I can get it off."

"*What?*"

"I think the paint will come off."

"Oh." He really needed to get a grip on himself. "Um, good." He cleared his throat as she turned and dipped the rag in a bucket of water behind her, then set to work again on his boot.

"There." All too soon—or not soon enough, depending on which part of his anatomy was doing the thinking— she sat back on her heels. "Almost as good as new."

The leather on the boot was dull and cloudy, as if it had a cataract, but Rand didn't dare say a word. He reached out his hand to help her to her feet, then immediately regretted it. Electricity zinged between them, scattering his thoughts like sparks from a blown transformer. From the dazed look in her eyes, she felt it, too.

A loud bleat sounded from the driveway. Celeste pulled her hand away and turned toward his pickup. "Good grief. Is that Dr. Freud in the cab of your truck?"

He wished to God it really was. He needed the psychiatrist to help him deal with his insane attraction to this wrecking ball of a woman.

"What's my goat doing inside your pickup?"

"The *doctor* there made an unwelcome house call to my ranch this morning," Rand said grimly. "I'd just coaxed a filly to finally take a bit when your goat strolled in and scared her half to death. She jumped back and nearly broke off her front teeth."

"Oh, dear!" Celeste's brows pulled together over her worried green eyes. "Is the horse okay?"

"Well, she's not physically injured—but it was a close

call. And it's caused a real setback in her training. It'll be weeks before she trusts me again."

"I'm so sorry."

Damn it, she looked sorry. It was hard to hold a grudge against someone who seemed so blasted sincere, and he wanted to hold on to his anger. It was his best hedge against the growing attraction he felt for her.

"Both goats were in my field this morning when I fed them," she was saying. "I don't know how Dr. Freud got out."

"There must be a hole in your fence."

"I'll go check right now. If there's a problem, I'll get it fixed."

Oh, there was a problem, all right—and it wasn't just with her fence. Dad-blast it, why did she have to look damned earnest and appealing? "You do that." Rand scowled, not sure if he was more irritated at her or himself. "And while you're at it, you'd better make sure this doesn't happen again. An incident like today could ruin my business, and I won't put up with it."

"I told you I was sorry, and I told you I'd fix the fence." She leveled a steady gaze at him that made him feel like a jerk. "And speaking of not putting up with things—*I* won't put up with the way *you* treated me at the Chamber meeting."

Rand narrowed his eyes. "And just how did I treat you?"

"You were condescending and rude and presumptuous."

He glared at her. "I was doing you a favor."

She glared right back. "You could have just taken me aside and told me Larry was married."

"There was no way to do that, not when Larry was hanging all over you like Spanish moss on an oak. I figured the most diplomatic way to handle the situation was to make him think you were spoken for."

"That was your idea of *diplomatic?*"

Even to his own ears, the word was laughable. He shrugged.

Celeste's mouth curved into a small smile. "I hate to tell you this, but you'll need to brush up on your skills before you're ready for the UN."

Against his will, Rand grinned. The anger he'd tried to nurse kicked the bucket.

"You didn't have to be so rude to me afterward," Celeste continued.

Aw, hell—she was right. Rand looked away and hitched his thumb through a belt loop. "Yeah, well, you were spitting mad. I figured the best course of action was to get you seated, then get out of your line of fire."

She regarded him curiously for a moment. "You must really like Larry's wife."

The remark caught him off guard. He shrugged. "I don't really know her all that well. I just hate to see a decent woman publicly humiliated by a creep."

Celeste studied him, her head cocked slightly to the side, as if she were trying to figure him out. Rand had the odd feeling she was looking too deep, seeing too much.

A muffled bleat made them both turn toward his pickup.

"Oh, gee—we'd better get Dr. Freud out of your truck before he suffocates in this heat." Celeste started down the porch steps.

Rand walked beside her. "He's in no danger. I left the air-conditioner on."

She shot him an amused grin. "That was thoughtful."

"Yeah, well—you can't leave animals in a closed vehicle in the summer."

Celeste shot him a sideways smile as she walked down the porch beside him. "It was kind of you to drive him back in air-conditioned comfort, too."

"Believe me, I didn't do it for the goat's sake." Rand scowled at the beast silhouetted in the passenger window.

101

"I tried to tie him in the truck bed, but he kept jumping out. I was afraid the dumb thing was going to hang itself."

"I see he's even wearing a seat belt." Celeste's grin widened.

"That's just to keep him from climbing all over me."

"Well, it was awfully nice of you to take such good care of him."

"Too nice," Rand muttered. "I passed my banker on the road here, and he looked at me as if I'd lost my mind."

"You mean the stuffy banker I met at the Chamber meeting?"

Rand bobbed his head in a curt nod. "None other."

A noise that sounded suspiciously like a snicker bubbled out of Celeste's mouth. She covered it with her hand, but her eyes betrayed her.

"I didn't think it was all that funny," Rand growled.

"I'm sorry. I wasn't laughing at you. I'm just imagining the look on Mr. Adler's face."

"It defies imagination. I just hope he didn't think I was taking Freud here on a lunch date."

This time she made no effort to hide her amusement. She had a wonderful laugh: vibrant, full and infectious— so infectious that Rand found himself laughing, too.

Every time he got around her, he ended up acting as if he'd been out in the sun too long. No wonder; everything about her was overly bright and shiny—her hair, her eyes, her smile.

"I'd better get him out of your truck and go fix the fence before any other animals escape," Celeste said when she finished laughing.

"Do you have the right tools?" Rand found himself asking. He opened the truck door.

"Well, I have a hammer and some picture-hanging nails. I'll make do with those until I can get to town and buy some bigger ones."

Picture-hanging nails? Heck, she might as well use thumbtacks. Before he could tell her as much, Dr. Freud interrupted with an eager bleat.

Rand grabbed the rope he'd tied around the goat's neck and unbuckled the seat belt. The animal promptly lunged out of the pickup, knocking Celeste against Rand's chest.

Oh, man, there it was again—that incredible, intoxicating scent, that amazing, soft-firm body. Too soon she pulled away, but not before she had Rand's senses completely befuddled.

"I've got a toolbox in my truck," he found himself saying. "Let me grab it and give you a hand."

"Oh, you don't have to do that."

He handed her the goat's rope. "I know, but it's in my best interests."

And it was, he told himself as he circled around to the truck bed. Once her fence was fixed, her blasted animals would stay on her side of it. This was strictly a matter of logic. It had nothing to do with physical attraction. Absolutely nothing at all.

"There's the escape route," Rand said fifteen minutes later, pointing to a broken section of fence in the back pasture. "The bottom rail came loose. If you'll hold it in place, I'll nail it back."

"Sure."

Rand set his toolbox on the grass, pulled out a hammer and several long nails. Celeste picked up the wooden rail and held it against the weathered post. Rand stepped up beside her. He was standing close, so close that their shoulders almost touched. Against her will, Celeste felt a shiver of attraction course through her.

Rand expertly hammered in a nail, then added two more for good measure. "That ought to hold it for a while."

He straightened at the same time as Celeste. She found

herself standing a scant inch away from him, so close that she could smell the faint scent of his shaving cream. They were inside each other's personal space, too close for polite company. Convention dictated that one of them should have stepped back, but neither of them moved. They just stood there, looking at each other, and attraction had flamed between them like a marsh fire. Heat radiated from Rand's eyes, setting off a blaze low in Celeste's belly.

His eyes fell to her lips. Her gaze slid to his. He had a full, sensual mouth, a mouth surrounded by beard-darkened skin. She wondered how he would taste, how he would feel—wondered about pressure and texture and temperature, wondered about angle of approach and duration. The ground seemed to shift and slant, so that it took a tremendous effort not to fall into each other's arms.

He was going to kiss her. She was sure of it. Her heart pounded so hard it should have bruised her ribs.

And then Dr. Freud interrupted with a loud bleat.

Rand abruptly pulled back, turned away and strode to his toolbox. He crouched down and placed his hammer inside. "The wood in your fence is getting rotten," he said curtly. "You're going to need to replace the whole thing before long."

"Hopefully it'll hold until I can start making some money."

Rand clicked his toolbox closed and straightened, held it in his hand. "How can you be so sure that'll happen?"

"What? That the fence will hold?"

"No. That your zoo will *ever* make any money."

Celeste squared her shoulders. "I refuse to consider any other possibility."

"Well, you need to consider it, because it's not just possible, it's likely. You're going to run through your savings, then you'll still wind up selling. Only then you'll be broke and desperate, and you'll end up settling for less than the place is worth."

She shot him a teasing look. "Not if you outbid the other buyers."

His expression held no hint of humor. "Don't delude yourself. No one but me is going to be making an offer on this place."

Celeste placed her hands on her hips. "So what are you saying? That if I don't sell it to you now, you'll screw me on the price when I'm really desperate?"

He gave a long sigh. "I'm saying that your place isn't likely to bring all that much, but I'm willing to offer more than the appraised value because it's worth it to me."

"Well, then, I assume it'll be worth just as much to you three months from now."

A muscle flexed in Rand's jaw. "I'm trying to keep you from throwing your money away on a pipe dream, but if that's what you want to do—well, it's your money."

"And it's my dream. Which apparently clashes with yours."

Rand's face grew dark as a storm cloud, the kind that a tornado might drop out of at any moment. Without another word, he turned and stalked toward his truck.

Celeste was unable to resist calling after him, goading. "So . . . what time are you picking me up for the dance?" she'd called.

He froze in his tracks, then slowly twisted around. "I thought you didn't want to go."

"I've changed my mind. Sara convinced me it would be a great way to get to know more members of the community and get the word out on my petting farm." She flashed him her sweetest smile. "Of course, if you no longer want to take me, that's fine. I'm perfectly happy going by myself. I'm sure everyone will understand that you didn't really stand me up—you just changed your mind."

She could practically see his blood pressure rising. A vein visibly pulsed in his temple.

"I'll pick you up at seven." His voice was a low, dangerous growl. "Seven sharp."

"I'll be ready," Celeste replied.

But would she? she wondered as she watched him stalk back to his pickup. How on earth could she ever get ready to deal with a man who could simultaneously be so discouraging and so helpful, so infuriating and appealing?

Chapter Eight

Celeste fastened the tiny buckle on her strappy tan sandal, then straightened and smoothed her sleek, butter-colored sundress, eyeing herself critically in her bedroom mirror. She'd intended to back out of going to this dance with Rand; she really had. She'd even picked up the phone and gotten Rand's phone number from Information for just that purpose. But for reasons she didn't care to examine too closely, she'd never followed through and actually canceled.

Celeste glanced at her watch. He'd said he'd show at seven, and it was almost that time now. Against her will, a shiver of anticipation rushed through her. She smoothed her hair in the mirror, then turned to Mr. Peepers, who was sitting on her bed. "What do you think, fella? Do you think I'll do?"

Mr. Peepers bounced up and down. Smiling, she scooped him up and headed for the living room just as a loud knock sounded on the door. Bite Me growled, Mr. Peepers made a parrotlike squawk and the poodles yapped in unison. "Quiet down, guys," she told the animals as she headed for the door.

Celeste was unprepared for the way her body responded to the sight of Rand standing in her doorway, dressed in pressed chinos and a starched blue shirt. His face was freshly shaved, yet he still had the faint shadow of a beard. The physical attraction that had knocked her for a loop in the pasture was back in spades.

"Hi," she finally managed.

"Hi, yourself."

Her mouth felt dry. "You, um, look nice."

"You, too." His gaze warmed her skin. "Except for that ape accessory. People don't wear a lot of fur in these parts, especially in the summer."

Celeste looked down, surprised to discover that she was still holding Mr. Peepers. The monkey grunted, then pulled back his teeth in an imitation of a smile.

She looked up at Rand and laughed. "He seems to be warming up to you."

"I think I'll stay out of spitting distance all the same."

Celeste laughed again. "Let me put him in his kennel, then I'll be ready to go."

Despite what he'd said, Rand followed her down the hall, admiring the way Celeste's dress skimmed the curves of her body. Hot damn, but she looked good—too good.

Okay, so she looked sexy as hell. That was not—repeat, *not*—going to affect the way he behaved toward her. He was going to keep his head and his distance. He'd spent a lot of time thinking about her—too much time—and he'd decided getting involved with her would only make things more complicated. If they started dating and got along, she wouldn't want to sell him her ranch because she wouldn't want to leave. If they dated and had a falling out, she wouldn't want to sell him the property out of spite or anger.

No, his best course of action was to be friendly but detached.

He followed her into a spare bedroom, which was unfurnished except for an enormous cage. The thing had to be eight feet wide, ten feet long and six feet tall. "You call this a kennel?" he said.

"Monkeys need a lot of space." Celeste opened the door of the large wire enclosure. "The Joneses took very good care of their animals."

"They traveled with this huge thing?"

"It comes apart pretty easily. Too easily, actually. Mr. Peepers is becoming quite an escape artist."

"I can't imagine why he'd want to escape," Rand remarked, looking at the collection of plastic toys, the toddler gym set and the pile of fresh fruit in the cage. "Most kids don't have it this good."

"I try to keep him happy, but he gets lonely when he's by himself." Celeste set Mr. Peepers on the newspapered floor and fastened the latch. The monkey put his hand to his mouth, made a loud smacking sound and extended his arm toward Rand. "Oh, look—he's blowing you a kiss!"

Rand shook his head. "Sorry, fella—you're not my type."

The monkey whimpered.

"Don't worry Mr. P.," Celeste said with a laugh. "I'll give you some extra lovin' when I get back."

Lucky monkey. Rand scowled at the thought and turned toward the door. "Well, we'd better get going. George is waiting in the truck."

"George is going with us?"

She didn't have to sound so damned happy about it, Rand thought as he followed her out of the house. He'd asked George to ride with them because he'd figured it would make the outing feel less like a date. He hadn't really thought about how Celeste was likely to react, but he hadn't expected her to be so darn pleased.

Her reaction rankled—and his response to it rankled even more. Damn it, what was the matter with him? It wasn't like he wanted to get anything started with her. Every time she entered his air space, she brought chaos and calamity. God only knew he'd had enough of those in his childhood to last a lifetime.

So why the heck was he so attracted to her?

"Good evening, George." Celeste gave Rand's trainer a smile and a wave as the older man climbed out of the pickup.

"Evenin'." George tipped his tan cowboy hat and held open the passenger door, his gaze sweeping Celeste with open admiration. "Wow—you look like a million bucks!"

"Thank you." Celeste smiled in a way that made Rand's gut tighten. "You look quite dashing yourself."

"I cleaned up as best I could." George gave a lopsided grin. "I'm not accustomed to bein' social. I spend all my time with horses, and they're not real particular about how I look."

"I heard you have a way with them." She gracefully climbed into the passenger seat as George crawled into the back of the four-door pickup. "Apparently you're the local horse whisperer."

"Oh, I just listen. The horses do all the whispering."

Celeste and George chatted about animals all the way into town. Rand listened sullenly, an odd tightness gripping his chest. Surely Celeste wasn't interested in George. Why, he was old enough to be her father!

The thought made Rand scowl. He was being ridiculous. George hadn't shown the slightest interest in women since his wife's death four years ago. He was just making conversation with Celeste, that was all, and Rand should be grateful. It kept him from having to talk to her himself.

All the same, Rand sneaked another sideways glance at her, the same way he'd been sneaking glances ever since they'd left her house. Good grief, but she looked good. She was wearing makeup, but not a lot—just a little lipstick and something to accentuate her eyes. Her hair fell just below her shoulders in tousled waves over the narrow straps that held up her dress.

And what a dress. It wasn't blatantly provocative, but it was cut low enough to show a teasing hint of cleavage. It stopped a couple of inches above her knees, but it had ridden up when she climbed into the truck. She wasn't wearing stockings. Her naked legs had a shiny, polished look, as if she'd put on some kind of lotion.

The thought conjured an intensely erotic image. He pulled his eyes away and forced his gaze back to the road.

She was a good-looking woman, that was for sure. Maybe George was doing more than making polite conversation after all. How could he not be?

The thought made the constriction in his chest squeeze tighter, and he was relieved when he finally pulled into the parking lot behind the VFW building.

"Looks like we're going to have a good crowd," he remarked as he guided the truck into one of the few remaining parking spaces.

"Good," George said. "Every admission ticket brings us that much closer to gettin' that fire truck."

It also meant there were more people to circulate among, Rand thought—which would hopefully keep him from obsessing about Celeste and her sundress.

111

Chapter Nine

The dance was in full swing when Sara walked into the VFW hall a little after nine. She paused by the door, letting her eyes adjust to the dim lighting. The room throbbed with a loud, accordian-heavy rendition of "Two-step Mamou." The scent of cigarette smoke, beer and perfume hovered in the air.

"Wow, this place is packed," she remarked as she handed her ticket to the grocer's wife, Maude Lamont.

"Sure 'nough," the middle-aged woman agreed, her two chins multiplying to four as she grinned. "I believe just about everyone in the parish is here."

Certainly just about everyone in town, Sara thought as she looked around. The dance floor was packed with couples two-stepping and twirling under an old-fashioned disco ball, and the sides of the room were packed with people in conversation.

Mrs. Lamont narrowed her eyes and shot Sara a sly look. "Even George Wright is here."

Sara's stomach felt as if she'd swallowed a bullfrog. She fought the urge to turn and flee. A dance was the last place she'd thought to run into George. He'd hated dancing in high school.

"Is that right?" she managed to murmur.

Mrs. Lamont's chins bobbed again. "He's over there, in the corner." She pointed a sausagelike finger.

Sure enough, there he was—standing against the wall with Susie and Frank Villere, along with the mayor and a group of other people Sara didn't recognize.

For that matter, Sara barely recognized George. He was wearing khaki slacks and a navy sports jacket, and he looked so handsome he took her breath away.

"Heather used to say she couldn't drag that man to a dance with a team of mules," Mrs. Lamont continued. "Guess he'll do anything for the fire department. He's the volunteer chief, you know."

Sara hadn't known. Her father never mentioned that little detail.

"This whole fund-raiser, it was his idea."

Another surprise. Apparently there was a lot about George she didn't know. She certainly hadn't known he could look so dashing or act so at ease in a social situation. A lot about him had changed in twenty-eight years.

But then, she'd changed, too, she reminded herself. She was no longer the scared child who'd fled town in her wedding gown, too timid to stand up for herself. Now she was a grown woman—successful, sophisticated, independent and confident.

Though right now, she didn't feel any of those things. Right now she felt awkward and out of place, surrounded by people who knew her only as the girl who'd left George Wright at the altar.

How sad and awful and funny that her weakest, most desperate moment was the one that would forever define her here.

George looked up and glanced in her direction, as if he sensed her presence. Her heart jumped to her throat. When they were young, he'd always instinctively known her whereabouts. He'd always been able to instantly find her face in a crowd, to sense it when she entered a room. Apparently that hadn't changed.

Their eyes met with the force of a head-on collision, making Sara feel as if the breath had been knocked out of her. Time and space fell away, and for a hairbreadth of a moment, she was sixteen again—her heart on fire, her stomach quivering, her pulse throbbing. She gave a tentative smile and took a step toward him, lifting her hand in a small wave.

George's eyes hardened into granite. Without so much as a nod of acknowledgment, he turned his back to her.

It felt like a slap. Sara stood there, rooted to the spot, shocked and hurt.

"Sara!" said a soft, familiar voice beside her. "Are you okay?"

She turned to see Celeste and forced a smile. "I-I'm fine."

"You sure?"

Celeste was too perceptive. "Not really," Sara confessed. "I just saw George. I didn't know he was coming here tonight." She tried to change the topic. "I wasn't sure you were coming, either."

"Well, here I am," Celeste said. "I changed my mind."

"So you came with Rand?"

"And George. He rode with us." Celeste looked at her closely. "You ought to try to talk to him."

Sara blew out a sigh. "We just made eye contact, and he deliberately turned his back on me."

"Oh, dear."

"Oh, dear, is right." Maybe she should just leave. She

hated the thought of being in the same room with George, trying to avoid him all night.

The thought made her back stiffen. No. She wouldn't run from him. She was no longer the timid young woman who couldn't bear confrontation.

She gazed at George's back, and her heart galvanized with indignation. "You know what? I'm sick of this. I'm sick of feeling apologetic about returning to my own hometown." Pressure built in Sara's chest like steam inside a teakettle. "I'm sick of feeling as if I can't go places where I'm likely to run into George, and sick to death of being avoided and slighted when I do. I'm going to march right over there and talk to him."

"Good for you," Celeste said.

Sara lifted her chin. She might not be able to trap him in an elevator, but she bet she could make this room seem just as confining. Her mouth tightened into a determined line. "Wish me luck."

Celeste squeezed her hand. "You've got it."

Sara straightened her spine and strode across the room before she had time to lose courage.

Sara was walking toward him—George sensed it even before he angled his body to catch a glimpse of her in his peripheral vision. Sure enough, here she came, gracefully as always, heading straight in his direction. His stomach tightened like the cinch on a rodeo bull. The old fight-or-flight instinct kicked in hard, and the urge to flee was winning hands down.

Yet the mayor was explaining a complicated sales tax issue, and since George was the one who'd brought up the subject, he couldn't very well walk away. He had to stay put and stand his ground. He had to act calm and cool and unaffected.

He tried to force his attention to what the mayor was

saying, but his mind was too preoccupied with Sara's advance.

She had perfect timing. She sidled up to the couple beside him just as the mayor wrapped up his monologue and the band played the last note of "Jolie Blonde."

"Hello, Fred . . . Susie." Sara greeted both of the Villeres with a hug. "How are your boys?"

"Fine," Fred said. "Just fine."

"I'm so glad to hear it." Sara smiled at Mrs. Villere. "You look wonderful tonight. I love what you've done with your hair."

Susie touched her freshly curled locks and grinned shyly. "Thank you."

George braced himself as Sara turned toward him. "Hello, George."

There was no avoiding her. She was right in front of him, less than a foot away, close enough that he could see the blue facets in the irises of her gray eyes.

Oh, God—why did she have to be so lovely? The youthful prettiness he remembered had ripened into a distinctive beauty. She exuded an aura of confidence, poise, strength, that hadn't been there when he'd known her before. It fit her as exquisitely as her slim black dress.

"Hello," he managed to respond. Even to his own ears, the word came out gruff.

She tilted her head slightly and smiled. "I understand you're responsible for the dance tonight."

George shrugged. "A lot of people worked on it."

"No, no. George is being far too modest," the mayor said. "It was his idea. He got the VFW to donate the hall, he found the band, and he handled all the publicity. All the rest of us did was show up."

The band started to play again, this time a plaintive ballad.

George decided it was his cue to move on. "Well, if you'll excuse me—"

Sara put her hand on his arm. A jolt of heat went through him, burning like a brand. "I was wondering if you wanted to dance," she said.

The group looked at him. George's stomach knotted again. He wouldn't let on that Sara rattled him. He refused to give her that victory.

"Thanks, but I don't dance."

"I remember you danced at our senior prom."

Yeah, and I was going to dance at our wedding. But since you stood me up, I didn't get the chance. "That was a long time ago."

"Dancing's like riding a bike. It'll come back to you." She tugged gently on his arm.

Hell. He had two choices: politely go along, or refuse and create a scene. If he created a scene, it would mean he'd be the topic of gossip for weeks to come, just like he'd been after she'd stood him up at the altar.

He knew people were speculating about how he felt about her, now that she was back in town. He'd heard the whispers; he'd seen the pitying looks. It was bad enough now, but if he made a scene tonight, it was sure to get worse.

Everyone would think he wasn't over her.

Damn it all, she had him cornered. He had no choice but to follow her out to the dance floor. He froze as she turned toward him and put her hand on his shoulder.

Oh, jeez—there was no way of keeping his distance, not when she was facing him, not when she was touching him, not when her scent filled his nostrils. He tried to staunch the flow of memories, but they poured out like blood from an arterial wound.

He hesitantly put one hand on her waist and took her extended hand with the other, trying to keep her at arm's length. She wouldn't let him. She stepped closer as his feet began to move in a slow two-step. "You've been avoiding me, George."

"I don't know what you're talking about." His voice sounded as wooden as a fence post.

"You do, too."

He did, of course. But what the hell did she expect him to do? Seek her out? Date her again? Hell, he wasn't a friggin' martyr. He had no desire to have his heart stomped into dust again.

"You turned around and left the Chamber meeting when you saw me," she said quietly. "And you've quit coming to the store."

He cut to the chase. "What do you want from me, Sara?"

"I don't know. To be friends, I guess."

Friends? She wanted to be *friends*? He clenched his jaw and moved stiffly around the floor, avoiding her eyes. If he told her no way in hell, she'd think she could still affect him. He wouldn't give her that satisfaction. He remained stubbornly silent.

"I was so sorry to hear about Heather," she said.

It hurt, hearing Heather's name on her lips. He didn't mean to glance down, but he did anyway. He immediately regretted it, because Sara's eyes were soft and troubled, and the sight assaulted the protective wall he'd erected around his heart.

"I sent you a card, but it came back unopened," she said.

"Yeah, well . . ." He hadn't needed her sympathy then, and he didn't need it now. He didn't want her to try and comfort him, didn't want her assuaging her guilt so easily.

"I heard you have children," she continued.

"Two boys."

"Tell me about them."

Maybe talking about his kids would let her know he'd managed quite well without her. "One's an engineer with an oil company in Houston. The other's a lawyer in Baton Rouge."

"You must be awfully proud of them."

Her voice held a note of wistfulness. He risked another glance at her face, then wished he hadn't. "I am."

"George . . ."

Oh, God—here it came. He steeled himself.

"George, I'm so sorry for the way I left you. It was a horrible way to handle things, and I've never forgiven myself for it."

Yeah, well, that makes two of us. Holding his body aloof, he held his words in check.

He could feel her looking up at him. He refused to meet her gaze.

"I tried to call," she said. "And I wrote letters. Dozens of letters. I wanted to explain . . ."

He couldn't resist looking down again. Damn her eyes— they were so full of emotion, so full of regret and pain. It was her own friggin' fault, he told himself. She deserved whatever regret she felt.

"There was nothing to explain," he said tersely, navigating a corner of the dance floor a little too sharply. "You made it all pretty clear."

"Still, I . . ."

Mercifully, the song was drawing to a close. "Look. There's no point in rehashing the past. Things worked out just fine, and I really don't want to discuss it." He drew away the moment the music ended, gave a stiff smile for the sake of anyone who was watching, then walked away. He didn't look back, but he knew she was standing there, following him with her gaze—he could feel the heat of it, the way he used to feel her looking over at him years ago.

"What's a pretty lady like you doin' sittin' on the sidelines?"

Celeste looked up to see Larry Birkman standing beside

the small table where Rand had parked her. He was dressed like Garth Brooks, in a western-cut striped shirt and tight jeans. He moved in close, close enough that she could smell the bourbon on his breath.

"I figured Rand would have you out on the dance floor nonstop," he said.

"He's been pretty busy." *Talking to everyone in the room but me.* Celeste's eyes automatically drifted to Rand. He'd been working the room like a politician ever since they walked in the door.

It wasn't that he'd been impolite, exactly; he'd gotten her a drink, taken her around and introduced her to people— people, Celeste noted, who had a way of droning on and on about nothing.

And on. She'd spent half an hour talking to a man who'd insisted on telling her the pluses and minuses of whole life insurance versus term life, and she'd just extricated herself from a fifteen-minute monologue by a woman recounting every detail of her recent knee surgery. Celeste strongly suspected that Rand was deliberately hooking her up with the chronically long-winded so he could move about the room unencumbered.

Which he was perfectly free to do, she reminded herself. After all, this wasn't really a date.

There was no reason she should feel so annoyed to see him talking to that willowy brunette in the tight red dress across the room.

But she did. A fresh rush of irritation shot through her as the woman placed her hand on Rand's arm and laughed at something he said.

"You need a man who knows how to treat a woman," Larry said.

Oh, and I suppose that would be you. Celeste suppressed the urge to roll her eyes. "Actually, I didn't really come here to dance. I just came to meet some people in the community."

"Dancing's a good way to get acquainted."

"Not if you're trampling your partner's feet."

"I'm willing to risk injury." He gave a charming grin. "Come on. It's easy to learn. And I'm a good teacher."

Celeste arched her brow. "Won't your wife mind?"

Barely a flicker of surprise crossed his face. "Nah. We both dance with other people all the time. Why, half the people on the dance floor are married to someone besides the person they're dancing with right now."

It was true, Celeste thought. A dance was hardly an act of adultery. She was overreacting because of Rand's remarks about this man.

Celeste's attention darted back to Rand. The brunette was using his back to write something on a card. When she finished and he turned back around, the woman rose up on tiptoe, whispered something in his ear, then tucked the card into his shirt pocket.

Aggravation, hot and irrational, balled up in Celeste's stomach. This was the second time she'd caught Rand in a distinctly unbusinesslike exchange with an attractive woman. Earlier in the evening, a buxom redhead had been hanging all over him. No telling how many women in the room he was sleeping with.

That was probably why Rand disliked Larry so much, Celeste thought. They were two of a kind, cut from the same cloth.

Larry leaned in close. "You strike me as the kind of person who likes to do things instead of just watching others do them."

Across the room, Rand smiled at something the brunette said. A cord snapped inside Celeste. It wouldn't hurt to show Rand that he couldn't control her behavior. What the heck—it was just a dance.

She turned to Larry and flashed a big smile. "If you're brave enough to teach me, I'd *love* a dancing lesson."

Larry took her by the arm and led her to the dance floor. Putting his hand on the small of her back, he pulled her flush against his body, so close that her breasts flattened against his chest.

Alarmed, she took a step back.

"You can't learn if you're halfway across the room." He tightened his arm around her. "Just relax and follow my lead."

"I really think . . ."

He squeezed her so tightly that his belt buckle dug into her belly. It threw her off balance, making her lurch against him.

"That's more like it," he said.

His bourbon-scented breath curled up her nose like paint remover. Apparently he'd had more than a few. She tried to keep things light. "Easy there. We're dancing, not making a porn movie."

He leered down at her. "Maybe we should give that a try."

Oh, dear. This had not been one of her better decisions. "I need to back up a little so I'm not standing on your toes."

"I like where you are just fine."

"Well, I don't." She jumped as his hand moved down to her buttocks.

"Get your hands off me," she hissed.

"Relax, sugar. You can't learn how to dance when you're all stiff."

"Come on, Larry. You're embarrassing me." He was practically mauling her, right in the middle of the dance floor.

His arm was like a steel band around her. "If you relax, you'll be just fine."

"Look—I-I've changed my mind. I don't want to dance."

"Loosen up. Why are you so uptight?"

"Because you've got your hand on my ass," Celeste snapped. She hadn't realized how loudly she'd spoken until she saw several couples turn and stare at her.

Larry was oblivious. He gave her bottom a hard squeeze. "And it feels real nice, too."

"Cut it out," Celeste ordered.

"Do as the lady says, Birkman, or you'll wish you had," said a stern, masculine voice.

Celeste looked up to see Rand standing behind Larry, his eyes unsmiling, his jaw clenched.

Larry immediately dropped both hands. He gave Rand a conciliatory smile, his eyes wide with feigned innocence. "What's the big deal? I was just giving her a little dance lesson."

"Looked to me like you were trying to give her something else."

"Aw, c'mon. I was just being neighborly."

"Save it for your wife."

"Hey, it was just a dance," Larry said. "I was trying to teach her the two-step."

"Lesson's over. Beat it."

Larry turned and disappeared into the gawking crowd. Celeste sighed.

"If you don't want to call more attention to yourself than you already have, you'd better dance with me until everyone settles down," Rand said in low voice.

Celeste looked around at the sea of curious faces. Rand was right. His palm curled around hers, warm and large and slightly rough. He put his other hand on her waist, and she placed hers on his shoulder. He stepped toward her, and she automatically found herself stepping back.

"I warned you about him," Rand said, moving them across the dance floor.

"I didn't think there'd be any harm in just one dance."

Rand ignored her. "So what's the big attraction? The fact that he's married, or the fact that he's trouble?"

"Attraction?" She pulled back and regarded him with indignation. "What are you talking about?"

Rand lifted his shoulders. "I turn my back on you for one moment, the next thing I know you're out on the dance floor getting felt up in front of the whole town."

"I was *not* getting felt up!"

"Felt down, then."

"I didn't think there'd be any harm in one dance. I didn't realize he was drunk, and I had no idea he'd be so pushy."

"You looked awfully cozy out there."

"Yeah, and you looked awfully cozy with that brunette," she shot back.

Rand pulled away and looked down at her. "You mean Charlotte? She's a Chamber member." He guided Celeste around a turn. "I told you this was a working occasion for me."

Celeste arched an eyebrow. "You didn't mention what kind of work you'd be doing."

His mouth slid into a maddening smile. "What's the matter? Jealous?"

"In your dreams." She wasn't jealous, she told herself; she was insulted. That was all. It was rude of him to bring her to the dance, then to spend all his time with other women.

She missed a step and stumbled on his boot. Her breath caught as her breasts pressed against his chest. The usual attraction, heady and knee-weakening, hit her with stunning force. Rand smelled of starch and shaving cream and something else—something subtle and intoxicating that made Celeste's brain feel all fogged up, like a window on a steamy day.

"Sorry," she muttered.

"Don't be. You're doing fine." He tightened his hold on her.

She looked up, and the heat in his gaze burned away all thoughts of insult or anger. Her heart pounded. She breathed in his heady scent as he guided her around the dance floor.

All too soon, the music ended. Celeste dropped her arms and backed away, trying to act normal even though she felt anything but. "Thanks for the dance lesson," she said, moving off the dance floor.

"You didn't seem to need a lesson at all," Rand said as he followed.

It was true, she realized with surprise. Aside from that one stumble, dancing with Rand had been easy and natural.

"Are you sure you've never two-stepped before?"

Celeste shook her head, which still felt muzzy.

"Well, then, you must just be a natural."

She stared up at him, surprised. "Boy, that's not what my ex-husband used to say," she said.

Rand lifted his eyebrows. "You were married?"

Why in the world had she brought that up? "Very briefly, a few years ago."

The concept of Celeste, married, was jarring. Rand hadn't thought of her as the settling-down type. Not that he'd thought of her as the out-every-night type, either. The truth was, he'd tried not to think of her in romantic terms at all, but dancing with her just now had sure blown that plan to pieces.

"My ex refused to dance with me because he said I was so terrible at it." Celeste brushed a strand of hair out of her face and gave a wry smile. "But then, he used to think I was terrible at everything."

"So why did you marry him?"

"Good question. I've wondered that myself."

Rand was intrigued. He wanted to ask her more, but the band cranked out another song, a loud and rowdy honkytonk tune that made conversation impossible. He leaned close to her ear. "It's awfully stuffy in here. Want to go out and get some air?"

"Sure."

They threaded their way through the crowd to the exit at the rear of the building. Rand held the heavy metal door open for her, then followed Celeste out into the parking lot. The night was warm and heavy with humidity, but a slight breeze ruffled it. A faint scent of night jasmine floated past.

Rand led Celeste to his pickup at the back of the parking lot and pulled down the tailgate. "Have a seat on my 'cowboy balcony.'"

Celeste laughed and perched on the edge, her legs dangling. Rand sat beside her, close but not touching. She gazed up at the sky and swung her feet.

"You were telling me about this guy you married," Rand prompted.

"I was?"

"Yeah. What was he like?"

Celeste leaned back on her elbows and stared at the half moon. "Well, his name was John. I met him about five years ago, when I was at a really low point in my life. My parents had just been killed in a car crash."

Rand was shocked. "Oh, wow. You lost them both at once?"

She nodded somberly. "It was horrible. I was an only child, and we were really close. I can't tell you how it devastated me." She looked over at him. "Are your parents still alive?"

"No." And his parents were a can of worms he had no intention of opening tonight. He steered the conversation back to her. "So, how did you and this John guy meet?"

"At a fund-raiser for the SPCA in Houston. He was a plastic surgeon, and his office was one of the event's sponsors. He was twelve years older than me." She paused. "Like I said, I was at a low point. I guess I was looking for someone to lean on, and he seemed really strong and supportive. Looking back, though, I can see that what I'd thought was support was really controlling behavior."

"Controlling how?"

She gazed up at the stars. "John wanted to mold me into his idea of the perfect woman. I was so torn up over my parents that I guess I was like putty in his hands. Looking back on it, it seems like some kind of makeover experiment by Dr. Frankenstein. He started out suggesting that I change my hair and my clothes and my hobbies, then he moved on to wanting me to change my friends and my job. He even wanted me to change my nose."

"Your nose? Why?"

She gave a wry grin. "He said the way it tilts up is undignified."

Rand wanted to say, "You look pretty perfect to me," but something made him hold back. "I think your nose is fine," he said instead. As a matter of fact, he thought her nose was adorable.

"Thank you, kind sir." She dipped her head in a mock bow. "I find your nose to be the very essence of olfactory dignity as well."

Rand laughed. "So your marriage ended over your nose?"

"More or less. The nose campaign coincided with the get-a-classier-job campaign and the let's-make-your-bustline-perkier campaign."

"He thought something was wrong with your *bustline?* Man, the guy must have been mental." Rand stared into her eyes.

Celeste gave an embarrassed grin and looked away. "I

finally realized what he really wanted was someone else altogether." The wind blew a strand of hair across her face. She tucked it behind her ear. "So I left. And I made up my mind I'd never do that again."

"Never do what again? Get married?"

"Get involved with a control freak. The next time I fall in love, it'll be with a man who loves and accepts me as much as I love and accept him." She shot Rand a curious glance. "What about you? Ever been married?"

"Nope."

"Ever come close?"

"No."

"Ever been in love?"

He shook his head.

Her eyebrows rose. "Why not?"

"I don't believe in it."

"*What?*"

He shrugged. "Love is really nothing more than sexual attraction all mixed up with jealousy and possessiveness and a lot of other stuff."

"Wow. Not too jaded, are you?"

He'd known she'd have a negative reaction, but he hadn't known it would bother him. He leaned back on his elbows and tried to keep the defensiveness he felt out of his voice. "People lose their heads when it comes to romance. They control their finances, their careers, and a million other aspects of their lives, but they lose the ability to reason when it comes to love."

"Everyone except you, I suppose," she said with a dry smile. "So let's have it: How do you keep your love life reasonable?"

"Well, first of all, I'm realistic about what I am looking for."

"And what's that?"

"Well, sex. Without all that sappy emotional stuff about love and commitment."

"Oh, riiight." Sarcasm dripped from her words. "Love and commitment just kill the romance, don't they?"

He grinned at her sarcastic tone. "Look—I'm just being honest here. And I suspect at least ninety percent of the male population agrees with me on this, but won't admit it."

She shook her head, her expression incredulous.

"People act as if emotion is some kind of great, noble, desirable thing. It's not. People do all kinds of irrational, irresponsible things when they get swept away by their feelings. That's why I don't do emotion."

"You don't *do* it?"

"I avoid it. I prefer to use my head."

She looked at him as if he'd just grown a third eye.

"I take it you don't approve," he said.

"It's a free country. My approval isn't needed." She kicked out with her legs, swung them like a little girl. "I'm curious about one thing, though. How do you go about finding women for these nonrelationship relationships?"

"It's not hard. Lots of women are looking for the same thing." *At first, anyway.* "It helps that I don't usually date women from around here. Long-distance relationships are a lot easier to manage."

"You 'manage' your relationships?"

A defensiveness crept into his voice. "I manage the logistics—how often we see each other, how often we talk, that sort of thing. Long distance means less pressure."

She lifted an eyebrow. "Long distance means more distance."

"Well, sure. That's part of it."

"The biggest part, from the sound of things." She looked at him curiously. "So basically, you just want sex without any emotional involvement."

"Well, there can be *some* emotion." Jeez, she was making him sound like a heel. "I mean, we can like each other."

"Oh, well. *That's* good to hear." She gave him a now-I've-heard-everything shake of her head.

It was high time to turn this conversation around. "So what are *you* looking for?"

"All the stuff you're not."

"That figures."

She leaned back on her elbows and gazed up at the sky. "Actually, I'm looking for my soul mate."

That figured, too. "Come on. You don't really believe there's such a thing, do you?"

"Sure I do. My parents were soul mates. So were my grandparents."

She stated it with a matter-of-fact certainty that piqued his curiosity. "What makes you think so?"

"They were so happy together. Each lit up when the other one walked into the room. They were affectionate and supportive, and they loved to make each other laugh. They were best friends, but a whole lot more." Celeste smiled up at the sky. "They tried to make each other's dreams come true. You could just feel the love between them. It kind of overflowed and spilled out and spread onto the people around them."

An odd wistfulness tightened Rand's chest. He'd seen long-term couples that seemed happy like that, but never at close range. He'd always thought that he was just seeing them at a good moment. "They never fought?"

"Oh, they'd have disagreements, but not often, and they never stayed angry for very long. They never left or threatened to leave each other. There was a bond between them that was stronger than any difference of opinion."

It sounded too good to be true. In Rand's experience, when something seemed too good to be true, it was. At least for him. "It must have been nice, growing up in a home like that."

"Yeah. It was."

"So how do you plan to find this so-called soul mate of yours?"

"Oh, I don't have to find him. When the timing is right, divine providence will bring us together."

He should have seen that coming. "So how does that work, exactly—you just sit home and wait for Prince Charming to knock on your door?" He shot her a teasing grin. "That might work if you're looking for a plumber or a pizza deliveryman. But you'd have to make a few calls first."

"Very funny."

"Did you think so? I thought it was only mildly amusing."

She playfully pushed his arm. "For your information, I'm not just sitting around. I'm living my life as fully as possible. It'll happen when it's meant to happen."

"So you just leave your life up to the whims of fate?"

"No. I trust in divine providence."

"That's an awfully unrealistic approach to life."

"It's no more unrealistic than thinking you can control everything." She shot him an amused smile. "And a whole lot less stressful."

She could hold her own, he had to give her that. "So how will you know you've met your soul mate and not just a guy you've got the hots for?"

"I'll know." She looked over at him with those bright, earnest eyes. "I'll just know." She placed her hand over her heart. "In here."

"Why didn't you know with your ex that he was wrong?"

Her expression grew somber. "I did, but I ignored it. Deep inside, I had a bad feeling about marrying him—but I let grief and loneliness drown out what my heart was trying to tell me." Her voice dropped. "I'd just lost my parents, and I was at an all-time low. It was like I had a hole in my chest and a cold wind was whistling through it."

Rand had known that kind of loneliness. It had dragged him into a hellhole of self-destructive behavior, and when he'd crawled out, he'd vowed he'd never go there again. That was what happened when you got emotionally attached to people.

"I married John for all the wrong reasons," Celeste admitted. "I wanted to belong to someone, to have someone to love who loved me back . . ." She blew out a sigh. "I guess I just deluded myself into thinking something was there that really wasn't."

"That's why decisions need to be based on logic."

"All decisions?" she asked.

"Sure."

"Oh, come on. Some things just aren't logical."

He slanted a grin at her. "Like you?"

She rolled her eyes, then smiled back. "Yeah, like me."

"Okay, well, I admit that some things"—he shot her another teasing grin—"and some people aren't logical. But there's a logical *response* to everything."

"Oh, yeah?" Her eyes held a playful challenge.

"Yeah."

"So what's the logical response to this?" With a mischievous grin, she put her hands on his chest and pushed him backward on the pickup bed.

"This." Grabbing her arms, he pulled her down on top of him. She laughed as she landed on his chest.

And then he heard her breath hitch. Or maybe it was his—because as he gazed into her face, a surge of desire kicked in, hard and fast and urgent. Her eyes were all smoky need, her lips a plump, parted invitation. His arms wound around her, and the next thing he knew, he'd pulled her close and covered her mouth with his.

And then he was a goner, swept away by sensation. *Hot. Wet. Sweet. Soft.* The scent of her perfume, the taste of her mouth, the feel of her breasts pressed against him—he was drowning in her and not even caring. He cradled the back of her head. Her soft hair spilled through his fingers and her scalp warmed his palm. He drew her closer, deepening the kiss. She flooded his veins, heated his blood and erased every thought from his head, except how to get closer. He angled his mouth to cover hers more fully, and she moved against him, kissing him back, threading her fingers through his hair.

He teased her lips with his tongue and she opened for him with a little groan. Desire, strong and hot and wild as a forest fire, raged through him, sweeping him up in a reckless heat. Celeste undulated against him, pressing her pelvis against his painfully hard erection. His mind shut off and his hands reached beneath her skirt. Her thighs were smooth and soft. She let out a whimper and moved her legs apart until she was straddling him.

Dear God, he wanted her. Right here. Right now. He was on fire, aflame, burning up with need. His fingers climbed higher to the silk of her panties. He could feel her slick heat, feel her hot readiness. She moaned and moved against him, giving him better access.

The sudden blare of music, followed by the loud slam of a metal door, penetrated the thick fog around his brain. *Voices.* Someone was coming.

Reluctantly, he pulled back. Celeste moaned and reached for him. The hungry look in her heavy-lidded eyes tempted him to throw caution to the wind, but he put a finger to his mouth. Footsteps crunched on the oyster-shell parking lot, headed in their direction.

"Wanna go to the Waterin' Hole for a nightcap?" called

a male voice that Rand recognized as belonging to the owner of a local auto parts store.

"Nah, Penny and I need to get on home before we owe the baby-sitter more money than we'll earn all week."

The footsteps headed toward them. Celeste tensed, her expression alarmed. Rand silently tugged down her skirt.

The footsteps stopped. A car door opened and closed. "Thank heavens," Rand whispered, holding her still. Brake lights cast a red glow on the shell parking lot, then tires crunched as the car backed up, then pulled away. A moment later, headlights flashed on across the street, an engine cranked and a minivan pulled away from the curb.

As soon as the two vehicles had driven away, Celeste scrambled out of the pickup bed. Rand rose, too, adjusting the painfully constricting crotch of his pants.

He cleared his throat and rubbed his jaw. "I, um, didn't mean for that to happen."

"Me, neither. I was just kidding around, and . . ." Her voice was breathy, as if she'd just finished a jog.

"Me, too. Guess I had too many beers."

It was a bald-faced lie. He wasn't drinking, because he was driving. They looked at each other, awkwardness as thick as swamp mud between them.

Celeste ran her hand down her dress, then reached up and smoothed her hair. "Well, I guess that proves my point."

"What point?"

"That not everything is logical."

"Oh, that was logical, all right." A dry smile played across his lips. "*Bio*-logical."

Celeste gave a weak laugh. "I meant it wasn't rational."

"Well, you've got me there." It was physical, pure and simple. A case of hormones calling to hormones in the dark.

Well, his hormones needed to put a lid on it. This

woman was a danger to his business, his reputation and his mental health. When he was around her, reason and caution went out the window and he found himself behaving in ways that baffled and alarmed him. Good Lord, he'd nearly made love to her right there in the parking lot, when practically the whole town could have come out and caught them in the act!

It was completely unlike him to indulge in such reckless behavior. She was like a mind-altering drug—dangerous, seductive, addictive.

It was clear that he needed to stay the heck away from her.

So why did she stir him more than any woman had in years?

Chapter Ten

"Yum. Smells like someone's baking bread," Celeste said as she followed Sara through the door of the Forest Manor Nursing Home two weeks later.

"Believe it or not, the food here is excellent," Sara confided, pausing to sign the visitors registry. "They've just built an assisted-living wing, and they brought in a chef who used to work at one of the big New Orleans hotels."

The place looked more like a hotel than a nursing home, Celeste thought as she followed her friend through the entry hall to a large room decorated in gold, burgundy and green. Two elderly women sat on a large floral sofa, a gray-haired man played checkers with a white-haired lady in the corner and three other people sat in wheelchairs by the large windows.

"He's over there," Sara murmured, indicating a slim man in a wheelchair by the window, who sat staring out at the atrium garden. The late afternoon sun shone on him like a stage light, making his hair gleam like polished sterling.

"Hi, Daddy." Sara bent down and kissed the man on the cheek. "I brought a friend to meet you. This is Celeste Landry."

Eyes the same shade of gray as Sara's turned toward Celeste. Unlike his daughter's, the older man's gaze seemed flat and disengaged.

Celeste smiled. "Hello, Mr. Overton."

"Hell-o." The man spoke in a rough, almost inaudible whisper, moving only the right side of his mouth. He lifted his right hand a scant inch off the wheelchair arm.

"He wants to shake hands," Sara told Celeste.

Celeste reached for his hand and gave it a gentle squeeze.

"Nice to meet you," he whispered haltingly.

"Very nice to meet you, too," Celeste said.

"Celeste is the friend I told you about who's opening the petting zoo at Miss Lizzie's old ranch," Sara explained. "She's been painting and fixing up the place, so I stopped by on my way here to see how it was coming along. When I said I was coming here to see you, she wanted to come, too."

"Sara said you like animals, so I brought one of my pets for you to see," Celeste said. She opened her large bag, and Mr. Peepers poked up his head.

Interest lit the elderly man's eyes. "A monkey!"

"This is the little guy she brought to the store," Sara said. "His name is Mr. Peepers. Isn't he cute?"

Mr. Peepers made the whimpering sound that indicated he wanted to be picked up. Sara lifted him from Celeste's purse.

"Can I hold him?" Mr. Overton asked.

"He'll need to get used to you first," Celeste warned. "He used to belong to a man who abused him, so it takes him a while to warm up to most men. But you can pet him while Sara holds him."

Sara held the tiny monkey close to the right arm of her father's wheelchair. The elderly man slowly lifted his hand and stroked the monkey's head. "Poor thing."

Sara nodded. "It's hard to believe anyone would be cruel to something so little, isn't it?"

"Yes. Does he bite?"

"No," Celeste said. "But if he's upset, he spits."

The right side of Mr. Overton's mouth curved up, and he gave a raspy chortle. He looked at Sara. "Just like Mr. Burns."

Sara threw back her head and laughed. "Yes." She turned to Celeste. "Dad has a customer who's addicted to chewing tobacco. He brings a coffee can with him everywhere he goes."

"What a nice little fellow." Mr. Overton's eyes were bright as his hand crept slowly down the animal's back.

"Oh, look, Ethel—there's a monkey!"

Celeste looked up to see two small elderly women shuffling into the room on walkers. The one with the tall beehive of teased gray hair had stopped in her tracks and stared at Mr. Peepers.

Her white-haired companion slid her walker forward, continuing her slow progress into the room. "Now, Doris, you know there aren't any monkeys around here. You must have taken too much of your medicine again."

"No! There's a real monkey over there."

"Last week you were seein' snakes in your shower."

"This is different! Jack Overton is petting him."

"Go back to your room. I'll call a nurse for you."

"Quit being so stubborn and just take a look."

The white-haired woman craned her head toward Mr. Overton. Her eyes widened behind her thick bifocals. "Well, I'll be!" she said.

By the time Celeste and Sara were ready to leave an

hour later, nearly every resident in the place had fawned over Mr. Peepers.

"That was the first time I've heard Daddy laugh since his stroke," Sara said as she and Celeste walked to the exit. The pleasant-faced nursing home manager walked with them.

"I don't know when I've seen our residents so alert and lively," she said.

"Animals have a way of drawing people out," Celeste agreed. "When I was in Houston, I was a volunteer with a program that took pets to visit patients in nursing homes and hospitals. The patients loved it, and the doctors said it was therapeutic."

"Anything that stimulates them and gets them to interact is wonderful."

Celeste bit the bullet. "I was wondering . . . would you be interested in a similar program here?"

"Oh, absolutely." The manager's round face beamed. "That would be terrific. But I'm afraid we don't have anything in our budget to pay you."

Celeste shrugged. "I wouldn't expect money. It would be a volunteer service."

"Well, then. It sounds fantastic."

"Good! I'll start making weekly visits, and I'll see if I can find some other pet owners who're interested in coming, too."

They reached the door. The manager smiled widely and shook Celeste's hand. "Thank you. Our residents will love this."

The sun was sinking behind the tall pines to the west of the nursing home as Celeste and Sara stepped out into the parking lot. "That was awfully sweet of you," Sara said.

Celeste lifted her shoulders. "My grandmother was in a nursing home for the last year of her life, and I know how much she enjoyed visitors. Especially the four-legged kind."

As always, the thought of her grandmother sent a pang through her heart. If only she'd had a chance to do things differently. . . .

She pushed the old regret aside and tucked Mr. Peepers into her purse as Sara pulled out her keys and unlocked her father's Ford Explorer.

"Well, it's very kind of you. People in the nursing home get awfully lonely."

Celeste climbed into the vehicle. "Well, I do, too. I can't wait for my business to get going so I'll have people to talk to on a daily basis. The animals are great, but they're not much on conversation."

Sara started the engine and backed out of the parking space. "Maybe you should invite your nearest neighbor over."

Celeste rolled her eyes. "I'm not *that* desperate for company."

Sara looked at her curiously. "I thought you two were getting along better."

Celeste sighed and gazed out the window. She hadn't seen Rand since the dance. After the episode in the parking lot, they'd both pretended nothing had happened. Rand had resumed his earlier pattern of introducing her to long-winded people and excusing himself to work the room. He hadn't said a word on the ride home, and when he walked her to the door, he'd said a polite good-bye without so much as a peck on the cheek.

"It's hard to get along with someone who can't wait for my business to fail so he can pounce on my property," Celeste said.

Sara pulled onto the highway, then shot her an amused grin. "Judging from the way he looked at you at the dance the other night, he wants to pounce on more than just your ranch."

Celeste shifted Mr. Peepers on her lap as she shifted the

topic. "So . . . how are things going with you and George?"

"Don't ask."

"You haven't seen him since the dance?"

"I've avoided him," Sara admitted. "I even saw his car in the grocery store parking lot the other day and decided to shop later."

"You need to talk to him," Celeste encouraged.

"I tried at the dance. He wouldn't listen."

"You need to keep trying."

There was a pause, then Sara nodded.

The conversation drifted to other topics, and before Celeste knew it, Sara had pulled up in front of her house. Celeste opened the passenger door. "Well, thanks for stopping by and taking me with you."

"Are you kidding? Thank you for coming." Sara gazed at Celeste's freshly painted front porch. "Your place is looking great."

"Thanks. I've been working my tail off, and it's starting to come together." Celeste blew out a hard sigh. "But the barn needs a new roof, which will cost a bundle, and I've run into a problem with the advertising."

"What kind of problem?"

"Highway billboards cost a lot more than I anticipated. I'm going to have to see about a loan after all."

"There's no shame in that. A banker is every small businessperson's best friend." Sara smiled. "Go see Mr. Adler. And be sure and put me down as a reference."

"Thanks, Sara." She gave the woman a hug. "That'll be a big help."

And Celeste had a feeling she was going to need all the help she could get.

The daily calendar on Mr. Adler's imposing mahogany desk was open to Thursday. Every line was completely filled— which meant, if Celeste was reading it correctly upside down, that he had an appointment every fifteen minutes all day long.

Her fifteen minutes were about a third of the way over, and Mr. Adler had barely said a word. Neither had she. She'd sat there with her hands tightly clasped in her lap, watching him study her loan application as he alternately leaned back in his tall leather chair and hunched forward to run some numbers on the electronic calculator on his desk.

Celeste studied the old masters prints on the paneled walls of the banker's office, her stomach a mass of knots. She'd been appalled to learn the cost of billboard advertising. The fifteen hundred dollars she'd budgeted for marketing wasn't enough to buy a sign in the middle of the swamp, much less on an interstate highway.

Mr. Adler put down her application, took off his reading glasses and folded his chubby hands on his desk, his expression somber. "Let me ask you a few a questions, Ms. Landry."

Celeste nodded. "Sure."

"Do you have any stocks, bonds or securities?"

"No."

"Do you have any funds at another bank?"

"I transferred everything here."

"I see." Mr. Adler drummed his fingers on his leather-lined desk pad. "It says here that you're divorced. Do you receive alimony?"

"Absolutely not!" Her attorney had wanted her to ask for a settlement, but Celeste had refused to even consider it.

"Hmmm. Well, do you own any other property?"

Celeste shook her head.

The heavyset man leaned forward on his elbows, steepling his fingers, his forehead creased in a frown. "Do you have *any* source of income whatsoever?"

Celeste felt like sinking down in her chair and sliding under the desk. "Well, not at the moment. I'm living on my savings until I get my petting zoo started."

Mr. Adler lowered his hands to his desk and sighed. "I'm sorry, Ms. Landry, but the bank will need proof of income before we can qualify you for a loan."

Celeste gripped the arms of her chair and leaned forward. "But I need the loan in order to start making an income."

The banker turned his hands palm up, his expression apologetic. "I'm sorry. That's not how things work."

Celeste's fingernails dug into the leather upholstery. "Can't you use the ranch as collateral?"

Mr. Adler shook his head. "The bank doesn't make loans, even secured loans, without some evidence that you'll have the means to pay the money back." His chair squeaked as he sat back and folded his hands over his belly. "It's for your own protection, Ms. Landry. We don't want to foreclose on your property. We're in the business of lending money, not selling real estate. I suggest you apply for a loan through the Small Business Administration."

Celeste had already checked into the possibility. "But that'll take months! I don't have months to wait. Can you suggest another bank that might be more lenient?"

"Not in good conscience. You can probably find a lender who'll make you a short-term loan, but they'll charge exorbitant interest rates, then wait like vultures to foreclose. I can't caution you strongly enough to stay away from them."

Mr. Adler droned on about the perils of unscrupulous lenders, then segued into a monologue on other financial factors. At length he glanced at his watch. Her fifteen minutes were apparently at an end.

"Isn't there any way you can help me?" she asked, a note of desperation in her voice.

"Well, if you could bring me some evidence of substantial business on your books—say, enough bookings to meet your expenses and your projected loan payments for several months—well, then, I'd be happy to reconsider your application."

How was she going to book business if she couldn't advertise? Celeste rose from her chair, her heart lower than the soles of her sandals. "Well, thank you for your time."

Mr. Adler rose and shook her hand. "I wish you the best of luck."

She was going to need it. Only two months remained before she'd be out of money. She could probably find a low-paying job to help her stretch out her funds; but a regular job would barely pay her bills, much less give her the money to advertise, fix the place up and pay the taxes that would be due at the beginning of October. And then there was the matter of the new roof on the barn. . . .

Tears clouded her eyes as she made her way through the lobby. She tried her best to restrain them, but by the time she'd reached the bank's front door, she could barely hold them back.

She pushed on the door, only to have it fly open, causing her to collide with a hard male chest in a blue striped shirt—a chest that felt all too familiar.

Strong hands caught her arms, steadying her. "Whoa, there!"

Great, just great. If there was one person she didn't want to run into right now, it was Rand Adams. She couldn't bear the thought of hearing him say "I told you so." "Sorry," she said, sniffing back her tears.

"No problem." Rand looked into her face and frowned. "Are you okay?"

"Sure. I-I'm fine." His hands were still on her bare upper arms, and the heat of his palms seemed to go all the way through her. She looked up at his face, but that only made

things worse. There ought to be a law against a man looking so good. It gave him an unfair advantage.

She hadn't seen him since the dance two and a half
weeks before, but that didn't mean he hadn't been on her
mind. He had been—all too frequently. She didn't know
what had possessed her that evening; she'd never behaved
so rashly in her life. She couldn't believe how rapidly
things had ignited and blazed out of control. How could
she feel so attracted to a man who was everything she'd
vowed to avoid?

Rand peered into her face, his forehead creased. "You
sure don't look fine."

The last thing she wanted to do in front of him was
cry—but to her mortification, the tears swimming in her
eyes spilled down her cheeks.

He rubbed his hands up and down her arms. "Hey, it
can't be that bad."

"Yes, it can. For me, anyway." She wiped at her face, but
the tears kept falling. "I'm sure you'll be elated, though."

He put his hand on the small of her back. "Come on.
Let's take a walk and you can tell me about it."

"Why? So you can gloat?"

"I won't do that." Even with her tear-blurred vision, she
could see the sincerity in his eyes. "Come on."

She might as well go with him. He was bound to find
out soon enough, anyway.

They walked down the block to the town square. The
weather was as gray as her mood, but the overcast sky and
late morning breeze cooled the August air. They sat on a
bench under a long-limbed magnolia.

"So what's going on?" he asked.

She wouldn't cry. She wouldn't. She drew a deep steadying breath. "You were right about the cost of advertising,"
she admitted. "It's a lot more expensive than I realized. I
knew that newspaper and TV ads would be beyond my

budget, but I thought I'd be able to afford a billboard on the interstate. I was shocked to find out that just one costs thousands of dollars. So I went to see Mr. Adler about a loan . . ."

It was pretty obvious what Adler's answer had been. From a logical standpoint, Rand knew he should be glad—but he didn't feel glad at all. "What did he say?"

Celeste picked at a thread on her black linen pants. "Pretty much that the bank only makes loans to people who don't need them."

Rand gave a small smile. "That sounds about right."

The dejected slump of her shoulders made him want to put his arm around her, but he figured it wasn't a good idea. "What are you going to do?"

"I don't know."

Rand sat beside her in silence, genuinely wanting to help. The longer she pursued this misguided plan, the more disappointed she'd be when she had to face facts. "I'll make you a good offer for the property," he said gently.

Her head jerked up. "Oh, I'm not giving up."

"Deciding to change your course isn't the same as giving up."

"It is to me."

"There's no shame in discovering where your talents lie. Maybe you're better suited to care for animals, than to run a business."

She stiffened. "Running a shelter is the same thing as running a business."

"No, it's not. A shelter doesn't need to make a profit. Making money requires a whole different set of skills."

"And you don't think I have them." She stated it in a challenging tone.

He didn't, as a matter of fact. But there was no point in

telling her that. "It's the sort of thing that usually takes years of study and experience to learn."

"And I suppose you're an expert."

He was trying to help her, but she acted as if he were her enemy. "I happen to have picked up a thing or two," he replied.

"Well, then, what would you do if you were me?"

"I'd quit while I was ahead."

"Aside from that."

"Get my head examined."

She rose from the bench. "I have better things to do than sit here and get insulted."

"Okay, okay." He motioned for her to sit back down and blew out an aggravated breath. "If I were you, I suppose I'd look at direct marketing instead of mass marketing. I'd aim my efforts at the people most likely to visit a petting zoo instead of trying to reach the whole world. It's a lot more cost-effective."

"So what would you do?"

"Well, first I'd figure out who was most likely to want to visit a petting zoo."

"That's easy. Children."

"Okay. Well, if children were my target market, I'd figure out where I was most likely to find large groups of them."

"*Groups* of children?" The hostility in her eyes began to thaw. "That's interesting. I've been thinking in terms of families."

She stared at the city hall, and he could practically see the wheels turning in her head. Her green eyes met his. "What would you do next?"

"I'd come up with a message that would make them want to buy what I was selling. And then I'd design a way of reaching them that fit my budget."

She jumped up, her eyes lit with excitement. "I could make up some flyers and distribute them to schools in some of the surrounding towns—maybe with a coupon giving families a discount." Her words spilled out fast. "I could even go talk to principals and teachers—and preschool owners. If I could emphasize the educational angle, maybe schools would even bring kids here for field trips. Classes might even come from Baton Rouge and New Orleans!"

Dismay filled Rand's chest as he rose to his feet. "You're getting a little carried away, don't you think?"

"Carried away? I'm just getting started." Her eyes were as bright as sparklers on the Fourth of July. She threw her arms around his neck. "Thank you! You're a genius."

I'm an idiot. He'd set out to dissuade her, but somewhere along the line it had backfired. And now her scent was invading his senses, curling its way inside him, wrapping around his brain like some kind of numbing agent. If he had any sense at all, he'd back off and make a fast getaway. The problem was, when he got close to Celeste, he *didn't* have any sense.

His gaze fell to her lips. They were parting, opening in invitation, calling to his in a silent, sensual language, begging to be kissed. Like a man in a trance, he started to lower his head.

She abruptly dropped her arms and backed away. His eyes flew open.

"I-I don't think this is a good idea." She sounded flustered, and her eyes wouldn't meet his. Two bright spots blazed on her cheeks.

He swallowed and nodded numbly. She took another step back. "Thanks for the advice," she said softly.

He nodded again, still feeling too doltish to speak.

"I really appreciate it." With a smile and a small wave, she turned and walked rapidly off.

It took a long moment before the blood began to circulate in his brain again. And when it did, it took another long moment before he realized what he'd done.

Chapter Eleven

George had just taken the first bite of his shrimp po'boy when the door swung open and Sara walked into the crowded sandwich shop. He froze, his sandwich in midair, and watched her take a place in line at the order counter, behind Harriet Hermann.

Thank goodness—she hadn't seen him. He was seated at a tiny table against the far wall, half-hidden by a large blackboard that proclaimed the special of the day. With any luck, she'd order her sandwich and leave without ever realizing he was there.

Man, he hated the way she affected him. Even after all these years, the sight of her made his pulse gallop like a racehorse in the final stretch.

It was unfair that she looked so good. Her hair was cut in some kind of a short, wispy style that showed off her long neck, and she wore a long tan skirt and matching sleeveless top that skimmed close to her slender body. Why couldn't she have gained fifty pounds and gotten all gray and frumpy like so many of her classmates? It sure would have made it easier to see her again.

He stared at her back, noting the curve of her waist, the flare of her hips. He remembered how right his hand had felt resting there. He remembered the softness of the nape of her neck, and how she used to shiver with pleasure when he'd kiss her ear.

She had a beauty mark below her right shoulder, right where the buckle of her purse's shoulder strap fell. He wondered if another man had ever kissed it, wondered if she had someone special waiting for her back in Chicago.

His sandwich suddenly tasted like sawdust in his mouth. With a hard scowl, he set it down and picked up his glass of iced tea.

The line slowly moved forward. Harriet looked around and spotted Sara behind her. "Well, hello, there. How's your father?"

"Well, this morning he was mad at the therapist for trying to make him do some leg lifts. I'm sure that means he's getting better."

Harriet laughed. "Yep, it's always a good sign when they start complaining. Any idea when he's going to get to come home?"

"No. The therapy is helping, but it's a slow process."

"He's awfully lucky to have you. Mabel says you're out at the nursing home there every morning and every night."

"I have breakfast with him every day, then stop by after the store closes to help him eat dinner. How's Wallace?"

"Oh, he's fine—but he's drivin' me crazy since he retired. It's like having a toddler underfoot again, only this one needs a shave."

The conversation shifted to Harriet's husband, then broke off as the two women reached the counter and gave their orders. They resumed talking a few minutes later, as they paused at the soft drink dispenser to get their beverages.

"How's business at the store?" Harriet asked.

"Good. For some reason, half the town decided to do their shopping this morning. I haven't sat down in five hours."

"Looks like you'll have a hard time finding a place to sit in here." They were walking his way. George looked down, not wanting to make eye contact. "Oh, look—there's George!" Harriet announced. "And he's got an empty spot at his table."

George cringed inwardly, but he rose to his feet as his upbringing dictated. "Hello, Harriet." He avoided looking into Sara's eyes, choosing to fasten his gaze on her chin. "Sara."

"It's your lucky day, George," Harriett bubbled. "Sara needs a place to sit, and you have the only empty chair in the place."

George reached for his plate and drink. "You two are welcome to the table."

"My goodness, what a gentleman—ready to give up his entire table, and he's barely started to eat." The older woman patted the back of his chair, indicating he should sit down. "That's very sweet, George, but I'm not staying—I'm taking lunch home to Wallace. But Sara's been on her feet all morning and needs a place to sit, so this worked out just fine."

Damn the old biddy. She probably wanted them to sit together so she could go gossip about it to the whole town. "Sure." George turned to Sara, still avoiding her eyes. "Have a seat."

Sara set her tray on the table and cast him an overbright smile. "Thank you."

Harriet clasped her white bag of sandwiches with both hands and beamed. "Look at you two! It's just like old times. I remember seeing the two of you together like this many a night."

If Harriet said one more word, he was going to throttle her, proper upbringing or not. He unclenched his jaw enough to speak. "Tell Wallace hello for me."

"Will do." The old woman turned to Sara. "So nice seeing you. Give my best to your father."

"I will."

The door jangled as the woman left the shop. George kept his eyes on his sandwich, but he was keenly aware of Sara taking her drink and sandwich off the red plastic tray, carrying the tray back to the stack on the counter, then returning to the table and sitting down across from him.

She placed a napkin in her lap. "How are you, George?"

"Fine."

"It was a nice dance the other week, wasn't it?"

He lifted his shoulders. "I'm not much on dances."

She took a sip of her drink, puckering her lips around the straw. He had a sudden flashback—the kind he imagined war veterans had, sharp and painful, so vivid it was almost tactile—of kissing those lips. A little shard of pain sliced into him.

"We never got to finish our conversation then," she said.

"We finished it as far as I was concerned."

"George . . ." She leaned forward. There was no avoiding her eyes. They pulled at him until he was staring straight into them. "I feel so bad about the way I handled things when we were young. It's been eating at me all these years." Her eyes were dark with misery.

He looked back down at his sandwich. Well, good. She deserved to feel miserable. That was exactly how she'd made him feel.

"I'm so sorry," she whispered. "I never meant to embarrass you in front of a churchful of people."

His head snapped up. "*Embarrass* me? You think that's what you did—you *embarrassed* me?"

A flicker of uncertainty crossed her face. "I'm so very, very sorry."

A wave of outrage, red and hot, flooded his veins as memories flooded his mind. He could still smell the scent of gardenias and roses, still see the sprays of creamy blossoms spilling out of tall white vases on either side of the altar, still hear the organ music reverberating from the arched ceiling as the guests filed in. He'd waited at the front of the church, peering through the tiny glass windowpane at the top of the door, his nerves dancing.

This was what pure joy felt like, he remembered thinking. He'd told himself to memorize the moment, to etch the details in his mind so that one day he could describe it to his children. He promised himself that if he lived to be a hundred, he'd never forget the way he felt that day.

And he never had. No, he'd never forgotten.

He stared at her through a haze of red across the table. She'd waltzed back into his life and dredged up twenty-eight years of pain, and now she wanted to apologize for *embarrassing* him?

If he'd been a violent man, he would have overturned the table right then and there.

"I'm so sorry." Her voice was a ragged whisper. Her eyes were full of tears. "I want to explain—"

"I don't want any damned explanations," he ground out. "I want you to leave me the hell alone." Without another word, he rose from the table and stalked out of the restaurant, leaving behind his uneaten sandwich and a café full of gawking onlookers.

The humidity in the night air clung to Sara's skin like Saran Wrap. Despite the cloying heat, a shiver passed through her as she climbed the stoop of George's house.

She had to do this. She had to do something to quiet the chaos inside her. She'd been haunted by her actions for twenty-eight years, and she simply couldn't bear it any longer. The whispers of guilt in her head had grown into shouts since she'd returned to Cypress Grove. They'd gotten even louder since the dance, but after seeing George at the sandwich shop yesterday, they'd crescendoed into a deafening roar.

For twenty-eight years, George had refused to listen to her. He'd hung up the phone when she'd called, he'd sent back her letters unopened, he'd refused to talk to her face-to-face.

The guilt was making her crazy. She was unable to sleep at night. She'd close her eyes and a wave of memories would wash over her, dragging her thoughts into a hellish hole of guilt and regret. The weight of it was crushing her.

She'd tried avoiding him, tried so hard that she felt like a criminal trying to elude the police. She jumped every time her father's store bell jangled. She found herself looking for George's truck every time she drove down the street. She checked the parking lot before she went into the post office.

This *had* to end. She had to get it off her chest. There were some things she needed to say, and she was going to say them, whether he liked it of not.

She wiped a bead of sweat from her upper lip, trying to gather her courage. The night was still and silent. Not a breath of breeze stirred the air. Only the hum of the air conditioning unit on the side of George's house and the rhythmic thrum of tree frogs relieved the almost oppressive silence.

When she'd first returned to Cypress Grove, she'd been surprised at the quiet. She'd forgotten how still the nights could be in a small town, a town where most folks worked hard and turned in early.

She was counting on that stillness to help her tonight.

She wiped her damp palm on her black slacks and drew in a deep breath of magnolia-scented air. He was still awake. She could see the flickering blue light of a television through a crevice in the living room window curtains. Drawing a deep breath, she lifted a trembling hand and pushed the worn doorbell button.

Her insides quaked as she heard footsteps approach, and she folded her hands behind her back. The door cracked open; then George stood in the light. His face creased in a scowl. "Go away."

"Please, George, I need to talk to you."

"You have nothing to say I want to hear." He started to close the door.

Impulsively, she stuck her sandal-clad foot in the opening and spoke with more bravado than she felt. "Too bad. You're going to listen to me anyway."

His scowl became a glower. "Jesus, Sara, get your foot out of the way."

"No."

"Do I have to forcibly take you off my doorstep?"

"If you do, I'll just go stand on your lawn and say my piece with a bullhorn." She held up her right hand, showing him a red battery-operated bullhorn, the kind referees use at ballgames.

His eyes widened at the sight of it. "Have you lost your mind? Give me that thing." He reached to grab it, but she stretched back her arm.

"If you take it away from me, I'll just scream my piece at the top of my lungs. I'm sure your neighbors will be interested in what I have to say."

He glared at her.

She glared right back. "I've tried to talk to you for twenty-eight years and you've refused to listen. I'm not going to accept that any longer."

"I'll call the police, Sara."

"You do that. If they arrest me, it'll make the newspaper, and I'll just tell the reporter what I came here to tell you. It's your choice, George. You can either listen to me now or read about in the *Cypress Gazette*. But one way or the other, George Wright, you're going to hear me out."

"Christ Almighty, Sara. What's gotten into you?"

"We have some unsettled business between us, and I refuse to let it remain unsettled any longer." She was breathing hard. "I look at my father—one minute he was fine, and the next he can't walk and he can barely talk. What happened to him could happen to any of us at any moment, and I'm going to get this off my chest while I still can. And you're going to listen to what I have to say, whether I have to make a total fool of myself to do it or not. So you decide, George. You can let me in and we can have a civilized private conversation, or I'll wake up your neighbors and spread our business all over town."

His eyes were full of fury. "I won't be blackmailed. Now get your foot out of my door or I'll get it out for you."

"If that's the way you want it." She removed her foot, and he immediately slammed the door in her face.

He didn't think she'd do it. Well, he was about to find out otherwise. She marched down the porch and into the middle of his lawn, flipped on the bullhorn switch and lifted it to her mouth. "*George Wright,*" she called.

The volume made her jump. Good heavens—she'd known it would be loud, but she hadn't known it would be *that* loud. Her voice resounded in the night like thunder.

What the hell. The louder, the better. She lifted the megaphone again. "*I need to talk to you, George, but you keep refusing to listen, so . . .*"

George's door jerked open and he stood in the entryway, glowering. "Damn it, Sara—have you lost your mind? What the hell are you doing?"

She lowered the megaphone. "Exactly what I said I would. It's your choice."

A porch light flashed on at the house next door. Across the street, a woman's face appeared in an upstairs window. Muttering a low oath, George held the door open, his mouth grim. "Get the hell in here."

A little thrill of victory pulsed through her. Sara scurried up the stoop and through the door before he had the chance to change his mind.

But once the door closed behind her, she nearly changed hers. Oh, mercy—she was in George's house, the home he'd shared with Heather. She hadn't thought of it that way before, but now that she was in it, the fact hit her squarely in the face. Over a small console table in the tiny foyer hung a picture of Heather and George on their wedding day. Heather's face was aglow, her expression radiant, her features beautiful with joy. George stood beside her, the smiling groom.

Sara felt as if a knife had just been thrust into her chest, forcing all the air from her lungs, creating a sudden, unexpected pain around her heart.

That should have been me. The thought left her lightheaded and nauseous. No. Not should have; *could have*, she mentally corrected. *Could have. Almost was.* She was the one who had run away. It had been her decision.

She just hadn't realized how final that decision would be. At eighteen, she hadn't known that life was a one-way street. No U-turns allowed. There was no going back.

She followed George into a small living room, gripping the megaphone with both hands to keep them from shaking. Her style-savvy eye surveyed the room: stark white walls, brown carpeting, beige and navy upholstery. Plain, practical, utilitarian—the decorative equivalent of white bread and vanilla pudding. For all it lacked in style and aesthetic appeal, though, it was clearly a home. Family pictures were everywhere. Boys in pajamas by a Christmas tree. A young boy on a horse, George by his side. Heather, George and two boys with George's parents. Heather, George and a gawky teenager. George and Heather with a young man in a graduation gown.

The knife in her chest drove deeper and twisted. All that he'd had with Heather, all that she'd never known—it had happened right here. The pictures documented it.

George stood in front of the fireplace mantel, his arms folded, his legs apart. "What the hell is so all-fired important that you're willing to make a fool of yourself to say it?" he demanded.

"I want to explain why I left."

His eyes were cold. "I couldn't care less."

"Well, too bad. Because I need to tell you." She seated herself on the blue, brown and beige plaid sofa with an aplomb she didn't feel.

"Will you leave me the hell alone after you do?"

"If you hear me out, yes."

His gaze was stony and full of disbelief. Another twist of the knife.

"Sit down, George," she prompted softly. "Please."

With a clearly exasperated sigh, he lowered himself into an armchair on the opposite side of the room. An old clock on the mantel—the same one that had sat on the mantel of George's parents' house, Sara noted with a pang—ticked in the silence, a loud heartbeat in the room.

She drew a deep breath. Now that she had his attention, she didn't know where to begin. "I hadn't planned to run away at the wedding," she blurted. "It was a rash, last-minute, moment-of-panic thing. Something inside me just snapped."

"If you didn't want to marry me, you could have told me."

"But I *did* want to marry you! I just didn't want to do it right then."

"You picked a hell of a time to come to that conclusion."

"I tried to tell you, George. Over and over. I tried to tell Daddy, too. But both of you just discounted what I had to say. I had spent my whole life pleasing people, going along and being agreeable, not making any waves. I-I guess I didn't know how to be forceful enough."

"You say you tried to tell me," he said flatly. "When?"

"Before you announced the engagement." He'd done it at a graduation party. He'd told the whole world they were getting married without giving her any warning. "I told you again when I got the scholarship offer. And when we set the wedding date. And lots of other times—right up to the night before the wedding. I tried and tried to tell you."

His jaw stuck out at a rigid angle. "You evidently didn't try hard enough."

"Every time I brought it up, you'd stop me."

"And how did I do that?"

"You—you'd kiss me."

He gave a derisive snort.

"I tried to tell you after the rehearsal dinner. Surely you remember that."

A memory floated up in George's mind, pushing through the layers of resentment and hurt, rising to the surface like flotsam from a long-buried shipwreck.

The rehearsal dinner had been held at an old antebellum mansion twenty miles away—a restaurant that had gone out of business a month later. How appropriate, George had thought at the time. The restaurant had had no future, just like the relationship they'd gathered to celebrate.

The occasion had been jubilant and joyful. Everyone was laughing and talking and joking—everyone except Sara. She'd been unusually pale and subdued all evening, and

George had been worried. It wasn't anything she did, but rather what she didn't do. No—not what she didn't do, what she didn't seem to *feel*.

George had been elated. Eager. Walking on air. And she wasn't.

"Are you okay?" George had asked on the drive to her house afterwards.

She'd shaken her head. His breathing had stopped.

"What's the matter? Are you ill?"

"George . . ." Her voice had been small and timid, thick with held-back tears. "I-I don't think we should get married right now. I don't feel ready."

Panic had welled up in his chest, but he'd pushed it down. He refused to allow it. He'd dreamed of this day ever since junior high. Other guys talked about scoring and fooling around and etching notches on their bedposts, but all George had ever wanted was Sara. She was the most beautiful, most intelligent, most kindhearted girl he'd ever known. He'd loved her since she'd sat beside him in seventh-grade social studies class and laughed at a cartoon he'd drawn for the school paper; and he could hardly believe that she loved him back. He wanted to make it official, to make it permanent as soon as possible. Now that he was about to make his dream come true, he wasn't going to let it slip away. By sheer force of will, he was going to make it happen.

"Of course you're ready, honey," he'd told her. "Your dress and the flowers and the church and the reception—it's all set. You're just nervous, that's all. It's perfectly normal."

"It's not the wedding I don't feel ready for, George. It's being married."

He'd put his hands on her upper arms and looked deep into her eyes. "Sara, do you love me?"

"Yes. More than anything. But . . ."

He'd raised a finger to her lips. "No buts. You love me and I love you. And we're getting married tomorrow." And then he'd kissed her until both of them were breathless, their young bodies throbbing. When he knew he'd shredded every fiber of her resistance, he'd pulled back and walked her to the door.

"Now go inside and get a good night's sleep. It's the last night we'll ever have to sleep without each other." She'd looked at him, her eyes full, as if she were about to cry. He'd kissed her gently on the forehead.

It was the last time he'd ever kissed her.

"I tried to tell you," Sara was saying now. He jerked his thoughts back to the present. "You just wouldn't listen."

"I thought it was just pre-wedding jitters," he said stiffly. "If you didn't love me, you should have said so."

"But I *did* love you."

"Yeah, right." Sarcasm dripped from his words.

"I did!"

"You sure had a funny way of showing it."

"It wasn't a matter of not loving *you*. It was a matter of not loving *myself* enough. How could I make a commitment to you when I didn't even know who I was?"

"Oh, please." George rolled his eyes. "Don't give me that 'I needed to find myself' crap."

"It was true! I *did* need to find myself—to stand on my own, to become my own person, to discover what I was made of. I needed to have my own life."

"You make it sound as if marrying me would have been a death sentence."

She stared at the megaphone in her lap. "I just needed to have my own identity, to make my own choices."

"If you didn't intend to go through with it, why did you bother even going to the church?"

"I *did* intend to go through with it. You know how timid I was—I never made waves, I always followed instructions,

161

I never upset anyone or caused any scenes. I was placid, passive Sara. I didn't know how to stand up for myself, because I'd never done it. I thought there was no way out."

Her words hit him like a slap in the face. "Well, you sure found a way. Right out the bathroom window."

She blew out a hard breath. "I'm trying to explain, George."

"I'm all ears."

She gazed down at the floor. The clock ticked loudly in the silence. "On the way to the church, Daddy drove past the lake, and I saw a big flock of ducks floating on the water, and . . ."

"Ducks?" He glared at her. "You called off the wedding because you saw a bunch of *ducks?*"

"You're not listening. You're looking for ways to block out what I'm saying."

It was true. He'd spent the last twenty-eight years trying to block her out, trying not to think about her, trying not to see her face when he closed his eyes or made love to his wife. Just because she decided to barge into his home tonight and try to clear her guilty conscience didn't mean he was going to let her.

He fixed her with a sullen stare.

She drew a deep breath and continued. "There was this large group of ducks on the water—the kind with those shiny, blue-green feathers—and a bunch of them took off flying. This one duck wanted to fly, too, but he must have been injured. He flapped and flapped his wings, but he couldn't get off the water. He looked so unhappy and frustrated—and then he started pecking at the other ducks around him. And all of a sudden, I realized I was going to be just like that duck."

Against his better judgment, George looked at her face. Her expression was so serious, her eyes so sincere that his sarcastic comment died on his tongue.

"I was going straight from one nest to another, without ever seeing if I could fly or how far I could go, without ever finding out if I were a lead duck or a follower. I didn't want to become like that: angry and resentful, taking it out on people around me. It wouldn't be fair to me, and it wouldn't be fair to you."

"How very big of you."

She leaned forward. "Look—I know I handled things horribly. I'll be the first to admit that. Running away was the coward's way out. I should have stayed and told you to your face. But the truth is, I'd *tried* to talk to you about it, and you always emotionally overpowered me. I was afraid you'd do that again. I wasn't strong or confident enough to stand up to you."

You always emotionally overpowered me. The phrase startled him. Was it true? Had he really done that? Against his will, he considered the possibility.

She mustered a sad smile. "Which is an awfully good reason in and of itself not to get married, now that I think about it."

Silence throbbed between them. She fingered the megaphone. "I'm so sorry. I don't think anyone ever felt worse about themselves than I did when I squeezed out that bathroom window."

"Well, you sure got over that."

"Not really." Her eyes held a sadness, a forlornness, a heartsick kind of grief. "It still hurts to know that I hurt you and your family."

"Well, I guess you did us both a favor."

"It seems I did you a bigger favor than I did myself." She gazed at the pictures of his children on the wall. "You had the life you always wanted, and you had someone to share it with."

Oh, God—she was starting to get to him. She was seeping through the wall he'd built around his heart, curling like smoke into all the little cracks and crevices. He steeled himself against her. "You had the life you wanted, too."

Her lips went through the motion, but it couldn't be called a smile. "In part," she conceded. "I'm not weak anymore, and I'm not a wimp. I've learned to listen to my heart and be true to myself. And I've learned to be upfront and honest with others, even when the truth hurts." She paused a minute. "I've become the person I needed to become before I was ready to marry. Unfortunately, I never had the chance to prove it."

She rose from the sofa. "Well, I've said what I came to say. If you can't forgive me, I'll just have to live with that, but I'm sick of feeling guilty, and I'm tired of driving through the parking lot at the supermarket to make sure your car's not there before I go in to get a loaf of bread."

"You do that, too?" He looked at her in surprise.

She gave a small, sad smile. "All the time."

She rose and headed for the door, not waiting for him to accompany her. And when he heard it close behind her, the house seemed emptier than it had in years.

Chapter Twelve

"Don't look now, but here comes your lady friend," George told Rand three days later.

Rand slipped the bit out of the mouth of a two-year-old roan and glanced beyond the corral to the gravel drive, where a plume of dust rose behind an old red Jeep. *Celeste.* A burst of adrenaline rushed through his veins.

He scowled, irritated at his body's reaction. "She's not my lady friend." Rand opened the metal bar gate that led to the pasture, unfastened the lead from the mare's rope harness and released the animal into the field. He slammed the gate harder than necessary, then neatly wound the rope into a tight circle.

"Whatever you say, boss." George deftly guided the mare he was riding around a barrel on the training course, an amused grin on his face. "Reckon she's wanting another dance lesson?"

More than likely she was wanting another marketing lesson, Rand thought darkly. He couldn't get over the way he'd practically written a business development plan for her. What was it about this woman that made his best intentions turn around and bite him on the butt?

"She's probably got an escaped animal or some other crisis," Rand said curtly. "That woman is more trouble than a crawfish in your shorts."

George laughed. "Well, she's the kind of trouble a lot of men wouldn't mind finding themselves in, that's for sure."

Rand shot the older man a sharp look. "What are you saying?"

"Just that she's not a bit hard on the eyes."

"You interested in her?"

George regarded him with surprise, followed by something that looked suspiciously like amusement. "Are you kiddin'? She's closer to my sons' age than mine."

Relief surged through Rand. He rapidly rationalized it away. Of course he was relieved; he didn't want his friend getting hooked up with someone who'd be history in a few months.

"Besides, I'm not in the market for a woman," the older man continued, reining the mare to a stop. His lips twisted in a teasing smile. "And even if I were, I wouldn't step out with the boss's girl."

"She's *not* my girl." The rope in Rand's hand was so tightly wound it was a wonder it didn't start fraying.

"Whatever you say." With a sly grin, George nudged the horse with his heels and cantered off to the obstacle course on the far side of the corral.

The Jeep drew up and stopped, and Celeste climbed out wearing a sleeveless white tank top and a pair of denim shorts. The outfit wasn't overly tight or lowcut and probably wouldn't be considered provocative, but it sure looked that way on Celeste.

She raised her hand in a wave, flashing a glimpse of bare midriff.

It was ridiculous, the way something so innocuous sent his heart rate soaring.

She headed toward the corral. Rand noted that two of his stable hands stopped in their tracks and stared at her. He shot them a dark scowl and ambled toward her.

"Good morning," she called. She ducked between the fence slats, joining him inside the corral. "It's a beautiful day, isn't it?"

"If you like it hot." He was pretty sure she hadn't come over to talk about the weather. He rested a cowboy boot on the bottom rung of the fence. "What's up?"

She leaned her bottom against the fence post. "I wanted to thank you."

"For what?"

"For giving me such good advice about marketing Wild Things."

His eyebrows rose. "Wild Things?"

"Wild Things Fun Farm. That's what I'm calling my place."

Things were pretty wild at her place, all right. "Is that Fun Farm or Funny Farm?"

She laughed. "Which do you think fits better?"

"Don't ask."

She grinned at him. "Well, you gave me a lot of really good suggestions. I've given a lot of thought to what you said about how it was going to be difficult to attract visitors here since I'm off the beaten path, and it occurred to me that instead of expecting everyone to come to me, maybe I should take the animals to them."

A buzz of alarm shot through him. "I didn't suggest that."

"No, but you kind of gave me the idea. You told me to try direct marketing, so I made up some flyers and sent them to some preschools." Her eyes sparkled. "And I got my very first booking."

"Oh, yeah? For what?"

"A child's birthday party. They want to have pony rides. Which is great, because Sheltie loves children."

One booking probably wouldn't even buy the Shetland pony a bag of feed, but Celeste looked so delighted that Rand couldn't bring himself to rain on her parade. "Well, congratulations."

"Thanks." She shoved her hands in her side pockets and rocked back and forth on the soles of her feet. "There's only one little problem, and I was wondering if you could help me with it."

Uh oh. Here came trouble. "What is it?"

"Well, the party's in New Orleans, and I don't have a horse trailer."

No. No way. He decided to toss the ball right back in her court. "You accepted a booking in New Orleans when you don't have a way of getting there?"

"Well, not yet." She flashed a winsome smile.

He was *not* going to fall for this. "That's not a very professional way to run your business."

She tilted her chin to a defensive angle. "Lots of businesses accept bookings knowing they'll have to rent or borrow equipment. If I have to, I'll drive into New Orleans and rent a horse trailer."

"That would wipe out any profit you could possibly make."

"Maybe. But every child at this party is another potential booking, and I have to start somewhere. And I don't have the funds to buy a trailer right now. I'm not even sure if I need one. Anyway, I'm just getting started, so I wondered . . ."

Here it came. He refused to make this easy for her. "What?"

"Well, I was wondering if I could borrow your trailer."

No. Absolutely not. He was *not* going to let Celeste borrow one of his most critical pieces of equipment. Still, it was hard to look into her clear green eyes and refuse her directly.

"What did the Joneses use?" he hedged.

"A trailer, but it belonged to the circus." She tucked a strand of hair behind her ear. "I promise I'll be careful. I won't damage it in any way."

Darn right you won't. Because you're not going to get your hands on it. It couldn't be that hard to find a believable reason to tell her no. Rand rubbed his jaw, pretending to consider the request. "When do you need it?"

"Saturday."

"This Saturday?"

Celeste nodded.

"Oh, gee, I'm sorry, but I'm going to be using it. I've got to pick up a mare in Luling on Saturday." It happened to be the truth, but he'd been fully prepared to lie.

"Oh." Her face fell. A second later it brightened. "Isn't New Orleans on the way? It's a two-horse trailer. You could drop me and Sheltie off at the party, go get the mare, then swing back and pick us up on the way home."

Oh, no. No way. The last thing he intended to do was to get further involved with her and her business. He shook his head. "That's not—"

"Please?" Those big eyes fixed on his. He tried to look away, but her gaze held him hostage. He vaguely remembered reading about a frog that paralyzed its victims by staring into their eyes. He could swear that's what was happening to him.

"I'll be happy to pay you," she said.

Ah, hell. She was making him feel like a jerk—especially since he knew how tight her money situation was. "I don't want your money."

"Why not? You'd be providing a service I need. It would be only fair."

He scowled, annoyed at how cheesy she'd managed to

make him feel. "I don't take money from neighbors."

"Well, then, I'll find some other way to pay you back."

One way immediately came to mind.

Before he could come up with a plausible reason why her plan wouldn't work, she'd flung herself at him, wrapped her arms around him and enfolded him in a hug. "Thank you *so* much! I really, really appreciate this."

"I didn't . . ." The scent of her hair filled his nostrils, somehow altering his brain functions.

She looked up, her eyes shining, her lips pink and parted. "What?"

"Huh?" Rand echoed, his brain fuzzy as a tennis ball.

"You were about to say something."

"Oh. Right. I didn't . . ." Lord, but she smelled good— and she felt even better. She was so close to him, close enough to kiss. The memory of the way she'd tasted sent an instant rush of arousal surging through him.

Hell. It *was* on the way. One little booking wasn't going to make or break her business. What harm could it do? If she thought he'd done his best to help her, it might even make it easier for him to acquire her ranch in a couple of months.

She looked up at him, still waiting for him to complete his thought. "You didn't what?"

He blew out a sigh and caved in to the inevitable. "I didn't catch what time you need to be in New Orleans."

Rand stared when Celeste opened the door on Saturday morning. "I didn't know this was a costume party."

She looked down at her outfit and grinned. She was wearing jeans and chaps, a fitted western shirt, a vest with a big sheriff's badge, a red bandanna and a straw cowboy hat. "The party's got a western theme, so I thought I'd get in character. What do you think?"

Rand's gaze was scorching. "I think that if the sheriffs

in the Old West had looked like you, the bad guys would have been lining up to get arrested."

Celeste felt her cheeks heat. Her feelings toward Rand were heating up, as well. He wasn't nearly as cold or detached as he pretended. He'd fixed her fence, comforted her when the bank turned down her loan request and given her some valuable advice. He stood to benefit if her business failed, yet here he was, helping her out yet again.

"Are you ready to go?" he asked.

"As soon as I put Mr. P. in his kennel." She scooped the monkey off the back of the sofa, headed down the hall and set the animal inside his enormous cage, where she'd already placed a papaya and some melon. She fastened the latch and headed back to the living room, where she found Rand squatting down by the door, looking into four gray kennels—one for each poodle, one containing four baby bunnies and a large one for the pot-bellied pig.

"Any reason these guys are in jail?"

"I'd like to take them with us, if it's all right with you. I promise they won't be any trouble. They'll stay in their kennels the whole way there and back."

"Fine. Let's get them loaded."

He picked up the kennels containing the pig and the bunnies, and she followed with the dogs. Rand carefully placed the kennels in the backseat, then turned and looked at Sheltie, who was tethered to the black wrought-iron lamppost by the driveway.

"Are we ready to load your pony?"

"In just a minute." Celeste hurried to the side of the house and picked up a large reflective metal sheet she'd propped against the brick.

Rand raised an eyebrow. "Planning on catching some rays?"

Celeste grinned. "This isn't a tanning bed. It's a funhouse mirror."

Rand's mouth curved up in amusement. "Most women just carry a compact, you know."

Celeste laughed. "It's not for me. It's for Sheltie. He's claustrophobic. If I tape it in front of the trailer, he thinks he's seeing a beautiful horse and he walks right in."

"You're kidding."

"Mr. Jones told me about it, and he was right. Sheltie refused to get into the cattle truck for the move here until I put the mirror in it."

Rand shook his head. "You sure have some weird animals."

She lifted her shoulders. "They all have their little eccentricities, just like people."

"Yours seem to have more than most."

"Well, that's only fair. So do I." She held up her arm, which was sporting a role of masking tape like a bracelet. "Do you mind if I tape the mirror to the front of the stall?"

He waved his hand at the trailer. "Be my guest. Need some help?"

She nodded. "It would help if you'd hold it while I tape it into place."

Rand stretched his arms on either side of Celeste, holding the metal mirror against the wall as she taped the top corners in place.

"There," she murmured. "I think I've got it."

Oh, you've got it, all right. You've definitely got it. He stepped back, giving her room to bend down and tape the bottom. At length she straightened, and they viewed their reflections in the wavy metal mirror.

"This makes us look like a pair of roly-poly midgets," Rand said.

Celeste's smile flashed in the reflective metal. "Maybe that's why Sheltie likes it. He's usually the shortest, fattest horse around—so maybe it makes him feel good to see a horse that's even smaller and rounder."

Rand laughed. "You think he has an inferiority complex?"

"Probably. Everyone feels inferior about something."

What did Celeste feel inferior about? Rand wondered. He wanted to ask, but she was already heading down the ramp and out of the trailer.

"There's one more thing I need to get before we load Sheltie." She hurried back to the side of the house, and returned in a moment with a bamboo fishing pole.

Rand lifted his eyebrows quizzically.

"Sheltie can be a little balky," she explained. "But if I put root-beer candy on the fishing line and dangle it in front of his face, he'll follow it anywhere. It works like a charm."

"The proverbial carrot on a stick?"

She nodded. "Except Sheltie hates vegetables and has a thing for root beer."

Rand watched her walk the pony to the trailer, the candy dangling in front of him. Poor sucker—he thought he was about to get a treat, but instead he was walking right into a trap. It occurred to Rand that there were some unpleasant parallels to his own relationship with Celeste.

Once the pony caught sight of his reflection, he eagerly walked into the stall. Celeste stood behind him, stretching the pole over his back, and let him reach the candy. He bit it off and crunched contentedly, eyeing himself in the mirror. As Celeste eased her way out, Sheltie rubbed his muzzle against the mirror, nuzzling his reflection.

Shaking his head, Rand closed and locked the trailer gate. "Ready to go?"

"As soon as I grab my bag from the house."

She reappeared a moment later with a large open duffel. Rand took it from her and loaded it in the backseat.

"What's in this thing? It weighs a ton," he said.

"Props for Killer and Bruiser's tricks, treats for Sheltie, rabbit food, a few books and flash cards."

"Books? Flash cards?"

She nodded as she climbed into the passenger seat and fastened her seat belt. "I like to sneak a little education into the fun."

"So what's going to happen at this party?"

"Well, I'll take the kids on pony rides and the dogs will do their tricks, then I'll give them a little lesson about the other animals while they pet them."

"Then what?" Rand shifted the pickup into gear and steered it out of the drive.

"That part's up to the boy's parents. I'm sure they'll have cake and ice cream, and the birthday boy will open his presents." Celeste gazed out the window. "I bet he's so excited. I just loved birthdays when I was a kid. I can still remember my favorite party."

"Yeah?" Rand found himself asking. "When was it?"

"The year I turned six. All my friends and I dressed up like princesses." He could feel her gaze on him. "What about you? Do you remember a favorite birthday party?"

"Never had one."

Celeste gazed at him in surprise. "Never?"

"No."

"Why not?"

Because my being born wasn't a cause for celebration. "I just didn't." Damn it, he didn't want to talk about this. He shifted on the seat, uncomfortably aware that she was looking at him with something in her eyes that looked suspiciously like pity. "So, how long did you work at the shelter?" he asked.

To his relief, she went along with his abrupt change of topic. "Seemed like forever. I started volunteering there when I was a fifteen." She looked out the window. "I always loved animals, and it was the one place I felt like I really fit in."

Rand looked at her, his eyebrows raised, but she continued before he had a chance to ask what she meant.

"The volunteer job turned into a paying one after high school, and I worked there while I went to college. I worked my way up from dog washer to shelter manager—which basically meant I got to wash the dogs *and* pay the light bill."

Rand laughed. She pulled one leg under her body and angled toward him, stretching her left arm across the back of the seat. "What about you? Did you grow up with horses?"

He shook his head. "I'd never even ridden one until I took a summer job on a cattle ranch outside of Shreveport." He steered the truck onto the highway. "One of the ranch hands was into rodeoing. I went with him, and . . . well, I got hooked."

"You rode in the rodeo?"

Rand nodded.

"What did you do?"

"I rode bulls."

"Bulls?" She stared at him, her eyebrows arched high.

Rand smiled. "And the occasional bronco. When I was sixteen, I'd have ridden the devil himself if the cash prize was big enough."

Her eyes were round and incredulous. "Your parents let you do that?"

"My parents weren't in the picture."

"Why not?"

Rand kept his eyes on the road. He hated to talk about his parents, but if he refused to answer, it would only pique her curiosity. Better to give brief answers, then change the subject. "My mom died when I was thirteen, and my dad . . . well, he wasn't really around."

He could feel her studying him. "So who raised you?"

He lifted his shoulders. "I mostly raised myself, I guess. After Mom died, I was in and out of foster homes and state institutions."

"Wow." He could practically see the wheels turning in her head. "Wasn't bull riding awfully dangerous?"

"Oh, yeah. But at that age, you think you're invincible." Especially when you have nothing to lose, and Rand had had less than nothing.

"Were you ever hurt?"

His lip twitched in a humorless smile. "Just about every time I rode."

"But you kept on riding?"

"Yeah. Until I lost a kidney."

She drew in a sharp breath. "What happened?"

"The bull went left. I went right. Then the clowns didn't get there fast enough."

Her hand flew over her mouth. "How horrible!"

That was the word for it, all right. And he had the scar to prove it.

"It put me out of commission for a good long while. But it gave me a lot of time to think."

He could still remember laying in the intensive care unit of Charity Hospital, in more pain than he'd known was possible, hooked up to all kinds of machines and tubes, floating in and out of consciousness.

"Have we located the father?" a nurse asked.

"In Baton Rouge. He's not coming."

"Does he know how serious it is?"

"The social worker said she told him." The nurse's voice had held a note of disgust. "He said the kid's not his responsibility. But he asked what happens to the boy's belongings if he dies. He wanted to know if the kid had any money or jewelry on him."

"Man—just when you think you've heard everything, huh?"

"Yeah. Poor kid. And the sad thing is, if he pulls through, he'll probably grow up to be just like his old man."

In his medicated, pain-fogged mind, something had kicked in—something dark and powerful. He was going to live just to spite the bastard, and he was going to prove those nurses wrong. He wouldn't be anything like his father. He wouldn't waste his life on booze and wishful thinking and get-rich-quick schemes. He would be a success. He would be respected.

"What did you think about while you were recovering?"

Rand lifted one shoulder. "What I wanted out of life, and how I was going to get it."

"And what did you come up with?"

"I knew I wanted to work with horses, and I'd always been impressed with reining competitions. It's a sport that takes a lot of skill, where the outcome is actually within your control. So I decided that when I got out of the hospital, I'd get serious about it. I'd learn all about reining and horse breeding and running a business. And that's what I did."

"Wow. How'd you go about it?"

"Well, I worked my way through college and earned a degree in business." It hadn't been easy, either; he'd held down two jobs to support himself. "I worked summers at a horse farm that specialized in reining horses, and I learned all I could about them. I scraped together a few dimes, bought a colt that had some potential and started winning some competitions. Then I used the prize money to buy some more horses and a little bit of land around Shreveport."

"How'd you end up in Cypress Grove?"

"I'd met George at the national show in Oklahoma City, and he knew I was looking for a bigger place in south

Louisiana. He called me when he was ready to sell his ranch. I fell in love with the ranch, so I bought it."

"George used to own your place?" she asked, surprised.

"Yeah. He sold it right before he took his wife to Brazil for some kind of experimental cancer treatment."

"Wow. And now he works for you."

Rand nodded. "I offered to sell the place back to him after his wife died, but he didn't want it. He said he didn't want the hassle of owning a ranch; he just wanted to focus on horse training and let someone else deal with all the headaches. So it's worked out fine for both of us."

"Fascinating how providence works things out, isn't it?"

"It wasn't providence that did all the work," Rand told her dryly.

"Oh, I'm not saying you didn't earn your success." Her green eyes were earnest and sincere. "I'm sure it was harder than I can ever imagine. But for you to have met George, and for you to buy his ranch, and then for him to come back and work for you . . . Well, it's all too much of a co-incidence to just be chance."

Rand had lost all belief in God a long time ago. If the world was under the direction of a kindly creator, why did He allow so many awful things to happen? But there was no point in arguing theology with Celeste.

"Tell me about reining horses," she prompted.

He was glad to latch onto a neutral topic. "Reiners are trained to compete in a series of maneuvers—sharp turns, circles, backing up and sudden stops."

He felt a soft touch at the back of his shirt collar. He glanced at Celeste, but she was listening intently, her arm stretched across the back of the seat. Apparently she was unaware she'd touched him.

"Are all reining horses quarter horses?" she asked.

"No. Any breed can be a reining horse, but I happen to think quarter horses make the best ones. They have the right mix of agility and responsiveness." He felt another brush along his collar—slower, with more pressure. A finger slid from the shirt onto the nape of his neck.

That was no accidental touch; that was a deliberate caress. A rush of arousal flashed through him. Startled, he looked over at Celeste. She was angled toward him, her arm stretched out, gazing at him with a thoughtful expression. "Agility and responsiveness," she repeated softly.

The words suddenly struck him as intensely sexual.

"So—are males or females usually more responsive?" she asked.

A fingertip moved down his neck, under his shirt. His nerve endings tingled. What was the deal? She was coming on to him but acting as if she wasn't.

"The . . . um . . . the females," he choked out.

"So how do you get a female to be responsive?" she asked.

"Well, you . . . you show her what you want her to do." Holy smokes—now she was playing with his hair. He glanced over to find her looking at him with a guileless expression, as if she were doing nothing more than having an innocent conversation. What kind of game was she playing? "You, um, try to get attuned to the horse, and get the horse attuned to you, so that the two of you move together."

"It sounds a lot like dancing." Her expression was placid, her eyes innocent, even as he felt a finger twirl the hair at the nape of his neck. His mouth went dry. The conversation was drifting into dangerously sensual territory, just like her fingers, but she continued to act like nothing was happening.

Well, if she wanted to pretend they were innocently talking about horses, he could beat her at her own game. In fact, he could play it hard enough to smoke her out and make her cry uncle.

But first he had to remember what they were talking about. He was more than a little distracted. "Yeah, reining's a lot like dancing," he said, cutting a sidelong glance at her. "Just like I danced with you the other evening. The only difference is, I have my partner between my legs and I'm directing her with my thighs."

Celeste's eyes widened, but the stroking on the back of his neck intensified. Fingers now swirled up his scalp, caressing the edge of his ear.

This Little-Miss-Innocent, I'm-not-doing-anything act was starting to get on his nerves. "While I'm riding her, I'm whispering to her and urging her on with my hands." He felt a gentle tug on his ear. "We get into a rhythm, and then we go faster and faster—in and out, in and out, in and out, in and out—"

Celeste's lips parted, and her eyes grew large and alarmed. She drew back against the door.

"—in and out of all the barrels."

Rand felt an abrupt tug on both ears simultaneously. He shot her a sharp look. "How the hell did you do that?"

She shrank against the door, regarding him as if he were a madman. "D-do what?"

He felt another yank on his ear, this time harder. "Come on—you're going to make me have a wreck."

The look in her eyes bordered on panic. "I don't know what you're talking about."

"Oh, right." He cast her a scowl, only to realize her arm was no longer draped behind him; it was folded protectively across her chest.

It wasn't her. Someone else was behind him, pulling on his ears.

Rand's foot jammed on the brake—hard. Tires squealed as he pulled the truck onto the shoulder of the highway, causing the trailer to fishtail behind him. Celeste let out a scream as he screeched to a halt.

"Why did you do that?" Celeste gasped. "What's going on? What's the matter with you?"

Rand reached up and grabbed at the thing tugging on his ears. His hands latched on to something tiny and furry. He was so startled that he loosened his grip. "What the . . ."

He heard a high-pitched shriek, felt a wet blob on the side of his face and saw a flash of brown dart across the front seat. He blinked hard. When he regained his focus, he saw a quivering brown monkey clinging to Celeste's western vest.

"Mr. Peepers?" Celeste stared from the monkey to Rand, then back at the monkey again. "What are *you* doing here?"

"Good question," Rand said. Spiked with adrenaline, his blood pounded hard and fast through his veins. He reached up and felt his neck. "The little bastard spit on me again!"

"Oh, no! Oh, I'm so sorry!" Celeste reached into the backseat and pulled a package of wet wipes out of her bag. She handed it to Rand. "H-he must have stowed away in my bag. I changed the latch on his cage after he figured out the last one, but he must have found a new escape route."

Rand ripped open the package and pulled one out. "That little monster could have gotten us killed!"

"You're scaring him," Celeste said, cradling the animal protectively.

"*I'm* scaring *him?*" Rand glared at her. "One minute I think you're playing with my neck, the next your ape is trying to pull bananas out of my ears."

Her eyes grew large as eggs. "You thought I was playing with your neck?"

"What was I supposed to think?" He cleaned his cheek, then wadded up the wipe and threw it in the backseat. "As far as I knew, we were the only primates in the car."

Celeste started to giggle. Rand stared at her, and the next thing he knew, he was laughing, too—laughing so deep and hard his belly ached, laughing in a way that was impossible to stop. Just as he thought he'd regained control, Mr. Peepers turned loose of Celeste's neck, bounced on her lap and let out a series of loud squawks, which set them both off again.

At long last Celeste drew a deep breath and wiped her eyes with the back of her hands. "I haven't laughed that hard in months."

Rand hadn't laughed that hard in years. Maybe ever. "Me, neither."

She placed her hand on his, her eyes filled with mirth. "I promise you I wasn't coming on to you."

"Too bad."

They sat there, grinning at each other. Rand impulsively reached out and put his hand on the nape of her neck. "What was I supposed to think when I felt *this*?" His finger snaked up the back of her neck. Her skin was soft—soft as the belly of a bunny—warm and smooth.

"And *this*." His finger wrapped around a silky strand of hair, then slid to her ear. "And this." He caressed the top of her ear, his finger tracing the outer rim.

"But I was entirely baffled when I felt this." Reaching out his other hand, he tugged on the top of both ears simultaneously.

She let out a fresh shriek of laughter. "I can see why you slammed on the brakes."

He ought to slam them on now. He ought to pull back his hands, turn away and put the pickup in gear. But the feel of her skin, so warm and downy and pulsing with life, made it impossible.

The laughter in her eyes deepened into something else— something aware, something sensual, something that sent a hot rush of desire coursing through him. She was close,

close enough that he could feel the heat of her breath on his face, see the gold facets around the pupils of her green eyes, inhale the mingled scent of soft perfume and herbal shampoo and the incredibly sexy undernote that was hers alone.

His heart thrummed against his ribs as his thumbs slipped over the smooth, warm skin between her ears and her hairline. Her pupils dilated and her lips parted. The memory of how those lips had tasted hurled a fastball of arousal, hard and rocket-rapid, straight through him.

His hands slid into her hair, cradled her head. Her eyes half closed. She leaned toward him, and his mouth covered hers.

Sweet. She had the sweetest, softest mouth—succulent as ripe peaches, delicious and tempting. With a little moan, her lips flowered under his: soft, full petals unfolding to offer up nectar. His tongue slipped between them. She wrapped her arms around him, straining to get closer, and made a throaty murmur.

That sound—low and hungry and untamed—set his blood ablaze. He hauled her toward him. She scrambled over the console and onto his lap, kissing him with a wild, frenzied passion, her breath coming in hot, erotic pants.

His hand moved under her shirt. She shifted to help him, pulling it up. His palm filled with a satin-covered breast, heavy and warm and sharply pointed. She groaned, then reached down to his fly. The feel of her hand on the zipper made his erection jerk.

Good Lord, but he wanted her. He craved her. He had to have her—right here, right now. His half-opened eyes saw everything through a red blaze of passion—a red, whirling strobe light of desire.

"Rand," she murmured.

He opened his eyes a tiny bit, still seeing a haze of red. "Yeah, baby."

ROBIN WELLS

"We've got to stop."

He opened his eyes further. The red light took on a more distinct shape.

"Rand . . . the police."

He opened his eyes more fully, and vaguely registered that the red light was twirling atop a state trooper's patrol car parked ahead of them on the shoulder of the road.

A rap sounded on the window. Rand jumped at the noise, then started again at the sight of a blue-uniformed officer in dark glasses standing beside the truck. Celeste rapidly slid off Rand's lap.

Rand lowered the window. The dogs in the backseat yapped inside their kennels.

"G-good morning," Rand said.

"Morning." The officer peered in the truck, ticket pad in hand. "Everything okay in here?"

"Yes. Just fine."

The officer looked from Rand to Celeste, then back again. "It's illegal to park on the shoulder unless it's an emergency."

"Oh, but it *was* an emergency," Celeste piped up. "He had to grab my monkey."

The tips of the officer's ears turned bright red. He pulled a pen out of his pocket. "That's not the kind of emergency I meant."

"Oh, please—don't write him a ticket," Celeste begged. "He couldn't help it. It was my monkey's fault."

Red spread from the officer's ears to his neck. He cleared his throat. "Yeah, well, maybe a ticket will help him show some restraint next time."

"You don't understand, Officer. She really does have a monkey," Rand said. He turned to Celeste. "Show him Mr. Peepers."

"No!" The officer held up both hands, his entire face the shade of a baked apple. "Please. I'm a married man."

184

Oh, sheeze. He thought "Mr. Peepers" was an anatomical part! "It's not what you think," Rand rapidly explained.

"Mr. Peepers gets shy around strange men," Celeste contributed. "He's hiding under my seat."

"L-let's just leave him there." The officer's Adam's apple bobbed as he swallowed. "Look—I'm going to let you two off with a warning this time. But if it happens again, you're either going to get a ticket or get hauled in. Understand?"

Rand nodded.

The officer leaned toward him. "There's a motel off the next exit," he said in a low voice. "If you want to monkey around, I suggest you get a room."

Rand bobbed his head in a curt nod. The officer stalked back to his patrol car.

"What was his problem?" Celeste asked indignantly. "Why did he think Mr. Peepers would care whether or not he was married?"

Rand wasn't about to attempt an explanation. He started the engine and was about to pull out onto the highway when his cell phone rang.

He pulled it off his belt and flipped it open. "Hello?"

"Hey, Rand—Peter Marston here," said a voice through the receiver. "The vet's coming by to check over my mare, but he can't make it until this afternoon, so I'm afraid she won't be ready to go until after four. Hope that's not a problem."

"No—no problem."

But it was. He'd planned to pick up the mare while Celeste was at the party. Her party would be over long before four.

Great, just great. Showing up with a pair of trick poodles, a bunch of bunnies, a pot-bellied pig, a sway-backed old nag and a monkey was not the best way to impress a new client.

He blew out a hard sigh and gazed at Celeste, who was

fooling with the damned monkey again. As soon as the cop had left, the little beast had crawled back into her lap.

The woman and her animals were an absolute menace. It was bad enough that they made him look like a fool at his own ranch, but now she had him taking her dog-and-pony show on the road.

Literally.

Why had he agreed to this? He knew she was a one-woman wrecking crew. Every encounter with her resulted in some sort of chaos.

And yet he kept coming back for more. Looking at her kiss-swollen lips, he'd be damned if he didn't want to kiss her again right now.

This was insane. It went against everything he wanted in life—peace and quiet and order and predictability. Every time he came within twenty yards of this woman, he seemed to abandon all rational thought.

He had to get a grip on himself. He blew out a hard breath and reclipped the phone to his belt. "We'd better get going. Hold on to your monkey."

Celeste grinned. "I think the normal phrase is 'Hold on to your hat.' "

"There's nothing normal about this situation."

Or any situation involving Celeste. And there was nothing normal about his response to her, either.

Chapter Thirteen

"Can I hold the bunny again?" The tow-headed boy turned big brown eyes to Celeste as she picked up the rabbit cage. "Pleeeease?"

Sheltie was already loaded in the trailer and Celeste was ready to go, but those five-year-old eyes were impossible to resist. She shot a questioning look at the boy's mother, a visibly pregnant brunette seated with a group of parents in lawn chairs. The woman nodded.

"Of course, Timmy," Celeste said with a smile. "Come sit on the grass and I'll put him in your lap."

"Me, too! Me, too!" cried several other children.

They jumped off the deck attached to the old Garden District home, their faces smudged with vanilla cake icing, and plopped onto the thick St. Augustine grass that covered the manicured back lawn. Celeste opened the kennel, lifted out a bunny and gently placed the animal in the nest of Timmy's arms.

The boy's parents smiled at each other. Timmy's father,

a lanky man in designer khakis, stepped forward with a camera. "Get in the photo, honey," he urged his wife.

It was a Kodak moment—a happy couple, their child's fifth birthday party, their friends and family gathered around to celebrate. Celeste's heart filled with an aching wistfulness. A husband, a child, a family. She wondered if the woman knew how lucky she was.

Celeste wondered if she'd ever have a family of her own. Not any time soon, she thought ruefully. The only man in the picture was Rand, and he'd clearly stated that he wasn't in the market for a relationship.

Although you wouldn't know it from his actions. The kiss that morning had been as hot as it was unexpected. It had left her aroused and shaken and confused, and Rand's attempt to apologize once they'd gotten back on the highway hadn't helped clarify anything.

"Look—I don't think it's wise for us to get involved," he'd said. "Cypress Grove is a small town, and we're next-door neighbors, and these things tend to get awkward when they end. I think it's best not to get anything started."

"I'm not the one starting things," Celeste had informed him.

"Yeah, well, you're sure not saying no."

"Like it's my job to keep you in line?"

"No, damn it." He'd blown out a sigh of resignation. "But I wish it was."

The remark had made her smile. Rand wasn't nearly as emotionally distant as he professed. The tough rancher had a kind, caring, almost tender side that attracted her even more than the physical pull she felt toward him. And boy, did she feel a physical pull.

A shriek on the lawn jerked Celeste out of her thoughts.

"He bit me! He bit me!" cried Timmy.

Celeste swooped down on the scampering bunny as the

boy's mother dashed forward, her dark hair bobbing against the shoulder of her sunflower-print dress.

The woman bent down as far as her belly would allow and looked at the boy's finger. "You're fine, honey. He didn't break the skin."

"But he bit me!" the boy whined.

"He probably thought your finger was a carrot," Celeste said. The other children giggled. "I'm sure Bugs startled you, but he couldn't really hurt you." Celeste looked at the children. "Does anyone know why?"

A little girl in a pink seersucker dress with an enormous pink bow in her dark hair held up her hand. " 'Cause they're gentle?"

"Yes, they are." Celeste nodded at the girl. "But what about them makes them gentle?"

A little boy held up his hand. "Their pers'nal'ties?"

The adults all laughed. "What a good vocabulary you have!" Celeste said. "Yes, they have shy, gentle personalities. But there's another reason. I'll give you a hint: What do bunnies like to eat?"

"Carrots!" said one little girl.

"Lettuce!"

"Fingers!" the birthday boy said.

Everyone laughed.

"They don't eat fingers," Celeste explained. "They only taste them to see if they're carrots, because rabbits are herbivores. That means they're plant-eaters. Is a finger a plant?"

A chorus of "No's" mingled with giggles.

"Because rabbits only eat plants, they have flat teeth. They don't need to tear into their food, so they don't have any sharp ones."

Celeste looked around the group. "Can anyone name some animals that *do* have sharp teeth?"

"Tigers!" called one child.

189

"Lions!" yelled another.

"Sharks!" contributed a brown-headed little boy in a blue-and-red-striped shirt.

Celeste nodded. "Those are great examples. And what do those animals eat?"

"Meat!"

"Fish!"

"People!"

The adults all laughed.

"Those animals are meat-eaters, so they need sharp teeth. Does anyone know what meat-eaters are called?"

"Carnivores!" called one father.

His wife gave him a sharp poke with her elbow. "The children are supposed to answer," she said in a loud whisper.

He grinned sheepishly. "Sorry. I got carried away."

Celeste smiled as everyone laughed. "He's right. Meat-eaters are known as carnivores." She looked around at the children. "Does anyone know what we are? Are people herbivores or carnivores?"

"We're both!" called a little girl.

"Excellent answer." Celeste beamed at the girl. "Yes, we're both. And creatures that eat both are called what?" She looked expectantly at the man who had answered earlier.

He cast a sidelong glance at his wife. "I'm afraid to answer."

"Go ahead, Joe. We'll protect you!" called another man.

The adults all laughed again.

"Omnivores," the man said.

Celeste nodded. "Exactly." She looked back at the children. "Now that you know about herbivores, carnivores and omnivores, let's play a quick game. I'll hold up a picture of an animal, and you say which you think they are."

Five minutes later, Celeste said her good-byes.

"You were wonderful," Timmy's mother said, handing Celeste a check. "The children not only had a fabulous time but learned so much! I'm going to tell all my friends about you."

"Thanks," Celeste said. "I can use all the referrals I can get. And I'm trying to get bookings for schools to come visit my petting zoo for field trips."

"What a great idea! I'll mention it at Andy's school. Thanks again."

"You were really something back there," Rand said as he pulled the pickup away from the curb.

"Thanks."

He glanced over at Celeste. He hadn't really known what to expect, but he'd been impressed at the smooth, professional way she'd handled the entire event.

"You're great with kids. Have you ever thought about being a teacher?"

"I like to think that in a way, I am."

"I meant in an elementary school."

She shook her head. "I'm good with animals and people, but I'm horrible with paperwork."

"Really?"

Celeste nodded. "I don't make a big deal out of it, but I'm dyslexic."

His eyebrows rose in surprise. "You have trouble reading?"

She gave a slight shrug. "It was more of a problem when I was a kid. I can read just fine now, but I'm slower than most people. My real weakness is writing. I'm a terrible speller."

Rand searched his mind, trying to recall what he knew about the disorder. "Dyslexics see letters differently, right?"

Celeste nodded. "Basically, my mind doesn't process the

written word the way other people do. School was something of a struggle."

"They have ways of helping kids with dyslexia, don't they?"

"Yes, thank heavens. But first you have to be diagnosed." She stroked Mr. Peepers's back. "Unfortunately, I'd made it to the beginning of third grade before anyone realized I really didn't know how to read."

"Wow." He looked at her curiously. "How come no one caught it until then?"

"I did a good job hiding it."

"How?"

"I'd memorize things."

"That sounds a lot harder than reading."

"It was. But I was ashamed. I thought I was dumb, and I didn't want anyone to know it."

The information took him by surprise. So did the matter-of-fact way she said it. Most people weren't so open about their feelings, so up front about their inadequacies. There was something brave and admirable about her blunt honesty. "So how did you get diagnosed?"

Celeste leaned back against the headrest. "My third-grade teacher discovered it the second day of school. She was having all the kids take turns reading a page of *Charlotte's Web* aloud. Just before it was my turn, I asked to go to the rest room." Celeste's mouth curved in wry smile. "That's how I always got out of reading aloud. It had always worked before, but this time I didn't stay long enough. The teacher called on me to read—and I couldn't."

Rand cut a glance at her. She was staring out the windshield, her mouth pressed in a tight, pained line.

"It was awful," she said. "I made a few false starts, then the kids started snickering, and I—well, I burst into tears. The teacher tried to smooth things over, but I wouldn't lift my head from my desk."

A pang of warmth shot through his chest like a flaming arrow. "Oh, man."

"It turned out to be a blessing in disguise. I was tested, and I finally got the help I needed."

"Didn't your parents suspect something was wrong?"

Celeste's mouth curved in a sad smile. "My mother was dyslexic herself, but she didn't know it. She'd just thought she was stupid." Celeste looked down at Mr. Peepers. "And she just thought I took after her."

"Oh, wow." Rand stared through the windshield, his mind sifting through the ramifications. The warmth around his heart intensified. "What about your father?"

"I hid it from him, just like I did from my teachers. I'd get him to read me picture books, and I'd memorize the words under each picture well enough to convince him I was reading it back to him." She gazed out the window. "I was ashamed. I thought it was somehow my fault."

"It must have been a big relief to find out other kids had the same problem."

"Oh, yeah. But it was even more of a relief to discover that dyslexia wasn't related to intelligence. Believe it or not, I scored pretty high on IQ tests."

"I have no trouble believing it."

Surprise flashed in her eyes; then she looked away, as if embarrassed. "Well, the normal kids never accepted me. I was in a class for kids with learning disabilities. They called it 'the retard class,' so I was always a 'retard.' "

"That had to be rough."

"It didn't help any that I'd try so hard not to come across as an airhead that I'd end up babbling on and on and couldn't seem to stop." Her lips curled in a sheepish grin. "Kind of like now."

"I don't think you're babbling."

She tossed him a grateful smile. "The truth is, the whole dyslexia thing left me with an inferiority complex. I hate for people to think I'm a dumb blonde. I even went through a period of time when I dyed my hair brown—but then I realized how ridiculous that was. I mean, there I was, pretending to be something I wasn't, so that people wouldn't think I'm something I'm not. It was all so convoluted that I couldn't stand it."

The warmth in Rand's chest grew and expanded. "For the record, I never thought you were dumb. Crazy, maybe, but not dumb."

"Crazy I can handle."

"Also for the record—I like your hair."

"Thanks." A charge of electricity crackled between them. She gave a shy smile, then looked away, tucking a strand of hair behind her ear. "Anyway, there was a bright side to this whole dyslexia thing. After I was diagnosed, my mother realized that she probably had the same problem, too, and she got some help. It was amazing, the difference it made in her. Dad and I were so proud."

An odd wistfulness joined the tender warmth spreading through him. "You and your folks were close, huh?"

"Real close."

He wondered if she knew how lucky she'd been. Her family intrigued him. "What were they like?"

"Upbeat. Fun. Always teasing and joking around—there was a lot of laughter in our house. A lot of laughter, and a lot of love."

It was like hearing about a foreign country he'd never visited. "Your folks got along with each other, too, huh?"

"Oh, yeah. They were crazy about each other. They had a really close relationship—the soul-mate kind I told you about."

The kind Celeste had said she was looking for herself.

"Did you have any other family?"

"My grandparents lived in a little town about twenty miles away. Granddad passed away when I was little, but

Gran was a big part of my life up until she died six years ago." Celeste's eyes took on a fond, faraway look. "She was originally from Scotland, and she was a real character—funny and spunky and a wonderful storyteller."

"What kind of stories did she tell?"

"True ones. Mainly about people finding love and happiness when they least expected it. Gran was a big believer in divine providence. She used to say that we're all threads in a big, beautiful tapestry. The problem is, we can't see the big pattern." Celeste adopted a falsetto Scottish brogue. " 'Follow your heart,' she used to say. 'Your heart knows where you're supposed to go. Your head only thinks it knows.' "

Rand couldn't help but laugh. So *that* was where Celeste got her skewed view of the world.

"Gran always insisted that there's no such thing as coincidences, so when I heard her words coming out of Mr. Jones's mouth, my ears perked up," Celeste continued. "Especially when I learned he'd promised his wife practically the same thing I'd promised Gran."

"What was that?"

"Well, Gran wanted to go back to Scotland for one last visit, and I'd planned to take her. But I kept postponing the trip because of things at work—things that seemed really urgent, that I thought I had to handle personally. And then Gran had a heart attack and died." Celeste sighed. "And now I can't even remember any of the things that seemed so all-important."

The regret in her voice moved him. "Don't be so hard on yourself," he told her. "You couldn't have known what would happen."

"No, but I felt like I'd let her down. And Mr. Jones felt like he'd let down his wife, too, since she died before they could move back home. I know it sounds funny, but when he asked me to help him fulfill his wife's last wishes about the animals—well, I kind of felt like I was getting a second chance with Gran."

Rand glanced over at Celeste, seeing her with fresh eyes. For the first time, her whole petting zoo plan made a weird kind of sense. Not the logical, measurable kind of sense he was accustomed to, but sense all the same.

She wasn't motivated by money or status; she was motivated by love and a sense of honor. The prospect of financial failure didn't faze her, because that wasn't her yardstick of success. She felt like she'd been entrusted with a sacred duty, and she was determined to carry it out.

Rand's heart suddenly felt soft and mushy, like the inside of a roasted marshmallow. Celeste was sentimental and sappy and undoubtedly misguided, but she was also genuine and kind and true—true to her beliefs, to herself, to her word. Against his will, she was digging up things he hadn't felt in a long time—tender, green, hopeful things. At the same time, though, she was unearthing feelings he'd thought were long buried—dark, painful feelings, like that hole-in-his-soul emptiness.

"You need to fill up," she said softly.

"What?" He jerked his head toward her, wondering for one surreal second if she were reading his mind.

"You're nearly out of gas."

"Oh." He glanced at his gas gauge and frowned. It was completely unlike him to overlook a detail like that.

"Pull over at the next gas station and I'll fill your tank," she said. "It's the least I can do to thank you for the ride."

He didn't want Celeste filling any part of his life—not his thoughts, not his heart, not even his gas tank.

"Nah," he said, slowing to turn in at a Shell station. "I had to make the trip anyway."

A few minutes later he was screwing the gas cap back on his tank. He turned to Celeste, who was holding two Cokes she'd bought inside. "Ready?" he asked.

She handed a can to him. "Maybe I should just wait here with the smaller animals."

Rand's eyebrows rose. "What?"

"Well, I know this is a new client, and you're anxious to make a good impression. And you hadn't planned to have me and all my critters along. So, why don't I just wait here with my animals, and you can come back and get us when you're done."

"No."

"Look, I don't want to be a burden to you. I really appreciate your helping me out today, and—"

"No. No way. Forget it. I'm not going to just leave you here like a bunch of refugees from Noah's Ark. That's crazy. And it's not even safe."

"We'll be fine." She shot him a confident smile. "Who's going to mess with two vicious poodles and an attack bunny?"

"No." He yanked open the passenger door. "Now get in the truck so we can go."

Celeste climbed into her seat. Rand slammed the door, circled the vehicle and climbed behind the wheel.

"If you don't want to leave us here, maybe you could leave us in the parking lot of a mall," she suggested.

"No."

"Why not?"

Because I know all too well what it feels like. A memory, as unwelcome and intrusive as a midnight burglar, stole into his mind, taking him back to the summer he was seven years old.

He could practically smell the crop-duster spray that had hung in the air that hot August morning as his father had braked his beat-up old Chevy Fairlane on the side of a two-lane highway. They'd been somewhere in Alabama, about an hour out of Mobile. The sun had been a fiery chariot riding high in the sky.

"Why're you stopping?" Rand had asked.

"I've got a little business meeting to go to. You stay here with your mother, and I'll be back in a little while."

Rand's seven-year-old heart had sunk. "Take us with you, Dad. I'll be good. I promise."

"No can do. Now get on out. I'll be back in an hour or two."

"But . . . it's awful hot, and I'm hungry."

"When I get back, I'll buy you a steak. The biggest steak you've ever seen. Now get out. Go on."

Rand's mother had hesitated. She looked at her husband, her brown eyes worried and ringed with deep purple shadows. "Pete, I don't think this is a good idea. That's the last of our money, and . . ."

"You trust me, don't you, sugar pie?"

Rand had felt his mother's hesitation. "Of course, Pete, but . . ."

"Takes money to make money," he'd said in a firm voice. "This is our big chance. You'll see." He'd nodded toward an orchard. "You can sit in the shade over there—maybe even find some ripe peaches while you're at it. I won't be long. And when I get back, we'll be all set."

"Can we sleep in a bed tonight?" Rand had asked. The family had slept in the car for the past three nights.

Rand's father had flashed a big smile. "You bet. We'll get us a big motel room with air conditioning and two big beds. Better yet, we'll get two rooms." He'd given a wink to Rand's mother.

"And a pool?" Rand had asked. "Can we go to a motel with a pool?"

"Sure. Anything you want." He'd reached over and ruffled Rand's hair. "Your daddy's about to hit the jackpot. This is my lucky day. I feel it in my bones."

"Petey, if we go back to Mobile, I'm sure I can get my job back," Rand's mother had said. "And you could probably get on with a construction crew, and we could rent a little place. . . ."

Rand's father's face had hardened. "Can't get anywhere workin' construction. We need a couple of lucky breaks, that's all. Leave it to me."

With a heavy sigh, Rand's mother had climbed out of the car, motioning him to do the same. She'd led him off the road to the orchard. They'd sat under a peach tree, the sweat running down their faces, and that's where they'd stayed. The sun had climbed higher and higher in the sky. An hour went by, and then another. Rand's mouth grew parched and dry. His mother kept looking at her cheap plastic watch, her face pinched and tight.

"What if he never comes back, Mom? What'll we do then?"

"He'll come."

But he hadn't. There was no steak, no air-conditioned motel room, no bed to sleep in. As the sun had set, they'd started walking toward town, and hitched a ride with a couple of men who kept looking at his mother in a way he didn't like. The men had finally dropped them off at the bus station. Bus stations were usually open all night, and it wasn't unusual for people to sleep there, his mother had said.

It wasn't unusual for them, anyway. They'd done it more than once.

Celeste's voice broke into his thoughts. "Maybe you could put us out in the parking lot of a fast-food restaurant, or . . ."

"Forget it," Rand snapped. "I'm not putting you out, and that's the end of it."

He kept his eyes on the road, but he could feel her gaze on him, could sense her bewilderment. The lump in his throat was back. He swallowed hard and turned on the radio, deliberately turning his thoughts to his business.

Chapter Fourteen

Celeste was still pondering Rand's vehement refusal to let her wait for him when he turned the truck through an impressive iron gate beside an elaborate stone sign that read MARSTON FARMS. They'd driven in silence for the last thirty minutes, with only the radio to break the oppressive quiet.

It was apparent that Rand was battling some demons—the big, bad kind, the type with fangs and claws and prickly scales. Equally apparent was the fact that he had no intention of sharing them with her.

She wondered if he'd shared them with anyone. Did the girl on the horse-show circuit know his secrets, know his heart?

The thought stung. *Now stop that*, she ordered herself. She had no claim on him. They'd shared a couple of kisses and some strong chemistry, but he didn't want a relationship with her any more than she wanted one with him.

She *didn't* want one with him, did she? She was no

longer quite sure. Come to think of it, she was no longer sure she was buying his explanation of why he didn't want one, either. If they got involved and things didn't work out, they were mature enough to handle it.

He'd said he didn't do emotions, but he wasn't as unfeeling as he claimed. In fact, she was beginning to think that his whole I-don't-believe-in-love, I-don't-do-emotion speech was just defensive posturing. It was more likely that he'd been badly hurt and wanted to prevent it from happening again.

Maybe he'd been more serious about the horse-show girl than he let on. Maybe she'd broken his heart and he wasn't quite over her.

The thought gave her a stronger stab of distress. Not that it mattered, she reasoned with herself. It was none of her business, and it didn't affect her one way or the other.

Liar, a little voice in her mind mocked. *Liar, liar, pants on fire.*

With deliberate intent, Celeste turned her attention to their surroundings. Rand drove past an imposing two-story home—a mansion, really—that looked like a modern version of Tara. He followed the winding road another quarter mile through tall pine trees and gorgeous landscaping to a clearing where a large, whitewashed brick stable stood beside a lush pasture.

"I'll wait here," Celeste said as Rand braked the truck by the stable doors.

"I won't be long." He lowered the automatic windows and unfastened his seat belt. As he climbed out of the truck, a man who looked like Crocodile Dundee loped out of the stable, his gait so bowlegged it looked as if he spent all his time on horseback. Beside him was a dark-haired boy about seven years of age.

"Hey there, Rand." The man shook Rand's hand, then

peered through the truck window at Celeste. "I see you brought your lovely wife."

"Oh, I'm not his wife," Celeste said quickly. "I'm just his neighbor."

The weathered rancher ambled around toward her and stuck his hand through the window. "I'm John Marston. And this is my grandson, Justin."

"Nice to meet you." Celeste smiled and shook his hand. "I'm Celeste Landry."

The boy tilted up his freckled face and stared at her. "Are you a sheriff?"

Celeste glanced down at her big plastic badge and grinned. "No. This is just a costume. I just finished giving pony rides at a child's birthday party in New Orleans."

"Pony rides, huh?" Marston regarded her with interest. "Is that the business you're in?"

"Actually, I'm opening a children's petting zoo. I do parties as a sideline. Rand was kind enough to give me and my pony a ride to a birthday party today."

"What's a pettin' zoo?" Justin blinked big blue eyes.

"A place where children come to pet and feed animals, and see them do tricks."

"What kind of animals?"

"Well . . . like Mr. Peepers here." Celeste lifted the monkey, who was crouching at her side.

The boy's eyes got huge. "Oh, wow! Can I pet him?"

"Sure."

"Well, would you look at that!" the boy's grandfather exclaimed, reaching out to pet the monkey. Mr. Peepers gave a warning hiss.

"He loves children and women, but he's afraid of men," Celeste explained. "He seems to be warming up to Rand, though."

John grinned at Rand. "Well, that's a pretty special character reference."

"Actually, it is." Celeste smiled. "Mr. Peepers is a good judge of people."

The little boy peered into the backseat. "What other animals do you have in there?"

"A pot-bellied pig, some bunnies and a couple of poodles that do circus tricks."

"Oh, cool! Can I see?"

"Sure—if it's okay with your granddad and Rand."

Marston looked at Rand. "Do you have the time? I'd like to see her critters' tricks myself."

"Mr. Marston was awfully nice," Celeste said as Rand drove away twenty minutes later.

"Yeah." Far nicer than Rand had ever seen him before. Celeste had thoroughly charmed the usually sour-faced man and his grandson.

Damn it all, she was charming him, too. The more he got to know her, the more he grew to like her.

The thought made him frown. He didn't want to like her; he wanted to distance himself from her.

Didn't he?

She tucked a knee underneath her bottom and angled her body toward him. "I told you about my childhood, but I still don't know much about yours. Where are you originally from?"

"Here and there."

She grinned. "Gee, that's specific."

"That's about as specific as it gets."

"Look, if this is something you don't want to talk about, I understand. I don't want to stir up a bunch of painful memories."

Too late.

"Sorry I brought it up," she said softly.

Aw, hell—now she'd think he was some kind of pathetic, poor-me, touchy-feely sad sack. He was over it. "I was born in Shreveport, but my dad moved us around a lot," he said flatly.

"Was he in the military?"

"No."

"So . . . what was your dad's job?"

"He didn't have one."

Celeste's eyes grew warm and concerned. "Was he disabled?"

Rand's mouth twisted in a mirthless smile. "You might say that."

"What was wrong with him?"

You'd be better off asking what was *right* with him, Rand thought. It would take a lot less time to answer. "He was a selfish SOB."

Celeste's voice grew soft and worried. "Was he abusive?"

"Yeah. Not the way you're thinking, though." The old anger filled his chest. It used to be a red-hot rage, but now it was just coals and ashes. It no longer consumed him, but it still smoldered. It probably always would.

"What did he do?"

"He was a con man. But the only people he was any good at conning were my mom and me and himself."

Celeste's eyebrows knit together. "I don't understand."

"He was a compulsive gambler. He conned himself into believing that he was going to strike it rich and life would turn into a bowl of cherries." Rand's fingers fisted around the steering wheel. "We were always on the move, running from bill collectors and gambling debts. After a month or two in a new place, Dad would gamble away the rent money, and in another month or two, we'd get evicted."

"That must have been awful for you." Her eyes were warm and soft, like a blanket on a cold day.

"It was worse on my mother."

"What was she like?"

His mother. Memories gathered over him like a thick gray

cloud. "She was a good woman—a good mother, a good wife. Too good a wife, considering the jerk she was married to." Rand moved his hands up on the steering wheel. "She worked two, sometimes three jobs to support us. She was always exhausted."

That was the thing he remembered most about her: the way she dragged around in a fog of fatigue, with gray circles under her eyes. "No matter how tired she was, she always made sure I did my homework, and she made sure I didn't get behind at school, even though we moved two or three times a year."

He fell silent for a moment. "She was a good woman," he repeated. "Her only flaw was her taste in husbands."

Celeste gazed at the stiff set of Rand's jaw, at the flat line of his mouth. "Did she ever think about leaving your father?"

"She threatened it from time to time, usually when she found out about one of his other women, but she never followed through."

Celeste's heart flooded with sympathy as she studied his rigid face. The information about his father explained a lot about him, such as his dislike of philandering husbands like Larry Birkman.

"I remember one time when I thought Mom was really going to leave. I was young—eight or so—and we'd just gotten evicted from our apartment in Slidell. We'd been there longer than I remember ever being anywhere. It was a furnished apartment, and I had a real bed." He shot her a grin smile. "I usually slept on a sofa or a heap of clothes on the floor."

Celeste's heart turned over. She couldn't imagine a childhood like he was describing.

"My parents had a big argument when Dad told Mom we had to move. Mom said that was it, that she'd had it, that she was leaving him. But then Dad started in on her, reeling off all these big dreams. He had a way with words, a way of painting a picture so pretty and real you felt like you could just step right into it." Rand's voice came out harsh as a Brill-O pad. "So she stayed. She always stayed. Sometimes he'd go off for months at a time and leave us on our own. Those were our good times. Things always went bad when he came back."

"Did you ever ask your mother why she didn't leave him?"

"Yeah. She said she *loved* him." Bitterness dripped from the word like battery acid. "She loved him, all right. Like a prisoner loves a ball-and-chain."

The pieces suddenly clicked into place. Oh, heavens—no wonder Rand had such a negative concept of love. What he'd seen didn't have much to recommend it. Love must look like a weakness—a weakness and a burden.

"Know what I think?" he continued. "I think she'd invested so many years believing in all of Dad's big talk that she couldn't admit to herself that his wild dreams were just that: dreams."

He'd said the word *dreams* as if it were a dirty word. And it probably was to him, Celeste thought. His father must have built up his hopes time and time again, only to let him down.

The thought of Rand as a disappointed little boy brought a lump to her throat. "So what happened to your mother?"

"She died of pneumonia." He stared through the windshield, unblinking. "She thought she had the flu."

Celeste's heart ached with sympathy. "How old were you?"

"I'd just turned thirteen."

"That had to be so hard," she murmured.

She watched Rand guide the truck onto the highway, his eyes stony. "The hardest part was finding out that if she'd just seen a doctor, she could have been treated easily. There was no reason for her to die." Rand's eyes were dark, his mouth a hard slash. "But money was tight and we didn't have insurance, and she probably didn't want to get docked pay for the time off work it would have taken to go to a doctor, and, hell . . . It happened."

Celeste's chest felt tight, as if a fist were clenching around her heart. "Where were you?"

"At school. I got called into the office. They wanted to know how to reach my dad." One corner of his mouth turned up in a sardonic snarl. "Of course, I had no idea. He was away on one of his so-called 'business trips.'"

"Where was he?"

"No one knew for a long time. Turned out he was in jail in Mississippi. He'd been picked up on a bunch of check-kiting charges."

"So what happened to you?"

"I got swooped up by child welfare. Spent my teens in a series of institutions and foster homes." A vein pulsed in his neck.

"Did you ever see your father again?"

Rand shook his head. "He was in prison off and on after that. Turns out he'd been in prison before, but I hadn't known it. He wrote me once. He wanted me to send him money for cigarettes."

"Did you?" Celeste asked softly.

"Yeah." There was a hint of self-disgust in the word.

Celeste's heart shifted like a seismic plate. The thought of Rand as a young boy, deserted and disappointed over and over by his father, still wanting his father's love . . . Tears formed in her eyes. "Where is he now?"

"Dead. They found him stabbed in an alley in New Orleans, less than two months after he got out of prison the last time. Apparently he messed with the wrong bookie."

Celeste sat perfectly still, the weight of his words settling over her. She looked for something reassuring to say and came up empty. "Most people couldn't rise above a past like yours," she finally murmured.

Rand lifted his shoulders. "I didn't want to be like my old man. My goal was to be the exact opposite."

"Is that why you work so hard?"

His lips twisted in a mirthless grin. "Well, it's definitely opposite behavior."

"You would have made your mother proud," she said softly.

He glanced over at her, then shifted uneasily. "How did we get on this topic, anyway?"

"I asked you about it."

"I can't believe I answered. Let's talk about something else."

He was embarrassed at having told her so much. The fact made her heart shift again.

He shot a glance at her. "So how do you like Louisiana?"

"I love it. But it's not what I expected."

"In what way?"

"I was expecting Cajuns and swamps and alligators."

"We've got a 'gator or two and a few transplanted Cajuns, but the area you're thinking of is farther south and more to the west." He looked over at her. "Ever been there?"

Celeste nodded. "My parents took me on an adventure there once."

Rand's eyebrows rose quizzically. "An adventure?"

Celeste smiled. "That's what we called them. Once a month or so, we'd all pile into the car on Saturday morning and head out to a surprise destination."

"How was it a surprise?"

"Because only one person knew where we were headed. Mom or Dad would pick a place and just drive there. I'd always try to guess where we were going. Sometimes, there was no destination at all—we'd just stop and explore whatever interested us."

"And you thought that was *fun?*"

"It was a blast."

"Sounds like the stuff I most hated about being a kid," he said. "Not knowing where we were going, not knowing what would happen when we got there. I don't like to do things that are nonproductive, and I never do anything without a purpose and a plan."

No wonder, Celeste thought. And no wonder he was wound so tight. He was probably afraid that if he let his guard down, everything would fall apart.

"There *was* a purpose to our adventures," she told him. "To spend time together and enjoy each other's company."

"That's still nonproductive."

"It was fun, and fun is productive. It produces happiness and warm memories." But she could tell by the expression on Rand's face that he wasn't buying it. "Even workaholics like you need to recharge your batteries."

"I love what I do, so I don't need to recharge."

"Oh, come on. Everyone's got to have something they enjoy besides work. What do you like to do when you're not working?"

"Well, I enjoy working with the Chamber."

"You're president of the group. That's got to be work, too."

"Maybe, but I enjoy it."

"Yeah?" She looked at him curiously.

"Yeah. I like feeling like I'm doing something good for the town. It makes it seem like I'm a part of the community, like I belong."

"You never had that as a kid, did you?" Celeste asked softly.

"We moved too much. Even if we'd stayed in one place,

though, we were still poor. When you're poor, people treat you like you've got a contagious disease."

So many things about Rand now made sense. He tried to control his life and his emotions so he wouldn't get hurt, but that control was preventing him from getting the very thing he longed for most—love and acceptance. Inside the big, tough, always-in-control man was a little boy who just wanted to belong.

Celeste blinked back tears. Everyone needed love and acceptance, whether they knew it or not. Maybe especially if they didn't know it.

"Well, all work and no play makes Rand a dull boy," she said with a lightness she didn't feel. "I'll have to take you on an adventure and show you what you've been missing."

"No, thanks."

"You can't say no to an adventure. It's a rule."

"Sure I can."

"Well, then, I'll have to figure out a way to make sure you won't." She'd enlist George's help. Apparently Rand had never learned how to have fun, and she intended to teach him.

Chapter Fifteen

Sara seated herself opposite her father's wheelchair in the nursing home's garden room two weeks later and watched the right side of his mouth pull up in a smile. Celeste had just placed her tiny gray poodle in his lap. It was wonderful to see him smile again, even if he could only do so faintly.

The stroke had damaged his spirit as much as his body, leaving the usually outgoing man silent and morose, but Sara had noticed a significant improvement in his mood this past week. The physical therapist claimed her father had made huge strides in his physical rehabilitation as well.

"He seems to have a new sense of purpose," the therapist had told her. "He's trying a whole lot harder."

Which was a big relief to Sara—and would no doubt be a big relief to her business partner, as well.

Christine had been hinting broadly that she was eager for Sara to return. "I'm having to turn away business from some of our regular clients. It's all I can do just to keep the shop doors open," she'd said in their phone conversation yesterday. "And our inventory is starting to run low. You're still planning to go to Milan next month, aren't you?"

"I hope to, Christine," Sara had told her. "But I just can't leave right now, not while Dad's still in this shape."

"I hate to keep turning away design business."

"Why don't I call Margaret Manning and see if she can help out for a few weeks? She's been out of the workplace for several years, but she's got exquisite taste, and she's wanting to get back in the business now that her kids are in college."

"If you have her number, I'll call her myself," Christine had said.

Sara's father laughed, jerking her thoughts back to the present. Celeste's little dog had placed its front paws on his chest and was licking his cheek.

"I believe that little dog likes you, Jack," said a large elderly woman in a purple-flowered mumu seated beside Celeste on the green sofa.

"Of course she does," said a sprightly voice from the doorway. "Dogs are good judges of character."

The smile flickered on Jack's face again. He strained to turn his wheelchair to the door. "Daisy! Come in, come in. I want you to meet my daughter."

Those were the most words Sara had heard her father string together since his stroke. Gazing wonderingly from her father to the petite white-haired woman entering the room, Sara rose from her chair and held out her hand. "Hello. I'm Sara."

"And I'm Daisy Phillips." The tiny woman's eyes were as bright as buttons. She wore a rose-colored sweatsuit, matching lipstick and a charming smile. "It's so nice to meet you. Jack has told me a lot about you."

"Is that a fact?" Sara looked again at her father. His face

was animated, his expression engaged and alert. He almost looked like his old self.

"Daisy just moved in," he volunteered.

The woman nodded. "I took an apartment in the new independent living wing. My daughter was worried about me living alone, and to tell you the truth, it was getting to be a bit much for me, taking care of a big old house by myself."

"Daisy used to live in New Orleans," Jack explained.

"So what brought you to this part of the state?" Sara asked.

"My daughter and her family live here. She's a teacher at the high school, and my son-in-law is a veterinarian."

"Dr. Thomas?" Celeste asked.

"Why, yes. Do you know him?"

"He came out and checked my animals a couple of weeks ago," Celeste said. "He's very nice. He told me my llama is pregnant."

Daisy smiled. "So is my daughter. She's forty-one, and pregnant with her fourth child."

"Oh, my! I'm sure she's glad to have you nearby," Sara said.

Daisy nodded. "She and her husband asked me to live with them and help out, but I like my independence. This is *perfect*." Daisy turned to Celeste and held out her hand. "You must be the petting-zoo lady. My son-in-law has talked about you."

"Yes. I'm Celeste Landry."

"I can't wait to take my grandkids to your place when it opens. Jack has told me all about you and your animals." She looked at the poodle in Jack's lap. "It's so nice of you to bring them by. The residents here just love your visits."

"I enjoy them, too," Celeste said. She gestured to her spot on the sofa. "Please—have a seat."

"I'll sit over here by Jack, if you don't mind."

The woman crossed the room and sat near Jack's wheelchair. Sara noticed with surprise that her father rolled his wheelchair closer to her.

"You'll never guess this little dog's name," Jack said.

"I wouldn't even venture a try," Daisy replied. "What is it?"

"Killer!"

Daisy's laughter was bright and musical.

Jack gave a crooked grin. "Would you like to hold her?"

The woman beamed. "Why, yes. Thank you, Jack—I'd like that very much."

Celeste jumped up from the sofa and transferred the dog from Jack's lap to Daisy's. Killer promptly licked the woman's wrinkled cheek.

"Oh, she's a sweetheart!" Daisy crooned, stroking the dog's fluffy head.

"Takes one to know one," Jack said.

Sara stared at her father, her mouth falling open. He was flirting! Her father had been single for nearly forty years, and in all that time, she'd never heard him express interest in any woman.

Two thin ladies shuffled through the door, a blue-haired one leaning on a cane and the other one shuffling on a walker. The one with the cane abruptly stopped. "Oh, Violet—look! There's a poodle!"

The woman with the walker peered down at the vinyl floor. "It's not my fault this time," she said in a loud voice. "I'm wearin' my Depends."

"*Poodle*, Violet. Not puddle. Poodle."

Sara heard her father chuckle, lifting his right hand off the arm of his wheelchair. That was a good sign. She usually had to coax him to make the slightest movement. She noticed that he was smiling at Daisy, who smiled right back.

Was Daisy the reason for his recent progress? Well, well,

well. This was certainly an interesting development.

"Where is it?" Violet demanded. "I don't want to step in it."

"I said *poodle!*" The blue-haired lady jabbed her cane in the air again, pointing toward the dog in Daisy's lap.

Violet lifted her gaze. When it landed on Killer, her sour expression sweetened into a smile. "Well, I'll be! Why didn't you say there was a dog in here?"

The blue-haired woman rolled her eyes and let out a long sigh. Jack and Daisy looked at each other again and exchanged a grin.

Something was definitely brewing between the two of them, Sara decided.

"I bet that dog's responsible for the puddle," Violet announced.

Celeste glanced at her watch and rose. "I'm afraid I need to go. It's nearly feeding time, and my animals will be getting hungry."

Sara rose from her chair as well. "I'll be back tonight," she said to her father.

She came back every evening to help him with dinner. His arm movement was limited, and although it was improving, it was still jerky and erratic. He always ate in his room because he was embarrassed to be seen in public being spoon-fed like a baby.

"No need," he said.

Sara looked at him in surprise. "You don't want help with dinner?"

"I want to try to do it myself. The therapist said I should give it a go."

"Well . . . all right." Sara bent and kissed him on the cheek, feeling baffled and slightly rebuffed. "Be sure and call the staff if you need some help, though."

"Okay."

Daisy reached over and put her hand on Jack's arm. "I'll

be right back." She followed Sara into the hall. "I hope your feelings aren't hurt. He just doesn't want you to see him make a mess as he tries to feed himself."

Sara didn't know if she was more surprised by the woman's remark or the fact that she'd made it. "But I'm his daughter!"

"I know, I know. But he's got his pride." Daisy took her arm and walked beside her down the hall. "My late husband had a stroke, so I know a little about how it affects a man. It's humiliating, having a body that won't do what you want it to. No grown man wants anyone to see him dribbling food all over himself."

It was odd, having this stranger tell her about her own father's feelings. "He's let me feed him up until now."

"That's because he had no other choice. Now that he's getting better, he's getting his pride back, too." The older woman patted Sara's arm. "It's hard to back off and let him struggle on his own, but he needs to do it. It's kind of like a parent with a teenager."

"Except the roles are reversed."

Daisy grinned. "And you don't have those high car insurance premiums."

Sara laughed. She liked the elderly woman, even though she wasn't so sure she liked being told how to treat her own father. She'd just met Daisy, yet the woman acted as if she were more of an insider than Sara.

Daisy leaned forward conspiratorially, a shy grin on her face. "Your father wants to be able to feed himself so he can take me to dinner on my birthday in a couple of weeks."

Sara's mouth fell open. She forced herself to shut it. "I—I see."

Daisy patted her arm. "You're a good daughter. He's lucky to have you." With that, she turned and headed back into the sunroom.

Sara turned to Celeste. "Can you believe that? He can't have known her more than four or five days."

"It's good for him, don't you think?"

"Well, yes," Sara admitted reluctantly. "But they seem awfully close to have just met. I think they're moving a little fast, don't you?"

Celeste shifted Killer in her arms and gave a teasing grin. "Now, Sara, you're really sounding like a parent."

Sara grinned back as they turned the hallway corner. "I suppose I do. It's just that . . ." She stopped in her tracks. "Oh, no," she breathed.

"What?"

Standing on a ladder in the entryway was George. Sara hadn't seen him since their conversation at his house. How would he react to seeing her? Was he still angry that she'd forced her way in?

For a brief moment, she considered turning around and fleeing back to the garden room, but it was too late. He'd seen her. It didn't make her feel any better that, from the look on his face, he wanted to flee, too.

She had no choice but to walk down the hall toward him.

"You'll be fine," Celeste murmured. "Just say hello like you would to anyone else."

George climbed down from the ladder and nodded politely as they approached. "Celeste. Sara."

"Hi, George. What brings you out this way?" Celeste asked.

"I'm checking the smoke detectors. The fire department does that every few months."

"What a great service!"

George lifted his shoulders. "Yeah, well, we have to do something to stay busy, especially in a town with as few fires as this one."

"I promised Mrs. Andrews I'd bring Killer by her room

before we left," Celeste said. "If you two will excuse me, I'll go do that." She headed down the opposite hall, leaving Sara alone with George.

Traitor. Sara suppressed the urge to run after her.

They stared at each other awkwardly for a moment. "I, um, checked the detectors at your dad's store right before his stroke," George said.

"That was nice of you."

He gave a shy shrug. "It was part of a free fire-prevention evaluation we offer businesses. I told your dad he needed to upgrade his sprinkler system. It's really old, and his store is full of combustibles."

"I'll remind him," Sara promised. "Thanks."

George nodded. Another moment of silence fell between them, then George cleared his throat. "How's your dad doing?"

Sara played with the strap on her purse. "Better. He's talking more and he's trying to feed himself."

"Well, good. That's good." George shoved his hands in his pockets. "I, um, didn't see your car in the parking lot."

Sara smiled. "So you thought the coast was clear, huh?"

He cast a sheepish grin at the floor. "Something like that."

"I came with Celeste. But I thought we weren't going to scout parking lots for each other's cars anymore."

He lifted his shoulders. "I just don't like awkward situations."

"Me, neither." Sara gave a shy grin. "When I saw you standing here, I nearly ran into the nearest room and hid under the bed."

He chuckled.

"What's so funny?"

"The thought of you in that outfit hiding under a bed. You would have been the best-dressed coward this town has ever seen."

Sara looked down at her white pants and sweater set, then looked back at George. He was smiling, and Sara couldn't help but smile back. They stood there like that for a moment, while a buzz of warmth hummed between them.

"Do you know a veterinarian named Dr. Thomas?" she asked.

"Sure. He takes care of Rand's and my horses."

Sara's eyebrows flew up. "You still have horses?"

"Does a leopard have spots?"

Her smile widened. "I should have known. Do you keep them at Rand's?"

He nodded.

"Is it weird, having someone else own the place?"

"Nah. It's actually a big relief. This way I get to focus on the training, which is the part I love. Plus I have more time for the fire department."

"I was surprised to learn you'd sold your grandparents' farm."

"Heather and I thought we'd be in Brazil for a year or more. The treatments were supposed to take a while."

The mention of Heather's name introduced a fresh awkwardness. Silence gathered between them, yet neither of them made a move to leave.

"Why did you ask about Dr. Thomas?" George finally asked.

"Oh—I just met his mother-in-law. She's moved into an apartment in the assisted living wing. She and my dad seem to have developed quite a friendship."

"Is that so?"

Sara nodded. "They're really hitting it off. Especially for people who've known each other less than a week."

"Hitting it off . . . romantically?"

Sara lifted her shoulders. "Well, it's hard to think of my

father being romantic, especially in his current condition. But he sure seemed flirtatious."

"Really?" George looked surprised.

"Yes. It just struck me as . . . well . . . odd. And I wanted to know if you knew anything about her."

George's eyes gleamed with amusement. "Sounds like you're worried your father's taking up with a fast woman."

"I guess that's kind of how I feel," Sara said sheepishly. "Dad's had women throwing themselves at him all my life, and he's never been interested. It just strikes me as odd that he suddenly seems to have a crush on this woman, when he's at his most vulnerable. I hate the idea of anyone taking advantage of him."

"And you're worried she's going to?"

Sara's brow furrowed. "Well, he seems pretty smitten. He's wanting to learn how to feed himself so he can take her to dinner for her birthday."

"Well, well, well." George laughed.

"You think it's funny?"

"Not particularly. But your reaction is."

Sara found herself chuckling, too. "I guess it is."

"Look, if you're worried that she's a gold digger, you can relax. Doc's wife comes from old money. From what I've heard, your dad's new friend is very well-heeled."

"Oh." Sara smiled nervously. "Well, that's good to know."

They stood there for a moment, just looking at each other.

"Look, about the other night . . ." she began.

George held up his hand. "That's history. Let's leave it there. We've got to live in the here and now."

"You're right." Sara fiddled with the strap of her purse again, her stomach tense. "Well, I'd better go find Celeste."

"And I need to finish checking the smoke detectors." He

hesitated for a moment, and she saw his Adam's apple move as he swallowed. "Nice seeing you."

She nodded. "Yes, it was."

It was a banal exchange, and between herself and anyone else, it would have been nothing more than polite social pleasantries—*"Nice seeing you," "Yes, it was."* But between George and herself, the words were profound and they both knew it.

George folded up his ladder and tucked it under his arm as if it were no more than a newspaper. Sara started down the hall, then paused to look back. George stopped at the corner and looked back as well. They hesitantly grinned at each other, then quickly looked away.

The realization that he'd turned to check her out sent a little thrill chasing down her spine. She headed on down the hall, a spring in her step and a smile on her lips.

Chapter Sixteen

"What's all this?"

The displeased look on Rand's face gave Celeste serious second thoughts. But it was too late to back out; she was standing in his amazingly tidy stable, holding the reins to two saddled horses.

Rand looked at George, who was standing beside her. "What's going on?"

George grinned broadly. "You're being kidnapped, my friend."

"*What?*"

"I promised to take you on an adventure, remember?" Celeste piped up. "Well, today's the day."

"No." Rand shook his head. "No way."

Celeste's smile never wavered. "Yes, way."

"I can't. I've got a million things to do. Besides, I've got a client coming in half an hour."

"He rescheduled," George said. "He's coming tomorrow."

Rand's gaze flashed to George. "When did that happen?"

"When I called him yesterday."

"You *what?*"

"Called him and rescheduled."

Rand's mouth flatlined in displeasure. "Damn it, I don't need anyone trying to run my business."

"I'm not trying to run your business. I'm trying to get you to take an afternoon off. And as late as it is, there's not even much afternoon left."

The roan mare behind Celeste snorted. Rand shook his head, his eyes still on George. "I can't believe she roped you into this."

"There was no talking her out of it. But the fact is, I didn't even try. A fellow who's all work and no play is a slave driver of a boss."

"Amen to that, brother," called out a grizzled stable hand who'd helped saddle the horses.

"That's no lie," agreed a shaggy-headed young man in baggy shorts pushing a broom near the front entrance.

George gave Rand a calm smile. "If you can't take time to go on a trail ride with a pretty gal on a beautiful day, well, you might as well be dead."

"I don't see *you* takin' any trail rides," Rand countered.

"I did my share when I was younger."

"Come on, Rand," Celeste urged. "It'll be fun."

He blew out a sigh. She could tell he was weakening, but he wasn't quite ready to concede.

"How long will this take?" Rand asked.

"Just a couple of hours." She gave him her best smile. "Besides, it's after four o'clock. It's almost quitting time."

"It's not quitting time until the sun goes down. That doesn't happen this time of year until after seven."

"Believe it or not, we'll manage just fine without you for the rest of the day," George said. "We do okay when you're out of town, don't we?"

"Well, yes, but—"

"The only butt you need to be concerned about is the one you're about to set on that saddle."

The stable hands laughed and applauded.

Rand raised his hands in a gesture of surrender. "Okay, okay. I seem to be outnumbered."

Celeste heaved a sigh of relief as she stepped into the stirrup and swung her leg over the roan named Sugar that she'd borrowed from George. Rand climbed on his mount as well, a large black horse called Blue Moon.

George walked beside them as they rode out of the stables into the corral, then opened the gate to the back pasture. "Don't do anything I wouldn't do," he called.

"Well, that gives us a lot of leeway," Rand retorted.

George laughed and closed the gate behind them. Celeste and Rand rode side by side through the pasture where they'd first met.

"I told you not to do this," Rand snapped as soon as they were out of earshot.

"Well, I went ahead and did it anyway, so just relax and try to enjoy it." Celeste reached forward and patted the auburn neck of her horse, feigning a nonchalance she didn't feel.

She'd been unable to get Rand off her mind since their trip to New Orleans. So many things about him now made sense. No wonder he tried to control everything; he'd grown up in chaos and confusion, so he craved order and predictability. No wonder he didn't "do" emotions; he'd experienced so many negative ones that he'd built a wall around his heart.

He'd never really had a childhood, never learned how to lose himself in play. Well, she hoped to give him a taste of that today. Hopefully he'd learn that a little fun and spontaneity wouldn't make his world fall apart.

"What's this all about?" Rand asked.

"It's just my way of thanking you for taking me and Sheltie to New Orleans the other day."

"What if I don't want to be thanked?"

"Tough cookies. You're getting thanked anyway."

"What if I decide to thank *you* for thanking *me* by hauling you over my knee for a spanking?"

"I'd say you have a kinky way of showing appreciation." She gave him a grin. "But I'm not worried. I'm pretty sure I can handle you."

"Oh, you are, are you?"

"Yeah. Because first you've got to catch me." She tapped her heels against Sugar's side, and the horse took off at a canter. Rand tore out after her. Celeste urged her horse into a gallop, her heart galloping, too, the pure exuberance of being chased by Rand coursing through her like the wind. Rand caught up as she reached the gate in the fence that separated his property from hers.

"I won!" she said.

"No, you didn't. That wasn't a race—it was a chase. And I've got you cornered."

"Not for long." Celeste swung out of the saddle. Holding her horse's reins, she opened the gate and led her horse through. Rand followed. She closed the gate behind him and climbed back on her horse.

"Where'd you learn to ride like that?" Rand asked.

"At my grandmother's place. She had a horse named Peanut."

"That's not much of a name."

"He wasn't much of a horse." Celeste smiled. "But Gran loved him to pieces. She used to bake batches of peanut butter cookies just for him."

"Maybe pampering animals is hereditary," Rand said.

"Maybe so."

"Speaking of pampered animals, how are things going with your zoo?"

"They're going great. I'm finalizing my plans for the grand opening extravaganza."

"Extravaganza?" This was news to Rand. He urged his horse to catch up with hers as she headed down a trail through the woods. "What are you talking about?"

"I've come up with the coolest plan! I'm holding a big grand opening with free admission for teachers and their families. I'm hoping that if I can get them to come see the place, they'll want to bring their classes on field trips. And I'm going to give discount coupons to distribute to their students, to encourage their parents to bring them here for family outings and parties."

"That's not a bad plan. Not bad at all." Actually, it was very clever. "What's going to happen at this big event?"

"Well, the kids can go on pony rides and pet the animals, and the dogs will do a show. And I'm putting together interactive display boards that explain things about the different animals: where they come from, how they're useful to people, what they eat, etcetera. I've ordered a bunch of picnic tables and a big playset with swings and a slide and a fort, and I plan to build a little stage for the dogs to perform on. Plus I'm going to serve free hot dogs and popcorn and soda, and maybe some finger sandwiches."

"Sounds like it's going to cost an awful lot of money."

"All I have left," she said cheerfully, apparently unfazed at the prospect. "And I'm sure I'll end up maxing out my credit cards, too."

"You're going to go into the hole for just one day?"

"I've got to, if I want to make a big splash. If you've convinced me of anything, it's that I can't just sit and wait for business to come to me."

He had somehow inspired this latest lunacy? A sinking feeling hit Rand's gut. "When are you planning to hold this thing?"

"The third weekend in September."

"That's only about a month before your taxes are due. Are you going to be able to make enough of a profit in that short a time?"

"I won't need to. I just need to get the bookings. Mr. Adler said that if I can get enough commitments to show that I can make a profit, he'll reconsider my loan."

" 'Reconsider' means he'll think about it. It doesn't mean you'll definitely get it. And you'd need to get an awful lot of bookings." Why couldn't she see that she was likely to lose all her resources and be heartbroken in the bargain? "Those are a lot of ifs, Celeste."

She ducked her head to avoid a branch. "My grandmother spent every penny she owned on a boat ticket from Scotland to the United States because she was certain that an American sailor she'd known for less than twenty-four hours was the love of her life. She said that if you truly believe in something, you've got to give it everything you've got."

"If you're planning on running up big credit card bills, you're giving it what you *haven't* got," he told her.

"Gran used to say that when destiny opens the door, you have to have the courage to walk through it. And sometimes you have to climb over a whole lot of obstacles piled up on the threshold."

"What if some of the obstacles are too big to overcome?"

"They won't be. If the door is there, there's always a way through it."

"What if the door was never there in the first place?" he demanded. "How do you know you're not like Sheltie, just looking in a funhouse mirror?"

"Because I just know, that's all. I know it in my heart."

It was a lost cause. There was no talking any sense into her.

Well, fine. It wasn't his business. She was setting herself

up for failure, and the sooner she failed, the sooner she'd sell him the property.

Which was what he wanted. Wasn't it? A weird, unsettled, anxious feeling flapped in his stomach. Suddenly he wasn't so sure.

Of course it was what he wanted, he argued with himself. He just hated to see her fall flat on her face, that was all. Knowing Celeste, she'd be all upset to think that she'd let down the old man.

Well, that was just life. The whole idea had been impractical from the very beginning. If Celeste wanted to ignore basic business principles and believe a bunch of stuff about destiny and signs and divine providence, that was her right, but sooner or later, she'd have to face the truth. Castles in the air always crashed down on the people who built them.

She'd be fine once she sold him the property, he reassured himself. He'd make sure she made enough of a profit to get back on her feet.

But knowing Celeste, she was likely to turn around and lose her shirt on some other softhearted, harebrained scheme.

There was that feeling again—that strange, pit-of-the-stomach flutter.

Hell. It was her life. It was none of his business. If she wanted to take every dollar she owned, shred it up and use it as garden mulch, it should make no difference to him.

But it did.

"This is the end of the trail," Celeste announced. She reined her horse to a stop, causing Rand to rein in his thoughts. They were at the back of her property, near the Owa Chita River. Not that it was really a river; except for flood season, it was a lazy, spring-fed stream with a sandy bottom. Celeste's land backed up to a wide spot that had been an old swimming hole.

She slid off her saddle. "We're walking from here."

"We're going to the river?"

"It's an adventure, so I can't tell." She shot him a mischievous grin. "You'll have to wait and see." She looked gleeful.

Rand dismounted and tethered both horses to a low branch on a red oak. He looked up to find Celeste standing beside him, teasingly dangling a red bandanna from her thumb and forefinger.

"What's that for?"

"It's a blindfold."

Rand shook his head. "Oh, no."

"Come on," she wheedled. "It's part of the adventure."

"I like to see what I'm walking into."

"I promise not to hurt you. I promise you'll even like it."

His thoughts flashed on a few things he'd like to do with Celeste. The afternoon might hold some promise after all. "How much will I like it?"

"A lot, I hope."

He shot her a rakish grin. "Are you going to take advantage of me?"

"Afraid not."

"Well, then, forget it."

Celeste laughed. "Turn around and shut up."

"Are you sure I'm going to like it?"

"Absolutely."

What the heck. He turned around and let her put the folded bandanna around his eyes.

"Can you see?" she asked.

He peered at her from under the edge of the scarf. "No, not at all."

"Liar."

He grinned as she tugged at the bandanna, adjusting it until he couldn't see anything but a small patch of light from the bottom. She put her hands on his shoulders and turned him around in a circle two times, then took his hand in hers. "Okay. Let's go."

He was a little disoriented, but he was pretty sure they were still headed toward the water. "You're not going to make me walk the plank, are you?"

"I might, if you keep asking questions." She tightened her grip on his hand and led him slowly down through the woods. "Okay," she said at length. "Now stand there for a minute."

"Don't I get last words or a cigarette?"

"You're really paranoid, aren't you?" He could hear the smile in her voice.

"Yeah, well, this is all pretty weird."

"Just relax and trust me."

"Easy for you to say."

"You don't have to always be in control, you know," she said gently. "You ought to try letting go of the reins once in a while."

"You're just full of advice, aren't you?"

"And you're just full of it, period."

Rand grinned.

"Now stay put and don't peek."

Rand heard her walk away, her feet crunching on leaves and pine straw. He liked the way she held her own with him, sassing him back and not taking any guff.

He just liked her, period.

As a friend, he quickly added. Strictly as a friend.

A friend who turned him on to an unbelievable degree. He tilted back his head and tried to see out from underneath the blindfold, but she'd done too good a job. He heard her footsteps grow fainter, heard some odd sounds he couldn't quite identify, then heard her footsteps returning.

"Ready?" she asked.

"For what?"

"You're about to find out." She stepped behind him, untied the blindfold and pulled it off with a flourish.

He blinked against the daylight.

"Ta-da!"

Stretched between two trees was a large banner proclaiming "Happy Birthday." Beyond that was a large picnic blanket festooned with a balloon bouquet and two birthday-themed place settings. And in the middle of the blanket sat a tall, rather lopsided chocolate cake blazing with candles.

He stood there, too stunned to move.

Celeste took him by the arm and guided him to the blanket. "Happy birthday to you, happy birthday to you," she sang in a slightly off-key soprano. "Happy birthday, dear Ra-and, happy birthday to you." She gazed at him, her eyes bright and expectant. "What do you think?"

"Wow. I—I'm speechless."

She sank down on the blanket. "Are you surprised?"

"Completely." He slowly sat down beside her, staring at the balloons and the cake. "Especially since . . ." He hesitated. Her face was so excited and happy he couldn't bring himself to put a damper on it.

"Especially since it's not your birthday?" she prompted.

"Yeah."

"I know. I had George look it up. But I didn't want to wait until December. You've waited too long for a birthday party as it is."

Oh, jeez—he'd made that offhand remark about never having had a birthday party when they were on the way to New Orleans. It amazed him that she remembered.

Amazed him . . . and moved him. Rand stared at the cake, speechless.

Stop it, he ordered himself. He didn't do emotions. He would not—repeat, would *not*—let Celeste know how deeply this touched him. It was disturbing enough for him to know it.

He cleared his throat, searching for something logical to focus on. "How many candles did you put on that thing, anyway?"

"Thirty-two. That's your age, right?"

She'd done her research. "That's a lot of candles. We'd better hurry and put them out, or else George and the rest of the fire department will show up to hose them down."

She grinned. "Well, then, make a wish and blow them out."

He drew in a deep breath and leaned over.

"Not so fast!" She put her hand on his arm, stopping him. "You haven't made a wish."

"How do you know?"

"Because you didn't take enough time. You have to silently say it in your mind."

"Let's pretend I did."

"Come on. There's got to be something you want."

Yeah. You. The thought disturbed him. He raked a hand through his hair. "I believe in hard work, not wishes."

"Because of your childhood?"

Damn it all—why had he told her all that stuff? He never talked about that part of his life, and this was why. Now she was going to psychoanalyze everything he said or did.

And the really annoying thing was, she was right on the money.

She looked at him, and something in her eyes made his throat close up again.

"They're not mutually exclusive concepts, you know," she said. "You make your wish, then you work hard to make it come true."

What the hell—she'd gone to a lot of trouble, and this

was obviously important to her. It wouldn't hurt him to fake a wish.

He'd better do it fast, because the candles were making the icing run down the sides of the cake. He did his best to look thoughtful. His eyes lit on her lips, and despite his best intentions, a wish immediately formed in his mind. Irritated with himself, he filled his lungs and blew.

The fire disappeared, leaving smoldering wicks and smoke.

"Good job."

"I was afraid we were going to need a ladder truck."

Laughing, Celeste pulled a bottle of champagne from an ice chest resting against the tree and handed it to him. "Would you do the honors while I cut the cake?"

"Champagne, too?" Another rush of emotion shot through him. "You really shouldn't have gone to so much trouble."

"It wasn't trouble. It was fun."

He unwrapped the foil and pried up the cork, glad of a task to perform, glad to focus on a solid, identifiable object. She slid an enormous slice of cake onto his balloon-printed paper plate, then cut another for herself.

The cork flew off with a loud pop. He filled the two plastic champagne glasses and handed one to her.

She lifted hers in the air. "To you. To many more birthdays and much happiness. May all your dreams come true."

A big chunk of emotion filled his throat, making it hard to talk. "Thanks," he managed to croak. He took a gulp of champagne and was relieved when it slid down and hit his belly. After another sip or two, maybe his throat would unknot enough for him to eat some cake.

"That was the best trail ride grub I've ever had."

Celeste grinned as Rand smashed the last cake crumbs

onto the back of his plastic fork, then slid the fork in his mouth.

"Don't you like chocolate cake?" he asked.

She looked down at her nearly full plate. She'd gotten so much pleasure watching him eat that she'd barely tasted her own.

Uh-oh. It was a bad sign if she enjoyed watching a man eat chocolate more than she enjoyed eating it herself. "I'm not very hungry," she said. "Do you want some more?"

He patted his stomach. "Not at the moment."

"Well, then, it's time to open your present." She reached behind her and pulled out a brightly wrapped blue and red package from a plastic bag by the ice chest.

Rand self-consciously rubbed his jaw. "Ah, hell—you shouldn't have gotten me anything."

"I wanted to. Every birthday boy needs a gift." She handed the wrapped box to him. "Besides, you're going to need it once the party games start."

"Party games?"

She nodded. "Open it. It won't bite."

He gave her a lopsided grin. "I'm more concerned about whether or not it spits."

She laughed. "It won't. I promise."

He ripped the paper off the box, then lifted the lid. He pulled back the tissue paper, then looked at her quizzically. "I'm going to need clean underwear?"

Celeste erupted in laughter.

"Wow, this *is* an adventure. What kind of party games do they play where you come from?"

She playfully threw the bow at him. "It's not underwear. It's swim trunks."

"I don't know if I should be relieved or disappointed." He pulled the navy trunks out of the box. "Where's your swimsuit?"

"I've got it on under my clothes."

"So if I put these on, you'll take off your clothes?" His voice was teasing, but his eyes held an unnerving gleam.

"No! I mean—well, yes. I'll take off my jeans, but I won't . . ."

She was blathering. And he was sitting there grinning at her, enjoying the fact that he'd flustered her.

She picked up the swim trunks and thrust them at him. "I'm going to leave you alone so you can change. Let me know when you're dressed."

"You mean *un*dressed."

Celeste headed into the woods, wondering if she'd made a huge mistake. When she'd planned this party, she'd been thinking of ways to stay cool in the Louisiana heat. She hadn't considered the fact that swimwear was likely to raise their body temperatures more than fur-lined parkas.

Or had she? Maybe, on a subconscious level, she had.

Oh, dear. Well, it was too late to question her motives. Celeste pulled off her T-shirt and stepped out of her jeans. Her aqua and royal blue tankini had seemed modest when she'd donned it, but now that Rand was about to see it, she felt overly exposed.

"I'm ready," he called.

Celeste tugged up the zipper that ran down the front of her top and headed back to the clearing. The sight of Rand in his swim trunks made her stop short. She'd known he'd had a good body, but she hadn't known how good. She tried not to stare, but his muscular pecs and trampoline-taut abs made it hard to keep her eyes above his neck.

She felt Rand's gaze travel over her as well. The sun was riding low in the sky, but the temperature seemed to be skyrocketing.

"Now *that's* what I call a birthday present," he said appreciatively.

Celeste tried to lighten things up. "Sorry. I'm not part of the package."

"You sure?"

"Very."

"I thought the birthday boy got to pick the party activities."

She grinned. "You're sadly misinformed." She picked up two large plastic bags sitting by the ice chest, put one on the picnic table and carried the other to the edge of the river.

Rand followed. "What have you got there?"

"Stay there for just a moment and you'll find out." Celeste turned and ran along the sandy shore, carrying the bag.

Rand was so entranced by the sight of Celeste in her swimsuit that he was caught unawares when she turned and hurled something at him. It hit his chest and exploded, drenching him in water.

"One point for me!" she yelled.

"Hey! What's going on?"

"Water balloon fight!"

"No fair! I don't have any balloons."

"You don't?" She regarded him with feigned innocence. "Well, I'll have to give you some." She lobbed two more at him. One missed, but the other one caught him in the chest. "Two points!" she called.

"Hey—if only one person has ammunition, it's not a fight—it's a massacre!"

"Okay, okay. Your balloons are in the bag on the table."

He grabbed them up, and the fight began in earnest. By the time they'd exhausted their supply of balloons, both were drenched and laughing.

"Twelve to ten," Rand declared, plopping down beside her on the beach. "I won."

"Only because I let you," Celeste said. "It wouldn't have been nice to beat up the birthday boy."

Rand shook his head. "Wow, what a pathetic loser."

Celeste tilted up her head. "Well, if that's your attitude, I won't be so generous the next game."

"What's the next game?"

"A race. Swimming to the old dock and back."

"What's the prize?" Rand asked.

"The thrill of being a winner."

His gaze sent a hot chill down her spine. "I'll need more of an incentive than that."

"Okay." She jumped to her feet. "If you win, I won't throw your boots in the river."

"If I lose, you won't, either," he warned.

"You better just worry about winning."

"If I win, I get to determine the prize."

"That's a mighty big if." She tossed him a playful grin and started wading into the water. "Ready . . ."

He leapt to his feet. "Oh, no. You're not going to start without me again."

"Okay, okay." She waited until he reached her side at the edge of the shallow river. "Ready . . ."

He bent over, ready to make a fast start.

"Set . . ."

His legs tensed.

Before he knew what hit him, she'd grabbed the bottom of his trunks and yanked them down to his knees. "Go!" she yelled, dashing into the water.

"Hey!" He struggled to pull up his shorts, then dove in after her. She was several yards ahead, but she'd lost much of her head start by stopping to watch him deal with her mischief.

"You're going to pay for that," he yelled.

She lost more of her lead due to laughter. She was a good swimmer, graceful and strong, but Rand was no slouch. He deliberately held back, letting her reach the dock first.

"I wonder if your boots will sink or float?" she taunted.

"Too bad you'll never know." Rand pushed hard off the dock and easily passed her on the way back. He reached the shore and started to stride out of the water.

"Hey!" she called.

He paused and turned. She dove underwater, tackled his legs and tried to pulled him down.

He grabbed her, taking her with him. They both splashed in the shallow water and came up laughing. She tried to break free.

"Oh, no. You're not going to win that way." He swung her up into his arms and carried her to shore.

She shrieked with laughter. "Put me down!"

"Not until you agree that I am the World Champion Birthday Boy Swim Race Winner."

"Okay, okay. You're the World Champion Birthday . . . whatever you said."

"That's more like it." He adjusted his grip on her.

"I thought you were going to put me down."

"First I have to get my prize."

"What's your prize?"

"This." He rolled her body toward him and claimed her mouth with his.

It was like throwing a match on kerosene. The heat between them blazed into a rip-roaring fire in nothing flat. The next thing he knew, she was kissing him back, her lips lush and hot, her arms wound tight around his neck. Desire, fierce and fiery, swept through him with thought-numbing fury.

Cradling her in his arms was no longer enough. He needed her flush against him, needed to feel the soft pressure of her breasts against his chest, needed to press the hard heat of his arousal against her belly. Slowly, slowly, he set her on her feet, never pulling his lips from hers.

She gave a whimper and fitted her body against him,

standing on tiptoe, tilting her pelvis against his.

More. He needed more. His tongue mated with her mouth, plumbing the sweet, slick depths, intimate and hot and needy. His hands slid toward her sides, cupping her breasts, and she moaned and arched her back, giving him better access. Their points thrust through the thin swimsuit fabric, hard tips begging to be tasted. She moved against his hand, pushing her breasts more fully into his palms, her pelvis rocking against his erection. "I need . . ." she moaned. "Rand, I want . . ."

His fingers flicked over her hard nipples. "Tell me," he murmured against her mouth, sucking on her lower lip. "Tell me what you want."

"You." Her voice was a pleading whisper. "I want you."

The words were like wind on a wildfire. Desire flamed through Rand, hot and beyond restraint. He picked her up again and carried her to the picnic blanket. When he set her on the navy print quilt, she pulled him down beside her.

He tugged at the zipper at the top of her swimsuit. His mouth traced the zipper's path, kissing each inch of soft flesh it revealed.

Pleasure, pure pleasure—exquisite, excruciating, maddening pleasure. Celeste's hands stroked the muscles of Rand's back as his lips slipped across her skin. She loved the way he lingered, yet impatiently ached for more.

He slid the zipper all the way down. His lips slid with it. He kissed her belly button, then started up again, slowly pushing aside the fabric, revealing her breasts.

"You're beautiful," he murmured. "So beautiful."

He made her feel that way. His fingers tightened around one breast, and he lowered his head to the other. His tongue laved the nipple, moving over the taut flesh in soft, erotic circles, making her ache for him to take it in his mouth. At long last he did, grazing it gently with his teeth. And then his lips closed around it, tugging on it with a hot, wet pressure that sent a surge of heat searing down her belly.

She moaned and moved against him, her hands caressing his muscled back.

He turned his attention to the other breast until she breathed in soft pants, then reclaimed her lips with his own. She felt the hard heat of his erection against her. She slid her hands to the waistband of his trunks and tried to push them down. He rolled to the side and quickly stripped them off.

He was huge and aroused. She started to peel off her bikini bottom, and he placed his hand over hers, stopping her.

"Let me." His voice was low and rough. "I've fantasized about taking your clothes off for weeks."

His large hand moved down her belly. Instead of immediately removing her bikini bottom, though, he slowly caressed her exposed skin around it. His fingers shifted to her inner thighs, languorously stroking her, unbearably exciting her, making her throb for a more intimate touch.

She reached down again and tried to push down her bikini. "Please," she murmured. "Oh, please."

Once again, his hand stopped her. "Not yet."

His fingers drifted to the fabric between her legs. He slid his finger back and forth, building her desire until she whimpered with need. When his finger finally slipped under the elastic and onto her slick, aching flesh, she was on fire.

She curled her hand around his thick length. It was his turn to groan.

"I want you in me," she whispered.

He eased down her swimsuit bottom. She pulled him close, wrapping her legs around him, but still he took his time. Slowly, slowly, he entered her, stretching her, filling her, solid and hard and hot. She was so ready that her release began on the first upstroke, a white-hot burst of unbearable pleasure that left her shaking and shaken.

She opened her eyes to find Rand watching her, drinking in her pleasure as if it were his own, his gaze rapt and intense and enthralled. His expression was so unguarded, so open and warm and enraptured, that it made her heart turn over.

It was the way she'd always wanted to be looked at by the man she loved.

Loved? The thought set off a faint warning clang in the back of her mind, but then Rand lowered his mouth and kissed her, and all thought melted away. He moved inside her, reigniting the fire he'd just quenched. She closed her eyes and surrendered to sensation—the scent of his skin, the taste of his mouth, the deep, hard heat of his body urging her upward.

He carried her back to the summit, back to the edge of the precipice. This time, she wanted to take him with her. She longed to make him lose control, to make him surrender—to the moment, to her, to the love they were making.

She teetered on the brink. He pushed, she pulled—and then they were free-falling together.

"That was amazing," Rand whispered long moments later, nuzzling her neck.

"*You're* amazing," she murmured back. She moved her hands up his back, loving the feel of his skin, loving the hard muscle under it, loving *him*.

Oh, dear God, it was happening. Against her will, she was falling in love, and she was more than halfway gone. She didn't know when or where it had begun. It had started out like wisps of a cloud, unconnected and harmless—but somewhere along the way, the wisps had banded together and strengthened like a tropical storm in the gulf.

The thought made her body tense. He sensed it, and all of a sudden the spell was broken. She could feel his guard going up, could sense his emotional withdrawal.

Physical withdrawal followed. He pulled back and rolled over. He lay beside her for a moment, then abruptly leaned up on one elbow, his forehead tensed.

"Are you using anything?" His eyes willed her to say yes. "The Pill or something?"

It took a second for her mind to process the question. When it did, she froze, horrified at the oversight. "I-I used to be. But I haven't had sex since my divorce, so . . ."

He stared at her, his mouth a rigid slash. "So you're telling me we just had completely unprotected sex?"

How could she have had such a lapse in judgment? Her stomach felt as if she'd just swallowed a cannonball. Another one felt lodged in her throat.

He blew out a harsh breath and sat up. "Damn it, I can't believe I didn't use a condom. I *always* use a condom."

"I-I think it's a safe time of the month," she said weakly. She had no idea if that was true or not, but saying it might make him feel better.

"There's no such thing as a safe time of the month." He jammed his hands through his hair. "I can't believe I was so careless. This is exactly the kind of thing that happens when you go off half-cocked and don't use your head."

Celeste considered informing him that he'd been fully cocked and that he had indeed used his head, albeit the wrong one, but she didn't think humor would be welcome at this juncture.

He shook his head, his mouth grim. "This was all a big mistake. I never should have gone along with this whole insane adventure idea."

A *mistake*. The word richocheted through her like a stray

bullet, finally lodging in her heart. She'd just had the most emotional, tender, profound experience of her life, but he saw it as nothing more than a big mistake.

She drew in a deep, steadying breath. "Look, I accept full responsibility. If anything happens, I'll deal with it on my own."

He sat up and reached for his jeans, his face tombstone somber. "Like hell. It takes two to tango. If you're pregnant, I'll live up to my responsibilities."

Hurt rose in a red-hot wave. That was all she was to him—a potential responsibility?

She felt as if a trap door had just opened under her feet. What had she been thinking? He'd told her how he viewed romance, told her that he didn't want commitment. Had she thought she would somehow change that? She'd promised herself she wouldn't fall in love with someone who didn't love her back, and Rand didn't believe love existed.

How could she have been so stupid?

She snatched a beach towel from the bag by the ice chest and wrapped it around herself. "I don't know why we're even talking about this. Chances are, everything's fine. This is a ridiculous conversation."

"Not nearly as ridiculous as what we just did."

"You thought it was ridiculous?" Anger flashed inside her. She was grateful for its heat, glad of its burn. Anger was easier to handle than hurt.

"Ridiculously irresponsible," he amended. "Completely out of character for me."

She arched an eyebrow. "Oh, but I suppose it was right in keeping with *my* character."

"I didn't say that."

"You didn't need to." She wrapped the towel more tightly around herself.

"I didn't say that. Damn it, Celeste. . . ."

She snatched up her clothes and started for the woods to put them on. "As soon as I'm dressed, I'm heading back," she tossed over her shoulder. "As far as I'm concerned, this party's over."

Chapter Seventeen

"Oh, dear." Sara's brow puckered in a frown as she gazed at Celeste across the table at the Cajun Café three days later. "Do you think you might be pregnant?"

"It's too soon to tell," Celeste said, looking down at her half-eaten blueberry muffin. "I won't know for a week or so. But probably not. It's a long shot I'd get pregnant from just one time."

"It only takes one time." Sara worried the silver necklace around her neck. "What will you do if you are?"

"Why, I'll have the baby." Celeste didn't tell her friend, but the prospect gave her a secret thrill.

"What about Rand?"

"What about him?" Celeste broke off a bite of muffin, feigning an indifference she didn't feel.

"Well, where does he fit into the picture? Do you think he'd want to marry you? Would you want that?"

Celeste shook her head. There was no way she'd marry a man who considered her a *responsibility*.

Sara's eyes were warm and worried. "So . . . how did you leave things between you two?"

"Not good." After she and Rand had left the picnic site, they'd ridden back to Rand's ranch in silence. Anger had braced her, but as soon as she'd left his place, her heart had felt like a newly sprouted sprig trampled by a heavy boot.

"Rand said he'd be away at horse shows for two weeks and that we'd talk when he got back. And he said he was sorry about what happened." Bitterness edged her voice as her fingers tensed around the coffee cup. "Sorry! Now that's a real nice thing to hear from the man who just made love to you, don't you think? That he regrets the whole thing."

"I'm sure that's not how he meant it," Sara said in a soothing tone.

"I think he does. He sounded all stiff and angry when he said it."

"He was probably mad at himself, not at you."

"Well, I'm sure mad at myself." Celeste blew out a frustrated huff of air. "What was I thinking? I mean, for Pete's sake—I kidnap a man in late afternoon, serve him champagne, strip him down, make him engage in contact sports . . . I literally threw myself at him." She shook her head in disgust. "Why wasn't I honest enough to just admit to myself that I was trying to seduce him?"

Sara's eyebrows rose. "Were you?"

"No! Not consciously, at least. I thought I just wanted to give him a birthday party because he'd never had one, and I wanted to . . . oh, I don't know—show him how to play. I don't think the guy ever had a childhood. But I must have had the wrong kind of play in mind, because look where things ended up."

"It's obvious you care deeply about him."

Celeste felt her eyes fill with tears. "That's the thing that upsets me most. He doesn't want a relationship, Sara. He doesn't want any emotional involvement. He says he doesn't *do* emotions." Celeste shook her head. "What kind of man doesn't do emotions?"

"A man who's spent a lot of time hurting."

Sara was right, Celeste thought glumly. Rand had been disappointed and hurt so often as a child that he'd shut off his emotions in self-defense.

"He's drawn these boundaries around himself," Celeste said. "He'll get *this* close"—she held her hands about a foot apart—"but no closer. And he'll take *this* much of a chance"—she moved her hands about half an inch apart—"but no more. And he makes these exchanges, like someone on a Weight Watcher's diet. Instead of an intimate relationship with one woman, he's substituted the respect of the whole town. Instead of the roots of a family, he's trying to put down roots with land."

"You have a lot of insight into him."

"Too much." Celeste blew out a sigh. "I'd be better off thinking he's cold and heartless. Unfortunately, I've gotten to know him well enough to realize that behind all his walls and barricades, he's a terrific guy."

Sara's eyes were warm and sympathetic. "Sounds like you've got it bad."

Celeste nodded glumly. "Yeah, well, fat lot of good that'll do. I'm his worst nightmare."

"How do you figure that?"

"I don't play by his rules. I won't stay at arm's length, I'm thwarting his whole property expansion scheme and I follow my heart instead of cold-blooded logic. And worst of all—heaven forbid!—I think I make him *feel* things, which threatens the safe little world he's created for himself."

"And he's drawn to you because of it."

"He avoids me because of it." Celeste stared into her

coffee, wishing the grounds at the bottom somehow held answers for her.

Sara leaned forward. "How many times have I heard you say that everything happens for a reason? If that's the case, there must be a reason you and Rand came together."

"Sometimes the reason is to teach us a lesson."

"So, what do you think you're supposed to be learning?"

"Not to repeat past mistakes, I guess." She took a last sip of coffee, then set down her cup. "After my divorce, I told myself I'd never fall for another man who didn't love me as much as I loved him. And look at me." She turned her hands palm up on the table. "Rand isn't even capable of love."

"It's not that he's not capable," Sara said softly. "He just deliberately avoids it."

"The result is the same. Either way, I've made a big mistake."

"You were following your heart. Sometimes the heart knows things before the head."

"You sound just like my grandmother!"

"Well, there you go." Sara smiled. "We can't both be wrong."

The waitress stopped by and dropped the check on the table.

"I'll get this," Celeste said, reaching for it.

"No, you won't. It's my treat." Sara pulled out a credit card and handed it to the waitress. As she looked up, she froze. "Uh-oh. Speaking of past mistakes, one of mine just walked in the door."

"George?"

Sara nodded.

"I thought you two had cleared the air."

"We did, but I still feel awkward around him. I don't know what to say."

"I'm sure you'll think of something." Celeste gave her a

teasing smile, then glanced down at her watch. She reached for her purse. "Time for me to go."

"But . . ."

Celeste pulled the strap up on her shoulder and scooted out of the booth. "I need to drop off some flyers at the elementary schools in Bogalusa and Folsom, and I'm hoping to get the chance to talk to the principals."

"You don't need to rush off and abandon me, do you?"

"I'm afraid I do." She glanced in George's direction, then gave Sara a soft smile. "Besides, I'd only be in the way."

"No, you wouldn't!"

Celeste lifted her hand in a wave. "Thanks for breakfast—and for lending an ear and a shoulder."

"Any time."

Sara's heart pounded as she watched Celeste speak to George on her way out the door, then gesture toward her booth. George looked straight at her and bobbed his head in a greeting. Sara gave a wan smile and lifted her hand, wishing the waitress would bring back her credit card so she could pay up and leave.

George stopped to talk with four men at a table by the window. Sara took a sip of coffee and pretended to be studying the label on the bottle of Tabasco, all the while surreptitiously watching George. He looked good—too good. He wore jeans, boots and a blue-and-white-striped polo shirt that accentuated his tan. Blue had always been his favorite color. She wondered if he'd always selected his clothes himself, or if Heather used to buy them for him. The thought sent a funny pang through her heart.

He wasn't going to sit with the men after all. Sara's pulse skipped like a child with a jump rope when she realized he was heading straight toward her.

He stopped beside her booth. "Hi there, Sara."

Her heart beat a fast staccato. "Hello."

"Busy place."

"Yes. Yes, it is."

He looked as ill at ease as she felt. Sara suddenly realized that every table in the small café was taken. "I'm getting ready to leave as soon as the waitress brings back my credit card. You're welcome to have my table."

"Okay. Thanks." He slid into the booth opposite her.

Silence stretched between them, awkward and self-conscious.

George leaned his forearms on the table. Sara gazed at his hands, taking in the clean, short nails, the tan skin, the light dusting of masculine hair. The hands of her first love. She could still remember the way his hands had felt on her skin, the way they'd set her on fire.

Sara pulled her eyes away, only to have her gaze slam straight into George's.

He cleared his throat. "How's your dad?"

"Better. He's had a big burst of improvement this week. He's feeding himself, and he can even walk a short way with a walker. His therapist says he seems to have found new motivation." Sara smiled. "I'm pretty sure it's his lady friend."

"So you gave him permission to keep seeing her?"

Sara laughed and nodded. "You talked me into it. She's very nice, and she's definitely good for Dad."

"Well, good. That's great."

Silence settled between them again. George looked around and cleared his throat. "Sure is busy in here," he said again.

"Yes, it is. It's the only coffee place in town." She fiddled with the silver bangle on her arm. "I've been toying with the idea of putting an espresso machine in the store. I don't know if it would go over in Cypress Grove or not, but I sure miss my morning cappuccino."

"I think that's a great idea."

"You think so?"

"Yeah. I could use a good Americano or double latte now and then."

Sara stared at him. "You drink latte?"

"I'm not quite the country bumpkin you probably imagine."

Sara's face heated. "Oh—I didn't think you were. I didn't mean—I mean, I wasn't trying to imply . . ." Oh, dear. She hadn't meant to insult him. "I-I just . . ."

He watched her, his expression inscrutable.

"I just have trouble remembering that twenty-eight years have gone by," she finally blurted. "I keep thinking of you the way you were when I knew you, which is ridiculous. I know you're not eighteen anymore. And of course your tastes have changed, just as mine have." She gave an embarrassed smile. "A lot happens in twenty-eight years."

"Yes, it does."

"People change."

He nodded, his expression still guarded.

"The truth is, I guess we really don't know each other anymore."

"No, I guess not." His face was getting the shuttered, closed-off expression he'd had when she first hit town.

Something seized her, some frenzied sense of now-or-never. "But I'd like to." The words came out breathy and fast, as if her mouth wanted to slip a fast one past her mind.

Once she'd said them, she immediately wanted to take the words back.

George's eyebrows rode up. "What?"

She felt as if she'd just hung her pride out to dry and it was flapping in the wind for all to see, like ratty underwear on a clothesline.

"I-I'd like to get to know you. Pla-platonically, of course." Her face flamed. Dear heavens—how long had it been since she'd blushed? A decade, at least. Maybe two.

"I was thinking it'd be good to talk, to catch up on things, to just . . . you know—visit a spell."

Boy, now there was a phrase she hadn't used since she'd left here—*visit a spell*. Next thing she knew, she'd be talking about Jethro and the cement pond.

"Of course, if you don't want to, I understand. I understand completely. I'm sure you're very busy." Her tongue seemed to stick to the roof of her mouth, and she stumbled over it. "It was probably out of place for me to even ask. I'm sorry if I put you on the spot."

"You didn't." His dark eyes thawed. "I'd like that."

She was so braced for a refusal, so intent on offering him an easy out, that it took a second for his answer to register. "You would?"

He grinned in the funny, lopsided way she remembered, showing the dimple in his left cheek. The boyish dimple in his rugged man's face made her heart turn over.

"Sure," he said.

Her face heated further. "Well . . . well, great." She fought to regain her poise, feeling as flustered as she had at thirteen, the first time he held her hand. "So . . . would you like to come to dinner some evening?"

"Sure."

Her heart thudded hard. She hadn't had a chance to think this through. It was all so spur of the moment. Which was just as well; if she'd had time to think it over, she never would have had the courage to ask him. "Well . . . how about tomorrow?"

"Fine."

"Around seven?"

"Sounds good."

The waitress chose that moment to return Sara's credit card and receipt. Sara was so nervous that she scribbled her name on the tip line. She scratched it out, added a ten-dollar tip to a seven-dollar tab, then scrawled her name on the bottom in a hand so shaky that she wouldn't have recognized her own signature. She stuffed the card back in her wallet, placed the wallet in her slim Italian purse and scooted out of the booth. George rose to his feet as she did.

The gallantry gave her an odd little thrill. She pulled her purse up on her shoulder. "Well, it was good seeing you. I-I'll look forward to tomorrow."

"Me, too."

She could feel his gaze on her as she walked away, and it put a smile on her face.

Chapter Eighteen

George killed the engine of his pickup and stared at the
ranch-style house where Sara had grown up. It was the
same—red brick, white trim, black shutters and a shake
shingle roof—but the landscaping had changed. The flow-
erbeds that used to bloom year-round were no longer there,
overgrown by shrubbery. The enormous old elm that had
shaded the east side was gone, a victim of Dutch elm disease.

But the change that struck him the most was the magnolia tree that now towered over the front of the house.
Magnolias and pink roses were Sara's favorite flowers, so
instead of a bouquet, he'd given her a rose bush and a
scrawny twig of a tree one Valentine's Day. Her eyes had
filled with tears when she'd read the note: "These will
bloom and grow over the years, just like my love for you."

A lump formed in his throat at the memory. *Man, we
were so damned young,* he thought. *Young and foolish and
green as grass.*

His palms felt damp on the steering wheel, just the way they used to feel when he'd pulled into this driveway as a teenager. Annoyed at himself, he picked up the bottle of wine he'd brought and climbed out of the car. Maybe this was all a big mistake.

No. He squashed his lips together in a rigid line. This was something he needed to do. He'd spent way too much mental energy on Sara since her return to Cypress Grove. At first he'd burned with resentment and bitterness, and his thoughts had primarily centered on avoiding her. But lately, his feelings had mellowed and he found himself thinking about her in a new way.

Funny—he'd been certain that nothing she could say would make a difference in the way he felt, and yet it had.

Part of it had been the way she'd said it. The memory of her standing in his front yard with a bullhorn, so tiny and determined and defiant, ready to go to jail if he refused to talk to her, made him smile. The very fact that she cared enough to make a public fool of herself had touched him.

So had the grief and guilt that he'd seen in her face. It had never occurred to him that he wasn't the only one who had suffered. She had, too.

She'd made him see the whole situation in a different light. All these years, he'd thought it was all her fault. He'd been so blinded by hurt that he'd never considered the possibility that he might have had some role in things.

It had shocked the socks off him when she'd said he emotionally overpowered her. He'd never thought of himself as doing that, had never considered the possibility that he was pushing her into commitments she wasn't ready to make. Was that what he'd really done? It was a hard pill to swallow, but he couldn't discount it.

He strode up to the front door and punched the doorbell. Before he could finish drawing a deep, bracing breath, the door swung open and she was standing in front of him, backlit by a lamp in the entry hall. God, but she looked gorgeous. She was wearing a long dress in a soft purple-gray color that buttoned all the way down the front. It skimmed her curves, hinting at them without really revealing them, casual but classy. Her smile left him feeling as if a camera flash had gone off in his eyes.

"Hello!" She stepped forward and held out her hand. It was odd, shaking her hand—the soft, fine-boned hand he'd held so often as a teenager. The gesture seemed stilted and formal, but a hug or a kiss were beyond him. Just touching her hand made him feel all tangled up inside.

"Come in, come in." She moved back from the door and he stepped into the foyer.

"This is for you," he said, handing her the wine bottle.

"Why, thank you!" She looked at the bottle, then up at him, her face beaming. "This is one of my favorites. It'll go perfectly with dinner."

George felt an easing in his chest. He had spent an inordinate amount of time selecting it, not sure of her tastes, insecure about his own, not wanting her to think he was hopelessly unsophisticated, then irritated at himself that he cared.

A delicious spicy aroma filled the air. He inhaled deeply. "Mm—something smells delicious."

"I hope you still like Italian."

"It's my favorite."

"Great! Let's go open this, shall we?"

"Good idea." He needed a drink in the worst way.

He followed her into the kitchen and leaned against the counter, watching the fabric of her dress swing against her body as she crossed the room and extracted a corkscrew from a drawer. He'd forgotten the graceful, feminine way she moved, forgotten how watching her could mesmerize him.

Good grief, he was mesmerized now. He was standing

there like an oaf when he should be opening the wine.

"Here—I'll do that." He jerked forward and took the corkscrew from her hand, glad of a task to perform.

"Thanks." She checked the contents of a large covered pan on the stove, then turned and watched him peel the foil off the neck of the bottle. "That's quite a step up from the stuff we used to drink," she remarked.

George grinned at the memory. "Boone's Farm was your favorite."

"That's right. We used to think that good wine tasted like cherry-flavored cough syrup."

"There were a couple with real wino names. What were they?"

"Easy Nights and Mellow Days." Her laugh sounded exactly as it had when she was a girl: light and floaty as a helium balloon. She leaned her hip against the counter and fixed him with a smile. "I ought to ask for one of those the next time I'm with a hoity-toity client at the Ritz."

George turned the corkscrew. "Is that one of your regular hangouts?"

"It's where I stay when I'm in Paris and Rome."

It sounded like they lived on different planets. "I've been to Paris and Rome," George said. "Paris, Texas, and Rome, Georgia."

Sara laughed.

"My idea of upscale lodging is the Holiday Inn instead of a Motel Six," he said. "Your life sounds just a tad more glamorous."

She opened a cabinet, stood on tiptoe and pulled down two stemmed glasses. "I guess it sounds that way, but it's like anything else. After you get used to it, it loses its glitter."

"Well, I imagine you're ready to get back to it." He eased out the cork, then set the bottle on the counter.

She lifted her shoulders. "My business partner's ready for

me to get back, but I'm actually enjoying my stay."

"How much longer do you think you'll be here?" He asked the question in an offhand manner, but he cared about her answer more than he wanted to admit.

"It depends on Dad's recovery. Until he's released from the nursing home, certainly. Then I'll need to make arrangements for in-home assistance and for the management or sale of the store." She pulled a plate of antipasto out of the refrigerator. "Maybe two or three more weeks."

"By then you'll be champing at the bit to get out of this boring little town." His voice held a harder edge than he intended.

"I don't think Cypress Grove is boring. I think it's peaceful." She picked up the bottle, filled a glass and handed it to him, then poured another for herself.

Her words surprised him. "You were sure in a hurry to leave after high school."

She leveled him a long look. "I always intended to come back."

"So, why didn't you?"

"Because you'd gotten married." She looked away, as if she were embarrassed. "After that, I-I just couldn't."

Dear God in heaven. He stared at her, trying to determine if she were lying. "You were really planning to come back?"

She nodded.

He felt as if he'd been hit by a freight train. "I . . . I never knew that."

The corners of her mouth lifted, but her eyes were too sad to call her expression a smile. "You would have, if you'd opened any of my letters."

Was it true? Had she really intended to come back?

"I-I was too angry." *And hurt.* He'd been so damned hurt, he'd thought he'd die.

Her eyes grew bright with tears. "Well, I guess I gave you plenty of reason to be."

Dear God. If he'd waited for her, Sara would have come back? A dizzy, nauseating feeling washed through him. He took a long sip of wine, but it did nothing to ease the constriction in his chest.

Was it true? *He* was the reason they hadn't ended up together? All those years . . .

Feelings, twisted and confused, guilty and ashamed, poured through him. It was disloyal to Heather to be thinking this way. He wouldn't allow himself to do it. She'd loved him unconditionally; she'd given him two sons. They'd had a good marriage, a good life.

He took another gulp of wine, his mind racing in circles. He'd married Heather on the rebound, there was no doubt about that. He'd married her to stop the pain. And she'd known it. She'd asked for it.

Hell, she'd begged him for it.

"I know you don't love me like you loved Sara," Heather had said, "but I love you enough for the two of us. I've loved you all my life, but you never looked my way or gave me a chance. You never looked at anyone but Sara. I can make you happy, George. All I'm asking for is a chance."

"Well, that's all in the past." Sara's voice broke into his thoughts.

She refilled his glass, then lifted hers with a tremulous smile. "Here's to letting bygones be bygones."

Yes. That was the only way to look at it. Deal with the here and now. Don't think about what-ifs. The what-ifs would drive him crazy. Besides, just because she'd written it in a letter didn't mean she'd have really come back.

George gently clinked his glass against hers. "To bygones."

They both took a sip of their drinks; then George watched her turn to the stove and lift a lid. He grabbed at a here-and-now topic.

"That smells wonderful. What are you making?"

"Chicken marsala. With Caesar salad, angel hair pasta and garlic bread. And a really, really decadent chocolate dessert."

"Sounds great."

She lifted the antipasto platter. "Come on—bring your glass into the living room. I want to hear about everything you've been up to the last twenty-eight years."

Three hours later, the candles on the dining room table had burned down to stubs, but their conversation was still going strong. They'd talked about college and work and travel. Sara had told him about her business and her friends and her life in Chicago, and he'd told her about his sons and his business and his parents' deaths. She was sad but not surprised to learn that he hadn't opened the condolence cards she'd sent.

He didn't talk much about Heather. When they'd drained the wine bottle and the candles had burned low, Sara coaxed him into telling her about Heather's fight with cancer.

"When we ran out of traditional options, we decided to go to a clinic in Brazil that was trying some new treatments."

"How long were you there?"

"Four months."

"That's a long time."

George nodded. "Seemed like a lifetime. It was our last hope, and so we stayed and prayed for a miracle. When she asked to come home, I knew the end was near." He toyed with the stem of his wineglass. "She passed away the week after we got back."

"Were you with her?"

He nodded. "So were both boys. She'd asked me to call them. She hung on until they got here, and then passed in her sleep."

Sara reached out her hand and covered his. "I'm so sorry."

George drained his glass. "At least she went the way she wanted."

"She was awfully lucky to have you."

He lifted his shoulders and shifted, as if he were uneasy. "I don't know about that. I did my best." He glanced up at her, then looked back down. He paused, then blew out a weighty sigh. "She always felt like she was second choice."

"What?"

"Because of you. She knew how much I'd . . ." He looked away, unable or unwilling to complete the thought. He drew a breath. "Hell, she was at our wedding. She knew the whole story about us."

Sara searched for the right words to say, her heart pounding hard. "Well, I-I'm sure that if she ever felt that way, she was long over it. You and Heather had something special." She swallowed hard, choking back all kinds of inappropriate emotion. What kind of person was she, feeling jealous of a dead woman? "I mean, she was your wife for twenty-something years, and the mother of your children. You and I never had that."

A heartbeat pulsed in silence.

"No. We never did." George's voice was low and flat, untainted by discernible regret. All the same, something in it was poignant.

He tossed back the last of his wine. "So, what about you?" he asked.

"What about me?"

"I've done most of the talking." He grinned. "You're going to ruin my reputation as the strong, silent type."

"I didn't know that you had a reputation as a strong, silent type," she teased.

"I do with everyone but you."

Dangerous currents were building between them. She rose and began to clear the table.

He stood to help her. "You haven't told me anything about your personal life."

She reached over and picked up his empty plate. "There's not a lot to talk about."

"I doubt that. Are you seeing anyone?"

She stacked her plate on top of his. "No one special."

He picked up the water glasses and followed her into the kitchen. "But you have." It was a statement, not a question.

"Not in a long while." She scraped a plate over the garbage disposal.

"Come on, you've got to tell me more than that. I've told you the whole story of my life."

"What do you want to know?"

"Did you ever come close to marrying?"

Only you. She put the plates in the sink. "There were a couple of near misses."

"Tell me about them."

"Oh, it's all ancient history."

"I still want to know."

Sara drew a deep breath and turned on the faucet. The words flowed out like the water. "Well, near-miss number one was an investment banker. I met him at a fund-raiser for a special exhibit at the Field Museum."

"When was this?"

"I was in my late twenties." She picked up a plate and rinsed it. "You'd been married nine years by then, and both of your children were in school."

His eyes locked on hers, and she realized she'd given away more than she'd intended. She rinsed another plate and smiled sheepishly. "My father used to keep me posted on your life and how you were doing." She turned and opened the dishwasher, then placed a plate on the bottom rack. "Anyway, Doug and I dated for about three years."

"Doug, huh?" George rinsed the silverware. "Three years is a long time. Why didn't you marry him?"

Because he wasn't you. "He'd been married before, and he didn't want any more children."

"And you did?"

"More than anything." She wedged another plate into the dishwasher rack. "Ironic, isn't it? We broke up because I wanted children, then I never had any anyway."

"Would you have married him if you'd known how it would turn out?"

"No." She shook her head.

"Why not?"

"It's hard to put into words."

"Try."

She reached for another plate. Her heart felt as if it had floated up to her throat, and it sat there, high and tight. "Well, we got along great, and we had a lot in common, but we just didn't have the kind of deep connection that . . ." *That I had with you.* ". . . that I wanted." She jammed the dish into the dishwasher a little harder than she intended, making it clatter against a salad plate.

George stood rock still, his expression giving away nothing, just watching her with his dark, dark eyes. She wondered how much he saw, how deep his gaze could probe.

"What about Bachelor Number Two?" he asked.

Sara laughed. "Well, he was a client. His name was Clayton, and he was a British earl."

"An earl!"

Sara nodded. "He'd inherited this huge old manor house in England. We met at an antique auction in Scotland, and he hired me to handle the interior design."

"Sounds like a big project."

"It was huge. The largest I've ever undertaken. It was an interior designer's dream. His family had lived there for more than four centuries, and he wanted it to reflect the different eras that they'd lived through. He pretty much gave me carte blanche to do whatever I wanted."

"He must have had lots of money."

Sara grinned. "Buckets full."

"What was he like?"

"Charming. Very charming. Outgoing, friendly, witty, funny."

"Not to mention wealthy."

"Yes." Sara pulled out the top rack of the dishwasher. "But that turned out to be a problem."

"How?"

She placed a glass in the top rack of the dishwasher. "You've heard the expression 'to the manor born'?"

"Yes."

"Well, he really was. He lived a life of leisure. He gave parties and went to parties. He sailed and played tennis and golf and polo. He didn't really work."

"And you found that a problem?"

"Most definitely. He just wanted to have fun and be amused, and after a while—well, it grew tiresome. It was like trying to live on nothing but sweets. After a while, you crave meat and vegetables."

She jammed a handful of silverware into the dishwasher. "I found it hard to respect a man who didn't do an honest day's work. He didn't want me to work, either, and I'm not a person who's happy to sit around and do nothing productive. He was like an overgrown, spoiled little boy." She slid the bottom rack into the dishwasher. "He sure behaved like one when I left."

"What did he do?"

"Well, I'd done all of the work on the place—the design, letting the contracts, selecting the furniture and fabrics and accessories—the whole thing. It took more than a year. All that was left was the actual installation of the drapes and rugs and furnishings. He hired someone else to supervise

that, and then he gave her full credit for the whole project." Just thinking about it still twisted Sara's stomach into
a knot of indignation. "His home was featured in all the
design magazines, and this Johnny-come-lately—or maybe
I should say Janie-come-lately; her name was Jane . . ." She
gave a sardonic smile. ". . . got all kinds of awards and
praise and fabulous offers."

George blew out a low whistle. "Man, that must have
been hard to swallow."

He got it. He understood. A burst of unexpected emotion pulsed through her, making her throat dangerously
tight. Sara nodded. "It really ate at me. For a long time,
every time I picked up a trade publication, there was her
lying, smiling face. She was the hot new designer of the
jet-set crowd."

Sara pulled out the top rack of the dishwasher. "After a
while, though, I realized that she and Clayton had actually
done me a favor, because the truth is, I really prefer doing
more modest projects. I like helping people turn their
houses into homes. If I'd stayed on the fast track, I'd just
be helping multimillionaires try to impress each other."

George's eyes were warm, but something about the way
he was looking at her sent a chill chasing down her spine.
His mouth slid into a slow smile. "You know, you haven't
changed as much as I thought."

She looked away, rattled, and dried her hands on the
dish towel. "I don't quite know how to take that comment."

"Take it as a compliment. That's how it's meant."

She gave a nervous smile. Sexual tension coiled in the
air, so thick she could practically reach out and touch it.

"So who came after this earl?" George asked.

"Nobody, really. He's the last man I dated seriously."

"Why?"

"I don't know." She turned back to the sink and busied

herself wiping down the faucet. When she looked up, George's eyes held a speculative light.

"I don't get it."

"Get what?"

"Why a beautiful woman like you never married."

Beautiful. He still thought she was beautiful? An electric jolt raced along her nerve endings, making them feel raw and exposed. She needed to move, to create some distance, to change the subject.

"I-I'll wrap up the chicken so you can take it with you." She crossed the room, then stood on tiptoe to open the top cabinet.

She felt him behind her. His arm reached up, extracted the box of plastic wrap she was reaching for, then closed the cabinet door.

"Th-thank you." She turned around, but he didn't step back, and he didn't hand her the box of plastic wrap. Instead he set it on the counter behind her, then leaned against it with both hands, trapping her with his arms. He was close—close enough that she could see the individual dark whiskers on his chin, smell the faint scent of his aftershave, feel the warmth of his breath on her face.

"You didn't answer my question," he said.

The counter pressed behind her, and he stood in front of her. His eyes were like searchlights; relentless, bright, impossible to ignore. They scoured her face, leaving her no place to hide. She tried to buy some time. "What question was that?"

"Why didn't you ever marry?"

She couldn't look him straight in the eye and lie. She tried to turn away from his gaze, but it pierced her soul like a phlebotomist's needle, drawing out the truth. "I-I never found another man I cared about the way I cared about you."

By all rights, he should be glad, Sara thought. After all,

she'd left him at the altar. It was only natural he'd get a sense of satisfaction from knowing that it was the biggest mistake of her life, that she'd never found his equal. But there was no gleam of triumph in George's eyes. Instead, they glistened with pain.

"You were the gold standard," she found herself saying, "and no one else ever measured up."

"Sara . . ."

A panicky feeling gripped her. Her heart hammered hard in her chest. This was getting way too intense, way too emotional. She needed to lighten things up. She pulled her mouth into what was meant to be a smile, but her lips quivered so badly she was pretty sure she didn't pull it off. "I guess I finally kissed enough toads to realize none of them were going to turn into a prince."

Oh, dear—she hoped he didn't take that to mean she'd been promiscuous. "Not that there were all that many toads—especially not lately." She made a weak attempt at a laugh. "In fact, it's been so long since I've kissed a man that I doubt I'd even remember how."

His eyes were dark, his voice a gruff rumble. "Let's see." His mouth came down on hers, hard and possessive.

It was like being thrown into a swimming pool with her clothes on. Stunned and shocked, she was suddenly over her head, out of her element and unable to breathe. Surprise immobilized her for a split second, and then instinct took over. Before she knew it, she was curving her arms around him as if he were a life preserver, seeking his mouth like oxygen.

His fingers threaded in her hair, gripping her head, angling her face toward his as if he'd never let her go. "Sara," he murmured as his mouth moved over hers. "Sara."

Her name on his lips. The sound of it opened her soul like a floodgate. Emotion, deep and dark and powerful, rushed out—years of pent-up longing and yearning, bursting out of the airtight compartment where she'd kept them pressure-sealed for twenty-eight years. The force of it made her knees weak.

No other man had ever made her feel the things she felt with George. No other man's mouth had ever heated her blood to such a fever pitch. No other man's arms had ever felt so right. No other man's scent and taste and texture were so deeply ingrained in her memory that they were a part of her.

No other man was George.

He drank her in like parched earth soaking up an unexpected shower. His lips moved greedily over her face, down to her neck, then back to her mouth—claiming, tasting, savoring, devouring. His kisses were hard and punishing, deep and demanding—the kisses of a man too long denied, a man making up for lost time. He kissed her as if it were a life-or-death matter, as if he'd die if he didn't. She kissed him back the same way, reveling in the sweet, brutal force of his mouth. She kissed him as if he were the only man on earth, because for her, he was.

He always had been. And, oh, God help her—he always would be.

She wrapped a leg around his, straining to get closer. He cupped her bottom and lifted her to the counter. It equalized their heights, aligning their bodies so that she could feel the hard length of his arousal against her own aching need.

She wrapped her legs around his hips, threading her feet between his thighs. He groaned and deepened the kiss, his tongue mating with her mouth.

Reaching between them, she unbuttoned his shirt. Crisp masculine hair tickled her palm as she ran her hand over his skin. His chest was firm and hard-muscled, the stomach below it still as taut as a snare drum. He groaned as she moved her fingers up to his flat brown nipples.

His hands slipped to the sides of her breasts. He filled his palms with her soft, aching flesh, then lowered his head and rained kisses down her throat. She reached down and unbuttoned her dress, desperate for his lips to follow his hands.

He needed no urging. He whispered her name, caressing her nipples through the sheer fabric of her bra, then unfastened the front hook. His gaze was hot, his mouth hotter still. She leaned back and closed her eyes as his tongue circled a hard dusky tip. When his mouth closed around it, she moaned with delight. He pleasured one breast and then the other, going back and forth until she thought she would die. She was on fire, burning with desire, aflame with passion. She reached for his belt and began to unfasten it.

He abruptly pulled back, putting his hands over hers, stopping her. His breath came in hot puffs. He leaned his forehead against hers. She could feel his labored breath on her face.

"Sara . . . I-I think I'd better go."

She pulled her hands from his and cradled his face. "No. Don't. Stay here."

He shook his head, his breathing labored. "I can't."

"Why not?"

"I just . . . can't." His voice was rough as gravel. "I can't do this again."

He stepped back, out of her reach, and buttoned his shirt. She slid off the counter, clutching her dress together, her knees weak, her heart aching.

"I better go," he repeated.

She followed him as he strode toward the door. "Can't we talk about this?"

"No." He paused at the door and turned toward her. "Look—I'm sorry. I—I . . ." He abruptly stopped, as if the words wouldn't come or he'd changed his mind about saying them. He blew out a breath, not meeting her eyes. "Thanks for dinner. I better go."

With that, he pushed the door open and walked out into the night, taking her heart with him.

Chapter Nineteen

Rand rounded Celeste's barn to find her bent over a large stack of lumber, tugging on a twelve-foot piece of timber as thick as a railroad tie. "Looks like you could use a little help," he said.

Celeste stiffened at the sound of his voice. She looked up but didn't straighten. "I can manage." She gave the log another tug, barely budging it.

Yeah, she could manage, all right, Rand thought dryly. If she pulled for a couple more hours, maybe she'd move it six inches.

Rand wordlessly strode over to the other end of the log and lifted. "Where do you want it?"

She blew out an exasperated breath, and for a moment he thought she was going to protest. "Over there," she finally said, pointing to a spot several yards away.

Rand dragged it where she indicated. "So, what are you building?"

She folded her arms and looked at him. "Why do you

want to know? So you can tell me how *ridiculous* it is?"

From the sarcastic emphasis she put on the word, he must have used it in a way that ticked her off the last time they were together, but for the life of him, he couldn't remember what he'd said. He was pretty sure it wouldn't improve her mood to ask. "Actually, I was going to offer to help."

"I don't know why you'd want to."

To tell you the truth, neither do I. He shrugged and gave her a grin. "I can't help it. I'm a compulsively nice guy."

She rolled her eyes.

"Okay, okay. I confess: I'm actually an evil sonofabitch who wants to sabotage your every effort."

Her mouth quirked at the edges. "That's more like it."

"I woke up this morning and asked myself, 'How can I make Celeste miserable today?' so I decided to come over and really irritate you. Apparently I'm doing a pretty good job."

She was fighting it, but her mouth no longer had that rigid set. She bent and began hauling a smaller log near the first one.

Rand picked up two more and walked beside her. "This is obviously a top-secret project. Maybe a missile launcher. Only instead of firing scuds, you're planning to shoot goats at my place."

She put down the logs and shook her head. "You're a regular laugh riot."

"You're just saying that to flatter me."

"Actually, I'm saying it to make you shut up and go home."

"Sorry, but the only way to accomplish that is to tell me what you're building."

She blew out a sigh, set down the log and pushed a strand of hair behind her ear. "It's one of those big swing sets with a fort and a slide and a glider, okay?"

"Okay by me." He set down his logs and shoved his hands in his pockets. "Why didn't you return my phone calls?"

He'd called her four times from the horse show, leaving his cell phone number on her answering machine each time. He hadn't known exactly what he'd intended to say; he'd only known that not phoning her would have made him feel like an even bigger jerk than he already did.

She tugged at the bottom of her pink cropped T-shirt. "I've been busy."

"I can tell." Rand looked around. The barn had a new coat of russet paint, and the back of the house had been painted a fresh white. She'd planted flowers and shrubs around the backyard and enclosed it with a picket fence. Six picnic tables sat under the shade of the live oaks near the barn.

The place looked inviting and rustic and charming.

"I figured you were busy, too," she said stiffly. "I didn't want to risk calling at an inopportune moment."

Rand narrowed his eyes. She was insinuating something, but he didn't have a clue what it might be. "What are you trying to say?"

"Oh, nothing."

"Didn't sound like nothing."

She tilted up her chin. "Just that I didn't want to inconvenience you by calling when you were with your girlfriend."

"Where'd that come from? I don't have a girlfriend."

She bent and picked up a board. "That's not what I heard."

Comprehension dawned. "Oh, *that*—that ended last winter." How the hell had she heard about that, anyway? The Cypress Grove grapevine was better at collecting information than the CIA. "I'm not seeing anyone but you."

She stood stock-still, her eyes guarded. "I wasn't aware we were seeing each other."

He wasn't, either, but hell—they'd made love, hadn't they? They'd seen plenty of each other. Just about one hundred percent.

He looked down at the toe of his boot and cleared his throat. "Look . . . about what happened the last time we were together—"

She lifted her hand. "There's no need to talk about it."

"There sure as hell is!"

"I'm not pregnant."

He was unprepared for the blunt declaration. "Oh. Well . . . well, good." He swallowed. "That's good."

So why the hell didn't it feel good? He should feel hugely relieved. He'd been obsessed with the thought that she might be pregnant for the past two weeks.

He'd thought about it from every possible angle, and he'd reached a decision. If she were pregnant, he'd insist on marrying her. He wouldn't take no for an answer. They didn't have to stay married long, but marriage would give the child Rand's name and make joint custody easier. If he had a child, Rand was going to be a part of its life. He had no idea how to be a good father, but at least he knew what to avoid.

But she wasn't pregnant. There would be no child. The point was moot.

"So . . . you're sure?"

"One hundred percent."

He nodded, feeling oddly deflated. Which was absurd. He'd just dodged a bullet. He should be thanking his lucky stars.

This was probably the same way a soldier felt when he was ready to go into battle, only to have the war end before he got his marching orders. Rand had spent so much time thinking about the situation, analyzing the best way to handle it, then imagining life with Celeste and a baby that he actually felt something akin to disappointment.

Akin to. Not actual. He wasn't really disappointed, he told himself.

Was he?

He raked a hand through his hair, not quite sure where to take things from here. An apology was probably in order. "Look . . . I'm sorry about the way we left things."

She picked up another piece of wood. "Like you said, it was a mistake. We both got carried away. Let's just put it behind us and forget about it."

Oh, like *that* was going to happen. No way was he going to forget a single minute of that afternoon. He needed a cold shower every time he thought about it. Hell, he needed one right now, watching her bend over in those cutoff shorts.

She picked up a small piece of timber and straightened. "If you don't mind, I've got a lot of work to do here."

"I can see that." He grabbed a couple of boards and followed her. "Are you planning to put this thing together yourself?"

"I was going to, but it looks like I'll have to hire someone."

"Be sure it's not Larry Birkman."

She shot him an annoyed glance. "Give me credit for having *some* sense." She stalked toward the swing set site. "Believe it or not, I'm not stupid."

"I never thought you were."

His answer again seemed to disarm her. She hesitated a second before turning back to the pile of timber. "Surely there's someone else around here who does odd jobs. Do you have any suggestions?"

Rand walked along beside her. "Yeah. Me. I'll come over Saturday and do it for you."

She shook her head stiffly. "No, thanks."

"Why not?"

She avoided his eyes. "I just don't think it's a good idea."

"Why not?" he repeated.

She lifted her shoulders. "I don't want to feel beholden to you."

"You wouldn't be." He followed her back to the stack of wood. "Look, if it'll make you more comfortable, we can work out some kind of exchange."

She shot him a wary look. "What have you got in mind?"

"I'll put together your swing set, and you can fix me a home-cooked meal."

"That's not much of a deal."

"Sure it is. Do you have any idea how sick I get of frozen dinners, the Cajun Cafe and my own cooking?"

She gazed at him uncertainly. He could tell she was wavering.

He needed to close the deal before she had a chance to refuse. "I'll see you Saturday morning. If we work hard, we should have this thing put together by dinnertime."

He turned and strode rapidly away, whistling loudly so that he could claim he hadn't heard her if she tried to tell him no.

Saturday dawned clear and hot. Rand showed up early, before the sun burned the dew off the grass, and set right to work. Celeste worked beside him, holding boards and beams as he drilled and nailed and bolted the frame together. They shared a friendly, joking camaraderie, but beneath the surface, sexual tension bubbled like lava inside a volcano.

As the sun climbed higher in the sky, Rand pulled off his shirt. Maybe working shirtless helped *him* feel cooler, Celeste thought, but it sure did nothing to help *her* body temperature. It was a struggle to keep her eyes averted, especially as they shared a quick sandwich lunch. It didn't help that she kept catching Rand surreptitiously watching her, as well. As the afternoon wore on, she took on the solo task of assembling the metal glider as he nailed the fort together, thinking it might keep her gaze from drifting in Rand's direction.

It was a little after four when she gave the bolt under the glider seat a final twist. "There. The glider's ready."

Rand looked up. "You made fast work of that."

"It was pretty simple." She put the wrench in Rand's tool set and straightened. "When you get a chance, would you help me hang it from the crossbeam?"

"Sure." He ducked out from under the fort and strode over to her. "Where'd you learn to use tools so well?"

"From my dad. I used to help him do chores and odd jobs around the house when I was a kid." Celeste grinned. "I always preferred that to helping with housework. Mom used to fret that I was too boyish."

"I'd say she had nothing to worry about." Rand's gaze warmed her skin.

Celeste tried to focus her attention on the swing set instead of the way her heart was knocking against her ribs. She took an end of the glider and helped steady it as he lifted it.

"Your dad was around a lot when you were growing up, huh?"

Celeste thought she heard a hint of wistfulness in the question. Her throat tightened. "Yeah. We did a lot together."

He squinted against the sun as he tilted the glider, aligning it on the heavy metal eye he'd bolted into the beam earlier. "Did you grow up in a house with a yard and everything?"

It was all so unfair. She'd had so much, while Rand had had so little. "Yeah," she said.

He inserted the bolt into the top of the glider. "Did you have a playset like this?"

"I had a swing set, but it wasn't this fancy. It was one of the old metal ones."

Rand slid the nut onto the bolt. "One of the foster homes I was in had one like that for the younger kids."

"How many foster homes were you in?" she asked.

"Three, altogether."

"What were they like?"

"The first one was a joke. The foster parents were trying to make a living off the system, and they basically laid around and smoked pot all day." He tightened the nut with his fingers.

"What about the next one?" she asked.

"It was a war zone. The fosters argued all the time. One night the man started smacking his wife around, and I decked him." Rand reached into his back pocket and pulled out a wrench. "I should have known better."

"Why? What happened?"

"The woman complained to my social worker that I'd attacked her husband."

"You're kidding."

"Nope." Rand fitted the wrench around the bolt.

"What was the next home like?"

He turned the wrench. "The people meant well, but they drove me crazy. They were always hovering over me and trying to get me to talk, urging me to open up. It was annoying as hell. The harder they tried, the quieter I got, and by the end of the first week, I wasn't speaking to them at all." He gave a wry smile. "My social worker finally recommended I'd be better off in a group setting, so I stayed in a youth facility until I turned eighteen."

Celeste watched the way Rand's biceps mounded as he gave a final hard tug on the wrench. Everything about him

was so strong, so tough, so manly—and yet inside, part of
him was still a wounded little boy trying to avoid further
injury. If he kept his distance, no one could get close
enough to hurt him. If he stifled his emotions, he wouldn't
feel pain. If he didn't get attached, he couldn't be abandoned.

But he was deluding himself. Try as he might to deny
it, he wanted to belong; he cared about people, and his
actions weren't always based on logic.

After all, he was here helping her, wasn't he?

The thought sent a surge of hope pulsing through her
veins. "What was the group place like?"

"Kind of a cross between a dorm and a prison. I hated
not having any privacy, but at least I didn't have to deal
with any weird family dynamics." He shoved the wrench
in the back pocket of his jeans. "I told myself that one day
I'd have my own place—a real house surrounded by lots
of land."

"And now you've got it." Celeste pushed a strand of hair
out of her eyes.

He nodded. "The minute I saw the place, I knew I
wanted it."

"How did you know?"

He gave the glider a push, testing it, then climbed back
under the fort to tighten the second lug nut beneath the
slide. "It had plenty of pastureland and a stable, and there
was adjacent land that I thought I could acquire when I
was ready to expand."

That would be her place, she realized.

"But the home was the thing that clinched it," he said.

A picture of Rand's house floated into her mind. It was
a white two-story house, with a long, deep porch and dark
green shutters—unpretentious and welcoming. "It's a nice
place," she remarked.

Rand fitted his wrench around the nut. "Yeah. It looks just like the house in a book I had as a kid. When we were living out of the car, I used to pretend that Mom and I lived in it, and that we were just out for the day. So when I saw the place, well, it just seemed right."

A lump formed in Celeste's throat. His eyes locked with hers; then he abruptly looked away, as if he were embarrassed at having disclosed so much.

Tenderness, dangerous and sweet, swelled in her chest. Despite all his denials, Rand felt things. Deeply. And heaven help her, Celeste had deep feelings too.

Deep feelings for him.

He ducked out from under the slide, circled around the back of the fort, then hoisted himself up the ladder. He stomped on the fort's floor, pushed on the railings and tugged on the slide. "Seems good and solid."

"It looks wonderful." Celeste climbed the wooden ladder and joined him in the small enclosed area.

He pulled on a board, testing its strength. Satisfied, he turned to her. "Well, looks like we're done."

"Not quite." Celeste grinned at him. "There's still one thing left to do."

Rand wiped his forehead with his forearm. "What's that?"

"We've got to give it a test run." She started for the slide. "Last one down the slide is a monkey's uncle!"

"Oh, no." He caught her around the waist, his teeth gleaming in a sexy smile. "I refuse to claim any relation to that spitting little primate of yours."

The feel of his arm around her set her nerves ashiver. The attraction she'd been fighting all day dealt a knockout punch, making it hard to remember why she needed to keep her distance. "Well, then, I guess we'll just have to do the test run together."

"I already know you don't play fair, so I'm not taking

any chances." He picked her up, swung her behind him and set her down. By the time she turned back around, he was already seated at the top of the slide.

"Who's not playing fair now?" she asked.

"It's the only way I can make sure you don't try to jump the gun. Come on." He patted his lap.

She knew it was unwise, but she climbed into his lap anyway. His arms curved around her, pulling her against his bare chest. The intimacy of the contact sent a shock wave rippling through her.

She had the fleeting thought that she'd just stepped in over her head.

And then she felt a soft kiss on the side of her neck. Her blood roared in her ears. His hands slowly moved up from her waist, touching each of her ribs, until they rested under her breasts.

A soft moan escaped her lips. She twisted around to face him, and the next thing she knew, he'd pulled her back away from the slide and stretched her out on the floor of the fort.

He tugged at her lower lip with his teeth, then teased her mouth with his tongue. Her blood pounded as his lips moved to her temple, to her ear, to the pulsing vein in her neck. His mouth was both hard and gentle, demanding and giving.

She could no more have stopped herself from kissing him back than she could have stopped a freight train. Desire, hot and aching, pooled low in her belly.

He pulled off her black T-shirt and tossed it aside, then reached up and unhooked the front hook of her bra. "God, you're so beautiful," he murmured, pulling it off her. He cupped her breasts, one in each hand, and teased the tips with his thumb. When he finally lowered his head to suckle a hardened peak, the hot, sweet pressure sent a surge of heat straight to the core of her being. His mouth moved lower, grazing across her belly. He unsnapped the waist of her shorts, his breath blazing a hot, erotic path down to the top of her panties. And then . . .

She abruptly felt another blast of air, this one hot and fetid, straight in her face. Jolted, she opened her eyes to see Dr. Freud standing over her, her black lace bra dangling from his bearded mouth.

"Give me that!" she gasped, reaching for her bra.

"Whatever you want, baby," Rand murmured. "However you want it."

"Give it to me, Dr. Freud!"

Rand's brain was so fogged by lust that he didn't quite grasp what she was saying. Was she wanting to play doctor?

If she wanted to act out a fantasy, he was willing to go along—although making love to Celeste was more than enough fantasy for him.

"So, are you the doctor or the patient?" he mumbled, trailing a kiss across her belly.

"What?"

"What's the scenario?"

She tugged at his head. "The *scenario* is that the goat has my bra!"

Rand looked up and found himself staring straight into the hairy face of a goat.

Sure enough, a black lace bra was dangling from the animal's mouth. Rand made a wild snatch at the garment and latched hold of an elastic strap. The goat wheeled around and started down the slide, stretching the bra as he went. Rand held tight as the beast's hooves slid on the slippery plastic.

"Baaaaaa!"

The bra snapped back like a sling shot, hitting Rand squarely in the face.

"Ow!" His right eye felt as if it had been stung by a bumblebee.

"Oh, no!" Celeste jumped up. "Oh, dear! Are you okay?"

Rand held his hand against his eye. "I-I don't know."

Celeste peered into his face. "It looks like you're bleeding. Move your hand and let me see."

He cautiously did as she asked.

She touched his forehead, her fingers gentle. "It's not a deep cut—just a couple of small nicks right below your eyebrow," she said. "It looks like the bra hooks did it." Her brows drew together in worry. "Your whole eye looks kind of red and swollen, though. Can you see?"

He could see well enough to know that Celeste was hovering over him topless. It was quite a health-restoring sight. "Y-yes."

"Stay here and I'll go get some ice." To his dismay, she grabbed her T-shirt and pulled it on, then hurried down the slide.

She returned a few moments later, carrying a plastic bag filled with ice and a metal first-aid kit. Kneeling beside him, she unfastened the metal box, pulled out some cotton and moistened it with hydrogen peroxide. "This might sting a little."

He winced as she dabbed at the wound. Her touch was soft, her eyes full of concern. A warm, tender, unfamiliar sensation spread through his chest—a sensation of being cared for, looked after, cared about.

"There." She handed him the bag of ice. "You'd better put this on it. It looks like you're going to have a black eye."

"Oh, good," he said dryly, placing the ice against his eye. "I can't wait to explain how I got it."

She grinned. "You better not tell the truth or I'll come blacken your other eye."

"In the same way? It would almost be worth it." His good

eye moved to her braless breasts pressing against the dark cotton of her T-shirt. A fresh surge of arousal burned through him. "Let's just forget about the eye and pick up where we left off."

She shot him a teasing smile as she screwed the top back on the hydrogen peroxide bottle. "Aren't you worried you'll be attacked by more of my undergarments?"

He grinned back. "It's a risk I'm willing to take."

She hesitated. Her expression grew somber. "Well, I'm not." Her voice was soft, but all trace of playfulness was gone. "We're just too different, Rand. We want different things from a relationship."

"We seemed to be on the same page a few minutes ago."

She gave a sheepish grin. "We weren't thinking. We got carried away."

"Let's get carried away again."

She tucked the supplies back in the first-aid kit and snapped it closed. "I don't think it's a good idea for us to get involved."

"Celeste, we're already involved."

"Well, then, I want to take a step back." She brushed a strand of hair from her face.

He blew out a long sigh, but he didn't try to change her mind. He wouldn't make promises he didn't intend to keep, wouldn't mislead her, wouldn't tell her lies. "Okay. It's your call. The next move is up to you." He pushed himself to his feet. "Well, I guess I'd better get going."

"But I was going to cook you dinner."

He curled his lip in a wry grin. "I don't think an intimate dinner is going to help me adjust to a platonic mindset."

She nodded. Her eyes never quite met his. "I'm sorry."

"Me, too." Blowing out a rueful sigh, he climbed down the ladder and picked his toolbox up off the grass, then looked around. "Have you seen my shirt?" he asked. "I thought I left it right here."

From her vantage point in the fort, Celeste turned to survey the other side of the field. "Uh-oh."

Rand turned and looked where she pointed. Two goats stood by the fence, strips of white fabric dangling from their chomping mouths. A small white rag lay in the dirt between them.

"That's my shirt?"

"I'm afraid so."

Rand ran his hand down his face. Every time he got around Celeste, he ended up aroused, rejected and confused, not to mention spit upon or battered. Why should it surprise him that he'd end up losing the shirt off his back?

Celeste climbed down the ladder. "I'm so sorry."

Rand lifted his shoulders. "Don't worry about it—it wasn't worth anything. I just hope it doesn't make them sick."

Her brows pulled over concerned eyes. "Do you think it might?"

"Well, I've been told I have pretty bad taste in clothing."

Her frown dissolved into laughter. "They seem to like your taste just fine."

And I like yours. The memory of her sweet salty mouth made his eye lock on her lips.

"Maybe you shouldn't drive with that eye swollen shut," she said. "Do you want me to give you a ride home?"

"Nah. I can see just fine."

"You ought to keep some ice on it to keep down the swelling," Celeste said.

His gaze fell to her braless breasts. "I'll do that." He turned and headed for his truck, thinking that if he didn't get out of there soon, he was going to need to put ice on more painful swelling elsewhere.

Chapter Twenty

"Sara—I finally caught you! Don't you return your calls anymore?"

"Hi, Christine." Sara shifted the phone to her other ear at the sound of her partner's voice, feeling more than a little guilty that she hadn't called Chicago in nearly a week. She could just picture Christine in her red lacquered office, her dark swingy hair tucked behind her ear, wearing something ultrachic, accessorized with the oversized jewelry she favored. Sara looked down at her own clothes and grinned. Christine would faint if she could see Sara sticking price tags on bags of manure, dressed in jeans and sneakers she'd bought at the Covington Wal-Mart last Sunday.

"Sorry." Sara held the phone with her chin and stuck another tag on a bag. "The battery went dead in my cell phone and I kept forgetting to recharge it."

"Wow, you've really gone native."

Sara grinned. "I guess I have."

"How's your father?" Christine asked.

"A lot better. The doctor says he can come home later this week."

"That's terrific!"

"Yes." It *was* terrific news. His improvement since Daisy had entered his life was nothing short of astounding. "He's decided not to come home, though. He says he wants to sell his house and the store and move into an apartment in the assisted living center."

"Oh, Sara, that's even better! Then you won't have to worry about him living alone."

"Right."

"So what's the matter? You don't sound happy."

Good question. Sara wished she had an answer to it. "I guess it's because he's decided to change his life so radically, so fast. Did I tell you that Dad's fallen head-over-heels for a woman about his age?"

"Get out!"

"I'm serious."

"Don't you like her?"

"Actually, I do. I think she's very good for him. It's just . . ." Sara sighed, at a loss to understand her feelings, much less express them. "It's just so odd. It's hard to accept that he's fallen in love again at his age."

"I think it's wonderful. We should all be so lucky."

"You're right." *Maybe at eighty I'll finally find a partner*, Sara thought glumly.

"Well, this is fabulous news! He's doing well and he's where he'll be cared for. That means you'll be able to come back soon, right?"

"Oh, Christine, I just don't know." Sara switched the phone to her other ear. "It's not going to be easy, selling the business. And everything in the house will need to be packed up and sold. . . ."

"You can hire people to do that."

"I know. But Dad won't want strangers going through all his possessions."

"Well, it wouldn't all have to be done right away, would it? You could come back, go to Milan, then return to Louisiana later."

"I suppose. It's just . . ."

"Just what?"

How could Sara explain something to Christine that she couldn't even explain to herself? "I really don't want to leave until I get things settled."

She was greeted with a long silence. "How long do you think you'll be?"

Sara drew a deep breath. She wasn't being fair. Christine had been an angel to handle the shop all by herself all this time. Sara needed to set a firm date. "Give me two more weeks. That ought to give me a chance to get the store inventoried, and the house listed and in shape to show."

"Okay. Good." Relief resonated over the phone. "That's the week after Labor Day. So you're on for Milan?"

There was no reason she couldn't go. Her father was doing well, and he'd be settled in his new apartment by then. And yet she felt an odd reluctance. The world of interior design seemed so distant, so remote, so removed from the things that mattered here. Decorating elaborate homes in outrageously expensive fabrics and furnishings suddenly seemed stupendously silly.

Well, silly or not, it was her job. She handled the store's buying, and Christine handled the operations. "Sure. I'll be set to go."

Again, there was a long silence on the phone. "Sara, are you all right? You sound awfully reluctant."

"I'm fine. I'm just tired. And the thought of going to Milan seems pretty alien while I'm sitting in a seed-and-feed store in rural Louisiana."

Christine's laughter tinkled over the line. "I can imagine.

Just don't sprout roots and settle down with some Cajun cowboy, okay, girl?"

"Of course not." Sara wondered if Christine noticed how hollow her voice sounded. She'd been unable to get George off her mind since he'd left her house so abruptly two weeks earlier. The thought of leaving town without seeing him again made her stomach feel as if she'd swallowed a box of rocks.

"All the customers are asking about you. No one can believe you're down in Louisiana selling oats and corn to farmers."

For some reason, the remark rankled. "It cuts both ways, Christine. No one down here can believe women in Chicago pay two thousand dollars for a custom-made bedspread."

"It's two different worlds, isn't it?"

"Most definitely."

"Well, in two weeks you'll be back where you belong."

Would she? Sara wondered as she hung up the phone. She was no longer sure where she belonged, or if she really belonged anywhere at all.

George guided the mare in a tight circle, then urged it into a gallop. He waited until the animal gained maximum speed, then gave a sharp tug on the reins. Right on cue, the mare locked her back legs, skidding to a stop. A rooster tail of dust danced in the air behind her.

The two stable hands watching from outside the corral broke out in applause and whistles. Rand let out a loud whoop.

A sense of satisfaction expanded in George's chest. "Good girl, Sunshine," he murmured to the mare, loosening the reins and patting the horse's neck. The mare snorted and flicked her tail.

Rand climbed between the railings and headed toward

them, reaching up to shake George's hand. "Great job. That was amazing."

George nodded his thanks. "She's a terrific horse."

Rand rubbed the mare's nose. "I think we've got our next NRHA futurity winner."

George nodded. The National Reining Horse Association's annual futurity for three-year-old horses had an annual purse of six figures. "I think so, too."

"Too bad we have to wait a year before she's eligible."

"She'll just get better with practice. And in the meantime, she'll clean up in this year's two-year-old competitions."

The cell phone on George's belt buzzed. No one but the fire department had the number. He swung down from the saddle and put the phone to his ear, adrenaline starting to pump through his veins. "Yeah?"

The voice of the dispatcher sounded tight and stressed. "There's been an explosion in town. Both trucks are rolling."

"Where?"

"The feed store."

Sara. The image of her face flashed through his mind. Icy tentacles of fear gripped his gut. "Anyone inside?"

"I don't know. That's all I've got."

"Get the whole squad on this," George ordered tersely. "Alert the Folsom department, too. I'm on my way."

With a muttered explanation to Rand, George handed over the reins and ran to his pickup.

"I'll meet you there," Rand called after him.

George sped down the long, curved drive to the road and turned the truck toward town. Over the tops of the towering pines, black smoke huffed into the sky, forming a dark, ominous pillar. George's foot smashed down on the accelerator as he raced toward it, resenting the right angles of the roads, wishing he could just cut through the fields and forest and pastures to the store. His pulse drummed in his veins.

Fertilizer, grain dust and a building so old it would burn like matchsticks—hell, the feed store was a firefighter's nightmare. The window of opportunity to rescue anyone trapped inside would be damned small and closing fast, if it hadn't slammed shut already.

Sara. The thought of her trapped in the store sent a sickening bolt of terror charging through him. *Please, God—no. Not Sara.*

George's car screeched to a halt half a block away. The fire trucks were already there, brought from the station by on-duty drivers. The hoses were connected and pumping, manned by a half-dozen firefighters who'd been closest to the scene.

George climbed out of his pickup, grabbed his fire gear from the backseat and pulled it on. The rancid scent of burning plastic and chemicals stung his eyes as he raced toward the number-one truck, where the on-duty deputy chief, Andy Collins, stood talking on his walkie talkie.

"Anyone inside?" George demanded.

"God, I hope not. It's after closing time. But it's too hot to go in and see."

"Sara always parks on the street around back. Is there a white Explorer behind the store?"

"I don't think anyone's checked."

George took off around the corner. An old red Camaro, a blue Toyota, a silver Dodge . . .

Oh, thank God—no Explorer. Relief swept through him, turning his knees to pudding. His eyes watered and his throat thickened as he sent a grateful prayer skyward.

"Ain't this somethin'?" said a voice beside him. He turned to see Steve Whitton, the balding, burly owner of the café across the street. George swallowed hard and nodded, grateful the smoke gave cover to the moisture in his eyes.

"Happened out of the blue. I heard a big *boom*"—Steve threw out his arms—"and ran to my window. Saw smoke pourin' out of the back of the store, so I grabbed the phone and called it in."

"The store was already closed?"

"Yeah. Sara came in and got a Coke to go about twenty minutes before the noise. She said she was goin' out to Forest Manor."

Thank you, God.

Steve's brow furrowed like a freshly plowed field. "Think it's gonna spread? Is my place in danger?"

"We'll try to contain it. But the store's full of fertilizer and insecticide and all kinds of chemicals, and if there's another explosion . . ." George's voice trailed off, hovering in the air like the unspoken possibilities.

Steve's mouth twisted. "Anything I can do to help?"

"Yeah." George jerked his thumb at the vehicles parked by the curb. "Find the owners of these cars and get them moved."

George rapidly strode to the front of the building, relief singing in his veins. *She's safe.* The words repeated in his mind like a mantra, buoying his spirits, floating upward like a prayer. *She's safe, she's safe, she's safe. Thank you, God. Thank you.*

He knew his elation was all out of proportion to their relationship. He knew it and it baffled him, even as it danced through him. Until a few weeks ago, he hadn't seen her in twenty-eight years, for pity's sake—and yet here he was, as relieved as if she were a close family member.

As if she were someone he loved.

The thought made him stop in midstride.

No. She was someone he used to love. *Used* to. Past tense. Over and done with. Over and out.

She was leaving again in just a few weeks, and for all he knew, it would be twenty-eight more years before he saw her again.

He was over her. He *was*.

Wasn't he?

"Hell," he muttered through gritted teeth, breaking into a jog. He'd sort it all out later. Right now he had a fire to fight.

"Oh, my God!" Sara slammed on her brakes and stared at the smoking wreckage that had once been her father's store, her hand over her mouth. "Dear God in heaven!"

It was gone—all gone. No roof, no windows, no doors. A remnant of the clapboard front, all singed and jagged, stood like a sentinel over fallen soldiers. All that remained intact were the two brick side walls. Between them lay a rancid, smoldering heap of unrecognizable debris that yellow-hatted firefighters were flooding with water. The roof, the counter, the shelves, the merchandise—even the old cash register with the sticking key—all of it was now a sodden, smoking, scorched heap of rubbish.

It had happened so fast! She'd rushed down here as soon as she'd learned about the fire. She'd been helping her father move into his new apartment in the assisted living wing when an aide had called her to the phone. It had been the dispatcher with the fire department, telling her that the store was ablaze. She'd braced herself as she'd raced down here, expecting to see some damage. But she'd never expected *this*.

Rain hit her face, startling her. Sara hadn't even realized she'd climbed out of her car, much less that the sky had clouded over. She slammed the door of the Explorer and walked toward the gaping hole that used to be her father's store, not caring that she was getting soaked.

It was hard to believe, even as she stood staring at the

evidence. It was gone, ruined beyond recognition. The place where she'd grown up playing hide-and-seek, the store where her mother had first met her father, the source of her father's livelihood for more than half a century—gone, up in smoke.

One of the firefighters headed toward her, his yellow hat low on his forehead, his face smudged with soot. She couldn't make out his features, but her heart recognized him immediately.

"George!" She ran toward him, throwing herself against his chest. His arms closed around her and she held on tight, her hands clutching his slick, wet jacket. He smelled of smoke and charred plastic, but she didn't care. She clung to him, and the tears began. Big, sobbing, enormous tears, tears that seemed to come from the far side of her soul—tears for all that was lost, all that was ruined, all that would never be again.

"Hey, now," he murmured. "It'll be okay. No one was hurt. It will all be okay."

She held on to him, not wanting to turn him loose, not wanting to ever let him go. At length he pulled back, holding her by her forearms. "Sara, honey—the fire marshal is on his way. He'll need to ask you and your dad some questions."

"Questions?" The rain was pouring down now, hard and fast and furious, as if heaven had turned on a celestial fire hose. It pounded down on her head, running off the ends of her hair onto her neck, plastering her red tank top against her body, making her jeans and sneakers feel as if they weighed a hundred tons. "Why?"

"It's just routine," George said. "They always conduct an investigation when a business burns."

Despite the warm weather, a chill ripped through her. George must have felt her shiver, because he put an arm around her and pulled her close against his side.

"Oh, George—they don't think Dad or I had anything to do with this, do they?"

"It's just routine," he repeated. "But the fire marshal will need to ask some questions."

"I hope he doesn't upset Dad any more than he already is."

"How'd he take the news?"

"He was shocked. He kept wanting to know what part of the building was on fire. I don't think he really grasped the extent of it. Heaven knows I didn't." Fresh tears joined the rain streaming down her face. "Oh, mercy—I hate to tell him."

"He'll handle it better than you think." George's eyes held a reassuring certainty. "He's been through worse, Sara."

George was right. Her mother's death had been far worse. Sara had been only a child when her mother had passed away, but she could still remember the grief on her father's face, so black and bottomless that it had felt like her father had died, too.

And a part of him had. He'd done his best to be a good parent, but a light had been extinguished inside him. He never talked about grief or loneliness, but they'd taken over his soul. Five years later, Sara had been stripping the bed linens off his bed for the weekly wash and had discovered that he still slept with her mother's nightgown under his pillow.

She looked at George, the rain pouring off the brim of his hat, and wondered if he'd grieved Heather like that, wondered if he still did. The thought sent a spike of pain through her heart.

"This is a disaster, but it's not a tragedy," George was saying. "Your dad will be fine. He's stronger than you think."

Sara nodded, her throat thick.

"Why don't I have the fire marshal meet you at Forest Manor in a couple of hours? That way you'll have time to go home and dry off, and he can talk to both you and your father in one visit."

"Will you come, too?"

"Sure, if you'd like."

"I'd feel better if you did."

"I'll be there, then." His arm tightened around her, and he led her back to her SUV. "You need to get out of the rain."

He opened the door to the Explorer for her. She turned to him. "Thank you for being here."

"I'm a firefighter. Where else would I be?"

"I didn't mean in your official capacity."

For a fraction of a second, she thought she saw something in his eyes, something steadfast and enduring, something her heart remembered.

He looked away and took a step back. "You'd better go get dry before you catch pneumonia. I'll see you in a couple of hours."

The inspector closed the cover of his notebook and rose to his feet. "Those are all the questions for now, Mr. Overton. I appreciate your time."

Sara saw her father struggle to stand, and she jumped up from the sofa to help him. Daisy beat her to it, placing the walker in front of his chair.

"Oh, no need to get up," the inspector said.

Sara's father grabbed the walker and pulled himself to his feet anyway. "I want to thank you for all you're doing." Gripping the walker with one hand, he held out his other to the inspector. They shook hands.

Mr. Overton turned to George. "I want to thank you, too."

George crossed the room and shook the old man's hand

as well. "I wish we could have saved more of your store."

"I know you did all you could."

George turned to the fire marshal. "I'll walk you out."

He returned a moment later, a relaxed smile on his face. "He said it looks like an electrical fire," George reported. "Apparently, a wire shorted out in the storeroom. You should have no trouble with your insurance claim."

"Thank goodness," Sara said.

They talked a few minutes more; then Daisy glanced at her wristwatch. "It's time to take your blood pressure medicine," she reminded Sara's father.

"Oh, that's right. Thank you, dear." A lump formed in Sara's throat at the tender way her father smiled at the elderly woman. The affection between the two filled the room with a rosy glow.

"I'll bring it to you." Daisy started to rise, but Jack caught her hand. "Don't go," he said to her. "I want to tell them."

"Oh, Jack—it's been an awful day. Maybe we should tell them later."

Sara's father shook his head. "I don't want to do any more waiting."

Sara gazed at Daisy. She'd never seen a woman over the age of seventy blush before, but she could swear Daisy was blushing now.

"Wait to tell us what?" Sara asked.

Sara's father and Daisy looked at each other, their faces spreading into enormous grins. "Daisy has consented to be my wife," he said. "We're getting married."

"Married!" Sara gasped. "But . . . but . . . You've barely known each other a month!"

"I've known Daisy long enough to know that I love her." Sara's father gazed at the elderly woman with adoration. "And at our ages, we don't have any time to waste."

Sara stared at her father, a jumble of emotions tumbling around inside her.

He glanced at George, then looked her straight in the eye. "I've lived long enough to know that love doesn't come around very often. When it does, you need to grab it by both horns, wrestle it to the ground and hog-tie it before it gets away."

The truth of his words hit her smack between the eyes, so hard she blinked. He was right. Oh, dear God—he was right.

She was glad that George was smiling at Daisy, because she didn't have the wherewithal to face him.

"Sounds like you're in for some rough treatment," George teased.

The elderly woman threw back her head and laughed. George reached out and embraced her, then shook Jack's hand. "Congratulations. I'm very happy for both of you."

George looked at Sara and nodded his head toward her father, prompting her to say something. With a start, she realized everyone was waiting for her reaction. "I-I'm speechless. This is so sudden!"

Lines of tension creased around her father's eyes. He exchanged a worried look with Daisy.

"But it's wonderful," she added quickly, giving them a heartfelt smile. "Absolutely wonderful." Crossing the room, she engulfed her father in a big hug, then turned and embraced Daisy.

"What are your plans?" Sara asked after everyone was reseated.

"Well, we thought we'd get married next month," her father replied.

"Next *month?*"

Jack grinned. "I hate to wait that long, but I want to be able to walk my bride down the aisle after the ceremony. The therapist thinks I'll be walking with a cane by then."

Sara turned to Daisy. "Can you get a wedding together that fast? Where do you plan to have it?"

"Right here—in the music room of the new wing. And then we thought we'd go on a cruise for our honeymoon. We haven't decided where yet."

"Wow!" Sara looked from one to the other, amazed at the extent of their plans. "How long have you two been planning this?"

"A couple of days. We told Daisy's son last night. He was going to a veterinary conference and we wanted to tell him before he left."

"What was his reaction?"

"About the same as yours," Daisy said with a smile.

"I thought he was going to call me out for a few moments there," Jack said with a laugh. "He was worried I'd be a burden to Daisy." He gazed at her fondly. "I was worried about that, too, so I put off asking her until I talked to my doctor. He said it looks like I'm going to make a full recovery."

Sara's eyes grew dangerously moist. "Oh, Dad—I'm so happy for you. Congratulations!"

"Thank you, honey."

"We need to know your plans, Sara, so we can set the date," Daisy chimed in. "We know you've got a trip to Milan planned in three weeks, but we don't know how long you'll be there or what your schedule will be when you return to Chicago."

George's gaze turned to Sara. He'd known she'd be leaving, of course, but he hadn't known when. And he sure hadn't known how it would affect him. She was going to Milan—in three weeks? George felt as if the floor had just been kicked out from under him.

"Maybe we should get married before she leaves Cypress Grove," Mr. Overton said to Daisy. "That way she won't have to turn around and come right back."

"Now, Jack—I'm sure she'll want to go to Chicago before she goes to Italy, and we don't want to tie her down," Daisy said. "Now that the store's gone and you're moving into the assisted living center, she'll probably want to head back to Chicago next week."

Next week? The floor seemed to drop a few more feet.

"I-I haven't given it any thought," Sara said, her voice faint.

"Of course you haven't, dear. I'm sure you're still in shock from the fire. I was just pointing out to Jack that there's no way we can plan a wedding before you leave."

"Hmph. If we were to get hitched tomorrow, that wouldn't be too soon for me," Jack stated.

Sara was leaving. Soon. The room suddenly seemed close and stifling.

"I-I've got to go," George said abruptly. He rose to his feet and turned to Jack and Daisy. "Congratulations on your engagement." He edged for the door, needing to get outside, out where he could breathe.

Sara stood as well. "I need to get going, too."

Oh, God—it would be rude not to wait for her. He was trapped. He stood by the door as she quickly hugged her father and Daisy again, then walked beside her into the hall.

"It's been quite a day," she said as they headed toward the exit.

"No kidding." He held the door for her. The rain had stopped, leaving the air clean-scented and almost cool. A soft breeze scuttled the clouds across a nearly full moon.

He drew a deep breath. "So you're heading back north soon, I take it."

"I guess so." She ran a hand through her hair. "I haven't had a chance to really think about it."

"Well, if you've got an overseas trip planned, I'd say you've given it some thought." His voice sounded gruffer than he'd intended.

"It's an annual buying trip." Sara leaned against her SUV and looked up at him, her eyes as bright as the stars overhead.

Despair, loneliness, anger, longing, fear—it all balled up inside him, choking the breath out of him. He knew he should probably say something, but "Don't go" was all that came to mind. He couldn't say that. So he stood there as the silence lengthened and grew louder, roaring with unsaid things, unvoiced feelings, unspoken possibilities.

"You could come," Sara whispered.

George's heart reared like a startled stallion. "What?"

"You could come with me to Milan. It's a great place. Lots to see, and the food is great." Her smile was persuasive. "I know how you love Italian food."

Oh, Lord. George's heart galloped hard. "I-I can't do that, Sara."

"But we had such a great time the other night. I thought maybe . . ." She looked down, her gaze fixed on the wet asphalt, which was just as shiny-wet as her eyes.

"What?"

"I thought . . . well, with planes and faxes and phones and e-mail . . . well, I thought that maybe we . . ." Her voice trailed off.

George braced his hands on Sara's SUV, his head down, then pushed off it. "Damn it, Sara, I don't want to date you. I don't want to have a long-distance relationship with you." Anguish churned inside him, so roiling and hot that it boiled over. "You're like a drink to an alcoholic. If I get started with you, I won't know when to quit, and the last round with you damn near killed me. I can't do that again."

A tear slowly slid down her cheek. He started to reach out and wipe it away, then thought better of it. He didn't dare touch her. If he touched her, he'd end up holding her, and if he held her . . .

He shifted his weight to his other leg and shoved his

hands into his pocket. "Look, Sara—you've had a hell of a day and you're all wrung out. You don't really want to get anything started with me; you're just rattled by everything that's happened. Go home and get yourself a good night's sleep. You'll feel differently about things in the morning."

"What if I don't?" she said softly.

His heart took a big dip like a kite on a string. "You will. Now go on home."

George opened the vehicle door for her.

But instead of climbing in, she threw her arms around his neck, molding her warm, soft breasts against his chest.

Dear God—this wasn't fair. She smelled so good and felt so right—so warm and womanly and familiar, a perfect fit in his arms. Against his best intentions, his arms wound around her, and when she tipped her face up, his lips lowered to hers as if of their own volition. Desire swept through him, desire and need and a tidal wave of emotion so tall and strong it nearly swept him away.

What would one night hurt—one full night with her in his arms? He'd never held her all through a night. But, oh, dear lord, how he used to dream of it! How he used to fantasize about feeling her body flush against his, about breathing in the scent of her hair, about seeing her face on the pillow beside him when he opened his eyes in the morning. Even on his honeymoon with Heather, he'd lain in bed and pretended he was holding Sara.

Guilt ripped through him, hot and searing.

He pulled back abruptly. "You need to go home."

"Come home with me," she whispered.

"I can't."

"Don't you want to?"

Want to? Sweet Jesus, did she really have no idea?

His fingers shook as he clasped them around her forearms and removed her arms from his neck. "Damn it,

Sara—what do you want from me? You want me to make love to you so you can turn around and leave me again?" His voice was a low, angry rumble. She gazed up at him, her eyes wide. "Why don't you just ask me to open a vein and bleed to death right here in the parking lot? It would be a hell of a lot easier and hurt a hell of a lot less."

He turned on his heel and stalked to his truck, his chest tight, his breathing hard. He knew he'd said too much, but he was too upset to care.

He yanked open the door of his truck and climbed in, wondering why there was no rain on the windshield when both of his cheeks were damp.

Chapter Twenty-one

"It was so nice of you to invite me out here for lunch," Sara said the following Saturday. "I think this is the first real meal I've eaten since the fire."

"I couldn't let you go back to Chicago without seeing you again." Celeste poured some more iced tea in Sara's glass, then put the pitcher on the kitchen counter and rejoined her at the table. "Besides, I thought you might need a break from town."

Sara nodded, swallowing another bite of salad. "You're right about that. I had no idea a fire generated so much work. I've been up to my eyeballs with insurance people, fire inspectors and demolition contractors. And every time I look at the store—or the wreck that used to be the store—I feel like crying."

Come to think of it, she'd felt like crying pretty much around the clock for the last five days—ever since her conversation with George in the nursing home parking lot.

Just thinking about it now made tears threaten again.

Sara gazed out the window at Celeste's backyard and swallowed around the lump in her throat, trying to hold them back. "It's so nice to have a change of scenery. I can't believe all the work you've done to this place! It looks wonderful."

"Thanks."

"How are things shaping up for your grand opening?"

Celeste dabbed at her mouth with the yellow linen napkin. "I'll have to wait and see how many people actually show up, but I've gotten a lot of positive responses from teachers and principals and preschool owners. From all indications, I should have a big turnout."

"I'm so thrilled for you! You must be excited."

Celeste nodded. "Excited and scared. Everything's riding on this. If I don't get enough bookings, I'm going to have to sell the place."

Sara leaned forward, her expression serious. "I can make you a loan, Celeste."

"That's so sweet of you." Celeste's eyes filled with gratitude and affection. "And it means a lot to me that you'd offer, but I can't take you up on it."

"Sure you can. I'd be more than happy to help you out."

"I really appreciate it," Celeste said. "But I need to do this on my own, without leaning on anyone else. If it's not meant to be—well, I guess I need to find out sooner rather than later."

"My offer will still be good if you change your mind."

Celeste gave a teary smile. "I appreciate that so much."

"I wish I could be here for your grand opening."

"I wish so, too. Are you sure you can't stay?"

Sara sighed. "Christine is anxious for me to get back."

"So you're still planning on leaving on Monday?"

Sara nodded glumly.

"You don't look too happy about it," Celeste observed.

Sara toyed with the edge of the blue and yellow place-mat. "I'm not."

"Because of George?"

She nodded again. "I asked him to come to Milan with me."

Celeste's eyebrows shot up in surprise. "And . . . ?"

"He said he doesn't want a long-distance relationship."

Celeste leaned forward. "Does he want a close-distance relationship?"

"It wasn't discussed. There was no point." Sara put down her napkin. "We live in two completely different worlds. He loves horses and wide open spaces—he'd be miserable in Chicago. And that's where my business and my home and my life is."

"What about your heart?"

"Oh, it never left here." The words came out so fast that they took Sara by surprise. Was it true?

Dear heavens. She wanted to deny it, but the bald truth refused to wear a toupee. It stood in front of her, blatant and bare and glaring.

She'd given George her heart many years ago, and he still had it. No other man had ever made her feel the way he did. No other man had ever measured up. No other man had even come close.

And no other man ever would, because George Wright owned her heart.

"Well, you can't just go off and leave it again!" Celeste declared fiercely.

"I don't have any choice." Sara's voice wavered. "Celeste, I have shamelessly pursued that man. I've practically thrown myself at him, and he's done nothing but run in the other direction."

"That's because he thinks you're going to leave."

"Well, I am."

"Would you leave if he wanted to marry you?"

"No." Once again, the speed and firmness of her reply caught Sara by surprise. She sat still for a moment, pondering it, wondering at it, amazed at its rightness. "No, I wouldn't."

Celeste hit the table with her palm. "Well, then, you've got to go tell him that. You've got to let him know the depth of your feelings."

"Oh, Celeste—I can't." Sara worried the corner of her napkin. "I asked him to come home with me the other night and he just walked away."

"Do you love him?" Celeste persisted.

"I never stopped loving him." The truth of the words resounded in her heart, clear as a crystal bell.

"So, which is more important—risking your pride or losing the love of your life?"

"It's not that simple." Tears gathered in her eyes.

"It is if you let it be. You came back to Cypress Grove for a reason, I'm sure of it. And I think George is that reason."

"Oh, now, Celeste—"

"Did I ever tell you how my grandparents got together?" Sara shook her head, startled by the abrupt change of topic.

Celeste propped her elbows on the table. "They met on a train going from London to Edinburgh during World War Two. My grandmother stumbled on her way to the dining car and literally fell into my grandfather's arms. He said she felt so right there that he immediately knew he was going to marry her." Celeste grinned. "There were a couple of problems, though: My grandmother was engaged to someone else—in fact, she was on her way to meet her fiancé's parents—and my grandfather was about to head back to the States."

"Those sound like problems, all right," Sara agreed, wondering where this story was going.

"They sat together and talked the rest of the trip, and by the time they made it to Edinburgh, Granddad knew he was in love. He thought Gran felt it, too, but she was already committed to another man.

"Granddad had one night in Edinburgh before he shipped out. It was the same night that my grandmother was going to a big, fancy party at her fiancé's parents' house.

"To make a long story short, Granddad crashed the party. In front of the fiancé, his family and all the guests, he got down on one knee and declared his love for my grandmother. The fiancé was furious and tried to kick him out. Granddad refused to leave. A scuffle broke out. My grandmother went to my grandfather's defense, and, well . . . the rest is history."

"That's a wonderful story." *But I really don't see what it has to do with me.*

"People used to ask Granddad how he had the nerve to do that. And you know what he always said?"

"What?"

"He said he thought about the odds. What were the odds that they just happened to be on the same train on the same day and she just happened to fall in his lap? And how likely was it that they'd hit it off so well, and feel so strongly about each other so fast? There were too many coincidences involved for it to just be chance. So he decided that if God had gone to all the trouble to set them up, the least he could do was follow through."

Sara's heart began to beat fast and loud, like a fist knocking on a door.

"You've got to do what my grandfather did, Sara. You've got to follow through. You've got to go to George and bare your heart."

"I don't know if I can." Sara's voice came out so low it was almost a whisper.

"Think about what you stand to gain. And think about what you stand to lose."

All of the years ahead of her unfurled in her mind's eye, stretching out like a gray, deserted highway—all the lonely weekends, all the empty holidays, all the dark, solitary nights. The thought of traveling the long, cold length of it alone chilled her to the bone.

"Go talk to him before you leave," Celeste urged.

"What am I supposed to say?" Bite Me brushed against Sara's leg. She bent and picked him up, glad of his warmth, glad that he welcomed her touch. "I can't just trot over and say, 'Hey, George—you've been avoiding me like the plague ever since I hit town. I bet it's because you want to marry me.' "

"Well, you might want to word it a little differently." Celeste smiled that knowing smile of hers, the one that looked far too wise to belong on such a young face. "But I bet one thing—by the time you get there, your heart will tell you what to say."

Chapter Twenty-two

Rand reached out a drowsy arm and smashed the button on his alarm, but it didn't stop the shrill ringing. It erupted again, shattering the quiet dark.

It wasn't the alarm; it was the phone. Rand opened one eye and glanced at his bedside clock. Nearly one in the morning. He grabbed the receiver, wondering who the hell would be calling at this hour.

"Rand? It's Celeste."

He was pretty sure this wasn't a booty call, but his heart started pumping hard all the same. "What's up?"

"Dolly is having her cria, but it's not going well."

He sat up. "*Who* is having a *what?*"

"My llama, Dolly . . ."

Rand ran a hand down his face, wishing he were more awake. "The Dalai Lama?"

"No. Well, sort of. My female llama, Dolly. She's having her baby—they're called crias. But she's having trouble."

"Have you called Doc Thomas?"

"He's out of town at a conference. I called the veterinarian who's covering for him, but he's on another call in Folsom, and it's going to be a while before he can get here." Celeste's voice sounded thin and strained. "Her water broke around ten-thirty. She's been in hard labor for a couple of hours, Rand, and she's not making any progress. From everything I've read, llamas are supposed to have easy births, but . . ." Her voice trailed off to almost a whisper. "She seems to be getting weak. I'm really afraid I'm going to lose her."

Rand swung his feet to the floor. "I'll be right there."

It took him less than fifteen minutes to throw on some clothes, grab the birthing kit he used on his foals and drive to Celeste's place. It was a still night, still and hot and cloyingly humid. The sky was clear and the moon was nearly full. He saw a light shining in the barn, so he drove straight toward it and parked outside the gate, then grabbed the medical kit and climbed through the split rail fence.

Celeste ran out to greet him, her brow ridged with worry. She was wearing cutoffs and a sleeveless blue knit top. "I'm so glad you're here. She's really struggling, and I don't know what to do."

Rand followed her into the barn. The scent of hay and horses and leather wafted in the humid air. He found the llama lying in her stall, looking scared.

"Easy, girl," he murmured, moving slowly, letting her get used to his presence. The animal regarded him with huge wary eyes, but she lay still and let him examine her.

Things didn't look good. Rand looked at Celeste. "I'm no vet, but it looks like the foal—or whatever you call it—is sideways."

"What can we do?"

Rand blew out a rough breath. "I can try to turn it. I've got to warn you, though—I've never tried it on a llama. I can't guarantee anything."

"Please—will you give it a try?"

He couldn't resist the plea in her eyes. "All right. I need to wash up."

"There's a sink right over there." Celeste pointed to the back of the barn.

Rand headed toward it. "We'll need some clean towels."

"I've got some handy."

Rand scrubbed his hands and forearms, then returned to the stall. The llama was gasping for breath.

"Help her, Rand," Celeste urged.

"I'll do my best." The llama needed help, all right. From the look of things, they were likely to lose both the mother and the child.

Which would break Celeste's heart. The thought filled him with resolve. He ripped open a package of sterile birthing gloves, pulled them on, then rubbed lubricant all over them. "Stay by her head and do your best to keep her calm."

"Okay." Celeste moved to the front of the animal and crouched down, murmuring soft words of encouragement. Dolly blew hard, her nostrils flailing.

"You're doing great, girl," Celeste murmured, stroking the llama's neck. She watched Rand work, his mouth set in a hard line, his brow wrinkled in concentration. Dolly let out an otherworldly cry and writhed, nearly kicking Rand. He deftly dodged her back hooves, making reassuring sounds in a low, soothing voice.

After what seemed like an eternity, Rand sat back on his heels. "Got it! Here comes the foal."

Celeste didn't bother to correct his terminology. She was too intent on watching the miracle unfolding before her eyes. Two tiny feet and the tip of a tiny nose slowly appeared . . . then the head and legs, followed by a long neck. Celeste held her breath as shoulders slowly emerged. A minute later, a tiny llama—a wet, spindly miniature of Dolly—lay on a nest of towels.

"Is it all right?" Celeste asked, her voice a low whisper.

The cria wriggled and gave a snort. "Yeah, looks like it," Rand said. "It's female."

"Oh, she's so beautiful!"

Dolly struggled to her feet and nosed her baby.

Rand took a towel and gently wiped the cria's nose and mouth, then reached in his birthing kit and pulled out a small suction bulb, which he used on the baby's nose.

"She's breathing fine," he said at length.

Dolly licked her baby's head.

"Let me take care of the umbilical cord," Rand told the mother llama, "then I'll let you take over."

Celeste watched as Rand again reached into his bag, pulled out piece of string and tied it tightly around the cord about a half-inch from the belly. He dug back in his bag and pulled out a pair of scissors. Celeste winced.

He shot her a grin. "It won't hurt either one. I promise."

All the same, Celeste squeezed her eyes shut as he snipped the cord.

"All done. It's safe to look."

Celeste cautiously opened her eyes to see Dolly turn and nudge her baby with her nose, then nudge Rand's hand as well. "Oh, look! She's saying thank-you."

Rand grinned. "It's more likely she's saying, 'Get your hands off my foal.' "

"Cria."

"Right."

Their eyes met, and Celeste knew that this was a moment she'd remember all her life. It was a moment of miracles, a moment sparkling with new life and fresh chances, a moment when anything seemed possible—anything, anything at all.

Even love?

On, dear heavens, she hoped so—hoped so with all her heart. Because as far as Celeste was concerned, it was a done deal. She was in love with Rand—completely, utterly, heart-and-soul in love with him. There was no denying it, no pretending it was a crush, no wishing it away.

Was there a chance that he might feel the same way about her? The way he was looking at her right now, his eyes all lit up and warm, made her think that maybe, just maybe, there might be a chance.

The crunch of tires sounded in the drive, breaking the spell between them. "I bet that's the vet," Rand said, rising to his feet.

Sure enough, an elderly man with a gray beard soon appeared in the doorway. "Is this the place with the pregnant llama?"

"It was." Rand tossed Celeste a smile. "But not anymore."

"Both mother and child are doing great," the vet pronounced twenty minutes later as he snapped his medical bag closed. The cria was on her feet now, her long, skinny legs splayed out as she nursed. Dolly contentedly munched on a pile of hay, occasionally turning around to look at her baby.

The vet shook Rand's hand. "I couldn't have done any better myself. You're gonna put me and Doc Thomas out of business."

"Believe me, you have nothing to worry about," Rand replied. "I couldn't handle the hours."

The gray-haired man turned to Celeste. "You're lucky to have such a handy neighbor. You could have lost both animals."

"I know." The gratitude in Celeste's heart started to well in her eyes. She blinked, wanting to control her emotion.

"I'll swing by in a day or so and check on them," the vet said.

"Great. Thank you."

With a wave, the veterinarian strode out of the barn. A moment later, his van rumbled down the drive.

Celeste stuck her hands in her pockets as the barn grew silent. "I can't tell you how much I appreciate your help."

He shrugged his shoulders. "I'm glad it worked out."

It was probably three in the morning, but she didn't want the evening to end. He didn't appear in any hurry to leave, either. "Would you like to come in for a drink or some coffee?"

"Coffee sounds great."

Celeste snapped off the overhead light in the barn and walked out into the night with Rand. The tree frogs croaked a throaty chorus, rising and falling in hypnotic swells. Overhead, the stars punched holes in a black velvet sky.

"I can't believe how bright the stars are here," she said. "They never looked this big in Houston."

Rand looked up. "City lights make them harder to see."

"Life's a lot like that, isn't it?"

"In what way?"

"Well, sometimes you have to get away from the clutter in order to see what's really there." She bumped against him as she skirted a blackberry bush on her side of the trail. He put his hand on her back to steady her. The touch electrified the physical awareness buzzing between them.

He slanted her a grin. "Did you have something specific in mind, or are you just waxing philosophical?"

"I was thinking about Sara and George."

Rand looked at her questioningly.

"Sara had to get away from Chicago and all the business in her life in order to see what really matters."

"Which is what?"

315

"George. She's in love with him."

Rand's brows flew up. "You're kidding!"

"No. She's loved him since they were teenagers."

"I thought that was all over. I heard she stood him up at the altar."

Sara opened the gate to her backyard. "She never stopped loving him. And I think George still loves her, too—but he's scared to get involved with her again."

"Well, you can hardly blame him. Once burned, twice shy."

"The same fire that burns you can keep you warm," Celeste said. "You just have to learn how to handle it."

"Oh, that's a good one." Rand shot her a teasing smile. "Have you got a little homily for every occasion?"

"Pretty much. I got them from my grandmother."

"Did she throw out these little gems willy-nilly, or did she explain them?"

"She explained them. That one's about the nature of love."

"I thought it was about fire safety."

Celeste grinned. "In a way, it is."

"So what was Grandma's advice?"

"Well, she used to say that loving someone meant caring about him as much as you care about yourself. She said it meant giving his needs the same priority you give your own. It meant helping him realize his dreams, and being there for him, no matter what."

Like you were there for me tonight. The thought made her heart lurch like a capsizing boat.

In the middle of the night, in her moment of need, Rand had been there for her. Just as he'd been there when she needed to borrow a horse trailer and repair her fence and assemble the swing set.

And he might not be aware of it, but he was helping her realize her dreams, even though they clashed with his own. He might disagree with her ideas, he might think she was misguided, he might even think she was a kook, but he'd been there for her all the same.

Surely that counted for something.

Oh, dear Lord, she hoped so, because tonight had driven home an incontrovertible fact: She was head-over-heels, up-to-her-neck, crazy, madly, wildly in love with Rand. If there were a chance that he might love her back, shouldn't she do everything possible to make him realize it?

Her head was spinning as she opened her back door. They stepped inside, and the poodles darted toward them, yapping a greeting.

Rand squatted down and ruffled their fur. "Hey Killer, Bruiser." The dogs climbed all over him, their pom-pom tails furiously fanning the air. "You're acting mighty fierce tonight."

The dogs sniffed curiously at Rand's pants and shirt.

"You must smell like baby llama," Celeste remarked as she crossed the room to the coffeepot.

Rand looked down at his clothes. His mouth twisted. "Oh, man—why didn't you tell me I was such a mess?" He straightened and pulled out his blood-stained shirt, then frowned down at his filthy jeans. "I'm disgusting. Maybe I ought to just go on home and clean up."

"Why don't you clean up here?" Celeste carried the coffeepot to the sink. "You got up in the middle of the night to help my llama. The least I can do is wash the clothes you wore while you were doing it."

"It'll take too long."

"Mr. Jones was about your size, and I've got a trunk full of his clothes. I'll dig out some clean pants and a shirt. You can wear those home, and I'll drop off your clean clothes later."

Rand regarded his jeans as if they were an alien creature. "I really need a shower."

"Take one while the coffee's brewing."

"You don't mind?"

"No. There are clean towels in the master bathroom." She headed to the sink. "I'll put some clothes on the bed for when you come out."

"Okay. Thanks."

She opened a bag of coffee as his footsteps receded down the hall. She was about to measure out a scoopful when an idea seized her and wouldn't let go—an idea so thrilling and terrifying that it made her hand freeze in midair.

No, she couldn't.

Could she?

If there was a chance he might love her back, wasn't it worth taking? She was already taking a chance on her career, her finances and her future. Wasn't her heart worth a chance as well?

The thought made her insides quiver.

What if this was another of her big mistakes? What if she were deluding herself because she wanted it so badly?

But on the other hand, what if this was meant to be? What if everything in her life had been leading up to this moment and she didn't have courage to follow through?

Follow your heart. Celeste could practically hear her grandmother's voice whispering the words.

"Your heart knows the way," Mr. Jones had told her. And what had she herself told Sara just the other day? *"Think about what you stand to gain, and what you stand to lose."*

If you get the same message two separate times from two trustworthy sources, it's a sign from heaven, Mr. Jones had written.

Celeste decisively put down the coffee scoop and drew a deep breath. If she was going to make a mistake, she'd rather make it out of love than out of fear. When all was said and done, she'd rather be a fool than a coward.

Drawing a deep breath, she squared her shoulders and strode down the hall before she lost her nerve.

Rand ducked down under the showerhead and let the water sluice through his hair. He reached for a shampoo bottle in the corner of the tub and flipped up the lid, only to have the scent waft up and hit his nostrils. Oh, man, it smelled like Celeste—soft and fresh and delicious, like green apples and herbs. He inhaled deeply, breathing it in, and felt a surge of arousal sweep through him.

Oh, great, Adams—nothing like getting turned on by the scent of shampoo. Scowling, he flipped the lid closed and set it back down.

Damn it, this had been a mistake. He should have gotten in his truck and headed straight home, filthy clothes or not. He had no business being naked in Celeste's house at three in the morning. She'd said she didn't want to get involved, that they were too different, that they wanted different things. And damn it, she was right. He respected her decision.

So what the hell was he doing here?

He didn't know. He just knew he hadn't wanted to leave. He'd felt all jazzed up after delivering that llama. Hell, he felt jazzed up just being around Celeste. The way she'd looked at him after that foal—*cria*—had been born, like he were some kind of a hero . . . Man, that had made his insides feel like a soft, twisted pretzel.

He grabbed the bar of soap and rubbed it into his hair, working it into a lather, then stuck his head back under the showerhead. He needed to get cleaned up and out of here before he went back on his word and made a move on her.

The room abruptly went black.

Ah, hell—the power must have gone out. It was a frequent enough occurrence out here in the country, but usually only during thunderstorms.

But the room wasn't entirely dark. Through the opaque shower curtain, he could make out a small light flickering by the door.

"Celeste?" he called.

"Yes." Her voice sounded oddly breathless.

"Did the power go out?"

"Not exactly."

"What's going on?"

The light stopped near the vicinity of the sink. His sight adjusted to the dark well enough to make out a form moving toward him. The shower curtain parted, and Celeste stepped into the shower with him.

Naked. Stark naked. Completely, entirely, exquisitely, beautifully naked.

He was too stunned to speak. His body, however, had an immediate response.

Her eyes were dark in the flickering light. "You said I'd have to make the next move." She moved close, stood on tiptoe and stretched her arms around his neck. "Well, I'm making it."

Rand's heart sledgehammered against his ribs as her naked breasts pressed against his chest. His brain shut off and his body took over. With a groan, he pulled her closer and lowered his mouth to hers.

Oh, jeez—she felt even better than he remembered. Her lips were soft and slick and sweet as honey. His hands slid over her skin as warm water showered down. She was so soft, so smooth, so eager. He lost himself in the taste of her, thrilling to her woman's body pressed so intimately against his own.

When they drew apart, panting, long moments later, Rand reached for the bar of soap, lathered his hands, then slowly slid them over her body—her neck, her chest, then her breasts. Her silky skin slipped beneath his fingertips, and her dusky tips pebbled at his touch.

A moan of pleasure escaped Celeste's lips. She was on fire, aflame, melting from within. She leaned against the tile and gave herself over to pure sensation, to the exquisite feel of Rand's hands on her skin. He lowered his head and kissed her breasts, suckling each taut tip until her knees felt like puddles.

When he finally straightened, she picked up the bar of soap and slid it slowly across his chest, working up a lather. She worked her way down his chest to his belly, following the trail of dark hair. He gasped as her soapy hand gripped his erection.

"Celeste," he groaned.

He was enormous and rock hard, and she felt him throb in her palm. She slid her hand slowly up and down his shaft, while her other hand soaped the rest.

He gently gripped her wrists, stopping her. "If you keep that up, honey, things will be over way too soon." He took the soap from her hand, his eyes glittering with heat. "My turn."

He pulled her against him, her shoulders against his chest, his erection pressing hard against the small of her back, and slipped the bar of soap over her breasts. Both of his hands moved down her belly—down, down, down to the juncture of her thighs. His soapy fingers teased her triangle of curls; then, as the soap rinsed away in the spray of the shower, slid still lower, down to the sensitive flesh aching for his touch.

Celeste let out a moan at the first contact. It was exquisite, excruciating, exciting beyond belief. Tension crouched inside her like a cat about to pounce. She closed her eyes and leaned back against Rand as his fingers worked their magic, stroking, caressing, inciting her to a white-hot heat. Just as she thought she would die, he slid a finger inside her, continuing his rhythmic caresses with his other hand. She felt her muscles contract, heard herself cry out, then found herself swept away on relentless waves of pleasure.

Her knees wobbled as she turned toward him. His mouth lowered to hers, hard and hungry.

"I want to stretch you out and kiss you all over," he murmured. He turned off the water, grabbed a towel from the towel rack and gently wrapped it around her, then picked up another and rapidly ran it over himself.

He followed her out of the shower, then bent down and pulled his wallet out of the back pocket of his jeans. He extracted a small plastic packet. "Protection," he murmured.

Before she knew it, he'd picked her up, one arm under her knees, the other under her back, and carried her to the queen-sized bed in the adjacent room.

He gently set her down on the floral comforter, slowly pulling off her towel, then leaned over her. Her heart fluttered hard as his lips moved down her body, grazing her neck, her breasts, her belly. The rough prickle of his beard on her skin sent hot shivers chasing through her.

The heat burst into flames as his mouth moved still lower. "Let me," he murmured, nudging her legs apart. "I want to look at you. I want to taste you." Her fingers threaded through his hair as sensation, hot and sweet and unbelievably intense, ricocheted through her.

"I need you," she whispered at length, her arms urging him up. "Please. I'm dying for you."

He raised himself up. She heard the crinkle of plastic, and then he loomed over her, his eyes dark with passion. She wound her legs around his hips and pulled him down, gasping as he entered her.

He filled her heart as surely as he filled her body. She

loved him—loved him with all her being. The words welled up inside her as he sent her into a star-strewn galaxy where time and place no longer existed, where souls connected and hearts merged, where surrendering and conquering were one and the same.

He gasped her name as he followed her to that rapturous place. And for the moment, it was enough. For the moment, it was everything.

Chapter Twenty-three

Rand awoke slowly the next morning, coming out of a deep
sleep like a scuba diver slowly ascending from the ocean
depths. He couldn't remember the last time he'd felt such
bone-deep contentment, such a complete sense of well-
being. He'd had the most incredible, amazing dream about
making love to Celeste. They'd started out in the shower,
and then . . .

He shifted his arm and was startled to feel a hand on
the back of his shoulder. His eyes flicked open. White curtains, lacy and feminine, hung at unfamiliar windows. The
sheets beneath him were a delicate pink.

It hadn't been a dream. He was in Celeste's bedroom—in
her bed. And she was behind him, her hand on his skin.

The thought made him smile. At the same time, it
kicked his morning erection up several notches. "Good
morning, beautiful," he murmured.

She responded by caressing his shoulder. Desire socked

him in the gut like a kickboxer's foot. "What do you say we start the day off right?"

Warm lips nuzzled his ear. Grinning broadly, he rolled over and reached for her.

Only it wasn't Celeste. On the pillow beside him lay a tiny, white-faced monkey, his lips pulled back in a smiling grimace.

"Acccck!" Rand bellowed, scrambling out of bed.

"Eeeeek!" shrieked Mr. Peepers, diving under the covers.

Celeste rushed into the bedroom, wearing a short flowered robe, her face alarmed. "Wh-what's the matter? What happened?"

Rand grabbed last night's discarded towel off the floor and wrapped it around his waist. "I damn near kissed a monkey!"

"*What?*"

Rand yanked back the covers, exposing Mr. Peepers. The monkey jumped off the bed and into Celeste's arms, squawking like a parrot.

Celeste comforted the startled simian, looking rather startled herself. Rand started to grin. "First your monkey comes on to me in my truck, and now here in bed. If he keeps this up, people are going to talk."

Celeste fell on the bed, convulsing in laughter. Mr. Peepers did a cartwheel, and before Rand knew it, he, Celeste and the monkey were all rolling on the bed, laughing like hyenas.

The faint ring of a telephone interrupted. "That must be yours," Celeste said, rising from the bed, picking his cell phone off the dresser and handing it to him.

It struck him as vaguely odd that his phone was on the dresser instead of clipped to his jeans, but he was too preoccupied with answering it to give it much thought.

"Hey—I'm glad I found you," George's voice said

through the receiver. "The Osterlings are here waiting for you. They said they were supposed to meet with you thirty minutes ago."

"Oh, hell!" Reality hit Rand like an anvil. How could he have forgotten he had important potential clients coming first thing this morning? His hand tensed hard around the phone. "Tell them I'll be right there."

Rand flicked the phone closed. He turned to Celeste. "I've got to go. I've got some big-time prospects waiting for me."

"Oh dear—your clothes are in the wash."

"Well, you said last night that I could borrow some of Mr. Jones's clothes."

She nodded. "I have his trunk in the guest room closet. I haven't gone through it, but he was roughly the same size as you."

"Whatever's in there will have to do."

Rand strode into the bathroom. When he came out, Celeste stood in the bedroom doorway, her brow creased with worry, her hands behind her back.

"You'll be able to change into your own clothes before you meet your clients, won't you?"

He looked at her warily. "I don't know. Why?"

Celeste bit her bottom lip. "Well, the trunk only had Mr. Jones's work clothes in it."

"That's okay. I don't care if they're worn."

"That's not really the problem."

"Well, what is?"

Reluctantly, she pulled her hands from behind her back and held up a pair of enormous red-and-yellow-striped overalls. They were covered with bright green and blue patches, with buttons the size of golf balls marching down the front.

Rand's jaw dropped. "What the hell is that?"

"His work clothes." Her expression was apologetic. "He was a clown."

"This is a joke, right?" He looked at her, praying she was kidding. He even forced his mouth into what might pass for a smile. "At any other time, I'm sure this would be very funny, but right now I'm running late and I'm a little stressed, and I don't really have time to kid ar—"

"I'm not kidding."

She wasn't. She wouldn't have that hesitant, worried, apologetic look on her face if she were.

"There's got to be something else in that trunk," Rand said.

"The only other pants in there are purple satin, and apparently they're designed to fit over stilts."

Rand muttered a low oath. "Don't you have anything else?"

"I'm pretty sure you wouldn't fit in any of my clothes, but Mr. Jones's sister-in-law left some dresses in the closet. . . ."

Rand reached out and snatched the overalls from her hand. "I'd rather show up looking like a clown than a crossdresser." He put one foot in the overalls.

A noise that sounded suspiciously like a snicker escaped Celeste's lips. She put a hand over her mouth.

"Don't you dare laugh," he warned.

Mr. Peepers let out a loud squeal.

Rand shot the monkey a dark look. "That goes for you, too, you little pervert."

Celeste collapsed on the bed, her face in a pillow. Every time she looked up, she relapsed in another round of mirth.

"I'm sorry," she gasped. "I truly am."

"Not nearly as sorry as I am," Rand muttered, pulling on his cowboy boots.

He didn't believe in jinxes, but if he did, he'd swear that was exactly what Celeste was.

* * *

"A clown suit!" Sara erupted in a loud peal of laughter. She'd run into Celeste in the baking aisle at the local grocery store, and Celeste had just told her about the morning's misadventure.

"Oh, Celeste—that's hysterical! I can just picture it. Did his clients see him dressed like that?"

Celeste winced. "Apparently, they were waiting for him on the front porch of his house when he arrived."

"Oh, no!" Sara burst into another round of laughter. "What did he say?"

"According to George, he started to explain, then just gave up, excused himself and went inside to change."

Sara's heart quickened. "You talked to George?"

Celeste nodded. "I called Rand's office to see how things went, and George answered the phone. Rand was with the clients in the stable, so I guess he managed to overcome a less-than-stellar first impression." Celeste leaned forward. "How about you? Have *you* talked to George?"

"Not yet. But I'm taking your advice, and I'm going to." Sara gestured to her grocery cart, which contained two boxes of baking chocolate, butter and a bag of flour. "I'm baking brownies for Dad's poker game at the assisted living center tonight, and I thought I'd take some by George's place afterwards."

"I guess we're thinking alike," Celeste said. "I'm planning to surprise Rand with dinner tomorrow evening. You know what they say about the way to a man's heart."

Sara shot her a wry grin. "I always thought the path was located a little lower than the stomach."

Celeste laughed. "Good luck with George."

"You, too." Sara gave her a quick hug. "I'll give you a call tomorrow before I leave for the airport."

Celeste's brow creased. "Oh, Sara—you're still planning to leave?"

Sara nodded. "Unless something happens tonight to change my mind."

George sat in his pickup in Sara's driveway and stared at the clock in the dash of his truck: 12:14 in the morning. Where the hell was she?

Maybe Rand was wrong. Maybe Sara had already left town.

But if she had, she wouldn't have left the porchlight on. And there was a light on inside the house, as well.

George draped both arms over the steering wheel and gazed out at the tree he'd helped her plant, his mind drifting back to the afternoon.

"Celeste says Sara doesn't want to leave Cypress Grove," Rand had said as he'd unbuckled the saddle on the Anderson gelding.

George had tried to act nonchalant, but his heart had pounded like a farrier's hammer. "Oh, yeah?"

"Yep." Rand had hauled the saddle off the horse's back. "She says Sara's still carrying a torch for you."

George had made a derisive snort.

"Apparently, Sara wants to hook up with you permanently, but since you've been avoiding her, she's just gonna go back to Chicago and leave you in peace." Rand hauled the navy saddle blanket off the horse. "Just thought you'd like to know."

George managed to grunt an acknowledgment, but he felt as if he'd been kicked in the gut by a team of horses. He'd stood stock still as Rand carried the saddle into the tack room.

Sara wanted to be with him permanently? Permanently—as in marriage?

His thoughts had tripped all over each other as they scrambled through his head. She *had* made several over-tures. And she *had* invited him to Milan. But he'd thought she'd just wanted a fling.

He'd been so preoccupied with keeping up his defenses, so determined not to let her get back under his skin, that he hadn't even considered the possibility that she wanted something more.

Sara wants to hook up with you permanently. The words kept circling in George's mind, trying to find a place to alight. Hell, he hadn't even considered the possibility of getting back together for keeps. He'd been too busy hanging on to anger and resentment and—oh, hell, he hated to admit it—fear. The truth was, he'd been so damned afraid of getting rejected again that he'd been blind to what was really going on.

Was he going to screw up a second chance just because he was too damned stubborn and proud and afraid to admit what he really felt?

No way in hell. He'd acted like a fool for too long as it was. So here he was, sitting outside her house, holding a pink rose he'd surreptitiously picked from his neighbor's garden because he remembered that it was her favorite color and there was nowhere in town to buy one. He'd been waiting for her to show up for the last two hours.

He looked at the clock again. Make that two hours and twenty-one minutes.

A pair of headlights turned onto the street. Before he even identified the vehicle, his heart started pumping as hard as an offshore oil well. He could always tell whenever Sara was near. He had a sixth sense where she was concerned, an internal radar system that was set just for her.

Sure enough, a white Ford Explorer hesitated at the end of the wide driveway, then slowly pulled up beside him. He climbed out of his pickup, the drooping rose clutched in his hand, and walked over to the SUV.

She opened the door and stepped down. She looked

beautiful—as feminine and delicate as the flower in his fist. She wasn't wearing anything fancy, just jeans and a sleeveless black turtleneck, but she took his breath away.

Her eyes were large and a little alarmed. "George—what are you doing here? Is something wrong with Daddy?"

It hadn't occurred to him that she might think that. "No. He's fine, as far as I know. I just, um, wanted to see you before you left town."

Her lips parted in surprise.

"I've been waiting for you," he added.

"Really?" Her eyes shifted to the rose in his hand and widened.

George nodded. "For about two hours. I was getting worried."

"You were?"

"Yeah."

Sara's mouth curved in an amused smile. "That's funny. Because I was waiting for you at *your* house."

"You're kidding."

She shook her head. "I wanted to drop off some brownies. I made some for Dad's poker group, and I had some extra, so . . ."

"That was really nice."

"They're in the car. Do you want to come in and have some?"

"Sure."

She stretched across the driver's seat and retrieved a foil-covered plate from the passenger side. He started to take it from her, then realized he was still holding the rose. He held it out to her. "Here—let's trade."

"Why, thank you." He took the plate. She gingerly accepted the rose. "It's beautiful."

"I took all the thorns off it."

"You always did." She held it to her nose, closed her eyes and inhaled. "You were always so thoughtful."

George looked down, a lump forming in his throat. "Yeah, well, it wouldn't have been a very good gift if it hurt you."

God only knew there had been enough of that.

Sara nodded, her eyes on him. "So . . . what did you want to see me about?"

He swallowed hard around that lump, not knowing what to say or where to begin. "I, uh, heard you're leaving tomorrow, and I just wanted to talk to you before you left." He cleared his throat. "Do you think we could go inside?"

"Of course." He followed her to the front door and watched her insert the key, noticing that her hand trembled. So she was nervous, too. Good. If she were nervous, it proved she cared. The fact gave him courage.

She flipped on the lights as she opened the door. He followed her into the kitchen. "Let me find a vase," she said.

She opened a cabinet, then closed it and opened another one. It took three tries before she located a bud vase. She filled it with water at the sink and carefully put the flower in it. "It's lovely."

"I remembered that pink roses used to be your favorite."

"Is it from your garden?"

"No. Heather only liked white ones." Oh, damn—why had he brought up Heather's name? Awkwardness hovered in the air, as ungainly as a stork.

"Did she like gardening?" Sara asked, peeling the foil off the plate of brownies.

"Not a lot." George shoved his hands in his pockets and leaned against the kitchen counter. "Except for vegetables. She liked homegrown vegetables."

"That must have been nice for you and the boys."

George nodded. Dad-blast it, he hadn't come here to talk about Heather and zucchini. He'd come here to talk about. . . . Hell, what the dickens *had* he come here to talk

332

about? He pulled his hands out of his pockets only to shove them back in again.

"So . . ." they both said simultaneously.

They looked at each other and laughed.

"You go first," George said.

"No, be my guest."

"I, um, was just going to ask you why you were bringing me brownies."

"And I was about to ask why you were bringing me a rose."

Silence stretched between them again. They stood there, just looking at each other, then spoke in unison once more.

"—George."

"—Sara."

They both grinned sheepishly.

"Ladies first," George said.

Sara drew a deep breath, her insides quaking. "What do you want to drink with your brownies?"

"Milk." He was standing near the refrigerator, so he opened it and pulled a carton out.

Sara turned to the cabinet and took out two glasses.

"Those look delicious," George said, looking at the plate of brownies.

It was time to lay it on the line, but Sara couldn't quite bring herself to do it. She strode across the kitchen and opened another cabinet, this time pulling out two dessert plates. "I love to bake, but I don't like the way baked goods look on my hips. I thought I'd bring you these so you could help me resist temptation."

"You shouldn't look to me for that."

Something in his voice made her stomach tighten. She turned and looked at him. His eyes held an old, familiar heat—a heat that made it hard to breathe. The air seemed thick and heavy, vibrating with sexual tension.

She turned around and leaned her hip against the cabinet to steady herself. It was now or never. She wrapped her arms around herself, briefly closed her eyes and drew a deep breath. "Okay—the brownies were just an excuse. The truth is, I couldn't leave town without telling you how I feel. The other night . . ." She paused and swallowed. "Well, I can't get the other night out of my mind. I'd forgotten I could feel that way. And it made me realize how deeply I—how much I. . . ." Her voice wavered. Tears gathered in her eyes. Then words tumbled out in a rush, like water being released from a dam.

"I still love you. I never stopped loving you. I'd do anything to have you back in my life. I don't want a fling or a part-time thing or a long-distance romance. I want to stay here and do what I should have done twenty-eight years. I want to marry you. I know you probably don't feel the same. It's incredibly presumptuous of me to even be telling you this, but I just couldn't go without saying it." She turned away, scared and embarrassed, as tears rolled down her face.

"Sara—"

She braced her hands on the counter, unable to look him in the face. "I-I'm sorry if I put you on the spot. If you want, you can just leave. I'll understand."

"I'm not going anywhere." He crossed the room in three strides, turned her toward him and pulled her into his arms. "Sara—honey . . ."

She looked up at his face. Her vision was blurred with tears, but not so badly she couldn't see the tenderness in his eyes. Her heart leapt like a jackrabbit in her chest.

"Sara . . . sweetheart." He gently brushed the tears from her cheeks with his thumb. "I was coming to tell you the same thing."

"You—you were?" She blinked hard and studied his face, not sure she could trust her ears.

He nodded. His eyes were bright. "I've been a thick-headed, stubborn old mule. I was twenty-eight years ago, and I guess I still am."

He moved closer. "I've been thinking about what you said the other night, and you were right. I wouldn't listen to you about postponing the wedding. I shut it out because I just didn't want to hear it. I didn't want you to go away to college. I was afraid of losing you."

"Oh, George," she whispered.

"And then I couldn't bear to talk to you or read your letters. I was just so damned hurt. And angry. Man, was I angry! I was mad as hell at you."

"I don't blame you."

"Yeah, well, I think it was easier to be mad than to deal with the hurt."

She placed her palm against his cheek. "I'm so sorry."

He covered her hand with his. "I'm sorry, too." He lowered his head and kissed her, a tender, soft, loving kiss, then pulled back and gazed down at her. "I'm sorry for so many things. I'm sorry I boxed you in like that. I'm sorry I didn't listen to you. And I'm sorry I didn't open all those letters you sent me. I should have been more patient, more willing to bend. And I should have waited . . ." He abruptly stopped himself in midsentence.

I should have waited for you. Was that what he'd been about to say?

"George—I never felt about anyone else the way I felt about you. Ever. Did you . . ." She knew she shouldn't ask. She knew she had no right. But it gnawed at her like a pitbull with a bone. "Did you feel that way about Heather?"

He ran his hands down her arms, his eyes troubled. "She was my wife for twenty-four years. She was a good mother and a good woman."

Sara hung her head. "Of-of course."

His hands moved up her arms. "She used to ask me the same thing about you."

Tears rolled down Sara's cheeks.

"She used to worry about measuring up to you. She used to ask me if I loved her as much as I'd loved you."

"What did you say?"

George's Adam's apple bobbed as he swallowed. A glint of moisture gleamed in his eye. His voice was a sandpaper whisper. "I lied."

Sara pulled him close and clung to him, her heart unfurling like the wet wings of a butterfly emerging from a cocoon.

At length he pulled back and gazed at her, the look in his eyes so loving that she thought her heart would burst. "Besides telling you that I love you and that I want a second chance, I was waiting here to tell you something else. Sara, honey—I'm willing to move to Chicago or Milan or any other damn place on the face of the earth that you want. I don't care where I am, as long as I'm with you."

"Oh, George!"

"I mean it. You don't have to move here. I'll move up there."

"George, I know this may surprise you"—it was hard to talk with the lump of joy in her throat—"but the truth is, I *want* to stay here. I want to be near my father. I've even been thinking about rebuilding his store. Only instead of feed and seed, I'd love to have a little specialty clothing store. With maybe a cappuccino machine in the corner."

His hands ran up and down her back. "I want you to have whatever it takes to make you happy."

"*You're* what it takes, George," she whispered softly. "You're all it takes."

He lowered his lips to hers, and the years melted away. It was a kiss with no barriers, with no restraints, with nothing held back—a kiss that was deep and true and honest, full of wisdom and forgiveness and lessons learned. It was a kiss between mated souls, a kiss full of promise and hope—a kiss as ageless and timeless as love itself.

Chapter Twenty-four

The sun was starting its descent behind the tall pines the next day as Celeste tentatively tried the knob on Rand's front door. It was unlocked, just as George had said it would be. Celeste had called George to ask if he would let her into Rand's house so she could surprise him with a homemade dinner.

"He never locks his front door, but I gotta warn you—he's not real fond of surprises," George had cautioned.

"He'll like this one," Celeste had replied confidently.

She hoped that her evening would go as well as Sara's had last night. Her friend had called that morning, bubbling with the news that she and George were back together. Sara was planning to stay in Cypress Grove, and had already talked to her business partner in Chicago. It looked like the woman who'd been helping out during Sara's absence was interested in buying her interest in the business.

That just went to show how easily things worked out

when something was meant to be, Celeste thought. Problems that looked like mountains turned out to be nothing more than little bumps in the road. She hoped that would be the case with Rand.

Celeste returned to her Jeep and pulled a bag of groceries out of the open door. She could hardly wait to see Rand's face when he walked in after a long day and discovered a delicious homemade dinner waiting for him. She hoped to show him that a relationship didn't have to be a burden—it could also be a blessing. She wanted to contribute to his life, not take away from it.

She set the bag on the counter and smoothed down her short red dress, a sense of anticipation flooding her veins. Before the night was over, she hoped Rand would realize that she was the best thing that had ever happened to him.

Rand jerked his attention back to the horse breeder standing across the corral. Stuart Jamison had just asked him something, but Rand would be damned if he knew what it was. He'd been woolgathering again.

Make that cloudgathering. He'd been daydreaming about Celeste pretty much 24/7 for the last two days. He'd been unable to get her out of his mind. He kept thinking about the way she'd looked when she stepped into the shower with him, kept remembering the texture of her skin and the taste of her mouth. He kept seeing her rolling on the bed, convulsed in laughter at Mr. Peepers's antics. Oddly enough, though, the memory that haunted him the most was the look of utter faith in her eyes as he'd tried to help her llama.

Man, that had gotten to him. It had been like a big fist around his heart, squeezing hard. She'd looked at him with such complete trust that he would have done anything, anything at all, to live up to the confidence she'd placed in him. He would rather have died than hurt her or let her down.

Yet that's what people did to each other if they got too close. They hurt each other; they let each other down.

Turmoil sloshed around in his belly. He shoved his hands in his pockets, trying to push aside his thoughts as well. Hell, he was standing here with a primo client, a man considering paying him fifty thousand dollars to buy a colt and thousands more to train a couple of foals, and all Rand could think about was Celeste. Something was very wrong with this picture.

"I'm sorry," Rand said. "I didn't catch your question."

"I wanted to know if you ever had any trouble breeding the dam."

"No. None at all."

A flash of movement on the roof of Jamison's pickup caught Rand's eye. Rand thought he must have imagined it, but a second later, a rope harness came flying out of the back of the bed of the truck. The next thing Rand knew, a small furry creature hopped onto the top of the tailgate and peered down at the harness on the ground.

Rand's stomach clenched like a pair of pliers. Oh, hell— Mr. Peepers! What was that damned monkey doing in Jamison's pickup? Rand watched in horror as the creature disappeared back into the pickup bed.

"Did the dam have any trouble foaling?"

Rand's attention jerked back to Mr. Jamison. "Wh-what?"

"The colt's dam. Any complications birthing her?"

"Um, no. We didn't have any problems." How the hell had that monkey gotten over here? Celeste would be worried sick if she discovered her monkey was missing.

The thought jarred him. Why the hell was he worried about *that*? He ought to be worried about his client, not about Celeste.

This was getting way out of hand. She was turning his life upside down, rearranging everything to the point that he was no longer quite sure who he was or what he wanted. He'd always prided himself on his ability to manage his emotions, but Celeste had him feeling things he'd never felt before.

He had to get a grip. He was jeopardizing everything he'd worked for. The reining horse community was a small one, and businesses lived and died on reputation. If word got out that Rand was running a slipshod operation, customers would disappear into thin air.

How the hell was he going to get that blasted monkey out of Jamison's truck without the breeder discovering him?

"You still own her?"

Another harness came flying out of the back of the truck, this one leather. The steel bit clunked on the oyster shell drive.

Rand abruptly coughed to disguise the noise, then forced his eyes back to the client. He'd completely lost the thread of the conversation. "Excuse me?"

Jamison looked at him strangely. "I asked if you still own the dam. If you do, I'd like to take a look at her. It'll give me an idea of what the colt's likely to grow into."

"Oh. Sure." But that posed a problem: Seeing the dam meant going to the pasture, which meant walking right past the monkey-occupied vehicle. He needed to buy some time. "Before we do that, why don't we stop by my office and go over the contract?"

Jamison stared at Rand as if he doubted his sanity. He spoke with the slow carefulness one might use when talking to a person who was a few bulbs short of a chandelier. "I want to see the dam first."

"Of course." Oh, jeez—now the monkey was standing on the pickup roof, doing deep knee bends. To Rand's chagrin, the creature swung down and climbed through the open window.

A pair of sunglasses soared out of the cab and into a puddle of mud, followed in short order by a tissue. Apparently the monkey had found an entire box, because Kleenex after Kleenex soon floated in the air. The monkey shrieked with glee.

"What was that?" Jamison asked.

Rand loudly cleared his throat, hoping to cover the sound. "What was what?"

"That noise."

Rand covered his mouth and coughed. "I, um, think I must be coming down with a cold."

A CD came flying out of the window, rapidly followed by another. Mr. Peepers jumped up and down and shrieked again.

Jamison turned toward the noise. Rand's blood froze in his veins as a tiny, hairy arm hurled another CD out the window like a Frisbee.

Busted.

Jamison lifted a meaty hand and pointed, his eyes bulging like a shih tzu's. "What the hell is that?"

Rand's stomach felt as if he'd swallowed a two-ton weight. "It's a monkey."

The breeder's mouth fell open. Mr. Peepers hurled another CD.

"I-I can explain," Rand said.

But he couldn't. He couldn't even explain it to himself.

Yet another CD sailed out the pickup window. Rand's carefully tended reputation sailed out with it.

Jamison's face took on a dangerous ruddy hue. "Is that your animal?"

"No. He belongs to my neighbor. He must have escaped."

A tan Stetson soared out the window, floated gracefully

in the air and landed in a large brown puddle. Jamison muttered a vile oath. "I'll teach that ape not to mess with my stuff." His face contorted in an angry scowl, the man started toward the truck.

Rand stepped forward, stopping him. "I'll get him."

Jamison muttered a foul oath and tried to sidestep Rand. "I want to get my hands on that little beast, and when I do, I'll . . ."

Rand moved again, blocking his path. "You're not going to touch him. I said I'd get him."

Jamison glared up, his eyes hot as coals. "You do that. And while you're at it, you'd better get your checkbook, because you're going to pay me for everything he's ruined. What the hell kind of place are you running here, anyway?"

Good question. Rand pondered it as he stalked toward the pickup. Why was he protecting a primate instead of his business? Where were his priorities? What the hell had happened to him?

Celeste had happened, that was what. Ever since she'd moved next door, his life had been in a constant state of chaos. It was bad enough that she'd made him postpone his expansion plans, she'd cost him clients and she'd endangered his horses—now she had him behaving in ways that defied his whole belief system. He was no longer behaving logically; he was acting on emotion. She made him feel all raw and unsettled and torn up inside.

This had to stop. There was no room in his life for this kind of confusion—no room for monkeys or wildcats or goats or llamas, no room for roller-coaster highs and lows, no room for a havoc-wreaking blonde who turned him inside out and upside down.

He needed to get his life back under control, damn it, and the only way he could do that was to get the uncontrollable forces out of it. Celeste had to go.

*   *   *

Celeste hummed as she stirred the jambalaya, bending down to inhale the rich scent of sausage, shrimp and seasoned rice. She'd just replaced the lid on the pot an put down the spoon when she heard the back door squeak open. Her heart quickened in anticipation. She couldn't wait to see the expression on Rand's face when he walked in and discovered her there.

She tucked a stray strand of hair behind her ear and turned around, a bright smile on her face.

The door slammed with ominous force and Rand strode into room. His mouth was set in such a tight, hard line that the skin around his lips was white.

"What's wrong?" she asked.

"*This* is what's wrong." He stretched out both hands A small white-faced monkey squirmed between them.

"Mr. Peepers! What are you doing here?" Celeste automatically stepped forward to take her pet. With a chirp, the animal leapt from Rand's arms to hers.

Rand folded his arms and glared at her. "I was about to ask you the same thing."

"Oh, dear—he must have stowed away in my bag again," Celeste said. "Where did you find him?"

"In a client's pickup, tossing everything that wasn't nailed down out the window and into a mud puddle."

Celeste's hand flew to her mouth. "Oh, no!"

"Oh, yes." His tone was low and icy. "The client—or should I say former client—demanded to know what kind of operation I'm running." Rand's eyes glittered with anger. "I was hard-pressed to tell him."

"Rand, I'm so very, very sorry!" She was more than sorry; she was mortified.

Rand advanced into the room and looked around the kitchen. "What the hell are you doing here, anyway?"

"I-I wanted to surprise you with a homemade dinner."

"Why didn't you call and ask me?"

"Because that would have ruined the surprise."

"Damn it, Celeste—I don't want surprises." His eyes snapped at her. "I want peace and quiet and calm and order. I won't have you ruining my life."

Ruining my life. Is that what he thought she was doing? The words were like daggers, stabbing her heart, slashing her soul, deflating all her hopes and dreams.

She'd been deluding herself. Rand wasn't ready to open his heart and let her in. Chances were he never would be. He wouldn't risk it. He'd told her he didn't want emotional involvement. Why hadn't she believed him?

"I want predictability, not chaos. I won't put up with this."

Tears clouded her eyes. She blinked them back, her arms tightening around the monkey. She wouldn't cry. She wouldn't let Rand know how deeply he'd wounded her.

"Fine. You can have all the predictability you want. From now on, I promise to stay out of your way."

Clutching the monkey with one arm, she grabbed her car keys and marched to the door. She paused, then wheeled around and faced him. "I hope you enjoy your calm, orderly, *predictable* life. Because you know what I predict? I predict you're going to end up a staid, stuffy, bitter old man, rocking all alone on your front porch, so bored and lonely you hate to even get up in the morning."

With that, she stalked out of his house, her legs shaking. She managed to climb into her Jeep, start the engine and drive all the way to the end of his driveway before she lost the battle to hold back her tears. It was a good thing she didn't have far to travel, because the rest of the drive passed in a tear-soaked blue.

Rand looked up as George strode into the darkened tack room a week later. "I thought you'd left with the rest of the crew." Now that George and his old flame were an item, he no longer stayed till after dark.

George straddled a sawhorse holding one of the saddles as Rand oiled the other side of the harness in his hands. "It might be none of my business, but I can't help but notice that something's bothering you. You've been acting crankier than a bear who ran into the business end of a porcupine."

Rand rose from the wooden stool and carefully hung the harness on the pegged wall. "You're right. It's none of your business."

George grinned. "I figured you'd say that. But I decided to talk to you about it anyway, because the boys are gettin' real disgruntled. You jumped all over Phil about the stalls, and it wasn't even his job to clean them this week. And you damn near snapped Kev's head off for using the wrong saddle blanket. So what if he used a green one instead of the blue?"

Rand started to reply, but George held up his hand. "It's your ranch and you can run it like you want, but if you keep this up, your whole crew is going to up and leave. I just figured you needed to know."

Rand blew out a breath and swallowed hard. He reached for another harness, dipping his head in a nod. "I appreciate the warning."

"I've always liked you, Rand, and I've always respected the way you run this place." George's voice was mild and nonjudgmental. "But lately you jump on people without giving them a chance to even open their mouths."

Rand's chest felt heavy. Damn it, he knew George was right. His breath hissed out in a sigh. "You're right. I need to lighten up." He sat back down on the wooden stool and picked up the oiled cloth. "It's no excuse, but I've had a lot on my mind lately."

"Does it have anything to do with a certain blond neighbor?"

It had everything to do with her, but he'd be damned if he'd admit it. By all rights, he should be glad she was out of his life. But the truth was, he'd started to miss her the moment she'd walked out his door.

He'd really missed her later, when he'd seen the dining table all set with candles and wineglasses, and discovered a fragrant pot of jambalaya on the stove. He'd found a loaf of homemade bread on the counter, and plates of salad and chocolate-covered strawberries in the refrigerator. The food had all looked and smelled delicious, but he hadn't had any appetite.

He'd felt sick about hurting her. She'd acted all angry and indignant, but he'd seen through it. She'd been hurt, and the thought of it gnawed at his gut. He'd never wanted to hurt a woman the way his father had hurt his mother. Especially not Celeste.

He'd picked up the phone to call her at least a dozen times, then set it back in the cradle. What good would it do? If he made up with her now, he'd only have to break up with her on down the road. It was better to leave things the way they were. He'd probably done her a favor by acting like a first-rate SOB. It would be easier to get over him if she thought he was a jerk instead of a guy who cared.

Not that he was. He didn't know the first thing about caring for a woman—not the way she wanted a man to care. But damn, it had torn him up, thinking about the way she'd been fighting back tears as she'd walked out the door. He'd felt even worse when he'd discovered a toothbrush, a bottle of massage oil and a sexy nightie in a canvas bag in the master bathroom. He'd spent the rest of the evening nursing a bottle of bourbon and a self-pitying sulk, and he'd been in a black mood ever since.

He was pathetic. He knew it, and he hated it, but he

seemed unable to stop himself. He'd sworn he'd never allow himself to get all carried away with emotion, yet here
he was, his heart feeling as raw as ground hamburger.

"Why don't you just go over to her place and apologize?"
George suggested.

"For what? Letting her screw up my life? No, thanks."
Rand poured more oil onto the cloth and rubbed it into
the harness. "Besides, as soon as her grand opening fiasco
is over next weekend, she's gonna be hightailing it back to
Texas."

"Don't count on it. From what Sara says, she's likely to
have a real good turnout."

"Yeah, well, it's a free event. It's going to take paying
customers—a whole hell of a lot of them—to pay her
taxes."

"She might just pull it off."

"No way."

George fixed Rand with a speculative look. "You know,
there are a lot worse things than bein' in love."

"Who said anything about love?"

"Nobody. But you're showing all the symptoms."

"Why? Because I'm miserable?"

George laughed. "It doesn't have to make you feel that
way."

Rand rubbed the leather so hard it squeaked. George's
new romance had him as giddy as a kid on the first day of
summer vacation. Rand was happy for him, he really was.
Sara was a terrific lady—smart, classy and beautiful, and
apparently she and George had been carrying a torch for
each other for most of their lives. But just because George
was riding the Love Boat didn't mean Rand had to jump
on board, too—especially not with a woman as ill-suited
for him as Celeste.

If he were interested in a long-term relationship—and
he wasn't, he assured himself—Celeste would be the last

person he'd pick. Oh, they had fun whenever they were together, and they had interesting conversations, and they made each other laugh. And they both loved animals and being outdoors, and as for the sex . . . well, Rand had never known it could be so hot.

But that wasn't enough. Celeste was an impulsive, emotional, fly-by-the-seat-of-her-pants kind of person, while Rand liked things logical and planned out and well ordered. She believed in divine destiny and happily ever after, while he knew damn good and well that life was no bowl of cherries. On the most basic, fundamental level, they were wrong for each other.

Rand worked the rag down the harness. "I'm real happy for you and Sara, but I'm not interested in pairing up to board the ark."

"Whatever you say."

"Well, that's what I say."

George's grin clearly said he was unconvinced. "Actually, there was something else I wanted to ask you."

"Fire away."

"Would you be best man at my wedding? I can't very well ask one son without hurting the other one's feelings, so—"

"Your *wedding!*" Rand looked up, startled. "Aren't you moving a little fast?"

George smiled. "This has been nearly three decades in the making. If you think that's fast, I'd hate to see what you call slow."

George looked so serene, so sure, so damned *happy*. Rand stared at him, wondering if anything in the world would ever make him feel like George looked. A blister of unexpected longing rose in Rand's throat. "Well, sure, I'll stand up for you. I'd be honored. When and where?"

"The nursing home in two weeks. We're having a double wedding with Sara's dad and Doc Thomas's mother."

"No kidding!"

"No kidding." George's smile was nearly wider than his face.

"Well . . . congratulations." Rand put down the harness, rose to his feet and held out his hand.

George shook it, that beaming grin still on his face. "Thanks." George glanced at the old yellowed clock on the wall. "I'd better get going. Sara's expecting me for dinner."

"All right. See you tomorrow."

George nodded. He'd no sooner walked out the door than he poked his head back in. "I know you don't want any advice, but I've lived a few more years than you, and every once in a while that entitles me to dole some out."

"You're about to use up your five-year quota," Rand warned.

George grinned. "I'll say this one thing and then I'll shut up." His expression grew serious. "I made some bad mistakes with Sara, and I want to pass along a lesson I learned the hard way: Stubborn pride won't make you happy; it'll only make you lonely. Sometimes a man has to realize he's been looking at things all wrong. There's no shame in admitting you made a mistake, but it's a hell of a shame to miss out on the best life has to offer because you're just too stubborn to admit you're wrong."

Rand grimaced. "Thank you, O Wise One. Now get outta here!" Rand pretended he was about to throw the oily rag at him. George ducked out of the doorway, his laughter echoing through the stable.

He doesn't know what he's talking about, Rand thought as he hung the harness on the hook and put away the oil.

George acted like happiness was some kind of a one-size-fits-all T-shirt. And hell—what was all that stuff about stubborn pride and being wrong? Rand wasn't wrong about anything. He just knew what he wanted out of life and had plans to get it, that was all. There was nothing wrong with that.

He snapped off the light and walked out of the stable, but George's words went with him. *Sometimes a man has to realize he's been looking at things all wrong.*

"Who the hell does he think he is—Aristotle?" Rand muttered with a scowl. "George is full of it."

And yet, as he made his way across the field, he was stung by the knowledge that George was heading home to the arms of a loving woman while he was heading toward a dark, empty house and another night alone.

As Rand drove home Friday night after another lonely dinner at the Cajun Café, the headlights of his truck gleamed on a group of round, silvery objects floating in the air at the turnoff to Celeste's drive. He slowed to take a look. The objects were a cluster of balloons, attached to the large "Wild Things Fun Farm" sign that Celeste had put up last week. A new banner flapped beneath it. "Grand Opening," Rand read. "September 20th."

Tomorrow. Her big event was *tomorrow?*

His chest suddenly felt full of buckshot, both heavy and full of holes. He didn't understand his reaction. He should be glad. When she failed to get enough bookings, she'd have to admit failure, sell him her ranch and leave town. He'd be able to expand as he'd originally planned, and his life could finally get back to normal.

Which was just what he wanted. Wasn't it?

Of course it was. He peered through the trees, trying to get a glimpse of Celeste's house. He could see lights gleaming through the branches, but he couldn't tell which room they were coming from. He wondered what she was doing. Probably making last-minute preparations for her big day. He felt a strong urge to pull into her drive and see if she needed some help.

Which was ridiculous. The most helpful thing he could do was stay the hell away from her, let her fall flat on her face, then make her a generous offer for her property. He pressed his foot to the accelerator harder than he intended and sped off toward his ranch.

He'd be glad when she was gone, he told himself. He was sick of feeling all torn up every time he drove by her place, sick of having his pulse race whenever George mentioned her name.

Hell and George wasn't the only person who talked about her. Everywhere he went, it was Celeste this, Celeste that. He was sick of hearing about her pet visits to the nursing home, or how she was helping the Girl Scouts organize a dog wash as a fundraiser, or what a great asset she was to the church choir. In just two and a half months, she'd somehow woven herself into the very fabric of the community. The town was going to miss her when she was gone.

He was going to miss her, he reluctantly admitted. Hell, he already did.

The thought made him scowl as he turned into his drive. He rounded the curve and gazed at his darkened house, feeling his stomach tighten at the thought of spending another night rattling around the place alone. Funny how life worked; when you got the things you wanted, they were never quite as good as you'd imagined. He used to dream about living in a big, old house. He'd thought it would make him feel warm and contented, but instead it just felt empty.

It hadn't felt that way before Celeste entered the picture. The woman was wrecking his life in more ways than one.

Rand climbed out of the truck and slammed the door harder than he intended, then impulsively headed for the stables. Horses were always good company—which was more than he could say about most people. Horses were predictable. Horses were manageable. Horses could be controlled.

He opened the stable door, flipped on the light, and breathed in the rich, familiar scent of hay and leather and horseflesh. Blue Moon neighed a greeting as Rand neared his stall.

"How ya doin', boy?" He rubbed the horse's nose. Blue Moon snorted out a hot breath and shoved his head further under Rand's hand.

The horse reminded him of the day Celeste had taken on that surprise birthday celebration. He hadn't ridden the animal since, relegating animal's exercise to stable hands.

"It's not your fault that woman makes me crazy, is it, Blue?" Rand murmured, patting the horse's neck. "Sorry I've been neglecting you."

Blue Moon nudged his arm. He'd take him for a ride now, Rand decided. It was late, but both he and the animal could use the exercise.

He grabbed a blanket and saddle from the tack room and hauled them to the stall. Blue Moon shied away as Rand tried to put them on him.

"Easy, boy," Rand crooned.

The horse lifted its head toward the overhead light and neighed.

"You're not used to going for a ride at night, are you, fella?" Rand placed the saddle on the animal, then tightened the cinch. "Well, it never hurts to try new things."

Celeste's face immediately floated in his mind's eye. She'd said the same thing when he'd tried to refuse her offer of an adventure.

He scowled and focused on buckling the cinch. It was annoying as hell, the way everything reminded him of Celeste.

Hopefully the ride would help clear his mind. Blue Moon balked as Rand led him out of the stable, but once

Rand climbed astride, the horse was so eager to go that Rand had to rein him in. A storm was brewing—clouds blacked out the moon, and the wind carried the scent of rain. After the cloying heat of the day, though, the breeze was a refreshing change.

Blue Moon pranced and snorted, eager to go, his hooves dancing like the treetops in the wind. Rand decided to give him his head. The horse set off at a gallop, heading for the back of Rand's property. Rand reveled in the roughness of the ride, enjoying the pounding of the horse's hooves beneath him and the whip of the wind in his face. He really ought to do this more often, he thought.

Too late, he recalled that Celeste had said the same thing.

Damn it, he couldn't get away from her. Everything he did, saw or thought somehow brought her to mind. He had to break the insane hold she seemed to have over him.

Fat raindrops hit his face, startling him out of his thoughts. Lightning flashed overhead, rapidly followed by a rumble of thunder.

"Time to head back, Blue," he murmured to the horse. Rand tugged on the reins, but Blue Moon wasn't ready to turn back. He tossed his head and tried to push on.

Another flash lit the sky, followed by a louder clap of thunder. It began to rain in earnest. Water showered down in a stinging spray, hitting Rand's face like needles.

Blue Moon still balked at returning.

"Stubborn, aren't you?" Rand said, tugging hard on the rein and leaning back in the saddle. "Well, I'm stubborn, too."

Unbidden, George's words floated through Rand's mind. *Stubborn pride won't make you happy.*

Hell. Stubborn was just another word for determined, Rand thought. George acted as if there were something wrong with knowing your own mind.

Against his will, the word "wrong" called up more of George's words: *Sometimes a man has to admit he's been looking at things all wrong.*

The thought made him clench his jaw. Everyone was so full of advice. Hell, even his horse was trying to tell him what to do.

He pulled hard on the reins, turning Blue Moon around. "There's nothing wrong controlling my own life," he muttered.

A flash of lightning zig-zagged across the sky like a jagged fluorescent light, followed by a deafening boom of thunder. Blue Moon reared up, and before Rand knew it, he'd slid off the rain-slicked saddle and landed in the wet field with a muddy *splat*.

The horse's back hooves kicked up a spray of mud as he cantered off toward the stables.

Rand gazed after him, stunned. He hadn't been thrown by a horse since he quit riding broncos at rodeos. It was a humbling experience.

Humbling, and eerie. One minute he was mumbling about being in control, and then, *boom!* The next thing he knew, he was on his ass in a muddy field. It was almost as if something or someone wanted to show how little control he really had.

Man, this was all a little spooky. He moved his arms and legs, and gingerly felt his tail bone. Nothing was broken, but nothing felt exactly whole, either.

Another jolt of lightning flashed across the sky, followed by another roar of thunder. Rand sat there, feeling small, as the storm raged around him, full of force and fury.

Hell. What, exactly, did he think was in control of? Not the weather. Not whether it was day or night. And not a 1400-pound horse—not unless the horse agreed to follow his lead.

He'd been deluding himself, thinking he was so in control. The thought knotted his gut. Ah, sheeze—he hated people who lied to themselves, yet that was exactly what he'd been doing. He rested his elbows on his knees and lowered his head. The rain pounded down, dripping off his hair in an opaque curtain.

Hell. The truth was, he wasn't in charge of anything that mattered. There wasn't a single thing he managed or owned that couldn't be struck by lightning or blown down or burned up or stolen or lost. Someone a whole lot bigger than him was calling the shots—and that Someone had just knocked him flat on his ass.

Celeste would say this wasn't a coincidence.

Celeste. The thought of her hit him like a bolt of lightning, illuminating all the dark corners of his mind.

Of all the things he'd been deluding himself about, his feelings about her were at the top of the list. Dear Lord—why hadn't he seen it? It had been right in front of him, and he'd refused to recognize it.

He'd twisted everything around. He didn't want Celeste out of his life, he wanted her right smack in the center of it. She wasn't the problem; she was the solution. She wasn't ruining his life; she was the key to completing it.

He loved her. How could he have been so blind?

A bolt of lightning lit the night, throwing everything into dazzling relief. He gazed up at the sky. It was suddenly all so clear.

George was right. Rand had been thinking about everything all wrong.

He'd been trapped in the very self-delusion he despised. He'd thought love was a weakness, when the truth was, love was a force of nature, as strong and real and powerful as the thunderstorm surging around him. Without it, life was as dry and useless and arid as land without rain.

Rand pulled himself to his feet and plodded toward his

house. The mud sucked at his heavy, rain-soaked boots, making each step a struggle, but Rand barely noticed. His heart was filled with new purpose.

He had to convince Celeste to give him another chance.

Chapter Twenty-five

"Gone?" Sara's voice sounded groggy through the phone receiver, as if the call had awakened her. "What do you mean, your animals are gone?"

"I went out to feed them this morning and the gates were open, and they're all gone." Celeste paced her kitchen floor, the phone to her ear. "Mr. Peepers must have let them out. I found him standing on the fence, jumping up and down, as pleased as punch. Evidently he got out of his cage, crawled out the window and opened all the gates."

"But today's your grand opening!"

"I know. It's supposed to start in two hours." Tears sprang to her eyes as Celeste's hand tightened on the phone. "This is supposed to be a petting zoo, and all I've got are two poodles, a monkey who spits and a wildcat with a skin condition."

"Stay calm," Sara said. "They can't have gone far. George and I will come over and help you round them up."

* * *

Celeste was trying to coax a bunny out from under an azalea bush half an hour later when she heard a vehicle pull into her drive. She rose to her feet and dashed to her front yard, expecting to see Sara.

Instead of a white Explorer, Rand's black Silverado and his horse trailer were parked in her drive. And profiled in the passenger-seat window were Bearded Lady and Dr. Freud.

Celeste's heart plunged like a high diver. Great—just what she needed to make a bad situation worse. She hadn't seen Rand in a week—not since Mr. Peepers had vandalized his client's truck—but he'd been stuck in her mind like a rock in her shoe. His words kept trampling around in her mind, beating down a hard path of pain. *I won't let you ruin my life, I won't let you ruin my life.*

Didn't he know that that was the last thing she wanted to do? She loved him. She didn't want to ruin his life; she wanted to share it.

But apparently, Rand didn't want the same thing. He didn't want a relationship. He didn't want her love. He didn't want *her*. He just wanted to be left alone.

Well, she'd done her best to accommodate him. Unfortunately, it appeared her goats had other ideas.

The sun was in her eyes as Rand climbed out of the pickup, making it impossible for her to see his expression, but she was sure he must be livid. How many times had he ordered her to keep her animals off his property?

She pulled herself to her full height as he walked toward her, bracing for an angry tirade. "I know I promised I'd keep my animals off your property, and I'm very sorry, but Mr. Peepers got out, and—"

Rand held up both his hands. "I know. Sara called and told me what happened, and I'm here to help."

"She did?" Celeste stared at him. Instead of the anger

she'd expected, his expression was downright friendly. "You are?"

"Yeah. You can't very well open a petting zoo without any animals, can you?"

He wasn't mad about the runaway goats? She gazed at him, completely bewildered. "N-no. I-I can't."

"That's what I figured. So I've organized a Chamber posse to help round up your animals. And in the meantime, I've brought over a couple of horses. I called some other neighbors, and they'll be bringing by some animals, too. You'll have a four hundred-pound pig, a couple of cows, some ducks, some chicks and who knows what else."

"I-I don't know what to say." *Or think. Or feel.*

Rand lifted his shoulders. "Hey, that's what neighbors are for. They help each other out in times of trouble."

Oh, God—this was so unfair. In fact, it was downright cruel. She'd heard about killing someone with kindness, but Rand was actually doing it.

"I-I'm so sorry Mr. Peepers messed things up the other day." The achy tenderness in her throat made it hard to speak. "Would it help if I called your client and explained that it was all my fault, that I'm getting a new padlock for my monkey's cage and it won't ever happen again?"

He shook his head. "Nah. I got kind of ugly with him when he threatened to hurt Mr. Peepers. He won't be coming back."

Rand had defended Mr. Peepers? The tenderness in her throat swelled to a hard lump. "I'm so sorry," she repeated.

Rand shrugged. "He was a jerk. Anyway—aren't you always telling me that if something is meant to be, it'll work out, and if it's not, it's because something better will come along?"

The swelling in her throat made it hard to breathe. Why, oh why did he have to be so agreeable? She could handle things better if he were acting like a creep.

He fixed her with a serious expression. "When your big day is all over, we need to talk."

A sense of dread clutched her heart. She knew what was coming: the classic you're-a-great-gal, but-it-could-never-work-out-between-us speech. That was why he was being so kind and helpful: He wanted to let her down easy.

The thought shriveled her soul.

She forced her head to wobble a nod. "Sure." Shading her eyes with her hand, she turned back toward the truck, hoping to blame any unnatural moisture in her eyes on the sun. "Well, I'd better get the goats out of your truck before they try to eat your upholstery."

"I'll help. And I'll unload the horses."

The pretty brunette preschool owner carefully ripped the check out of her checkbook and handed it to Celeste. "I can't wait to bring my students here. They're going to have so much fun, they won't even know they're learning!"

"That's the whole idea," Celeste said.

She smiled and waved as the woman, her husband and their two children climbed into their blue Suburban and drove away; then she let out a sigh and headed for the picnic table where Sara was wrapping up the last of the finger sandwiches and cookies.

"That was the last visitor. It's officially over." Celeste sank wearily onto the picnic bench and smiled at her friend, who had manned the refreshment table throughout the day. "I can't thank you enough for all your help."

"Hey, I loved it. I can't believe how many people came!" Sara shook her head. "How did the bookings go?"

"Great. Even better than I'd dared imagine."

"Oh, that's wonderful!" Sara gave her a hug, then held her at arm's length and looked at her closely. "So, why don't you look happy about it?"

Because I don't feel happy about it. The thought of staying here and living next door to Rand, loving him as she did and knowing he didn't love her, suddenly seemed unbearable.

Especially if he was going to be so blasted nice.

The group he'd organized to find her runaway animals had located all but one missing bunny before the guests even began to arrive. Rand had hung around for most of the day, giving children rides on his horses, answering questions and generally helping out. He'd been so kind, so patient, so doggone *nice* that her heart felt like thin ice, ready to crack at any moment. She'd wished he'd do something awful, something that would make her angry. Anger, at least, had heat and purpose. She'd rather feel anything besides this cold, free-floating despair.

"Here come the guys," Sara said.

Sure enough, Rand and George were rounding the house, heading toward them. Celeste busied herself gathering up the unused paper plates and napkins, steeling herself against the wave of emotion rising inside her.

The two men stopped at the end of the table.

"Looks like your day was a big success," George said. "Congratulations."

Celeste carefully avoided Rand's eyes. "Thanks. And thanks for your help."

"My pleasure." George walked over to Sara and looped his arm around her waist, looking down at her with such love that Celeste felt tears form in her eyes.

"Ready to go?" George asked Sara.

Sara nodded.

For a wild, desperate moment, Celeste considered begging them to stay. But that would only be postponing the inevitable. She had to face Rand. She had to get this conversation over with.

She watched them walk arm in arm toward George's truck, a sense of panic growing in her chest. Her pulse rate ratcheted up to the approximate speed of machine-gun fire as Rand slowly walked toward her.

"You had some turnout," he said.

Celeste nodded.

"Did you get a lot of bookings?"

He was no doubt hoping she hadn't. She lifted her chin. "Even more than I'd hoped. I had another meeting with Mr. Adler, and he told me how much business I needed to book to qualify for a loan. I got more than enough."

"Well, good. Congratulations." Rand's smile was warm, without the least bit of resentment or rancor. "I guess I'll have to look into buying the land on the other side of my place."

His response ripped a hole in the last of her defenses, sending her spirits plummeting to earth like a punctured hot-air balloon. Oh, Lord—she couldn't do this. She couldn't stay here and live next door to Rand, loving him as she did, knowing he didn't love her in return. There was no way she could pass him on the street, no way she could make small talk with him at the grocery store, no way she could listen to rumors about whom he was dating.

It was unbearable. It was undoable. It was impossible.

"I've got some things I need to talk to you about," Rand said.

There was another, more immediate thing she couldn't do. She couldn't stand here while he gave her the let's-just-be-friends speech. She was sure he intended to phrase it gently and couch it in all kinds of flattering terms, but she couldn't bear to hear him tell it.

"I've got something to talk to you about, too." The words came out in a fast, high rush as they squeezed around a lemon-sized lump in her throat. "I've decided to sell the place and move back to Texas."

"*What?*" His dark brows flew up.

"You heard me."

"But . . . why?"

She looked down at the ground. "Look—it's not going to work out, the two of us living next door to each other."

"Celeste, if this is about our argument the other evening . . ."

The lump in her throat swelled to the size of a cantaloupe. "You were right: This just isn't going to work. So I'm going to sell you the property. As soon as I honor the commitments I made today and find a place to move the animals, I'll be out of your hair." She paused and drew a breath. "By the end of October—or November at the latest—the place will be yours."

As she said the words, she realized there was no turning back. She had just committed herself to leaving—leaving her dreams, leaving her hopes, leaving Rand.

The stress of the long day, combined with the tension and dread that had built up in anticipation of this conversation, suddenly erupted into tears. She turned around, determined not to let him see her cry.

He reached out and stopped her before she could run to her house. "Celeste, I don't want your property," he said softly, his hand gentle on her upper arm.

Great—just great. Now that she'd decided to give him the place, he'd changed his mind about buying it. He wasn't just breaking her heart, he was breaking her pocketbook.

She gathered every shred of dignity she could find, determined to retain at least a scrap of pride. "Fine. I'll find another buyer." She tried to shrug off his hand, but he held firm.

He stepped closer and put his other hand on her other arm. "I don't want your property," he repeated. "I want you."

She stared at him, not comprehending.

His hands moved up her arm. "Celeste, I've been miserable without you. I haven't been able to think or eat or even sleep. So last night I saddled up Blue Moon and went for a ride. And something happened—well, actually, a couple of things happened—that made me look at things differently."

She looked at him, unsure where this was heading.

His hands slid down her arms. "When I went out to the stable, Blue Moon balked at first. He didn't even want to come out of his stall. He'd never been ridden at night, and he didn't want to go. But once he got outside, he had the time of his life. He tossed his mane and held up his head and high-stepped as if he were dancing. And it made me realize something."

"Wh-what?"

"You make me feel like that—all free and alive and willing to try new things. You bring out a side of me that I didn't know I had."

Hope rose in Celeste's heart like a hot-air balloon. She tried to keep it tethered, to keep it from rising, afraid to face the fall if she was wrong, but it floated high all the same.

"Anyway, Blue Moon and I rode to the back of my property, and all of a sudden, it started to rain. I hadn't been paying any attention to the weather—I'd been thinking about you and about something George said."

"What did he say?"

"That I was looking at things all wrong." He tightened his hold on her. "Just as Blue Moon and I started back to the house, a big bolt of lightning lit up the sky, followed by a big clap of thunder. And the next thing I knew, Blue Moon threw me and headed back to the stable, and I was sitting on my tail in the middle of a field." His Adam's apple jerked in his throat. "And then it hit me—like a bolt out of the blue." He gave a wry grin. "Literally."

"What hit you?"

"What I've been looking at wrong. I've focused on all the outside stuff, the stuff I thought I could control. And I tried to tell myself that the inside stuff—the stuff like emotions and wishful thinking and . . . oh, hell—*love* . . . well, I thought those things just messed with your head. I told myself I didn't need any of that. I didn't need anybody. And I never let anybody get too close."

He paused. The corner of his mouth tugged up in a grin. "Except for you. You somehow sneaked under the wire."

She tentatively smiled back, her heart gaining altitude.

"Anyway, there I was, sitting on my backside in a downpour. I've got to tell you—it was a pretty humbling experience for someone who makes his living training horses. And all of a sudden, I realized just how powerless I really am. Hell—I've been kidding myself, thinking I'm so in charge. I thought I could control my life and my emotions, and the truth was I couldn't even control what cheek I landed on when Blue Moon threw me."

Celeste grinned. Rand did, too, but his eyes remained serious. "I guess getting thrown last night was one of those signs you talk about."

Celeste's heart floated upward.

"Anyway, it made me realize that life isn't about control. It's about love and trust, about taking chances, about believing in something bigger than yourself."

His eyes were dark and full of emotion. "You made me see that. You made me want that. You make me want to let go of the reins and take a few risks."

Her heart soared into the sky. His eyes poured into hers like warm cocoa.

"I've gotta admit, I'm not big on risks. Risks seem a lot like gambling, and because of my dad . . ."

He hated gambling. He wanted to be the exact opposite of his father. "I know," Celeste murmured. "I understand."

He nodded, accepting that she did. "Look—I didn't grow

up with a good example of how men and women are supposed to love each other. From what I saw, love just caused a lot of hurt and disappointment. I thought that the way to avoid all that was to never get emotionally involved. But you made me see that I was also avoiding the good stuff." His hands moved down her arms to grasp her fingers. "You made me see that love is worth the risk." She saw his Adam's apple bob. "What I'm trying to say here is, I love you."

Celeste's heart rocketed into orbit.

He tightened his grip on her hands. "Celeste, I don't want you to move away. Heck, you're too far away as it is. I want you to move into my house. I want you to be my partner and my best friend and my soul mate." He dropped down to one knee, still holding her hands. "I want you to be my wife."

"Oh, Rand!"

"I love you." His gaze was so tender and earnest that Celeste's heart rolled over. "I want to spend my life with you. I want to care for you and support your dreams and do all that stuff your grandmother talked about. Celeste—will you marry me?"

Tears formed again in her eyes, but this time they were tears of joy. It took her a moment to find her voice. "I love you, too," she finally managed to whisper.

"Is that a yes?"

"Absolutely."

And then he was on his feet and she was in his arms, and nothing had ever felt so good and so right and so meant to be.

Long, breathless, kiss-filled moments later, Rand smiled down at her. "So I guess I don't have to worry about becoming that lonely, bored old man you predicted, huh?"

A metallic clink made her glance over his shoulder at

his Silverado. As she watched, a tiny, furry arm flung a wrench out of the pickup bed.

A monkey wrench, if she wasn't mistaken.

A grin spread across Celeste's face. "You won't be lonely," she promised. "And I guarantee you won't be bored."

Celeste rose on tiptoe to kiss him again, but before their lips met, she glanced over his shoulder and saw an enormous gray cat shoot past the truck.

"Bite Me!" she gasped.

"I'd much rather kiss you," Rand replied.

"I meant my cat."

Rand shot her a teasing grin. "I don't want to bite *or* kiss your cat."

Two gray fluffballs streaked past the truck as well. "Rand—Bite Me's on the loose, and Killer and Bruiser are chasing him. And Mr. Peepers is in your truck, and . . ." She gave him an apologetic grin. "I'm afraid things have gotten a little wild."

Rand smiled down at her, his eyes full of tender amusement. In their dark depths, she saw her soul mate, her heart's desire, her destiny and her answered prayers.

"They sure have," he murmured. "I'm absolutely, positively wild about you."

Christie Craig
Divorced, Desperate and Dating

Sue Finley murdered people…on paper. As a mystery writer, she knew all the angles, who did what and why. The only thing she couldn't explain was…well, men. Dating was like diving into a box of chocolates: the sweetest-looking specimens were often candy-coated poison. After several bad breakups, she gave it up for good.

Then came Detective Jason Dodd.

Raised in foster homes, Jason swore never to need anyone. That was why he failed to follow up after experiencing the best kiss of his life. But when Sue Finley started getting death threats, all bets were off. The blonde spitfire was everything he'd ever wanted—and she needed him. And though this novel situation had a quirky cast of characters and an unquestionable bad guy, he was going to make sure it had a happy ending.

ISBN 13: 978-0-505-52732-5

A Taste of Magic

Tracy Madison

"Fun, quirky and delicious!'
—Annette Blair, National Bestselling Author
of *Never Been Witched*

MIXING IT UP

Today is Elizabeth Stevens's birthday, and not only is it the one-year anniversary of her husband leaving her, it's also the day her bakery is required to make a cake—for her ex's next wedding. If there's a bitter taste in her mouth, no one can blame her.

But today, Liz is about to receive a gift. Her Grandma Verda isn't just wacky; she's a little witchy. An ancient gypsy magic has been passed through the family bloodline for generations, and it's Liz's turn to be empowered. Henceforth, everything she bakes will have a dash of delight and a pinch of wishes-can-come-true. From her hunky policeman neighbor, to her gorgeous personal trainer, to her bum of an ex-husband, everyone Liz knows is going to taste her power. Revenge is sweet…and it's only the first dish to be served.

ISBN 13: 978-0-505-52810-0

JANA DELEON

Maryse Robicheaux can't help heaving a sigh of relief at the news that her not-so-beloved mother-in-law has kicked the bucket. The woman was rude, manipulative and loved lording over everyone as the richest citizen of Mudbug, Louisiana. Unfortunately, death doesn't slow Helena Henry down one bit.

Being haunted—or more like harried—by Helena's ghost isn't even the worst of Maryse's problems. Close to making a huge medical breakthrough, she's suddenly been given an officemate, and the only thing bigger than Luc LeJeune's ego is his sex appeal. Maryse would bet her life the hot half-Creole is hiding something. Especially because it seems someone's out to kill her. But getting Luc to spill his secrets while avoiding Helena's histrionics and staying alive herself will be the ultimate bayou balancing act.

Trouble in Mudbug

ISBN 13: 978-0-505-52784-4

To order a book or to request a catalog call:
1-800-481-9191
Our books are also available at your local bookstore, or you can check out our Web site **www.dorchesterpub.com** where you can look up your favorite authors, read excerpts, or glance at our discussion forum to see what people have to say about your favorite books.

The **HIGH HEELS** *Series*

by

Gemma Halliday

National Readers' Choice Award Winner
Double RITA Award finalist
Booksellers Best finalist
Daphne DuMaurier Award finalist

"The High Heels Series is amongst one of the best mystery series currently in publication. If you have not read these books, then you are really missing out on a fantastic experience, chock full of nail-biting adventure, plenty of hi-jinks, and hot, sizzling romance."
　　　　　　　　　　　　　　　　　　—Romance Reviews Today

- *Spying in High Heels*
- *Killer in High Heels*
- *Undercover in High Heels*
- *Alibi in High Heels*
- *Mayhem in High Heels*

"A highly entertaining and enjoyable series."
　　　　　　　　　　　　　　　　　　—*Affaire de Coeur*

"Kate Angell is to baseball as Susan Elizabeth Phillips
is to football. Wonderful!"
— *USA Today* Bestselling Author Sandra Hill

KATE ANGELL

WHO'D BEEN SLEEPING IN KASON RHODES'S BED?

The left fielder for the Richmond Rogues had returned
from six weeks of spring training in Florida to find someone
had moved into his mobile home. That person was presently
in his shower. And no matter how sexy the squatter might be,
Kason wanted her out.

He had his trusty dobie, Cimarron; he didn't need anyone
else in his life. Not even a stubborn tomboy who roused all
kinds of wild reactions in him, then soothed his soul with
peace offerings of macaroni & cheese and rainbow Jell-O.
The bad boy of baseball was ready to play hardball if need be,
but with Dayne Sheridan firmly planted between his sheets,
he found himself . . .

SLIDING
HOME

ISBN 13: 978-0-505-52808-7

☐ **YES!**

Sign me up for the Love Spell Book Club and send my
FREE BOOKS! If I choose to stay in the club, I will pay
only $8.50* each month, a savings of $6.48!

NAME: _____

ADDRESS: _____

TELEPHONE: _____

EMAIL: _____

☐ I want to pay by credit card.

☐ **VISA**   ☐ **MasterCard**   ☐ **DISCOVER**

ACCOUNT #: _____

EXPIRATION DATE: _____

SIGNATURE: _____

Mail this page along with $2.00 shipping and handling to:
**Love Spell Book Club
PO Box 6640
Wayne, PA 19087**
Or fax (must include credit card information) to:
610-995-9274
You can also sign up online at **www.dorchesterpub.com**.
*Plus $2.00 for shipping. Offer open to residents of the U.S. and Canada only.
Canadian residents please call 1-800-481-9191 for pricing information.
If under 18, a parent or guardian must sign. Terms, prices and conditions subject to
change. Subscription subject to acceptance. Dorchester Publishing reserves the right
to reject any order or cancel any subscription.